"Learning doesn't just happen in the classrooms"

Looks can be deceiving. And that is certainly true in *The Quintet Approach*. What appears to be an elite collegiate institution out in the middle of coastal Oregon serving those privileged enough to be accepted to attend, is anything but.

Using a program of personalized self-development and universal academic subject matter combined with tasks like helping to care for rescued horses and other animals, these students will ultimately rise to the best of their unique abilities and values. Learning doesn't just happen in the classrooms, folks, and you can follow the trials and triumphs of several students (plus the academy's rather eclectic faculty) as they "step outside" themselves and truly become adults.

Following the developments of several students over two years, the story builds into that of a family moving towards a common end: the mission to create a project which will have a positive impact in the world.

Experience the joys and tragedies, the fears and hopes, the laughter and the tears, the love and the loneliness of these young people as they go forth into this bold new adventure.

The Quintet Approach

Pangolin Guild

The Quintet Approach
Pangolin Guild

by
Julie K. Starr

contributions by
James W. Hash

I Can Dream Publishing
A division of Rising Starr Enterprises, LLC
P.O. Box 414
Neotsu, Oregon 97364

The Quintet Approach
Pangolin Guild

Design and layout by Julie Starr. Photographs on cover taken in Lincoln City, Oregon on the 15th Street beach and Spring Lake Open Space.

Drawing on back cover by Jean Starr. All other artwork by Julie Starr. "Richard Hugo 23–82," "A Short Novel," and "The Inchworm" by James Hash, Jr.

ISBN-13 978-0692463529
ISBN-10 0692463526

Published by
I Can Dream Publishing
a division of Rising Starr Enterprises, LLC
www.icandreampublishing.info

First published on September 21, 2015 to celebrate the International Day of Peace.

The characters in this book are fictional. While most of them were in part influenced by one or more people, none of them represent any individual. Any resemblance to a person living or passed is not coincidental, but also not intentional.

At the time of writing, links to web pages were valid. Due to the nature of the internet, that can change. Always exercise due diligence when visiting these or any web pages. Neither the author nor publisher assume any liability.

for **Jolene Mae** and **Jennae Jing**
who made my heart sing
and always will

Table of Contents

SUPPLEMENTARY MATERIAL

Acknowledgments

About the Author

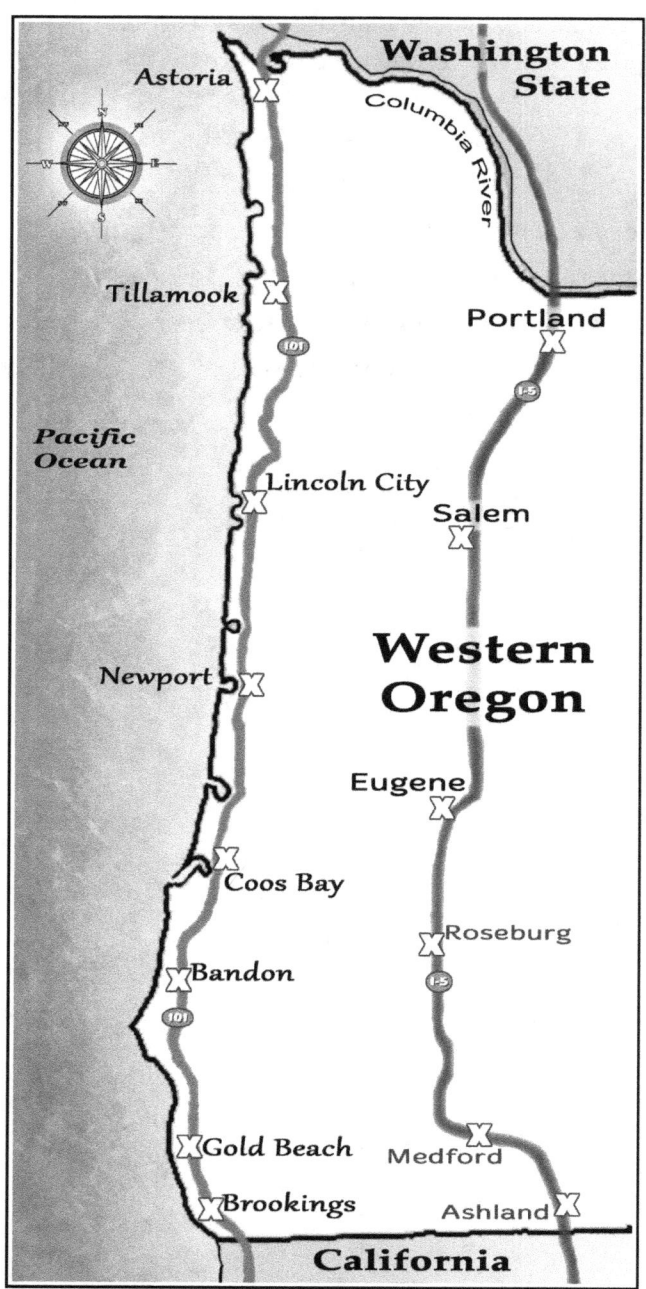

Paunder Avian Academy is on the coast between
Tillamook and Lincoln City.

Approximate locations of some Oregon towns.
Not to be used for navigational purposes.

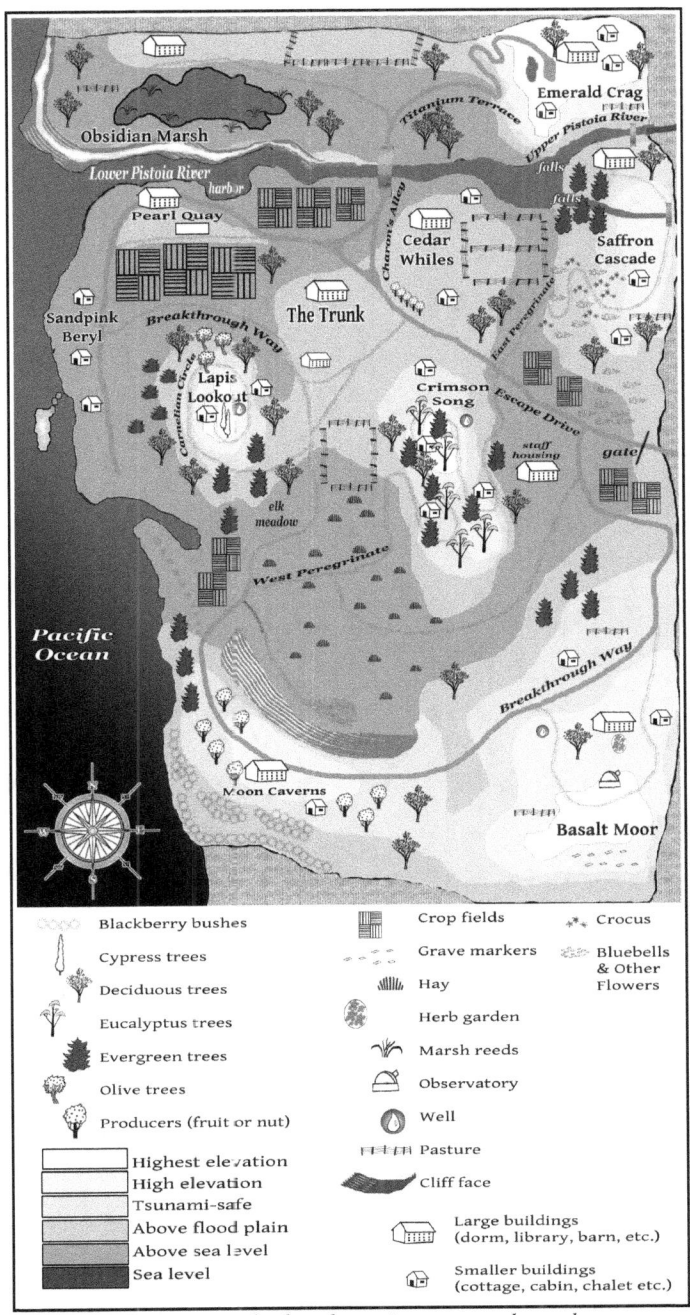

Blackberry bushes   Crop fields   Crocus

Cypress trees   Grave markers   Bluebells & Other Flowers

Deciduous trees   Hay

Eucalyptus trees   Herb garden

Evergreen trees   Marsh reeds

Olive trees   Observatory

Producers (fruit or nut)   Well

Highest elevation   Pasture

High elevation   Cliff face

Tsunami-safe

Above flood plain   Large buildings (dorm, library, barn, etc.)

Above sea level

Sea level   Smaller buildings (cottage, cabin, chalet etc.)

A full-size version can be found at quintetapproach.wordpress.com

Not to scale. Not all structures or vegetation are represented.
See online for the most recent version.

Part One

METHODI ET ADVENTU

Chapter 1

Acceptance

Safe!
Now let the night be dark for all of me.
Let the night be too dark for me to see
Into the future. Let what will be, be.

— *Robert Frost*

November

"Everyone, but especially you, should laugh every day, and I don't think you have for a while," Lorena said over the table. She took a sip of her warm saké. "I wish you could've moved here with me. We would've had so much fun! Plus, this is a great area for jogging. And the address is your birth date! How could you ignore that; it was a sign!"

"You know I don't believe in signs. I'm sure I would have loved living with you, but I have Oliver to think about. I couldn't give him up." Adele dipped her tempura into the sauce.

The girls were partaking in happy hour at Yama Sushi just up the block from Lorena's place. It was much easier to get around in San Francisco if one could walk to their destination. For most people, buses, streetcars, cable cars, delivery trucks, arrogant pedestrians, confused tourists, and both bicycle couriers and motorcycles—which had a habit of zipping between vehicles whether parked or in motion—made driving in The City overwhelming. But for Adele, it wasn't that difficult if she stayed in her space, was aware of other drivers and her immediate surroundings, avoided rolling the truck backwards down the steep hills with its manual transmission, and watched out for the traffic lights which seemed designed for wall-eyed people. Even she had to admit that it was a lot to take in.

Parking her 1983 Ford Ranger though, was another matter entirely: Between finding a spot that was on the same side of the street that she was on and long enough in both space and time—was a real headache. Even if she found a parking space where she could stay a few hours, she had to make sure the street sweeping schedule was in her favor as nearly every street in San Francisco is cleaned at least once a week.

But visiting her friend in The City was worth the hassle. Lorena was one of the lucky graduates of Piner High: Not only had she managed to get into San Francisco's City College, but she'd also found a rental on Jules Street to share with four roommates, the blue house protected by bars on the door. Though the neighborhood itself was clean and pleasant, one always had to be careful in any city. The arrangement could have been straight out of a sit-com script.

Lorena said, "Yes, I know. But you give up a lot for that horse. And I know you're unhappy at SRJC. I can't tell you what you should do, but if I were you, I'd be looking for an alternative. Just think about thinking outside the box, Adele."

The next week back in Santa Rosa, optimistic, dilatory Adele Stawski caught the toe of her Nike on the pavement as she crossed the community college's near-empty central plaza. Her books and iPad skittered on the wet concrete as she fell to her knees; the heel of her palm and an elbow painfully prevented a planted face, though not a twisted grimace. After catching her breath, she turned to sit on her haunches, clutched her skinned knees to her chest, dropped her forehead onto her ripped jeans, and shuddered silently against sobbing. Emotional humiliation needn't follow her pain and embarrassment.

It wasn't the tumble itself that upset her, or even the injuries; she'd fallen off of or been thrown from horses numerous times. On the other hand, she didn't usually fall on pavement. But Lorena was right: Adele was not enjoying her third month at her hometown college. She didn't enjoy the first month either, nor the second, and it looked as though there wouldn't be any hope of enjoyment in future months. With the fall, the disappointment of all this lost time hit her at once.

A kind bystander to her indignity helped gather her items together: her unharmed, overstuffed knapsack with folders of papers and a change of clothes; the books scratched and wet; the iPad's screen now cracked; and with a word of thanks, Adele resumed her walk to the bus stop. *I've got to stop carrying so much stuff with me, especially when the truck's in the shop*, she chided. *The iPad would probably have been okay if I'd had it in my bag.*

Adele wasn't a believer in signs, but this was the third indication in a single day that maybe she should consider Lorena's suggestion that she look into transferring to another school. The first sign was during this morning's class. The instructor responded to her question, but called her by the wrong name, again. *Ariel, really?! We're at the end of the semester, and you still don't know my goddamn name! So much for "low faculty/student ratio;" what good is it if you can't remember who I am?!*

The second sign came at lunch, if anyone could call it that. The cafeteria offered a choice of hockey-puck burgers...but of course no buns, they were fresh out, which seemed to be the only way food could be called "fresh" here; a quiche that was brown throughout, even its broccoli...at least she assumed it was broccoli; and gray fish dish in a gelatinous sauce of the same color that stank like a cannery. She opted for a non-descript flaky cereal, pulling the lever of a tall plastic dispenser. At first the cereal got stopped up, then came out all at once, overflowing onto the floor.

But her fall was the pièce de résistance, the rotten cherry on top of a shitty day. It wasn't anyone's fault, nothing the school had done. She simply took it as a punctuation on a day's—no, months'—worth of signs. Waiting for the bus, Adele resolved to look again at the junior college brochure that her guidance counselor had given to her the last semester of high school. After graduation, she'd taken a couple years off to work, saving for college. The money wasn't there for University yet, but she went to the junior college anyway to keep sharp and retain her study skills, weak as they already were.

As soon as she got home she'd go through her boxes and bags of paperwork to find the brochure, but only after tending to her wounds, hugging her horse in his dry, sawdust-filled stall, and indulging in a deep glass of local pinot noir.

mid December

Even though he had to come here formally every term, Radegast always felt out of place when he entered the executive offices at the academy's Trunk. It was the central campus to the academy's ten other schools or "branches," and he was the overseer of the entire twelve-hundred acre grounds. He was much more comfortable getting his hands dirty running the place than being in the polished, patrician coolness with its sense of decorum. For some it was a sanctuary; for Leonard Radegast, it was like being in an empty vault: boring and confining.

The lobby was populated with dark brown overstuffed leather chairs; deep, vibrant blue cushions; and wooden wall sculptures of each of the ten branches' avian mascots. The hub of transportation and administration, it was like no other building on campus; but then, they were each unique. This time, tasteful Christmas décor and greenery festooned the suite; the crisp scent of fresh pine infused the air.

He was the first administrator most incoming students—or "leaves," as students were cordially labeled—would meet; Radegast was always pleased to welcome them to the academy. A member of the core administration, he was also involved in this final selection process of students on the edge of eligibility. He hoped this meeting wouldn't take long, so he could get back to supervising the repairs at the Saffron Cascade stables. One of the horses had a temper tantrum during the night, kicking the hell out of a box stall and cutting his legs on the broken boards. The horse had been taken to the hospital barn at Cedar Whiles to recover from the wounds, but the stall was still waiting.

Radegast preferred to keep on top of maintenance before tasks piled up. That was one benefit of the concrete stalls here at the Trunk: though not warm and inviting, they rarely needed to be repaired. With dozens of stalls on the main level of the building and several outside paddocks, the Trunk had a capacity for over four hundred horses at any given time. Efficiency was necessarily at the top of the list.

Several other committee members were settling in the conference room when he arrived, comprised of both academic and management staff. The satin-finished live edge cedar plank table was empty except for two pitchers of ice water. Glasses were on a sideboard, along with a platter of cucumber-and-cream cheese finger sandwiches and other delectables. He took a seat next to Ms. Talbot, knowing this was her first time on the committee. She wore a tawny camel hair blazer over a crisp white mandarin blouse, and smelled slightly of leather and horse and fresh air. "Did you ride down here from Moon Caverns?" he asked her.

"Yes, I couldn't resist on such a beautiful day. You have to take advantage of them, especially in winter. Besides, I knew you'd appreciate it," she said teasingly, nudging him with her elbow. She was right, he did. After all, they expected the students to get around the campus as ecologically as was reasonable and realistic, providing them with horses, middleweight dual-sport motorcycles, and even bicycles. It was fair to have the same expectation of the staff.

"That's good; where'd you put your horse?"

"One of the stable attendants took him for me. He said the farrier's in, and it's time for a hoof trim so the timing works out well."

"Right, she's here every Monday. No appointment needed, though you may have to wait a bit," confirmed Radegast.

"Good to know. Their hooves grow so fast! Now, getting back to the meeting; please enlighten me, how does this process work?"

He twisted in his chair to turn to her. "I guess we have a few minutes, so I'll give you a run-down. Looks like we're still waiting on—" he scanned the room, "—five or six more committee members before we start. There's thirteen of us on the committee. Sydney Chevaux is our chairman this year, he's a culinary instructor at Crimson Song. Once he opens the meeting, Mr. Violo—he's the administrative assistant for the Trunk—will give us a verbal summary of the potential students who've applied or been nominated for two terms from now, which will be summer."

"Couldn't that take a while? There must be thousands of names."

"No, not that many. I mean, yes, we do receive a large number of applications, but by the time we get to this stage, most applicants have already been turned down. Some are ineligible—any known history of mistreating animals, for instance—others have terrible handwriting or grammar."

A bombastic man with a gaudy tie to match joined the conversation as he walked by them. "Can't be too tough, after all, they let *you* in, Leonard."

"Yes, well...uh, Ms. Talbot, this is Robin Fergus, he teaches some of the core classes."

"Welcome, my dear," Fergus said as he clasped Ms. Talbot's hand in both of his, and before she had a chance to respond, he took his seat at the end of the table.

Radegast noticed her confused expression. "You'll get used to him, he's harmless. As I was saying, Mr. Paunder was insistent that handwriting reveals substantial and important information about an individual's character, so a handwriting sample is a required component of every application. If that shows overwhelming characteristics that don't fit our program, or if they've omitted it entirely, their application is turned down. Same with poor grammar; if they state, for example, 'Me and my brother ran a lemonade stand,' they're going to have a tougher time getting accepted."

"Does that mean people with unique penmanship or poor grammar *can't* be approved?"

"Not necessarily, just that they are going to have to go through a process which has a higher probability of rejection."

He held his hand up to his face, palm out toward Fergus, quelling the glib comment he knew was coming. "However, if applicants meet all the requirements, their handwriting and language usage passes scrutiny, and the application is accompanied by qualified testimonials on behalf of the applicant, they are automatically approved. That accounts for about 150-180 of the 200 who'll be admitted. This meeting has a threefold purpose: to discuss applicants who are marginally qualified, those who've been nominated but not actually applied, and to plan an alternate list in the event of attrition. And there's always some of that, as priorities and situations can change in the next six months."

"Then this isn't a hard-and-fast process, more of a discussion?"

"Yep, you could say that. It's subjective, and that's why you're here, to make sure there's fresh perspective. There's someone new on the committee each term."

"And when did you join the committee, Mr. Radegast?"

"Oh, mmm, about five years ago, I'd reckon. But please, call me Leonard."

"Okay, Leonard," she smiled. "In that case you must call me Louisa. So you're old-hat at this procedure now."

"I suppose. As Trunkmaster, I'm obligated to be on it, so here I am."

As Mr. Radegast said that, Chevaux entered the conference room, with Mr. Violo behind him, carrying a large plastic tote. Violo set it on the floor, and pulled both deep blue and brown folders out of it, setting the folders on the table. As he did, Chevaux said, "Looks like we're all here. Thanks for coming, everyone. Please help yourselves to the water and hors d'oeuvres as you like. Let's get started." Violo handed him a short stack of the folders, then began passing around copies to the committee members. "This set will take us to our first break."

"Hot dog!" said Fergus. "That means we got a slew of line-walkers!"

Ms. Talbot heard Radegast muffle a groan.

"Next we have Adele Stawski," said Mr. Chevaux after they'd gone through several dozen files. "We received her application just under the deadline for summer term." The committee members opened her application folder in near-unison, and began to peruse the materials—which included several effulgent recommendations—while Violo gave the quick verbal summary.

"I like this girl," said Ms. Pepperburgh after several minutes. "She's hard-working, smart, has a great attitude, likes people and animals of all kinds."

"But those qualities aren't qualifiers. Does she know any languages?" asked Fergus, thumbing through the girl's file.

"The only fluency is in English, and in that she's quite proficient. Adele's taken several language courses. Obviously she has an interest in expanding her fluency, but you can see she never got a full grasp of any of them. I know the applicants are expected to have a minimum of handshake knowledge of at least one foreign language, but how do we decide just how fluent they need to be? And Sydney," implored Ms. Pepperburgh, "aren't we able to bend the rules a bit?" She turned with a raised eyebrow to Mr. Chevaux.

"It's what I understand this committee is about, anyway. Scrutinizing the borderline applications, right?" said Ms. Talbot. She turned to Radegast for validation. He nodded.

"I'll allow that we can consider it," Chevaux replied. "It's a guideline, not a rule, strictly speaking. Keep in mind that a second language is important to this program, so if we accept her, she'll have to commit to taking a language course while she's here."

The discussions continued throughout the morning. Of the one hundred twenty-four applications and nominations under consideration, thirty-eight were accepted, eleven were to be sent invitations, and thirteen were listed as alternates.

"That's it, then," Chairman Chevaux said. "Along with the one hundred fifty-one already approved, we have made our selections for the summer term, the...what is this bloc, Eddie?"

"The Pangolin bloc," replied Violo.

"Yes, the Pangolins are chosen." He pushed the remaining stack of files to Mr. Violo. "Letters will be sent out Wednesday, and they'll have till February fourteenth to inform us of their intentions. Now, my graduating culinary students of Crimson Song have prepared a holiday party for the staff and faculty. Let's go show our appreciation for their efforts in the best way we know how. Enjoy yourselves, it's quite a nice luncheon!"

Decades earlier, Sebastian Paunder had a dream, waking in the middle of a cold February night with philosophical topics and visions of all sorts of birds leaping from his inspired subconscious to paper, scribbling them down and drawing tables in which to organize his thoughts. Not just birds, but colors and major parts of their anatomy were used as symbols and inspirations, cross-referenced to provide a framework for expanded knowledge. The tail of a bird in silver suggested "Wisdom;" the eye in black suggested "Violence;" wing in yellow implied "Hope." Even the terms for campus divisions provided an "aha!" moment: The main building would be the Trunk, and the separate schools would be the "branches." Unofficially, students who were failing their courses were termed "falling leaves."

The inspiration was not unbidden; the futility and despair that he saw in people's eyes broke his heart; the selfishness, dishonor and meanness in the actions of crude people caused disillusion and distrust in the population. A long-time aspiration of his was to inspire hope, honor, and honesty in the world; in fact, he and his Italian wife had named their young children after these three principles. But how could their little family make any real difference? Though the circumstances were less than desirable, the opportunity was priceless.

Paunder had been chosen to administer the gift of this land from the Spreckles estate. The exchanges he'd had with the board of directors proved him to be a conscientious and fair man, a man who could be trusted. He was given the burden to decide its purpose, with the guidance of the board. The provisions were numerous: that it be free of federal aid; at least partially open to the public; while it could make a profit, it should be not-for-profit; 50-80% of the land could be utilized, in other words, mostly but not entirely; serve the greater good; and that no portion of it could be sold. Finally, whatever the land was used for, it was to include his family name in gratitude for the Paunder family's dedication and service, for it would be a multi-generational endeavor.

Within months of being appointed, Paunder and Bianca moved themselves and their three teenagers to the modest cabin that was built there. For several years he contemplated what to do with the property as they became acquainted with the land, its special features, and its limitations. Land, water, and geological surveys were performed. They entertained many ideas from friends, family, and the public. A state park was suggested, but there were already several nearby. His oldest friend proposed timber harvesting, but that was mostly a financial enterprise: while allowed by the provisions, it didn't really meet the letter of the intention. A research facility was a possibility, but Paunder wanted something more interactive for the public. His daughters wanted a horse facility, but the property was much too large for such a specific purpose. It was the same with retail outlets, his wife's suggestion—there wouldn't be enough to make the best use of the land.

His epiphany was simple but revolutionary: create an academy where the intention was not to produce students with financial reward and careers as a goal, but of like-minded students who wanted in some way to make a positive contribution to the world as well. Instead of the academic year starting at the same time for everyone, students could come in at the beginning of any one of four terms, blocs differentiated by unique names. During their two-year program, they would each take any twelve—no more, no less—of sixty "enhancement" classes, classes that weren't tied to any specific discipline, but designed to encourage students to think and make up their own minds on how the topics would apply to their degrees, and give them unique insight in regards to their chosen field. And finally, free to all who qualified for the program; at least financially.

Combined with his focus for the academy on humanities, animals, and the environment, and his daughters' love of horses, Paunder decided to integrate rescue horses into the school. A future adoption/training program would be developed to enhance the animal husbandry and business degrees. The academy must also have a foreign language component, because he believed that honoring and learning languages of other cultures was essential to cultivating an understanding between people. And he believed in reminding people of the magic of the world, from the enormous silicate crystals at Moon Caverns to the largely untapped power of the human mind.

Several areas on the grounds are preserved as a wildlife habitat. Elk freely roam through the grounds. Depending on the season, they can often be seen grazing in the unfenced field at the southern base of Lapis Lookout when not camouflaged amid the uncultivated woods of its hillside. Mammalian populations of raccoon, porcupine, opossum, bat, woodrat, skunk, coyote, deer, bobcat, and black bear also inhabit the grounds of the academy. To preserve their unaided nature, feeding or interacting with them is highly prohibited as it results in dependency and concentrated overpopulation, especially well-demonstrated with raccoons as they tend to become aggressive and demanding. Trout and salmon can be fished from the lower Pistoia River.

The board approved of Paunder's ideas, and decided after much debate and research—as well as vetting to the local community—on various associates programs. Initially, Environmental Science, Marine Biology, Animal Husbandry, and Physical Education degrees were offered. Later, Psychology, Art and Music, Humanities, and Emergency Medicine were added. As the academy grew, so did its list of offerings.

The final component was one of outreach. The board and Paunder agreed that there was a responsibility to give back to the community, a way to enhance and be accountable to the people of the Oregon coast, and beyond. Residents of Tillacoln County were welcome to participate at no cost in any of the enhancement classes. For the larger community, a uniquely formed small group of students would form irregularly—by chance and design—to develop a program to enhance the world in some way, large or small. This component was at the heart of what made the academy so special.

By the time the scope, purpose, and functions of the academy were established, the Paunder children were educated adults, and contributed to the growth of the academy. Their oldest, Naomi (Nao being Japanese for "honest"), had obtained a degree in architecture from the University of Oregon. She designed most of the academy's buildings. Honoré—French for "honor"—was their only son and a geologist. He gave the final names to the schools and landmarks, and chose several of the mascots. The youngest of the children was Nadja, whose name meant "hope"; an avid equestrian, she used her degree in business administration to establish the academy's horse rescue, education, and adoption program.

All three had subsequently left to take their places in the world. They would return to visit or help now and then, as need arose. Though the Paunder family no longer lived on the grounds, their legacy lived on in the spirit and intent of the school.

Chapter 2

Humility

Humility like darkness reveals the heavenly lights. The shadows of poverty and meanness gather around us, "and lo! creation widens to our view."

— Henry David Thoreau

January

The home that Phoebe Hugo shares with her mother is the most cheerful in the neighborhood, with pink and red sweet peas in the spring, bright orange nasturtiums in the summer, and in the fall, periwinkle asters blooming by the hundreds in the tiny front yard. Even in the winter the Hugo's flower bed is brilliant with sunshine-yellow forsythia shrubs. Where others her age spend hours on the internet, Phoebe tends to her profuse flower garden, bringing out of each plant its highest potential. The house itself is built like all the others on their street, single-story shotguns with exactly the same size narrow lots, but the Hugo house was painted rich poppy-yellow with bright purple trim. Depending on the season, theirs was one of the most colorful in all of Eunice, Louisiana[1].

Phoebe had recently graduated from high school, but with the Hugo's modest income coupled with Phoebe's average grades and a short list of extracurricular activities—none of which she excelled at—academic scholarships weren't a likely option.

---

1 www.city-data.com/city/Eunice-Louisiana.html

The library four blocks away offers air conditioning, a reprieve from the humidity of the Louisiana heat. Though not a voracious reader, Phoebe looks through books about different places, immersing herself in the pictures of perfectly manicured gardens, quaint European villages with multi-hued shops, and snowy alpine scenes with pure, untouched powder. When something grabs her attention, she reads the information thoroughly. She can be lost in here for hours, as she was this afternoon.

Returning from the library, she stopped at the white picket gate to collect the mail from the box and carried it to the house, thumbing through it as she walked. Her ash blonde locks were already starting to frizz in the mizzle.

"Cypress Hugo, Cypress Hugo, Resident, Ms. C. Hugo, Hugo Residence, Cypress M. Hugo …."

Her mother leaned over the porch railing. "Phoebe, stop being such a nosy butt and hand over that mail. Unless *you* want to pay the bills yourself, then you're welcome to them."

"Okay Ma, it's all for you anyway." She passed the mail up to the outstretched hand.

As Phoebe walked up past Cypress into the house, she thrust her hands into the kangaroo pouch of her hoodie. "Not like anyone writes me anyhow," she said softly.

Cypress thumbed through the envelopes. "Nobody gets personal mail anymore, you know that, girl. Nobody takes the time…Wait up, young woman!" she cried, following Phoebe into the house. "There's actually something here for you!"

Phoebe spun around, her eyes wide open. "Is it from the casino?"

"Nope." She handed the hand-addressed envelope to Phoebe. Cypress' voice went higher with each of her next words. "You expectin' something from *them*?"

Paunder Avian Academy
23000 Escape Drive
Gilded Sand, Oregon 97177

"Not really. I mean, I know the school was following several leads 'round here, but ... no, I didn't expect it."

Cypress sat down heavily in her chair as she watched her daughter stare at the envelope as though it were from a long-lost friend.

"Go on, girl; it can only be good news," urged her mother gently, catching her breath.

Phoebe looked into Cypress's eyes. "That's what I'm thinking. This could change everything!"

Phoebe gazed back at the brown-ink meticulous handwriting for a moment, then carefully opened the ivory-colored vellum envelope breaking the blue wax seal, as if she were afraid of tearing the golden ticket. She unfolded the letter, and silently read it, her eyes darting quickly across the lines.

"Well, what's it say, child?"

"I'll read it aloud to you, so I don't lose the meaning. 'Dear Miss Hugo,'" she began.

"So formal!"

"Shhh, Momma, let me read! 'Dear Miss Hugo, because of your care for your home, family and community, you were nominated to join the Paunder Avian Academy by one of your high school instructors, who asked to remain anonymous. After reviewing your records, and interviewing those in your community with whom you're acquainted, we are pleased to offer you a place in our two-year associates program, which is all-expenses paid. This invitation is to join us this summer in the Pangolin bloc.

'Once you've completed the program, you'll have two choices to fulfill your obligation to the academy: Commit to two years of field work at the academy in a support role, or Sponsor a new student. If you qualify for a guild, you'll have the additional option to be on special assignment.' My gosh, Momma, I'm gonna be in the program!"

She bent down and threw her slender arms around her mother's thickset shoulders. "No more wondering about my future. I'm on my way, and I'm going to make you proud."

Chapter 3

Sacrifice

Life at its noblest leaves mere happiness far behind;
and indeed cannot endure it.... Happiness is not the
object of life: life has no object: it is an end in itself;
and courage consists in the readiness to sacrifice
happiness for an intenser quality of life.

— *George Bernard Shaw*

May

Since childhood, Adele retreated next to a shallow creek whenever she needed time to herself; the tangled, thick roots of a gnarly old tree supporting a dirt bank somehow gave her the feeling of being in the presence of a wise being. This private shelter from the empty field above it was Adele's favorite thinking spot, away from her mothers and household chores. It's here in the raw, muddy earth with thick grasses that life is simple, undemanding, dependable. The water of the creek gurgles by, washing out noises of the street a hundred yards away. With the sun shining softly on her skin, she recorded in her journal, drawing horses and sharing thoughts with her future self.

The Stawski's moderate house looks out of place in the neighborhood, surrounded by horse estates. Although Adele has a horse, most of her friends come from multi-horse homes. Her parents support her interest, even indulging her with a Shetland pony when she was just seven years old. But they had no interest in building an equine center in suburban Santa Rosa[2]. Though the couple was dedicated to Adele, their dedication could only go so far.

In the afternoon Adele's bedroom is brightened by the post meridian light, partially shadowed by a massive willow tree off the patio. Although lacking a decorator's hand, there is clearly a horse theme: Pictures of horses torn from equine magazines clutter the door frame, the tacked-up pages folding down at the corners, fluttering at the slightest draft; a bridle hangs on a post of her brass bed, which is unmade, sheets wrinkled and cover askew. Her mother urges her regularly to redecorate, hinting not too mildly that the room was too adolescent for the now-adult Adele, suggesting that when she does come home, she might like to "visit" a mature bedroom.

Her friends said Adele had CPF, or "concentrating pissed face," because when she was working on a project, her scowl made her appear angry. Perhaps because of this, she didn't make friends easily, until they got to know her.

After a quick breakfast of toast and "candy white coffee"—a beverage with more milk and sugar than brew—she walked out to the one-horse stable in the backyard.

Oliver extended his neck out of the stall door and nickered as she approached. He nuzzled Adele's caramel-brown hair, blowing the soft curls off her shoulders. He was urging her to give him his ration of cob: corn, oats, and barley, an equine delight. Before he could have his breakfast, Adele put him in the paddock so she could clean out his stall. She used a pitchfork to lift the straw with piled manure into the wheelbarrow, followed by shovelfuls of urine-soaked sawdust. Going to the sawdust bin, she half-filled the wheelbarrow to replenish what she took out. There was still enough straw in the stall to cover the sawdust, so she spread it out evenly.

Despite the steaming manure, heavy five-gallon water buckets, and the occasional misstepped hoof on her foot, Adele would miss this early morning routine, but not the early morning. While she did appreciate the breaking light of day, the

---

2 www.city-data.com/city/Santa-Rosa-California.html

fresh smell of the air and earth, she also appreciated her warm bed and venting dreams. Life seemed to always be a decision between one good thing and another, balancing the scales on what one wanted most: to be happy, or to be comfortable.

She led Oliver back in when she finished. "I'm sorry I can't take you with me," she said to the four-year old, a grulla-colored Oldenburg gelding. "I can't believe I'm leaving you!" she said emphatically, choking on her words. She spoke as if Oliver could understand. Clearing her throat she said, "But, if I weren't going to the academy, I'd be going *somewhere* else." She lightly stroked his velvety-soft nose while he ate cob out of her palm.

Her family had a long history of being both proud and pragmatic, so they made plans for Oliver's care after Adele applied to PAA, even before she'd received the acceptance letter. Her "mother of origin" agreed to take over most duties willingly though begrudgingly, including feedings. Despite not being a horse person, she wanted her daughter to be happy. Adele made sure she committed to feeding him the same time morning and night. The easy part was arranging for her best friend Dorothy taking out Oliver in the morning, exercising him every day before she went to work.

Adele knew Oliver didn't understand what she was saying, but she was sure he was sensitive to her emotions. Her bags were ready, all the arrangements were made. She'd had months to prepare, plan, pack. But Adele was torn, leaving her parents' comfortable home and the horse she adored, yet excited about attending the academy and fully transitioning into an independent woman. If she'd known about the falls which were to come, she may have been even more hesitant.

Chapter 4

Security

In a multitude of acquaintances is less security, than in one faithful friend.

— *Herman Melville*

June

The elation of being accepted into a two-year residential college isn't quite as high for students and their loved ones as going to a university, although it still demands a major commitment and change in lifestyle. With its atypical admission requirements, low acceptance rate, and unique characteristics, the Paunder Avian Academy is an exception. By design, innervation is experienced even before the students step foot on the grounds.

The ocean journey to the academy was enjoyed by most, feared by others. To be sure, it was an adventure: exiting a major river to embark on the open ocean—even though they only went a few miles out—was an exhilarating or terrifying prospect, depending on point of view and expectations. The anxiety that the journey promoted was the same in everyone, though people felt it differently. Some experienced the anxiety as excitement, others as trepidation. But even if their apprehension was perceived as negative, most took the journey.

The academy provided the vessels itself, a "first gift" to new students. Those coming from Portland went out to the Pacific by the northwest-most city of Astoria, from the Columbia River; those who departed from southern parts—like Adele—came up the Oregon coast by way of Coos Bay, the largest city of the Oregon coast.

Adele and other "southern" new initiates boarded the ship at the Port of Coos Bay's Dolphin Terminal. The one-ship wharf's humble, white building for processing passengers and their luggage. The unassuming beige vessel was trimmed in blue and brown, lifeboats ominously suspended from its sides.

However, there was a surprise awaiting the students. Inside, the ambiance of each ship was posh, with sparkling clean windows, appointed with ecru and chocolate-brown striped drapes, long seats upholstered in the deep, intense blue of lapis lazuli; a sumptuous buffet was laid out, befitting the stateliest of cruise lines. It was a very special experience, and those who were anxious about the ocean voyage took comfort in the welcome atmosphere.

The ships rocked on the restless water. Although the ships stayed in sight of the land at all times, the vastness of the water under the sky's canopy made the students feel small and vulnerable. For most of the voyagers, it was a new experience, another world.

Not uncommonly, others decide to forego the oceangoing adventure and arrive via land vehicle. The academy paid for this transport too, since students were prohibited from bringing their own transportation. Of course, parents or other support people were welcome to deliver their students to the academy directly.

Her uncle and Cypress drove Phoebe to the airport in New Orleans. They left in the cool before dawn, and on the way, discussed breakfast options.

"Let's go to Dot's Diner," said Cypress. "I haven't had a crawfish biscuit in ages."

"Sounds good to me," said Phoebe. "A fitting last meal. I'll bet there's nothing like Dot's where I'm going."

"Okay, we can go to the one on Airline Drive," said Uncle Charlie as he turned the Lincoln onto Gum Avenue. "It's zip, zip, we're there. Just past the airport."

In the relative dark, Phoebe was already looking it up on her smartphone. The light from it bathed her skin in its white-blue glow. "No, we can't. It's too early. That one doesn't open till six am. But the one in Kenner is 24-hours, so it's open. May even be closer."

More than an hour later, they pulled up to the homey white building with cerulean and lipstick-red accents. A down-home style southern chain, Dot's was the family's favorite restaurant.

The biscuit was swamped with Crawfish Julie sauce, filling Cypress's plate. Despite the early hour, Uncle Charlie ordered his usual, Catfish Orleans with a side of sweet potato pancakes. Phoebe had a Popeye omelet, Beignet Stix with plenty of powdered sugar, and hot black coffee.

"It's not gonna be the same without you around pestering me, Phoebe," said her uncle after his third cup of coffee. "Not sure if that's a good thing or a bad thing, but it's gonna be different. Either way, I don't think I like it."

She leaned into his broad chest. "I'm gonna miss you too, Uncle Charlie." He didn't hear a word, but understood her completely.

Natali rented a car to drive to the Portland marina, traveling across the top of Oregon from Moscow, cutting a corner through southeast Washington. On the way, she stopped in Walla Walla to see her brother at Whitman College. He took her to breakfast in the cafeteria.

"Why are you going there, sis?" he said more than asked. "You should come here to Whitman; with your grades, I know you'd get in, and may even get a scholarship."

She sighed and explained to him again, "I'm getting my associates first. I may want to come here later; you know I've been interested in their Rhetoric Studies[3] program. But there's several directions I could go with my career; just let me get my feet wet at Paunder."

He furrowed his brow at her. "Do you think it's wise to go away from your family? You know, with your...problem? What

---

3 www.whitman.edu/academics/departments-and-programs/rhetoric-studies

will happen when you, you know, 'get upset' again?"

Natali knew his real concern. He was thinking of their cousin, how much she'd admired him; Ben was worried that even now she might be influenced by Dell. She furrowed back at him and playfully slapped down his hands. "Stop it, jerk; 'you know' I hate it when you use air quotes on me!" She pushed away from the table and grasped the tray. "I'll manage, really, just like I always do. Besides, it's not that far away. Speaking of which, hurry up Ben, and walk me to my car; I've got a boat to catch in four hours."

Once the ship exited the Pacific Ocean and entered the Pistoia River, the passengers saw S-curve-necked, long-legged snowy egrets and great blue heron standing still as statues along its bracken banks. Though the heron were larger and regal, the egret were more eye-catching in their elegant wedding-white plumage.

On the port side to the north was a black obsidian cliff that they'd seen while still at sea. Those who had read the map knew that it hid from view the Obsidian Marsh campus. Several people were walking along a wide ridge at the top of the cliff. The strollers waved to the ship as it glided by. Starboard, a rocky bank led to their first sighting of the buildings of Pearl Quay. As they neared the moorage, they saw the buildings revealed as a row of prismatic structures, all adjoining, and in an array of heights and levels. The ornate trims were mostly white, with vivid colors on the walls: shell pink, violet, periwinkle, Caribbean blue, and yellow the shade of buttercups. Cars were parked on either side of the road that divided the rocky ledge from the storefronts.

As they came to the harbor, several types of small to mid-size craft were moored: sailboats, sport-fishing boats, charter boats, river dories, and a pontoon boat or two. Most of the incoming students didn't know the difference between one vessel and another. However, some were disappointed that they didn't see jetboats; the academy didn't permit speeds more than thirty-five miles per hour.

Their ship pulled up to the main dock, bumping along the wharf. The roar of the engines reversing and the apparent shifting of gravity signalled a renewed surge of excitement among the passengers, those standing clumsily finding their balance. The captain said over the loudspeaker: "We have arrived at port. Please gather your belongings, and make your way in an orderly fashion to the starboard side of the vessel. For you landlubbers, that's the right side."

Holding tightly to his dufflebag, Zeb Caruthers barely kept his seat as the airport shuttle bounced on the westbound end of Highway 6. A major contributor, the illegal use of studded tires post-season caused the surface of Oregon roadways to deteriorate prematurely, costing taxpayers millions of dollars each year[4]. Fissures and cracks throughout portions of the asphalt were unavoidable by traffic, thus making the problem worse. For now, Zeb had problems of his own: In addition to the rough ride, the handles of the bag in his lap were cutting into his palms; the weight of it—mostly from his Latin books—all the way from Portland had made his legs numb.

His heart began to pound hard in his chest again: He'd never gone on a trip alone before, certainly not to the other side of the country. His father had driven him to the airport in the dark early morning, an awkward but not unfamiliar silence like soiled laundry lay between them the entire trip.

From his father cursing the parking situation to passing through Security at Roanoke, Zeb's stress level was nearly over the top. Sitting in the gatehouse for most people was an annoyance. For Zeb, now that his father was gone, it was a relief. Almost too soon, it was time to board the airliner.

People seemed as slow as sorghum as they boarded. He wanted the trip over quickly. The dawdling and backtracking of passengers finding their seats and shoving oversized bags in the overhead bins agitated him further.

At last, everyone was settled and new annoyances began.

---

4 www.ktvz.com/news/odot-studded-tire-use-down-road-damage-too/30320388

Jet engines roared, but still they did not budge. Finally they jolted forward, taxiing slowly on the ground, making turns on the side strips. It seemed to Zeb that the plane became heavier as it approached the runway. He looked out the window for a moment, saw nothing but low trees in the distance beyond the airfield. He quickly resumed his view to the front. The plane taxied into position, and halted again. After what seemed like eternity to Zeb, the engines roared and squealed; as little as he liked flying, he hated the anticipation of it even more. As the plane started forward, gaining speed, it shuddered. Babies were already crying from the change in pressure, passengers who'd been reading put down their materials, finding it too difficult to read the shaking words. Going so fast now Zeb wondered when they'd crash, they caught some air, lightly bounced once or twice, then were airborne.

As they gained altitude, Zeb continued to stare up to the wall at the front of the plane until it leveled out. All the way on the flight out to Portland he shut down as best he could, ignoring the young woman at the window seat. She was excitedly saying such things as, "Holy cow, we're up high!" and "Look at that, those cars look like ants!" Instead of slapping her across the back of her fool head, he folded his arms tightly over his chest and clamped his eyes closed. He only opened them to abruptly tell the flight attendant "no" when offered a beverage. A tremulous sigh escaped him when they hit a particularly hard air pocket, and Zeb squeezed his eyes shut once more.

Chapter 5

Hope

There is no coming to consciousness without pain.
People will do anything, no matter how absurd, in
order to avoid facing their own Soul. One does not
become enlightened by imagining figures of light, but
by making the darkness conscious.

— Carl Jung

June

From the vantage of the overlook, Kimiko Paunder watched the ship as it came around the jetty and into Pistoia River from the Pacific Ocean. It disappeared from view as it passed on the far side of the retail and residential buildings. It had been her grandfather's favorite pastime too, watching the arrival of the new students, from this very spot on Lapis Lookout. Oceangoing wasn't the quickest way to travel, but it was an opportunity for the students to mingle, receive some orientation, and perhaps most importantly, transition from the everyday world to the unique, self-contained environment of the academy.

Kimiko pulled the long cardigan against her slender body, tying the belt to protect her from the wind.

The butter-cream colored house at Lapis Lookout was the oldest building on the campus, though it wasn't the first built. Spreckles Manor had a large, half-ellipse balustraded balcony constructed on the west side. It afforded a vast view of the Pacific Ocean from the family quarters; the view from the enclosed patio below was lesser, but still majestic; a perfect place to storm-watch. The main entrance was at the lee of the house. Spacious enough for the Paunder residence, several classrooms, and a dining area, it was quickly proven inadequate as the academy grew. Five larger buildings were soon constructed in the same Spanish Mediterranean style, but none could quite rival the history, attention to detail, and view that Spreckles Manor enjoyed. Shore pines sculpted into sometimes twisted, always asymmetrical shapes by the buffeting winds provided some break for the grounds.

Honoré and his wife, Fujioka, raised Kimiko on the grounds; she remembered skylarking in the yards during the day, and at night, listening to her father's and others' stories about events, visitors, and exploits of the last or current guild.

Now she wondered—hoped—that a guild would form from this incoming summer bloc, by luck or timing or providence. The last guild to coalesce had completed their obligation two years ago. Although two had stayed on as staff at the academy— not all "leaves" leave, as they have the option to stay on as staff members—it was vital that a guild was active off-campus as often as possible, to keep the momentum of the academy's *raison d'être* strong; and to keep their benefactors, both present and future, interested. Was a guild necessary? Not necessarily, but it was a unique and beneficial tradition, the guild doubling as ambassadors for the academy. The academy was largely self-sustaining, with recent alumni sponsoring new students, income from Pearl Quay's rentals and moorage fees, and raising some of its own food as well as providing many of its other needs; but donors were an important source to fill in the inevitable gaps in expenses.

Kimiko learned last week that the previous summer bloc which just completed their fourth term wasn't eligible, simply because not all interactions were cross-reported. There had been students from almost half the terms eligible, but reported interactions weren't adequate to form a guild. Most had entered their convergences into the specialized kiosks, but not always both parties, a requirement for coalescence. It was disappointing: there were several students in that bloc who would've made excellent representatives, with charisma and presence. But Kimiko reminded herself that it wasn't all about ambassadorship, or even the perception of it. The guilds were out in the community, in the country, to promote expanse of thought and the virtues dear to her grandfather's heart; its purpose is not to self-promote, neither to promote ideals and "best" personalities, but that all types of people can contribute, regardless of talent or agreeability.

When she heard a crunch of rock, she turned to see a golf cart come up the circular driveway. The driver came out and approached her. "Good noon, m'lady," said a robust man in his mid-twenties, shirtsleeves rolled up to his elbows. His faded jeans were lightly stained, and there was a dusting of earth on his brow. "Beautiful day to watch boats come in, isn't it?"

"I agree ... and I hope it's a good omen, Luke." She glanced at the scene far below them. The ship had reappeared, and was coming into the harbor.

"Yep, I heard that it's time for some fresh blood," Luke jested.

"Now you know I don't care for that phrase, but you're correct. Having a guild form is good for morale, in addition to the infusing of new energy. Didn't your bloc have one coalesce?" asked Kimiko.

"It was the bloc after mine," said Luke. "The announcement came during my third term. It was exciting; I had just committed to serving two years instead of sponsoring. Truth be told, it's why I decided to stay on here after graduation, to be part of the energy. I may be 'just a groundskeeper,'"— exaggeratingly using air quotes—"but I use and share what I learned every day." He explained how the challenges of the enhancement classes made him aware of his perceptions, and preconceptions.

"Like what, for example?" she asked.

"Like grief. I always thought of it as a bad thing, something to avoid. While it is difficult to go through, it can heighten your senses, bring emotions out in the open, and help you to appreciate what you haven't lost, as well as what you did lose."

Kimiko looked at him directly. "I'm so glad to hear you say that. That's what it's all about, isn't it? It's not a philosophy; everyone determines their own beliefs. But it's a way of living." She shook her head, and turned back to the scene below. "I know this can't go on forever, but humanity needs every benefit it can get, every reminder and perspective about the good we can be and do. We've been able to provide some of that into communities across the country, and beyond. I'd hate to see that come to an end, just because of funding problems."

"Don't tell me you're giving up hope, Kimi? Is the academy having financial difficulties?"

"No, not at all." She paused. "It's just a momentary pity-party. I'm sure we'll be fine; after all, the benefactors aren't our only source of funds." A warm gust blew suddenly from the east. She pulled the sweater's collar further up her neck. "I'm going in for lunch of chamomile tea and cucumber sandwiches in a few minutes. Want to join us?"

"Thanks, but I came up to feed the peacocks, then I have a team of coeds coming to work on the pens. Enjoy lunch." He left Kimiko alone to watch the ship. It was now docked, and the passengers were starting to disembark.

Regardless of whether new students first set foot at Paunder Avian Academy at the docks—as most did—or coming in by land via the Oregon Coast Highway, everyone started their tour at Pearl Quay before heading off to the Trunk to orient for their first term. To please her mother, Naomi Paunder designed the buildings at "the Pearl" after Bianca's hometown of Portofino, Italy.

They were shown the harbor. "As you see, and experienced," said Branchmaster Amber Bootsma, "this is a working harbor. We have fishing charters, whale watching tours, and private boats docked here. It's one important stream of income for the academy; you might even say we help to keep it afloat." Amiable groans were audible—and understood—throughout the crowd.

As the new coeds completed their introduction to Pearl Quay, they were assembled at The Hip, an open area for all kinds of gatherings. At one end was a gazebo of weathered pine, large enough to accommodate a band or small wedding ceremony. At the other, an outdoor stage was used for plays, orchestras, graduation ceremonies, auctions, and provided an alternate location in case of surprise rainstorms, which are not uncommon on the Oregon coast. In the middle of the Hip was a wide lawn of dark, lush grass. In the more blustery months, an enormous white tent was erected for this and other events, and taken down after March arrivals. Spring weather was still unpredictable, but not severe. This day was beautiful. While the new students waited for the next phase of the tour, appetizers and beverages including coffee, water and juices were provided.

The students assessed one another in the warm sun. Even without asking, each knew something about the others already: that they were all about 17-24 years old, each had an interest in learning other languages, that they had an appreciation for science, nature, humanity, and animals—if not a love—and they had at least some of the attributes of being a leader. These were among the qualities for being admitted to the Academy.

Zeb felt much better after eating, since he hadn't had a meal since leaving Mullens[5] ten hours earlier. He'd refused the lunch his mother had packed, and didn't want anything to eat while flying. He'd learned the hard way that food in his belly made him nauseous when traveling.

A tall man with short-cropped jet-black hair and a trim goatee took the stage after all newcomers were accounted for. Many recognized him from the academy's literature as Mr. Radegast, the Trunkmaster. He tapped on the microphone to deliver the orientation instructions.

"Welcome, everyone. I trust you enjoyed your trip." He waited a few moments while the two hundred students hushed each other. Once he had their attention, he continued: "You'll begin your tour here at Pearl Quay, which most of you know is

---

5 www.city-data.com/city/Mullens-West-Virginia.html

the school of business. As I'm sure you've already noticed, this is first-and-foremost a working harbor. It's also the center of our commerce, as it's the only area of campus where the public can do business. In fact, all of the shops you see here," he gestured to the main storefronts, repeating what Bootsma had said, "are operated by local merchants. Rent from these businesses is crucial in helping to finance the academy. But enough about that; you'll be breaking up into groups here in a few minutes. Your guides will be instructors from each of the schools. We have ten shuttles to take you for flash-and-dash introductory tours, so you'll be at each for less than half an hour. Please board when you're called, or you'll miss dinner! Have fun, get to know each other, and I'll see you back at the Trunk."

A Word About the Bird

Mascot of Pearl Quay, the Snowy Egret[6] of the heron family has pure white plumage. Among other shorebirds, it shares the riverside and wetlands with the great blue heron, a larger cousin. They hunt small fish and other aquatic animals with their long, thin beaks, swallowing their prey whole. Though cautious, they are not shy, so can be viewed openly. If approached carefully, one can get a close-up look. A startling gesture will send them skyward, flapping expansive wings while stretching out or their long, curved necks.

Their throaty, loud call—which belie their elegant appearance—reminded Paunder of the sounds that are associated with dinosaurs, particularly when in flight. Because of this, he believed that they are descendants of pterodactyls.

---

6 www.allaboutbirds.org/guide/Snowy_Egret/id

Chapter 6

Wonder

...Composed of sand was that favored land,
And trimmed with cinnamon straws;
And pink and blue was the pleasing hue
Of the Tickletoeteaser's claws....
— Charles Edward Carryl, "A Nautical Ballad"

June, same day

Pearl Quay was the only campus open to the public on a daily basis. The harbor moored as many as forty fishing vessels, as well as several various charter boats. Visitors would come in hopes of catching their limit of tuna, salmon, halibut, and more. Or for the less macho, to catch sight of cetacean creatures of the deep such as Grey whales and orcas. Sharks were present too, but rarely spotted from land or sea.

Groups of initiates formed, glancing inside the windows of the storefronts and eateries as they were being led upstairs to the second-floor classrooms, and third-floor dormitories. Most were surprised at the layout of the four-resident dorm rooms: four sections for beds, which was not a surprise, but that they were set in an alcove with walls enclosing the beds on three sides, was. They formed an H shape, the sleeping alcoves forming the stems. Each of them had one window on the side, to the right or left, a shelf and built-in drawers on the other.

After they had toured the rest of Pearl Quay, the new students waited their turn to load onto a shuttle to tour more of the schools. Ten colorful shuttles were lined up along the dockside. Each was painted with one color in several shades to form an abstract composition. The academy's brochure explained that each summer—when humidity was lowest, and days longest—the Arts students from all current blocs would design and paint one of the shuttles.

Owlet was painted in seal brown, chocolate, beige, cedar, and rusty ochre; its streaks and knots resembled wood grain.

Canary, which was painted in shades of amber, citrine, daffodil, pale butter, and deep goldenrod, shone with rays inspired by the sun.

The *Peacock* shuttle, painted in azure, navy, cobalt, sky, and robin's egg blue swirls and dashes reminiscent of the sky in Vincent Van Gogh's "Starry Night."

Cardinal was enrobed in wide painted ribbons of scarlets, rubies, deep roses, lipstick red, and burgundy.

The black *Swan* shuttle's deep colors took the shapes of ocean waves at night in eggplant, indigo, coffee, ink, carbon.

Mallard's tall, narrow blades of forest, teal, emerald, olive, and even green-apple gave one the impression of being shrunk inside a psychedelic green lawn. This shuttle was the next slated for redesign.

The most recently painted shuttle, *Ostrich*, had elegant undulating bands, from the darkest gray to the lightest: somber gunmetal, battleship, titanium, silver, to the pale of dove.

The playfully colored squares of *Flamingo* created a checkerboard pattern in salmon, baby pink, cerise, crimson, and coral.

The purples of *Martin*—lavender, lilac, eggplant, plum, and amethyst—inspired its class to design circles, some overlapping, some transparent.

White *Egret's* design was the most representational, with shapes in ecru, smoke (a very pale lavender), pink pearl, vanilla, and honeydew, strongly suggesting seashells.

As each of the shuttles filled, they left for Sandpink Beryl. The drivers turned on the overhead speaker. "Welcome to the Paunder Avian Academy, also known as PAA. You each have a notebook. Inside the front cover you'll find instructions for using it if you have hopes of being eligible for a guild." Adele pulled out the eucalyptus-bound notebooks they'd just been issued and read:

> Your class is the Pangolin bloc. During your first year, you are encouraged to record and report interactions you've had with other students from your bloc.
>
> You have the responsibility and the discretion to report your interactions. Several kiosks are available on the grounds. You each have a code to encrypt your identity, in the event that you want to keep that information concealed. The code is the first two letters of your bloc, the day of your birth, your first and last initials of your name, plus a numeral. Your code is: PA19AS1. If this doesn't match you, discuss with the first branchmaster you see.
>
> You must have co-recorded and reported interactions to be eligible as a myrmidon for the guild. Only five of you will make the guild, assuming one is possible. The more interactions you have, the higher your chances, and ours. Remember, your participation is voluntary. Likewise, it is prohibited to coerce anyone into participating against their will.

The students knew how the system worked already, but it helped to be reminded. Most of the "fresh leaves" immediately listed their seatmates.

The shuttles came out of Pearl Quay on the ocean side down the tail end of Escape Drive, with crop fields on the left, and a pine forest on the right, the ocean unseen beyond the trees. As they made a turn through the end of the forest, it was common for the students to gasp and "wow" in unison at the unspoiled beach ahead of them. The sand glistened in a cool pink, as the beryl-blue waves crashed ashore. The drivers always paused at this wayside for their riders to drink in the scene before moving into Sandpink Beryl proper.

"It's so beautiful," Natali said under her breath, unaware she spoke aloud. She'd been to the Oregon coast several times, at the quaint but commercial town of Seaside. But never a beach like this, where feldspar, mica, and garnet particles infused the sand, capturing light and throwing it back in sparkling pinks.

The shuttle continued along the sand-dusted blacktop of Escape. Salty air was immediately evident, fresh and cool, not at all odorous like the students experienced at Pearl Quay. The shuttle pulled up to a large, sturdy round building walled with canvas. The roof came to a peak at the center; a wide cedar deck with built-in benches encircled the structure.

The driver opened the shuttle door. "Here we are, your beachfront campus. That building there is called a yurt. Your guide is around somewhere; should be here shortly. I'll be waiting for you over at that lot. Enjoy your tour of Sandpink Beryl, school of marine biology, and home of our mascot sandpipers. By the way, you're in luck: they're about to migrate for the summer. Once they do, we won't see them again till autumn."

Sure enough, on the flat, wet sand beyond the yurt Natali could see a large group of sandpipers commingling with plovers, all busy on the sparkling shore. The tiny, sensitive creatures scurried farther down the beach as the students disembarked. It was unbelievable that the fragile birds were hardy enough to make the long trip.

As the last student caught up to the tour, the shuttle was driven to the parking area.

"Hey, guys, take off your shoes. The sand feels amazing between your toes!" said a tall, red-headed hoyden, as she bounced on the sand like a child experiencing the beach for the first time. Several of the others slipped off their footwear, with the "ahhhs" following. The pink, fine sand oozed between toes, and soon fingers. It was soft and somewhat powdery, with a bit of grittiness. It reminded Natali of coarse cornmeal. She and several other students walked up the steps of the yurt, and strolled around on its wooden deck.

"Welcome, everyone! I'm glad to see you're making yourselves at home," said an older man. He seemed to come out of nowhere, but the sand sticking to his bare feet revealed that he must have just come from the beach. "Come on up here, we'll start with the great room." He walked up past Natali and into the yurt.

Inside the great open space, the students could see the structure of the yurt. Many beams radiated out from a circular hole in the peak of the roof. The beams met the tops of the lattice-patterned walls, which created a circle. Along with the opening at the top, windows let in abundant light. Brattebo led them to one of the walls and stood by a map of Sandpink Beryl.

"It's difficult to get to this beach from the shore, so we don't get many visitors here. But you should know that Oregon state law says that the beaches are for everybody, so we don't 'own' the beach. We own access to it, but the academy's land officially ends there at the grassline," he said as he pointed to symbols of the dune grasses. "Now, here you see our other yurts. The one we're in is the main meeting place. These plain circles mark our aquatic classrooms and labs. We're fairly spread out here, so I suggest you have a look at our other displays here instead of going out on the campus for now. I assure you, even if you don't take any classes here, you'll make time for it later." The students dispersed throughout the room, admiring the various maps and photos along the walls.

The red-headed girl bumped up to Zeb. "Hi, awesome place, huh?" she proffered. "We're both in the Canary shuttle. I'm Penelope, but everyone calls me Poppy. Hey, you wanna trade codes?"

"Uh, hi. Sure," he answered. He was taken aback by her forwardness and energy. They exchanged numbers.

"I didn't see you on my boat. Did you take the other one, or were you hiding?"

Zeb really didn't feel like being sociable. It'd been a very long day, and he wouldn't be able to relax till he got settled in his dorm room. The tour was important, but being chatted up wasn't, not to him. "Neither. I didn't come by ocean. I came by airport shuttle."

"Oh, too bad - it was really exciting. We even got to see a school of dolphins! It was *tres magnifique!*"

"Actually, a group of dolphins is called a pod," he corrected.

"Oh yeah, whatever. Irregardless, you shoulda seen 'em."

Zeb dropped his chin and rolled his eyes up as though he were spying on a cat atop a fence. He found it annoying when people who could speak a second or even third language couldn't speak their own. He saw no point in correcting her again. Besides, she'd already moved on to collect her next name, probably to fill her book to increase her chances of getting on a guild.

When Natali reboarded the "Owlet" shuttle, she took a seat up front, behind the driver. Another girl stopped, about Natali's same build and height. "Ya mind if I sit with you?" she said.

"Not at all, have a seat," said Natali.

"I'm Phoebe," said the girl. "Isn't this tour a great way to start our journey?!" Natali smiled. Combined with Phoebe's openness and enthusiasm, and the way she reminded her of herself in style and outlook, Natali instantly took a liking to her. She could tell that they'd be good friends.

The shuttles made the loop at the end of Escape Drive; a large, oblong cenotaph of sandstone with carvings of sandpipers created the road's end. Doubling back up towards Pearl Quay but before they reached the business campus, the shuttles turned onto a wide dirt road, the hillside now to their right, a crop field on the left.

They came around the hillside, then took Carnelian Circle to the right, beginning the winding climb to the top of Lapis Lookout, the school of humanities and communication. Appropriately, the cell tower was located here. Nadja Paunder had negotiated with the provider, insisting not only that it be built upon the donated land, but that it share the structure with other cell service providers since staff, students, and visitors used different carriers. As a result, cell phone coverage is available all over the campus, regardless of provider. The shuttles' drivers usually pointed out the tower because it was camouflaged to look like the cypress trees that led up to it.

"Hey, cypress, that's my momma's name!" Phoebe told Natali.

Drivers explained that while cellular service was available all over the grounds, internet access via wi-fi was only available at the main common building of each school. By design—to discourage high, distracting usage—the signal range is quite limited.

Kimiko waited for the shuttles in the driveway. She welcomed each group in turn, and directed them to tour guides —instructors at the school—inside the big house who would take them on a brief tour.

On the floor at the center of the foyer balanced a large lapis lazuli sphere, nearly four feet tall. Into the vibrant blue stone were etched images of peacocks and peahens. Suspended over it hung a Spanish-style chandelier dripping with crystals, lapis pieces embedded in its goldtone ornamentation. Beyond the foyer, sumptuous furnishings with rich embroidery, tapestries on the wall, over-sized house plants, and Persian rugs graced the space with its vaulted ceilings and creamy-white walls. Above them were balconies to the second story. They were led through arched doorways into the enormous family-style kitchen, meeting rooms, and other common spaces before being taken upstairs to the classrooms. All the rooms were roomy and bright, appointed with the same elegant furniture and accessories. But the feature that inspired the most awe was the view of the Pacific Ocean, for which the school had been named.

When they came back downstairs, a husky boy from the Martin shuttle came across a bright blue, boxy machine in the foyer. In a strident voice he announced, "Oh, look here; so *that's* what the kiosks look like." Several students began taking turns entering codes. They were hurried along by branchmaster René Miracle, a tidily-dressed older woman. "You'll have plenty of time to do that later," she patiently explained.

Back outside, the peacocks, olive trees, additional buildings were pointed out. But there was no time to visit them up close, as time was tight. Each group bid farewell to Kimiko before leaving.

As the shuttles rumbled back down the spiral on the east side of Lapis Lookout, the students noticed a large herd of horses in the ample pasture below.

The drivers announced, "The herd we'll be passing are retired horses. They were employed as academy transportation, or the PAA rescued them at the end of their usefulness. It is the belief of the academy that a horse's quality of life shouldn't end simply because their work has, so we provide them a forever home." He clicked off the microphone.

Phoebe admitted to Natali, "I've never ridden a horse in my entire life."

"That's going to change here. You are planning to ride, aren't you?"

Phoebe shrugged. "I don't know; I'm thinking I'll just take the shuttle. They run all day during the week."

"Sure, you could do that. There's one that makes a continual loop all day, and another that waits for a call, then runs the loop. But there are horses at each school that you can use to get to the next one. A stable attendant is always there to grab an available horse for you, and once saddled, off you go!"

"But by the time that all happens, the shuttle will probably arrive, so it doesn't save any time."

"True, but what's the fun in that?!"

Phoebe laughed. "You've got a point. I'll probably try it. But only on a nice, sunny day. If anything, I think I'm a 'fair weather rider.'"

"Fair enough. Uh, no pun intended." Natali feigned a shocked face at her poor if unintended pun. "I want to put you in my interaction log. Make sure you put your cell number in too. I definitely want to keep in touch." She handed it to Phoebe, and Phoebe reciprocated.

On Breakthrough Way as they headed to Moon Caverns, they

passed by a large herd of elk, with their dark furry necks and light beige heart-shaped fannies and stumpy tails. Few of the students had seen live elk, and they were stunned that the adults were about the same size of some of the horses; that there were so many, maybe 80; and the fact that though some of them moved off the road, they otherwise didn't seem to care about the shuttles at all.

"A few notes about wildlife," said the driver. "If you leave them alone, they'll leave you alone...for the most part." He explained safety tips, such as not approaching bear cubs, no matter how cute and cuddly they looked. "Anytime you see a cub, just remember that somewhere, a mama bear weighing up to three-hundred pounds—mostly muscle—sees *you*."

He explained how important it was not to leave food out; more dangerous than bears were coyotes, as they were not as shy. Raccoons also posed major problems when fed human food, as it contributed to higher birth rates, exploding the population in a concentrated area. The resulting overpopulation led to competition for food and aggressive behavior both to humans and their own kind.

When they reached the front of Moon Caverns, the students expected to see a cave opening like an Easter egg scene, with a view of enormous white crystals. The PAA brochure photo showed spelunkers sitting astride a glowing, slanted column, as if they were on a fallen log. But down here from the lower part of Moon Caverns, just a plain-looking rock wall loomed ahead. They craned to see the tops of the school's buildings on the cliff looming above them.

The shuttle stopped at the foot of the wall. "We don't have time to go into the caverns today," the driver announced. "You'll need half a day to explore it. But there, just past the ledge, you can see the entrance." Several stood to peer at the uninspiring and reticent entry. "You must have a guide to go inside; contact Branchmaster Lusk to arrange a visit. We'll go up top now and meet Ms. Talbot, one of our newest instructors."

The shuttle circled back then turned west; the driver paused their journey before continuing up to the school itself. "If you look to the right, you'll see that the land drops down to the shore. You can make out the very end of Sandpink Beryl on the other side. The road used to connect here, but about a decade ago, the road collapsed into the ocean. You may have noticed the tribute on the other side, a monument to those who perished in the accident. The rubble below created an interesting habitat for our native species. You're free to check it out on your own time, but exercise caution. "

Natali said to Phoebe, "That would be interesting to check out. I've seen some ravines and caved-in trails, but not into the ocean."

"I'll go with you sometime," said Phoebe. "But I think I'll wait to go to the caverns."

Arriving at the top, they drove through manicured fruit orchards. Branches were heavy with ripening cherries and plums; hard, immature small apples and pears grew on thick, gnarly branches. "Herded" blackberry vines were allowed to grow wild, creating a natural barrier at the southern edge of the property. Rambling trails were maintained through it to enable pickers to harvest big, juicy berries.

From up here, the view of the valley they'd traveled through was incredible. They could now understand why they couldn't see the buildings from below. They stopped on the drive between the paddock and the campus' buildings. The driver told them that this School of Healthcare was where they would come for basic medical services, such as weight monitoring, wound care, and physical exams, all at no charge. The clinic was on the main floor of the central building. "But each school has a first-aid office, so don't think you have to run all the way up here to get antacid when the culinary students or your roommate experiment with your dinner." The newcomers laughed easily; their anxieties and discomfort were disappearing with each new vista.

Talbot met the shuttles at the entrance. "I know you're moving right along, and indoors is mostly classrooms like you've seen before," she explained. "So let me just tell you about what's here." She pointed out the smaller buildings to the right and left. "Those are the dormitories. Behind that dorm, are blackberry fields. This of course, is the school. Its main floor is the stables. At that end is the garage with the motorcycles. Across the way are the open paddocks, obviously."

Continuing eastward, they began the gradual climb to Basalt Moor, the school of environmental studies. At the highest point of the entire PAA grounds stood a dome-shaped building. "What's that?" asked one of the students.

"It's an observatory!" cried another. "I didn't know the academy had one!" Turning to her seatmate, "I'm an amatuer astronomer, you know."

The driver said, "They don't advertise it; it's not part of any degree class that we offer. But the original board members of PAA felt that a knowledge of the stars was valuable, so it was built for anyone who's interested in stargazing to use. Astronomers who live in Silica City come up to give free classes on occasion, especially during an astronomical event, such as a comet, for instance. I recommend you sign up as far in advance as possible, because those classes fill up quick."

"*Quickly*," corrected grammatically-aware Adele silently.

The driveway ran in front of Balboa House, the large three-story all-in-one building of the campus. The main floor of the central section had glass walls at the front and rear, so one could see through to the herb garden on the back side.

Tours of Balboa were conducted by students. They brought their followers through the atrium, pointing out the classrooms above on one side, the dorm rooms above on the other. Directly above them the three-story tall room was capped by a massive skylight. On the main floor in one direction were the cafeteria and other service rooms, such as the laundry; on the other side could be found conference rooms, the library, and study centers. The students were then ushered out the back, treated to a walk-through of the large herb garden. "This is a working garden," they were told. "If you need any herbs for cooking or any other kind of project, come on by and help yourself. We only ask that you take no more than you need." Each group was then alternately circled around the building to meet their shuttles on the other side.

Rejoining Breakthrough Way, they began the descent toward Escape Drive, stopping before they joined it. "To your right you'll see the security gates," said each driver. Two wishbone-shaped gates consisted of two long joined boards painted yellow, with reflective tape striping them, and a metal arm to raise and lower them. "These are closed at night so a gate code to enter is needed after ten o'clock. A few hundred yards past it is the Oregon Coast Highway."

After half a mile on Escape, the shuttle turned up East Peregrinate into Saffron Cascade, the school of creative arts. The driver explained that they wouldn't be able to see the waterfalls from the road, they'd have to go on trails. They wound their way through rocky fields with carpeting clusters of flowering plants on the way to the campus. "This lower area is too rocky for horses, but it's a utopia for hummingbirds, butterflies, honeybees, and more. In a few months, it will be colored lavender with autumn crocuses. You can even harvest their saffron."

They slowly passed by the paddocks and barns. Mostly ungroomed, lanky horses watched them warily as they went by. These were not the types of horses Adele was used to seeing back at home. The horses in her neighborhood—including Oliver—were strong, well-trained, and healthy. These leery horses frightened her, as mistreated, unsocialized horses were generally the most dubious.

"This school also hosts the main library of the academy." Driving past the front of the modern, mostly-glass fronted building, sounds of approval and impressed students emanated from the shuttle. Phoebe couldn't wait to check out this beautiful library. She hoped that the books inside were as wonderful. She would have to wait though; the shuttle only let them out at one of the instructional buildings. No classes were in session (of course), but they were serenaded by bits of music and voice as they passed rooms with students practicing. As they walked by the art classrooms, they were greeted with the odors only art studios could produce: oils, clay, solvents, and indiscernible scents played their own kind of symphony of the senses.

The leaves dropped in on one group of residential chalets on their way to the shuttles. The quaint two-story structures with wide, eave-covered patios built on the hill was reminiscent of Swiss homes in the Alps. But the tight schedule didn't allow time to go inside.

Back on the shuttles, they made their way down the hill again, crossing Escape Drive onto West Peregrinate, and entered the Crimson Song campus, school of hospitality and culinary arts. Rainbow and red gum eucalyptus towered overhead, sharing the space from ground to canopy with Sitka spruce and alders. They wound around the serpentine road, viewing the front ends of the cottages, shrubbery and other vegetation dividing them.

They came to the clubhouse, a large log cabin. Sine Cameron waited inside the great room filled with tables and chairs. As each tour group came in, she said, "Greetings, please have a seat." She waited until everyone was settled. "Welcome to the school of hospitality and culinary arts. I am the branchmaster for this campus and director of hospitality for the academy. If there is any issue you experience or observe in regards to the way the academy is perceived by anyone, anywhere, I am the one who wants to hear about it. This is your last stop on the tour for today. I know you're all tired, so in front of you you'll find a map of our campus. I'm going to give you a virtual tour with it." Eric's smile spread across his face. The map was well-drawn, and he appreciated it better than most. Sine continued, "You've already seen our cottages. Now look on your map and you can see where the kitchens and classrooms are located. Our layout is quite different from the other campuses, because it works within our environment. We even have some classrooms up in the trees! I don't think you'll find that at an institution very often." She was clearly proud of the extraordinary setup.

She completed the virtual tour by taking questions.

"Do you have cooking classes in the trees?" asked one of the students from Adele's shuttle.

Sine laughed. "No, we're not quite that adventurous. Those classrooms are for discussion and study only. And yes, before anyone asks, they are handicap accessible. What other questions do you have?"

After answering a few more, she said, "It's time for you to go on to the Trunk to conclude today's tour of the academy. As you go out the door, please take a gift bag we've prepared for you. Have a good night, and I'll see some of you in a few days."

Chapter 7

Trust

The whole value of history, of biography, is to increase my self-trust, by demonstrating what man can be and do.

— *Ralph Waldo Emerson*

June, same day

As each shuttle arrived at the backside of the Trunk, they drove past what looked to be an apartment building with plants and toys on some of the balconies. "That is our family residence hall," explained the drivers. "Students with life partners or children live there, and are exempt from moving between campuses each term."

Once parked in the arena lot, the students were guided into the larger of two convention rooms adjacent to the arena. Radegast greeted the fading leaves with more instructions.

"You'll find that your luggage has been moved by our hospitality crew, and is waiting for you at your rooms," said Radegast. "We know you're tired from a long day and we've thrown a lot of information at you, but we have two points of business to attend to: giving you your living assignments—I'm sure you'd like to know where to drop tonight—and we're going to send you off to your dorms with a hearty supper, also provided by hospitality in concert with culinary students. Joining us will be some of the other current students as well. Feel free to pick their brains; just make sure you leave some for the rest of us." Several students politely laughed, more from nerves than the double pun. "If you forget or are confused about the schools you've visited today, don't worry—you'll find in your rooms an album with photos and information about each of them."

Radegast explained that tomorrow they'd complete their tour of the academy and be subjected to evaluations. Though the students had completed personal needs assessments at home in topics related to medical issues, any disabilities, allergies, or dietary restrictions, they knew other needs and limitations would be checked upon their arrival. At Cedar Whiles, they'd have their horsemanship tested; those whose skills were rated intermediate or higher, and who would commit to its care, would be assigned their own horse. During their tour at Obsidian Marsh, fluid reasoning ability would be appraised; and while at Emerald Crag, crystallized intelligence[7] would be assessed.

But for tonight, they could rest, or if they preferred, recuperate by sampling the night life of Pearl Quay. However, Radegast warned, "While you can leave the grounds anytime— you are adults, not prisoners, after all—I highly recommend you stay on campus tonight. You want to have an accurate evaluation tomorrow, and this has been a very long day." Radegast then explained the room assignment process. The students were directed to find the booth along the wall with initials of their last name. Eric Wholm found the "U-Z" booth at the far right.

Though never a wallflower, Eric had an inner dread that he was out of place. The bustling of finding room assignments vaguely reminded him of busy life back home, but it couldn't really compare. City life was constantly in motion, day and night. A major metropolitan city, Atlanta, Georgia[8] is full of people, especially in his complex. His family lived on the third floor of the Heritage Station Apartments. An exceptionally gregarious family, friends and neighbors move through the Wholm household every day, kids running and screaming up

---

7 study.com/academy/lesson/two-types-of-intelligence-fluid-and-crystallized-intelligence.html
8 www.city-data.com/city/Atlanta-Georgia.html

and down the stairwell. Eric was also sociable, taking part in the goings-on, but it drained him mentally. He sought solitude outdoors when possible, gaining energy from time alone.

When he'd been contemplating his impending departure, he looked down at the vacant soccer fields in a park near his home. It was about the biggest open space he usually saw. And now he'd be going to the Pacific Northwest, with more nature than he'd ever seen.

At seventeen years old, Eric was taller than most of the other boys in his class, but not awkwardly so. Far from gangly, an athletic assurance made him appear even taller than he was. He made friends easily, though not closely. Back home he had friends for years, but they couldn't have told you Eric's thoughts and dreams. Few knew he wrote poetry. He was thought of as the fun guy, not the deep guy. Although they thought they did, none other than his girlfriend Amara knew him well.

Outwardly he had the appearance of confidence. Inwardly he felt like he didn't know what he was doing, even a fraud … just like everyone else.

Eric also read poetry secretly. On an internet search for his favorite poet, Eric came across a poem about him.

"RICHARD HUGO 23-82"
blonde road…
i found his name in the book (the one i didn't buy)
23-82!
DEAD?
the voice of those small volumes
i accidentally found in a library or two
and read for hours in a kicking-horse reservoir

82?
one hundred and eighty-two pounds in a sailor suit
(back from the MED)
looking for girls
a major north pacific poet book in the lynchburg library

collecting dust
the big-bellied antagonist who quit a good paying job
is gone
a nothing in a norfolk bar knows nothing about the nothing,
loss

88, volumes read and read by an english major — extra A credit
    on a final exam — knowledge of a modern free verse poet
writing small little haikus
writing small little letters
writing small little papers
to present in class
(i wonder what Richard would say about this?
eating steaks medium rare
gallons and gallons of beer, long restroom stops — the tile on
the floor deep blue dust building a universe beneath his feet
do you believe in god?
can i borrow your book?
god helps me with my abstinence
where is your book?
thumbing through
RICHARD HUGO 1923-82
no more blonde road!
i almost got a book on Dylan's lyrics
no more blonde roads to fall upon
AMERICAN LITERATURE THREE-THREE-THREE
looking over the still waters of the reservoir
calm yet brown
filled with the same blonde earth he walked on
and dreamed on, finding himself along the groove cut between
    grasses
praying to a dead god.

The poem mirrored what Eric felt, that he was alone, no longer with his friends and family, the familiars of his life. The difference was, he was the one who left *them*. Did he make the right choice? He would have to trust that he had.

For many of the incoming, this was their first major trip away from home, often their first time out of their home states. It took faith, and trust, to leave their homes behind and get a new start in an unfamiliar place, with unknown people.

Between each term, a two-week break gave the current students time to pack up and move to another branch. The resulting scuffle as sometimes students were caught between residences was expected and tolerated as a life-lesson in patience, ingenuity, amiability, and resourcefulness. The Paunders believed life experience, not just classroom exposure, was educational. Frequent moving as well as attending enhancement classes at the different schools also prevented students from becoming "barn-sour": identifying so strongly with a particular school that rivalries between them would develop. Bianca in particular felt that unity was in the academy, not its separate campuses. "The schools may be independent of one another, but the grounds bind us all," she said.

But all new students started at the Trunk; previous occupants had moved out within the last two weeks, so the newcomers were spared that confusion. The Trunk was the hub of all transportation, and being centrally located, gave them easier access to the other ten campuses while they were learning their way around. Group horsemanship or dual sport motorcycle lessons were offered at the arena, so by the time their first term ended, the new students knew the grounds almost as well as any other student.

Natali held the map of the dormitory unfolded in front of her. The first meal she had on campus delivered on Mr. Radegast's promise: it was delicious, savory and juicy. A truly hearty stew, made with chunks of beef, caramelized onion, carrots, and spices. Accompanied by a flaky buttermilk biscuit and a green garden salad, with apple pie ala mode to finish it off, Natali understood why the way to a man's—or anyone's—heart was through their stomach. Now with her dorm assignment in hand, she was off to find the room she'd share with three other "newbies."

Others were also looking for their rooms. Males and females darted about, teasing and purposefully causing confusion while looking for their section of the residential building, the largest dorm on the entire PAA grounds. As they did, the men finding their rooms on the fourth floor and the women theirs on the third, the sexes were divided. Fountains of laughter gushed through the U-shaped hallways. Natali found her room and relative quiet near the laundry. One other girl was there, already making the bed she chose.

"Hi, nice choice!" Natali said.

"Yeah, thanks—the privilege of being the first to arrive," said the girl. She stood up and held out her hand. "Hi, I'm Amanda Wayfair, Williston, North Dakota," she said, using the introduction format Mr. Radegast had suggested.

"Natali, Moscow, Idaho[9]." Natali noted Amanda's strong grip. "Oh, Williston, that's where Sitting Bull surrendered, right?"

"Wow, you know your history! You are correct madam." Amanda flourished a polite curtsy. "And you're from Idaho, huh? Nice. Hey, you should grab a bed before the others get here. I had thought about the one by the bathroom, but I decided I'd rather be near the window." She turned back to her unpacking.

"Gotcha, thanks." Natali surveyed the room. The beds were arranged along the walls, head-to-feet in mirror image. There was a gap in the middle for the wide window. Directly outside was a view of the large parking lot; beyond that, Escape Drive up to Crimson Song. To her right, a third bed was closest by a few steps to the bathroom—could be handy for some in the quiet of the night, Natali thought, but not for her—and the last bed was against the back of their shared closet. She opted for the other window bed.

"Do you think we could move these beds around, maybe make a different configuration?" Natali asked.

"Nope, they're bolted to the floor. My guess is they've had

---

9   www.city-data.com/city/Moscow-Idaho.html

people try all kinds of crazy things. I don't know if the other rooms are like this."

"I think I'll go look, get my bearings around here anyway. Wanna come?"

"Not right now, I'm gonna finish unpacking. You can tell me what you discovered when you come back."

Natali walked to the next room, and introduced herself. She enjoyed meeting people, and it helped her to feel at home. The other beds were, for the most part, in the same setup as her dorm room, all bolted to the floor.

In the girls' locker room, Natali ran into Phoebe. "We meet again! How's your room? Do you have a view?"

Phoebe smiled and opened an empty locker. "I think all the rooms have a nice view. Ours looks over the horse paddocks." She took shampoo, conditioner, talc, and other shower supplies out of a satchel and placed them in the locker. "Did you get a locker yet?"

"No, I didn't think of it," said Natali.

"Oh, well here's an empty one. Why don't I put something in it and call it yours?" Phoebe advised.

"Cool, thanks. I was surprised that the hygiene class is a core requirement. Shouldn't everyone know how to take care of their personal hygiene by now, in this point in their lives?" said Natali.

"You'd think so, but not everyone is raised with the same standards," Phoebe said. "I guess the academy can't assume that they are; they can't say, 'This person would know about flossing, that one wouldn't,' so they have to treat everyone the same. After all, we don't know what we don't know, you know?"

Natali returned to her room to find Amanda settled in, reading a paperback. Amanda told her that one of their other roommates had made an appearance, but went to the cafeteria to get something to drink. Natali told Amanda that the cafeteria was on the other side of the building, and other details about the layout of the place.

"We had a couple visitors drop in too, I guess they were

checking things out, like you. One of the girls is a local, from Silica City. So how'd you know about Williston? Most people've never heard of it, let alone know anything about its history."

"That's just it, I'm a history buff, mostly about the US and ancient mythology. I think it's fascinating. For instance, the term 'myrmidon' is from Classical Greek. It was interpreted as 'ant-people.' They said Achilles' grandfather, a king, pleaded with Zeus to populate his country after a terrible plague. Zeus agreed, and said his people would number as the ants on his sacred oak. From the ants sprang the people of Aegina known as the Myrmidons. Now I know that's not real history, but stories are a part of history."

"That's cool. But I've never much got into 'real' history, memorizing all those dates and names."

"I get that, but there's a lot more to it." Natali became animated. "I mean, our lives are based on history! The way we do things, why we do them ... that's it, you're my project. I'm going to show you this term just how cool it can be!"

Amanda rolled her eyes. "Fabulous."

Natali's love of history had been ignited by her older cousin, Dell Derby. His degree was in History, specializing in the Italian Renaissance. He participated in the Society of Creative Anachronism[10], even making his own clothing. Natali often attended the events with him when she was a child. She enjoyed everything about Ren Faires, from the varied tents to the jousting exhibitions. Someone would even sneak her a taste of grog or honey wine now and again. These days had been some of the most pleasant of her life; she couldn't comprehend how Dell could choose to take his own. A wise aunt had advised her not to try to understand. Still, her childhood didn't end when she turned eighteen; it ended in the summer of her fifteenth year.

After a period of mourning both Dell and the loss of her

---

10 www.sca.org/

childhood naiveté, her interest in the future was reawakened. She dreamt of life as a horse trainer, traveling around the country, giving workshops, training people to train their horses. She believed in making friends with horses, gentling the animal so it would trust people. But she was discouraged to find that it was not a popular concept; gaining trust took time, and attention to each individual horse. The "industry" was impatient for results, whatever the cost. And the "cost" was often the horses who didn't learn quickly enough what was expected of them, dismissed and discarded as "difficult" horses.

This was a hard realization for Natali. The intrusion of realities into her comfortable world were unsettling. But she knew she needed to experience them, that there was more to personal growth than happiness and contentment. She only hoped it wouldn't hurt too much. Losing Dell was painful enough.

Her parents were divorced; for a while, she lived with them alternate semesters. But it was awkward and challenging, so she moved in with her grandparents who were only too happy to have her. Natali's brother chose to leave for college a year earlier than he'd intended. Once she graduated from high school, she wanted to be on her own too. With her earnings from her job at the print shop which was now full-time, she rented a studio apartment in downtown Moscow. The responsibility of having her own apartment was offset by not being the knot in her parents' tug-of-war, or taking advantage of her maternal grandparents. She missed her brother more than her parents.

On her way to work, she would stop at the coffee shop on East 3rd Street, sketching in her drawing pad, sipping inky-black espresso and pampering herself with a pastry to start the day, a lavender lemon shortbread, or if she was feeling particularly in need of self-nurturing, a thick napoleon with its layers of filo, whipped cream, strawberry filling, and glaze.

Before going in to work, she ground out her cigarette into the rim of the cement planter. *I can't afford this disgusting habit. What a nasty legacy from such a loving woman,* she thought, remembering her chain-smoking late aunt.

Natali was enjoying her lifestyle, but was still dissatisfied — she knew she needed to do more. She wanted to have a positive impact on the world, and not waste time. With Dell's death, she realized at that tender age something that people decades older learned: time was short, there was no time like the present. For the third time—after being rejected the first two times—Natali applied at PAA.

By nine p.m., the new residents of the Trunk joined in conversations in rooms, playing games in the activity room, or for those who'd been up since early morning, retired to their rooms; some of those of legal age decided to take a walk on Escape to have a drink at the Tilting Unicorn in Pearl Quay. Other groups went down to the beach and built fires on the sand. Two of his roommates chose the bar, and the other roommate went to take a long shower. Eric took advantage of the empty room and unpacked his belongings into his built-in dresser, then put on his work boots to go downstairs and explore the arena. He'd glanced into it as they walked the corridor, but he was curious about getting a feel for the place.

The large arena was now empty. Though there were horses in the stables on the other side of two of its walls, underneath the stadium seats, all was quiet. Only the security floodlights were on, dimly illuminating the arena. The *mise en scène* was an eerie contrast to the non-stop events of the day. Yet it was also filled with potential and memories that he knew existed, but had no knowledge of.

He walked through the soft, brown dirt, making large circles and crossing through it. Eric was pleasantly lost in woolgathering. His one prevailing, concrete thought: Would this be the place where he'd find sodality, a fellowship where he would not only be accepted, but cherished for all he was and would be, "warts and all"?

Chapter 8

Intimacy

*I would venture to warn against too great intimacy
with artists as it is very seductive and a little
dangerous.*

— Queen Victoria, in a letter to her daughter

June, next day

Coming out of sleep in a strange place is momentarily disorienting for anybody. As the mind resumes consciousness, bits and pieces of the surroundings are reorganized and recognized, reorienting to time and place. Until then, the reluctant riser could be any where, in any time.

The shuffling of feet and unfamiliar though muffled voices brought Eric to a higher level of wakefulness, just short of being cognizant. Fresh out of a dream, his confused mind interpreted the hard bed and strange voices. For a long moment, he thought he was in a military hospital, maybe in the midst of the Civil War. Then flashes of recent memory, reasoning, and the odor of "man smells," as his little sister called it, came to the forefront, and he was awake.

After their cafeteria breakfast, the students gathered again to continue their tour. They broke into groups, three shuttles going to Cedar Whiles—school of animal husbandry—for their horsemanship evaluation; three to Obsidian Marsh, the school of science and technology, to test their level of fluid reasoning; and four up to Emerald Crag, psychology school, for evaluation of their crystallized intelligence. When each was completed, they rotated to the next.

While Zeb was going through his CI evaluation, he thought that just getting to the academy would've been an adequate test, one which he would've scored relatively high. Despite numerous unfamiliar situations, he did get there, after all.

Phoebe was more than happy to return to the Trunk by the end of the day. Experiencing the campus and this new environment was wonderful and exciting, but by the time she'd finished her third evaluation, she was done in. She was rated "beginner" at horsemanship, no surprise there; "average" in crystallized intelligence, which was the rating most new students earned due to their short list of life experience; "exceeding" in fluid reasoning, which did surprise her. She'd never thought of herself as street-smart; but as she considered it on the shuttle ride to Cedar Whiles, she could see that she was pretty good at thinking on her feet.

She took a shower; the rest of her day was free. Cypress had given her some money when she left Louisiana. Phoebe tried to refuse it, but her mother was insistent. "Go on now, take it. Uncle Charlie and I've been saving it. I want you to buy yourself some logo stuff, get a sweatshirt and whatnot, show your team spirit." Phoebe reminded her that PAA didn't offer intercollegiate sports. "Ah, it don't matter. Show your support anyway."

With an hour to kill before dinner, she went downstairs to the bookstore next to the academy's postal station. It was quiet, with hushed voices looking for this textbook or the other. No one was looking at the clothing. There were six color choices: a deep, this-side-of-purple Persian blue, periwinkle, white, beige, cream, and a deep, rich brown. Besides the logo, design choices included feathers, horseshoes, sea stars[11] or bluebells.

She chose a cream t-shirt with blue trim, two sweatshirts—one brown with "P.A.A." in cream lettering, the other beige with a feather design in brown—and a satiny, vibrant Persian blue sleeping shirt which was an extravagance but on sale. She

---

11 animals.nationalgeographic.com/animals/invertebrates/starfish/

thought about a cap, but decided against it, for now, instead choosing socks in cream, beige, and navy blue to complete her outfits; her denim jeans would work with it all. At the checkout, she bought some ballpoint pens and a notepad with the academy's logo to send home. The gift money spent, she was satisfied that Cypress would be too.

By the end of the first week in the Trunk, relationships—both platonic and intimate—had already materialized, and even unrequited love had surfaced.

Zeb coveted time with Adele, though he didn't yet know her name, and she probably didn't know he existed. He had seen her while on tour, where her curvy figure and slightly lopsided smile initially caught his eye. She'd just come out of Spreckles Manor at Lapis Lookout as his shuttle was pulling into the driveway. At first he thought she was one of the staff, until he noticed the eucalyptus notebook she carried under her arm. She was laughing, and though he couldn't hear her, her risibility seemed easy and sincere. At least it wasn't the "hilarious" guffaws he'd noticed some of the girls display. He was intrigued.

He spotted her again at the arena during room assignments. But how could he get to know her, without seeming creepy? Someday, when the time was appropriate, he'd have to take a chance.

Intimacy comes in different forms: sexual, psychological, emotional, etc. But you can know someone *too* well.

The coeds aired their dirty laundry, literally. In the laundry room, there were no secrets. The girls were mortified when they'd had a messy accident; some boys didn't know how to run a washing machine, and needed help. Everyone had to work on getting over it, to not be embarrassed, and to be mature enough not to make fun of their classmates. Everyone farts. Everyone stinks, now and then. And in the gym, everyone sweats.

Part Two

ANNO PRIMO FOLIA

Chapter 9

Education

Education must, then, be not only a transmission of culture but also a provider of alternative views of the world and a strengthener of the will to explore them.

— *Jerome S. Bruner*

June

The break was over. The academy's grounds were now fully populated with returned coeds and teachers scurrying around to their first day of classes. Early summer was being cooperative: Other than a thin veil of morning haze, there wasn't a cloud in the azure sky.

Adele walked up the breezy concrete stairs to her core orientation class on the fourth level. The Trunk's main building was made of concrete, from the massive pillars supporting the structure and porticoes to the planter boxes and benches. It was a clean, high-tech industrial-type environment. She had an appreciation for it, but also an apprehension of it, as she recalled her humbling fall in the courtyard in Santa Rosa. Concrete was strong, and unforgiving.

The sound of tribal drums provided an unexpected counterpoint to the setting. As she neared Room 4C, it was apparent that the drumming came from inside.

She was the last to arrive, as usual. The instructor closed the door after her, gesturing flamboyantly for her to take a seat in the circle. Tall and lean, with a long hook nose, deep laugh lines and a loud tie, Robin Fergus stood at the front of the room and directed the drumming to stop. "Go ahead and set the drums down. I hope you enjoyed that exercise. As this is your first class at the academy, it's been my experience that music—especially that you make yourselves—is a language of its own that's conducive to relaxation, bonding, and can bridge the gap between spirituality and the mundane. That, of course, is for you individually to decide." He stood between two posters on easels: one listed all the required core classes for the students' first term, the other listed all the elective core classes available.

"A more pressing decision to make is the focus you want your degree to take. You have until the end of this term—if you haven't already—to choose twelve enhancement classes to complete by graduation. The purpose of those classes is to help you to expand your mind, to guide you in the best way for you to think for yourself. They are graded on participation and the effort you demonstrate to come up with your own thoughts and conclusions. These," Fergus theatrically smacked the poster of required classes with his keepsake wand, causing a girl in the front row to jump—Adele remembered hearing that he was a big fan of sci-fi/fantasy novels—"are not those kind of classes. You have no decision to make with these. Completion of these core classes are required in this term.

"Every one of you in this room is in your first term here. When you've completed this term and your core classes," he paused for more dramatic effect, "you won't be seeing as much of each other, so enjoy your company while you can." A student raised his hand. "Put down your hand, son, I don't stand on ceremony. I reckon you've got enough manners and intelligence not to interrupt. Now, whatever it is you'd like to know, just go ahead and speak up. This is your best time and place to ask any questions."

"I just want to know what you mean, that, uh, we won't see much of each other."

Fergus answered in one breath, as if it were all one long sentence. He'd explained it many times before, at least once with each new class. "After your core classes, you'll be taking classes to complete your degree, along with your enhancement classes. Some people prefer to take their enhancement classes as a block, others spread it out throughout the eight terms. For the most part, it's up to the student. So," Fergus noisily refilled his lungs, "you'll be taking classes with other students, whether they're in their second term or their last." He noted some confused faces. "Do you follow? You know, in the core classes, you're more condensed because you're all in the same bloc." He noticed there were still signs of confusion in the circle. "Eh, not to worry. It'll fall into place for you soon enough."

Fergus explained the academy's reasoning for core classes. "Intelligence in and of itself is not a factor in admission. High test scores will not provide the applying student any guarantee of admittance. But there are different types of intelligence, as well as different types of ignorance. For instance, a person with a high IQ may have terribly offensive body odor. While it may be due to a chemical imbalance or medical issue, it is more than likely a matter of personal hygiene." He threw an exaggeratedly high eyebrow to several snickering boys.

"Core classes, in addition to making sure everyone has the rudimentary skills for advanced learning, are designed to 'level the playing field,' so that everyone has if not the same, at least similar advantages." Fergus continued by having his students review the posters.

Required classes—regardless of the degree they were pursuing at PAA—are:

English / Grammar
Different dialects and accents across the country. Participants find an appreciation and tolerance for differences.

Writing Papers / Preparing Reports
Learn how to get your point across in such a way that your audience will want to take the time to read your papers or reports. This skill is critical to the academy's courses, however basic or advanced.

Personal Hygiene and Time Management
A light-hearted class which usually results in the students letting their guards down, getting to know each other better.

Public Speaking and Other Keys to Success
It is said that most people have a greater fear of public speaking than they do of death. This class will help you "feel the fear and do it anyway!" with the support of your peers.

Fergus continued, "Beyond these, you leaves must select at least three elective 'cores.'" He handed out a brochure that explained the current classes:

Computers
In the age of electronic communication and instant feedback, most students already know a good deal about computers. But some only know enough to play games or post photos, not word processing or how to do a spreadsheet. This class can fill in those gaps, or help students who are starting from scratch.

Cooking / Meal Planning
Processed foods, meals on the run, and microwave cooking have all but eliminated the need for learning the chemistry and art of cooking. This class will bring students back to the hearth to learn the skill of self-sufficiency in any kitchen.

Casual Conversation
Text messaging and "PMs" are efficient ways to communicate, but not the most rewarding. Learn how to start a one-on-one conversation, when not to, how to listen, and most importantly, how to end a conversation politely.

Parenting
Whether students are on their way to parenthood, already have offspring, or are preparing for their future family, this class reveals the dark and light side of bringing up children, and shares tons of tips and resources.

Gardening
Another in our self-sufficiency series, this class is taught by local certified Master Gardeners from Gilded Sand and Silica City.

Keeping House
Not everyone is raised with housekeeping duties. For those who've either had someone to do it for them, or who came from households which didn't make it a priority, this class will catch them up on the finer points of keeping a home. Household hints and shortcuts are offered as well.

Paying Bills
Back in the day, if one had a bill, a check was sent or delivered every month. Now with so many ways to be in debt and to pay, the choices can be overwhelming. This class will make sense of it all. Moreover, it will prevent our students from incurring unnecessary debt by showing ways to meet needs without someone else making a profit from it.

Family Planning
Most of our students are young adults. This course is designed to help them grow up without raising new people until they're ready, and help them to determine when that is.

Financial Planning
Planning for the immediate, post-academy, the golden years, and life beyond. From balancing checkbooks to a summary of the stock market, this course will give our students valuable insight into preparing for their—and their family's—future.

"Finally, you can take any of the following language classes at any time: English, French, Spanish, Italian, Japanese, German, or American Sign Language. I highly encourage you to do so, as this is a very important expectation of PAA graduates. I know most of you have a second language already," he looked pointedly at Adele, "but it never hurts to brush up or learn additional languages."

Fergus opened the classroom door and indicated the exit.

"Well, that's all from me, folks! If you have any questions for me during your stay here, I'm at your disposal. If you want to come relieve some stress by drumming, come on by anytime and hit the skins. Until then, enjoy your first term, and beyond!"

Adele hadn't learned much about meal preparation, as both of her mothers more or less "assembled" meals instead of looking up a recipe. This seemed like a good skill for not only her health, but her social life as well. She decided to sign up the cooking class right away. She would take a little longer to choose a language class.

Chapter 10

Innocence

*When I bestride him, I soar, I am a hawk: he trots the
air; the earth sings when he touches it; the basest horn
of his hoof is more musical than the pipe of Hermes.*
— Shakespeare, Henry V

July

Horses are widely considered to be the most noble of creatures. We often use them for transportation, sport, therapy, fun, food, and even medicine. For such nobility, we certainly treat them mean, disregarding their mental and physical needs. Man has so overrun and exploited creatures of the planet that—among others—the western black rhinoceros has been classified as extinct; hunted and discarded for its "magical" horn to the point that it no longer exists. But domestic horses have the opposite problem: There are too many.

Arguably, most little girls love horses. Some fantasize the horses, silver spiral-horned unicorns—reminiscent of rhinoceroses, if one cares to imagine it—or Pegasus, with pink manes and flowers in its flowing tail. Others read every horse-related story and novel, collect figurines, paste photographs and magazine clippings in notebooks. Still others are able to interact with the animal first-hand; the truly blessed have their very own steed. In whatever way they experience horses when young, usually they outgrow the love, forgetting the pleasant infatuation when schoolmates grab their fancy instead.

Eric had no horse experience, zero. The youth program in

which he'd been involved in Atlanta didn't offer equine exposure. When his horsemanship skills were evaluated, he was rated at the lowest end of the scale. But as an athlete, he was able to throw on a saddle—promptly removing it after being instructed that the blanket goes on *first*—bridle the horse, though he held it upside down; and finally, after someone else had tightened the cinch around the horse's girth, put his left foot in the stirrup "*oops, wrong one*" when he realized he'd end up in the saddle backwards; he finally hoisted himself up, throwing his right leg over the rear end of the horse, placing his bottom in the seat.

"Not too bad, some people end up kicking their horse in the rump, then holding on for dear life when it takes off, standing in the one stirrup!" laughed his evaluator.

When horses no longer serve their purpose, or when their owners tire of them, they're often abandoned or neglected. Sometimes they are sold for meat. In other situations, mares are bred and kept in deplorable conditions, treated worse than caged chickens, their urine collected and sold to pharmaceutical companies. Existing as pee factories, these mares are left standing for most of their gestation until they give birth, only to have their foals taken away: fillies to live out the same fate, colts to be disposed of, one way or another. While these facilities are now illegal in the United States, the manufacture of hormone replacement products using the urine are not. Although synthetic alternatives exist, some pharmaceutical providers continue to benefit from the heartless practice of harvesting the pregnant mares' urine. All so menopausal women and others who seek hormone therapy can have more comfortable sex lives.

Some of the horses at the academy are rescued from such inhumane "manufacturing" facilities—mares and their offspring, born after rescue; others were won at the auction yards; and the lucky ones, directly from owners who no longer want them, but care enough not to subject them to the frightening and at best, under-staffed auction yards. Although rescues from the latter are often in poor condition due to neglect and even starvation, it's favorable to being auctioned to kill buyers and transported en masse, crowded together in trucks designed for shipping cattle.

Because breed or purpose is not a prerequisite for rescue, many breeds are represented at the academy. Arabian pleasure horses, working Quarter Horses, Shires, appaloosas, flaxen-maned Belgians, donkeys, Oldenburgs; all these and more reside on campus. Except for aging and recovering horses, all are put into service of some kind, most for transportation. Even the small herd of miniature horses are put to work, providing entertainment and cuddling for young visitors during "Know Your Equine" days periodically held at Cedar Whiles.

Some students—even those familiar with horses—were surprised to learn facts about them:

- While horses' coats come in innumerable colors and patterns, the actual skin of most horses is dark gray or black.

- Horses have long memories. If a horse is abused by men for instance, it will learn to distrust men while responding positively to women.

- Because the anatomy of their eyes is designed to focus on objects at ground level and not in the sky, horses don't look up. They may point their nose in the air to change their field of vision (or to catch a scent), but it's not to see up higher.

Cedar Whiles is the school of animal husbandry. Here students learn to care for ranch animals such as alpacas, llamas, cattle, sheep, and of course, horses. The hospital barn is the shape of a cross; two arms are devoted to horse care, another to camelids, and the last to all other livestock. Community areas are separate in large, single-story cabins. They are identified with letters of the alphabet. "Vowel" cabins—Cabins A, E, I, O, and U—are lecture rooms. Cabin B is the boys' dressing room,

Cabin C is the cafeteria, Cabins D and F are for staff use, Cabin G is the dressing room for the girls, Cabin H is a small-scale infirmary, and Cabins J-N designed as classrooms. The largest and oldest cabin was multi-purpose, a large open space with a stone fireplace. It could be used as any gathering space from a meeting hall to an emergency shelter. It's cornerstone was made of granite, and depicted the school's mascot, the Western Pygmy-Owl.

Additionally, there's a stable and paddocks, and, as with all the campuses, pastures with shelters for protection from both sun and rain.

The students' rooms are on the second floor of the many residential bunkhouse-style cabins. The floors are divided into four rooms, housing up to six occupants each. On the main floor are found the kitchen, dining room, activity room with laundry, and reading room.

Other inhabitants of the grounds which frequent Cedar Whiles include pygmy-owls, elk, coyotes, and other wildlife.

Natali chose Event Planning as her first term's work study. There were several upcoming opportunities from which students could select, from weddings to a bloc's graduation ceremony. One event in the works was the academy's semi-annual horse adoption fair. Rehabilitated horses could be adopted through the academy's program at any time, but the fairs were an opportunity to network, tell stories whether successes or disappointments, share resources, and conduct workshops. Students also educate the public on why rescue is necessary, the difference between adoption and purchase, the reason for overpopulation of domestic horses, and how the public can get involved, even if they don't adopt.

A seminar specifically for the newcomers to the program was conducted. They learned what the public would learn, but more in-depth. The first portion was an overview of the program, its history, purpose, and success rate. The second portion was a slide presentation followed by a questions-and-answer session.

Natali ate up the information. She wasn't new to horses, but really hadn't been involved with them either, other than to go on rides with her "horsey" friends occasionally. The seminar ignited a new passion in her: educating people about the plight of horses may nip the problem in the bud. She signed up for the fair job on the spot.

A Word About the Bird

Mascot of Cedar Whiles, the Northern Pygmy-Owl[12] is a native year-long resident. It sits in treetops during the day to hunt small birds, such as hummingbirds, wrens, and even chickens. Small enough to fit inside a human's open palm, they also eat insects and small mammals, such as shrews. Watchfulness over a variety of species suggested to Honoré that they'd be an ideal mascot for the school of animal husbandry, despite its opposing goal.

The pygmy nests in hollows which are made for them, cavities created either by rotted out trees or previous nest builders, namely woodpeckers. Dark patches on the neck give it the appearance of having "eyes" on the back of the head.

The call of the pygmy-owl reminded Sebastian Paunder of water dripping from a faucet.

12 www.allaboutbirds.org/guide/Northern_Pygmy-Owl/sounds

Chapter 11

Truth

*Seldom, very seldom, does complete truth belong to
any human disclosure; seldom can it happen that
something is not a little disguised, or a little mistaken.*
— *narrator in "Emma" by Jane Austen*

July

Each and every person has their own idea of what truth is,
and what is true. But is it truly *every* person? Among billions of
people, there must be some—even a great deal—who have the
same ideas about truth. One thing must be true: What is true for
one person isn't necessarily true for another.

Zeb relaxed on Cabin E's porch after the "Truth" class at
Cedar Whiles. Most of the other students had gone in for
supper, or left to return to their dorms. Zeb didn't feel like
returning to the Trunk just yet. The rooms there were very
institutional; maybe they were a kind of litmus test of the
fortitude of the "fresh leaves." In any case, it was a far cry from
the hominess of his own bedroom back home.

In the warmth of the summer evening, he considered the
"truth" of his family. What a web of lies they had woven! But
did they lie to protect him from neglect or abandonment? There
was an off chance that they'd made the right decision, but he
still couldn't see how it could have been made with his well-
being in mind. Plus, couldn't they have *told* him at some point?
Why did he have to find out himself? Then there was his own
mother. So much for a mother's love—if that wasn't "true" love,

what could be? He couldn't remember anybody ever saying, "I love you" to him. If he would ever be told that in the future, would he ever be able to believe them?

The ocean breezes began cooling him. He gathered his satchel and headed back to the Trunk. "Truth" would have to wait a while longer.

Chapter 12

Contentment

I'd give all wealth that years have piled,
The slow result of Life's decay,
To be once more a little child
For one bright summer-day.

— *Lewis Carroll*

mid July

The Oregon coast has a temperate climate: rarely cold enough for snow to stick for more than a few days—if it falls at all—and summer is almost always comfortable, even cool. If it ever gets over ninety degrees, going down to the beach is a quick and easy way to find relief from the heat. Though the Oregon coastline is about 350 miles long and there are discernible differences in plant species and climate, it all falls within the comfort zone of humans, even if generally damp. Astoria at the north end was naturally colder and more hyetal than the southern end near Brookings, the "banana belt" of Oregon. It enjoys temperatures which are even milder, due to geographic and terrain conditions.

With about two-thousand people on the compound at any given time—as many as sixteen-hundred students, eighty-five instructors, and dozens of staff and support service members, not to mention visitors and shoppers—there was always something going on at Paunder Avian Academy.

A year 'round organization, the campuses are always busy with students attending classes, new students adjusting to routines, and everyone working for their jobs or work studies. Daily visits from the unpredictable public complicate the level of activity, particularly during the summer months. Part of the grounds are open to the public 6am to midnight, with the access gate closing at ten p.m. Most come for shopping and/or dining at Pearl Quay, or setting up for the weekend's community market.

Special events are held at different locations as well, such as weddings on the beach at Sandpink Beryl, horsemanship and other sports events at the Trunk's arena, and semi-annual adoption events of rehabilitated rescue horses at Cedar Whiles. Whatever the time, reason, or season, careful attention to securing the property and inhabitants is required.

Many of the work study jobs at the academy were interesting or exciting, such as incident response to handle emergencies of all conceivable types, and security patrol to contend with any threats (real or perceived). Others however, were mundane. In her first term, Adele was working in the maintenance department as a facilities worker, a cleaner. It wasn't a glamorous position, but it was solitary and undemanding. Dumping trash bins after classes had let out for the day, dusting offices, and sweeping staircases allowed her to think, mostly about her life, but when she was more disciplined, she mulled over what she'd learned in her core classes. She wasn't quick or terribly efficient at cleaning, but she felt a sense of accomplishment when done anyway.

One night, she'd been assigned to clean an instruction building at Emerald Crag, her home branch. She was taken aback when she saw someone there upon opening one of the office doors. The light was on, but teachers often forgot to shut them off. "Oh, I'm sorry, I didn't know anyone was here," she said to the man sitting at the desk, whose mature but still-smooth face was haloed in salt-and-pepper gray from his head to his tidy French beard. She began to leave the room, pulling the door shut behind her.

"It's okay, nevermind," he called out. "In fact, you could do me a favor. If you have the time, naturally."

"Sure, what do you need?" She assumed he'd want a cup of coffee, or to clean up a spill.

"I'm Wesley Peising, a teacher here in sociology. I'm developing a series of questions for my class on qualitative interviews of sexual mores." He leaned forward, putting his elbows on the desk, chin on his clasped hands. "You could be a good subject. Mind if I try some out on you? They may be somewhat probing."

Adele was genuinely intrigued. "Yeah, that could be interesting. I'll be starting my psychology studies next term. It might help to have some exposure before that."

"Oh yes, some exposure would be good for you." Adele had to admit to herself that his tone wasn't entirely pedantic. "You'll find that the study of the mind is improved when it includes the study of social intercourse. Come on over here and sit next to me."

He pulled out a chair from a side table for her as she leaned the broom against a bookcase. He said, "Go ahead and shut the door." She did, and took the seat. He turned to her, inhaling her scent. "It's up to you how long we do this. I could go for hours, but you may not have that kind of time," he repeated. "I'll leave the ball in your court, okay?" He patted her thigh; it lingered just a moment there after the second pat. Adele nodded her head. Though idealistic, she was also smart, and a realist: Adele knew he was deliberately choosing evocative words. Without conscious thought, she decided to ignore it. *You only live once.*

He asked her many questions, mostly in the "If this happened, what would you do of these three choices?" vein. She was actually enjoying the experience. From the scholarly aura of the room with books piled on every flat surface to his trim form under the gray shirt, unbuttoned to the top of his bare chest, she was intrigued. The attention from a man—though highly clinical and certainly calculating—was flattering. Some of the questions were a bit titillating, and she flushed more than once.

As a professional observer, Peising noticed her nuanced physical responses, such as her chest rising and neck pinkening when the question struck an erotic chord. He pressed on to continue disarming her.

"If you were pulled over by an unscrupulous officer for speeding and you couldn't afford a ticket, would you rather let him A, kiss you on the mouth; B, pat down your body; or C, grope your breasts?"

It was not an innocent question. She considered walking out, slapping him in the face, admonishing him for such unprofessionalism. But like a schoolgirl, she giggled. He found her nervous response enchanting; noticed her minute wiggle while she considered her answer. In turn, she noticed him, too.

When she finally said she needed to go, he took her hand but didn't let go when they finished shaking. "It's been a pleasure, I hope to know you more," he said. He released his grip slightly and slowly, lightly touching her palm all the way down to her fingertips.

Wide-eyed at feeling his touch in more than her fingers, she managed with great concentration to say, "I think you just might," before walking out quickly. The broom—still leaning against a tall bookcase—was forgotten.

She did see him again, the next week. He asked her additional questions; they were even more suggestive. The power of the "innocent" questions built from undoubtedly flirtatious queries to downright seductive phrasing. The warmth and pulsing building deep in her body was palpable by both of them.

By the end of their third encounter a few days later, she did not object to Wesley Peising exploring more than her mind behind the locked office door. Though he was a good twenty years her senior, mutual attraction ignited their chemistry. She saw a reflection in his eyes of how she perceived herself as a woman. *This would be an easy habit to keep*, she thought as he crossed the line, more than once.

Adele wasn't in love with him, though she couldn't deny falling into the sexual magnetism and her lusty response. But in her lonely disposition, a no-strings fling, she decided, was adequate for now.

Chapter 13

Growth

A noble craft, but somehow a most melancholy! All
noble things are touched with that.
— *Moby-Dick, chapter 16, by Herman Melville*

July

The empty horse trailer bounced Natali in her seat as it rattled on the rough paved road from Cedar Whiles to the PAA security gate. A winsome look flashed across her face at the name, Escape Drive. She wondered if the meaning was escape *from*, or escape *to*.

After an early breakfast, Natali and two other students in her event planning work study crew had climbed into the truck to be taken to an auction yard in Skinner's Ferry. They'd all been off the academy's grounds in the last month to run errands and pick up supplies in Gilded Sand or Silica City, and took a tour of the Three Capes[13]. But this trip would be extensive, in more ways than one. The drive just to I-5 would be over an hour itself, traveling through the winding roads of Siuslaw National Forest. Although it would be a long day, no one complained: Their mission was to rescue at-risk horses from being shipped to Mexico or Canada for slaughter, or save neglected, abandoned horses from living out a wasted life. There would be other rescue operations in attendance, but there were too many horses for all to be saved; some would make the brutal trip despite the efforts of the various agencies.

---

13 visittheoregoncoast.com/2013/01/three-capes-scenic-loop/

When they reached the academy's gate, Mr. Senpaku, branchmaster of Cedar Whiles, stopped the truck and turned to the students; he reminded them that this was not a pleasure trip. "This will be something you'll never forget. I encourage you to take notes, not just on the horses, but the whole experience."

Natali had been to auctions in Lewiston before, but only for livestock. She'd learned that horse slaughter bidders would often compete against people who just wanted a horse to love, and that—contrary to common belief—these horses weren't old and sickly, but were generally sound and broke to ride. They had more value per pound to the kill buyers, and were more able to survive the gruelling journey to Mexico. It was not a system for discarding elderly or infirm horses.

The academy's team had a $1,300 budget to bid on the horses, and a four-horse trailer. The two criteria for selection: the horses were well enough to make the long trip back to the academy, and not so ruined by mistreatment and cruelty to be deemed dangerous. Senpaku assured them that they'd fill the trailer, as most horses would fit these basic parameters.

"What else can we expect of today, Mr. Senpaku?" asked Jack.

"We'll have lunch in Corterram before we get to the auction. Once we get there and park, about one o'clock, watch your step." Natali wondered what that warning meant, but he didn't elaborate. "We'll go into the pens; you can take photos. Be sure to include in your notes the tag numbers of the horses you want me to bid on, and why. Obviously we can't buy every horse, so we're going to have to be selective. And let me warn you right now, we will not win every horse we bid on. At three o'clock, I want you to regroup at the café and compare notes. One strategy is to rank your selections; you should have about twenty horses on your 'wish list.' Auction starts about four. I'll be waiting for you in the stands, second row." He pulled off Escape Drive and turned south onto Highway 101.

"But Mr. Senpaku, how will we know if a horse is sound enough?"

"As far as health, we're only concerned with getting them back to the academy. You can go into the pen with the animals, check their legs and hooves, eyes, listen to their chests, etcetera. If you want me to check them too, come and get me. I'll be around."

On the way down and at lunch, the students shared their horse backgrounds with each other. Natali said that she'd done a fair amount of riding, but hadn't owned her own horse. "A lot of my friends had horses, so I'd ride with them," she explained.

A small woman with weather-washed skin, Alberta looked in the rear view mirror and said, "Horses are why I'm here, in the school I mean. I've been around them all my life, since I was a tot. The idea of going away to college really troubled me, till I found the academy. If any of you have questions about horses, any kind of question, you can ask me."

"I have something I've wondered about, " said Jack. "I'm like you, Natali. I've been around horses, but never had one of my own. Rode in boys' camp, brushed them down, stuff like that. But what's it like to own a horse on a daily basis?"

Alberta turned halfway around in the front seat to face them. "I won't pull any punches with you: It's a lot of work. If you keep them in stall, you've got to clean it out every day. At least one wheelbarrow full. Lots of water hauling—unless you're plumbed—'cause they drink about five gallons a day. And they need exercising and handling daily if you want a good horse. You have to check their feet often to see if they've picked up a rock, pick out any debris. Then there's feeding, at least twice a day."

Senpaku interjected, "The best way to find out, Jack, is to sign up for work study. After all, that's why you're in this work study: You'll glean valuable information as you learn how the auction runs their business. Especially when it comes to this sale, they are basically putting on an event. You're all in event planning for your work study, right?" Natali and the others nodded. "They are one of the most respected horse auctions on the west coast. Anyway, whenever you're ready, Radegast'll put you to work as a hand in one of the school's stables. He'll have you come in morning and night for an hour or so each. It'll give you a pretty good idea of what care horses need every day."

Lunch in Corterram was quick and economical. After they shared sandwiches and bottled tea at the deli, they were on the road again. A short while later, they pulled into the auction's gravel driveway. It was badly in need of repair, the numerous jagged potholes were filled with opaque beige rainwater as there'd been a downpour during the summer night. Some puddles were approaching pond status. The truck hit some hard, causing its passengers to bounce and the trailer loudly complaining, despite Senpaku's low speed. Now Natali understood what he meant about watching their step - they'd have to walk through and around those puddles soon.

Numerous cars, trucks, and trailers were already parked. Some had arrived early in the morning to unload horses. To Natali and Jack, the scene seemed chaotic, vehicles parked askew in every direction. But as she and the others got out, she realized that everyone had parked in such a way that vehicles could get around, not blocking anyone in. She was impressed: at the farmers market back home where she'd volunteered several summers, people often ignored lines, parking wherever they damn well pleased. They didn't care if they trapped people in, blocked off whole lanes, or even parked in the fire lane. The "chaos" here at the auction yard was quite impressive, and in its most positive sense.

Her group made its way into the covered pen area. The fences were mostly wood boards; some were made of pipe, which made it easier to view the horses. The flooring was concrete; not good for horses to stand on, but Natali reminded herself that this was mostly a livestock auction yard, and the animals weren't here for long anyway - sometimes just a few hours.

Natali had been enthralled that she could participate in choosing which horses to rescue, having seen miraculous transformations before. She'd felt a wave of anticipation and pride at their good works, especially since she was joining the effort. But now that she was at the auction yard, saw them in some cases crowded shoulder to rump, heads hung low, some with hip bones protruding, open wounds, or ridiculously grown out hooves, it broke her heart. Yet she was also appalled at the fit, hardy horses. Questions she'd never thought of before sprang to her mind: Why would an owner who had taken care of the animal bring it here, putting it at risk of being purchased by someone they couldn't verify? Did they ever relate to their horses, or did they always consider them "just livestock"? Finally, how could she select *any* horse, knowing the probable fate of those left behind?

Walking in the aisles between pens, Natali saw some of the horses bunched in a corner. Others were more curious and approachable, even friendly. Most stood unaffected; it was difficult to tell if they were naturally calm, were well-trained, had been given a horse sedative, or if their spirits were simply broken. Natali took note of one younger horse, a small nervous pinto with blue eyes. Natali imagined it had been an intermediate horse for an adolescent girl who outgrew it. Her parents probably didn't want to spend the time finding the horse a new home, so told their daughter that auction would be the best way when really, it was just more convenient. As a nice, healthy horse, it had a higher reserve on it, so it languished in the yard for months, wasting health and personality with each passing day. The owners didn't bother to have it ridden through the auction, which would have demonstrated to bidders that this was a broke animal. Maybe this wasn't this horse's story, but Natali learned that it was a common one. Or the horses that had served on a string: After years of patiently enduring the burden of kicking, screaming kids or tourists, when the boy's camp or dude ranch closed, the horses were sent all at once to the auctions, overwhelming them with too much inventory to be placed in forever homes. Lucky horses would be purchased by an individual or family; some would be bought to be rehabilitated then sold or adopted; the rest had about a 50% or higher chance of being sold to kill buyers.

Many people were wandering through the pens, some individuals, some clusters. Natali couldn't tell who were buyers or who were sellers, or even who were working for the auction house. Senpaku told her later that some were both sellers and buyers, having brought in a horse to sell for whatever they could get for it, then buy a new horse cheap. Senpaku disdainfully referred to them as "upgrade junkies."

Natali was looking at a bay gelding, trying to tempt him closer to the gate. Unsuccessful, she was about to open the gate to go to him when she heard from two pens over Jack call out to Senpaku. She walked to him as they waited for their instructor. "What's up?" she asked.

Jack said, "This horse is obviously in bad shape, but something's weird with his cheek. Feel it."

Natali did. "What's that crackling? It feels like cellophane under his skin."

"I know, huh? Here's Senpaku, maybe he'll know." Jack expressed his concern, and Senpaku went inside the pen.

He looked over the animal, felt along his neck, his ribs, his legs, and both cheeks. "This horse has been beaten. Often, and recently. That crackling you feel is subcutaneous emphysema[14], air trapped within the tissues. It's a symptom of blunt force trauma. I can feel it on several parts of his body." Natali fought to keep down her bile. She didn't speak in fear of losing it, physically and mentally.

"Can we bid on him?" asked Alberta.

"That's up to you kids. I think he'd make the trip, but there's no telling how long he'd live after we get him to the academy."

Jack pointed out that lifespan wasn't important. The girls agreed, but they'd discuss it after seeing all the horses. That would take them all the way to their meeting time, as horses were still being brought in. Natali wondered if there was ever an end to the line.

Jack and Alberta were in a booth when Natali joined them at the café. They took out their notebooks and began negotiations.

---

14 en.wikipedia.org/wiki/Subcutaneous_emphysema#Trauma

"Did you see the Belgian? He's the only big draft horse I saw. He looks pretty sound, but he's about twenty-six years old."

Alberta said, "Yes, a nice big guy. I'd like to see him at the academy." Natali agreed. Then Natali suggested another.

"There's a horse with one eye, due to damage when he was kicked by another horse when he was young. It's a gelding, never been broke. He's small-ish, feet look okay."

"I don't think we should bid on him," said Alberta.

"Why not? He's low-key, needs a home—"

Alberta interrupted, "Two points: one, he may be low-key now, but that may be due to a dose of Ace. Two, he won't ship because he's blind. There's a law about that. The kill buyers won't bother with him, when there's other 'legal' horses to choose from. Let some family buy him." Natali looked skeptical. "He may not sell this auction, but eventually he'll be purchased. Don't worry, we have plenty more to talk about. But we've got to hurry up, the auction won't wait for us."

"I'm sorry to disagree Alberta, but you're wrong. I don't know about the law, but the humane society[15] says that blind horses do ship," Jack said.

Natali was confused already; there were so many horses, she couldn't keep them straight. And at "only" eighty-three head, this was a *small* group.

They continued sharing notes, agreeing on the horses, then cutting down their list. Natali felt like she was in a scene of "Sophie's Choice," deciding who had a chance at life, and who would be sacrificed. With each number they crossed out, her desire for a cigarette grew stronger. It didn't help that occasionally some smoke would waft in from outside when a smoker came closer than the legally prescribed ten feet to the building. Just in time—for both Natali's craving and the start of the auction—they had a list of their twenty-one top picks.

Walking up the steps to the sales arena, Natali had not expected stadium seating, with steep concrete tiers and hard plastic seats bolted into them. But more surprising was the size

---

15 www.humanesociety.org/issues/horse_slaughter/facts/transport_to_slaughter_092909.html

of the arena; she wondered how the horses could possibly be exhibited effectively in such a small space. It only seemed to be about as big as her family's living room in Moscow.

There were a number of people in the stands. Customarily, before the horses come in, horse tack is sold. They had gone through a stack of western saddles; now they were auctioning the English saddles. The auctioneer's chant was rapidfire; the volume of the speakers uncommonly loud. With all the input, it took Natali a moment to figure out who was speaking. After about twenty minutes, the tack portion was completed. The auctioneer's stand was at the back center wall of the arena. It emptied for a few more minutes while workers reconfigured the arena for the horses, removing tables and adding handlers.

Several men and women returned to the auctioneer's booth, a couple of them opened laptops. A man in the center with the tan cowboy hat was the new auctioneer. The first horse was brought in, a stocky "cowboy"-type. After a quick review of the rules and procedures, the auctioneer began cantillating so fast Natali could only make out the verbiage here and there. His sing-song blending together of words with the numbers popping—the most important part—enhanced the excitement of the process, encouraging bidders to act.

Ringmen were pointing to bidders in the stands. Often their heads were seen turning in unison, looking at the bidders as they indicated their interest. It was like watching the spectators at a tennis match, Natali noted with amusement.

The horses usually were brought in one at a time. Most of them were ridden to some degree; horses whose skills were exhibited brought in more bids and higher prices, hopefully too high for kill buyers. Natali was pleased to see that the auctioneer gave plenty of time—in terms of auction minutes—for people to get a good look at the horses in motion. Sometimes the rider would reach over the horse's neck and slip off the bridle, then "steer" the horse with their legs alone. She was delighted when the tolerance factor of the horses was demonstrated, when the rider would stand up in the saddle, step onto the rump of the horse, then dismount by dropping off or sliding over the rear. Several times the crowd roared with laughter when the handler ducked under the horse multiple times or sat backwards in the saddle. Natali was sure that not many auction houses would allow such theatrics. She was very impressed with this one; they really seemed to care about the horses, as much as was possible for that type of business. Plus they had a sense of humor, which she appreciated.

A pair of ponies on Natali's wish list was brought in. The Highland pony was a gelding, a bay dun with three white pasterns. The pinto mare was a Shetland-Cob cross. Natali looked over and saw Senpaku note their lot number.

The auctioneer began. "We have here a pair of ponies who've been together for many years. The owner wants to keep them that way. Who'll give me a hundred dollars for this lot?" Senpaku lifted their number immediately. "ONE hundred dollar bid, now two, now two, will ya give me two? I got it. TWO hundred dollar bid, now three, now three hundred, will ya give me three? Two hundred, two and a half, two-fifty, How about two fifty? fifty? fifty? How about two and quarter? Two twenty-five?" Senpaku lifted his fingers and nodded. "Two twenty-five, I've got two twenty-five, now fifty? how about fifty? two-fifty? I've got two-fifty, do I hear two seventy-five?" Natali could feel her pulse in her neck; she felt like she was going to jump out of her seat. Why did Senpaku stop bidding? "Two seventy-five, who'll give me two and three quarters? Going for two fifty, two fifty, two fifty, SOLD to the woman in the green jacket, number three-five-one." Senpaku looked at Natali as he rolled his shoulders and raised his palms up in a gesture of resignation.

Natali's group won three horses: Cookie, an older flea-bitten white mare with a slight swayback and untrusting eyes who they won with an $80 bid; Loppy, a muscular faded palomino mare with very bad feet, for $200; and Viceroy, a small bay gelding with Morgan conformation. He was their big purchase, at $450. They also acquired a Welsh/Arab pony for $175.

Natali was disheartened that they didn't bid on the beaten horse. Alberta argued in their meeting that it was too hard a case, its outgrown hooves no small consideration. "There are too many horses," she said with kindness. "I don't want you to get hard, but you have to understand they can't all be saved. You have to learn to let go, to move on, to do what you can and not beat yourself up for what you can't do."

A woman in the audience won the animal for $20. She didn't seem like the slaughtering kind, but appearances could be deceiving. In the pens, Natali had seen five hispanic men ogling one of the distressed horses, a gorgeous smoky snowcap appaloosa stallion who was constantly, gingerly shifting his weight off his feet, especially the right fore and the left rear. Obviously in a great deal of pain, but she couldn't see why. She assumed these men were kill buyers, since the horses sent to the slaughterhouse would either go to Mexico or Canada. The way they surrounded his pen reminded Natali of vultures, waiting for the animal to expire. She asked Senpaku about it.

"Yes, you could be right. But maybe not; you can't make assumptions. I've seen very 'wholesome' families, with kids in tow, load up their winnings cattle-style, and ship them off. It's just a family business to them; horses are livestock, just like chickens or pigs." Natali frowned in anger. "I know you don't see horses like that, you feel that each one of them could be a friend. You see a soul. But not everyone has your vision, your sense of attachment. We'll do our best to save the ones we can, and hope that other rescues were successful. The rest...well, just send them off with a blessing."

After paying for the wins, Senpaku pulled the trailer around to the back of the auction yard. The auction was slowly winding down, but still in progress. Natali had wanted to stay to see what some of her choices would go for, if at all, but the auction would continue for at least two more hours.

"We've got all the horses we can take," explained Senpaku. "There's nothing more we can do tonight."

The trip back to the academy was gruelling and exciting and sad and frightening. At times Natali would hear a commotion in the back, when one of the horses slipped on a turn or tried unsuccessfully to reposition themselves. Senpaku assured her that not only all was well, but that they were having a perfectly normal day.

In the relative silence, Natali and the others thought about the other horses they saw, many of which they knew must have been won by "kill buyers." Seeing how the horses were treated, she realized that she had much to learn. In her mind's eye she could see the little brown and white pinto, its head hung down in dejection. It was probably a child's teaching horse, and now that the child was older, they'd moved on to more challenging horses, or some other interest altogether. Natali found that her imagination was highly active, and in this case, it was not a comfort.

Then there was the black gelding, big-boned and head held high, with flaring nostrils. Senpaku tried to get him but was outbid. He would've been a magnificent addition to the academy, but their goal was to save as many horses as they could, not get a great deal.

A horse came through in such deplorable condition, Senpaku didn't think it would survive the trip. Natali just wanted to gather it in her arms and allow it to pass peacefully while being loved, but of course that wasn't possible. Again she shook her head in disbelief that anyone would put a horse like this through the ordeal. Hadn't they suffered enough? She broke the silence by voicing her chagrin to Senpaku.

"You can't judge people for sending their horses to auction," he gently admonished her. "There are myriad reasons for choosing this option. Not all are noble, but you just can't know sellers' motivations or situations. Don't forget, without the auction, we wouldn't be able to see a fraction of the horses for sale, and neither would anyone else."

She grasped his meaning, but it was little consolation. She'd thought that after the auction, she would be excited at bringing back rescued horses. Instead of exhilarated, Natali's chest felt heavy, burdened with the knowledge of so many discarded, wasted horses. She couldn't understand why horse owners bred indiscriminately; so often didn't think of providing them with "forever" homes, just "for now" homes. Or at least to rehome them; didn't they deserve the trouble and expense? Although she was glad that they'd rescued the horses they won, Natali made two decisions: That it wasn't enough, and a little knowledge was indeed a dangerous thing, for her.

Chapter 14

Knowledge

Many are our joys
In youth, but oh! what happiness to live
When every hour brings palpable access
Of knowledge, when all knowledge is delight,
And sorrow is not there!

— *William Wordsworth*

August

Saffron Cascade is the "fantasy" school, where one can almost spot the woodland nymphs and faeries dressed in bluebell skirts as they dance in the lush old growth forest of gigantic evergreens, frolic in the shimmering waterfalls, and sleep in the abundant wild violets.

All incoming horses are quarantined at the remote north-most end of the grounds, behind Obsidian Marsh. This period gives the animal husbandry students time to evaluate the health of the animals, physiologically. It also gives the students the opportunity to evaluate their temperament. But after quarantine, horses rescued by the academy which continue to demonstrate signs of emotional distress or complete distrust of humans rehabilitate at the bucolic stables of Saffron Cascade. The stables are small, housing just four to six horses, each with their own turnout along with small adjoining paddocks. It could take several months to calm a horse. They were not assigned to a student for transportation nor eligible for adoption until they were deemed reliably safe. Every so often, a horse would come in that could never get over its trauma, unable to be haltered, led, or even caught without further stress; these horses are retired to another pasture at the north end of campus between Obsidian Marsh and Emerald Crag, to live out their days with no demands upon them, except to be free. At least once a year they were caught as humanely as possible, and sedated in order to tend to their feet, float their teeth, be wormed, and receive updated vaccinations.

Students were housed in chalets, a type of Alpine-inspired cabins. Low, wide eaves provided ample shelter to the open patios below them.

As the "quiet" campus, it had seemed fitting to Naomi Paunder that the main library of the academy would be hosted in the beautiful, tranquil setting, above and unconnected to the toil of the other schools. Work is done here, but most of it is mental, which can be just as exhausting as physical labor.

The library building is three stories tall. There are large windowed rooms, and smaller, more comfortable rooms with large overstuffed chairs. One wall has a mural depicting the message, "None of us is as smart as all of us." Its vivid yellow background and large ornate letters stood in contrast to the quiet of the space. Phoebe was delighted with the library. No one could accuse her of being an intellectual, but she loved absorbing knowledge.

As much as she loved the library, the pull of the outdoors was even stronger. Butterflies, hummingbirds, a "secret" clover patch, and a bluebell forest thrived on the south side of Saffron Cascade. She noted that bluebells were more beautiful as a group than as individual flowers. On the western slope—the ocean side of the campus—the crocuses were in bloom. In August, soft purple carpeted the hillside, following the babbling stream down to the shaded horsetail waterfall where the sweet violets took over in the moist, rich soil alongside of it. It was too dangerous to swim in the descending pools created by the falls, mostly due to the slick basalt columns over which the waters ran, as well as criss-crossing fallen logs. But one could perch on the natural seats to savor the intensely green surroundings.

Phoebe delighted in merging her two loves as she took books to read at the basalt tables built beside the water. The constant mist wasn't good for the books, but it cleansed her mind, diffusing any worries or cares. Before she reached the end of her time at Paunder, even the memory of this peace would serve her well.

A Word About the Bird

Mascot of Saffron Cascade, the Rufous Hummingbird[16] is a fairly small hummer or "buzzer," as some on campus call them. In the right light, it can seem to glow red or orange. A migratory species, it's seen at the academy from mid-spring to late summer.

While it feeds on the nectar of flowers and the feeders that humans provide, its main diet is small flying insects, either in-flight or those caught in spider webs—to the great consternation of the spider. A pugnacious species, it chases away all other hummingbirds, and sometimes cats. Its own most deadly enemy is said to be the praying mantis.

Honoré appreciated its tenacity, so he chose it as a symbol of tackling overwhelming challenges.

---

16 www.allaboutbirds.org/guide/Rufous_Hummingbird/id

Chapter 15

Purity

*We have to learn how to come out of unclean
situations cleaner than we were, and even how to wash
ourselves with dirty water when we need to.*
— *Friedrich Nietzsche*

August

Naturally, the power of water to cleanse Phoebe's mind isn't its only value. Paunder Avian Academy is outside of an incorporated area. As such, it must provide its own water supply. Emerald Crag and Saffron Cascade take their water from Upper Pistoia River, which divides the two schools before its waterfall plunges into a pool, suitable for swimming. The stream's waterfall also feeds into the pool. The confluence of waters form Lower Pistoia; the river then continues on toward the Pacific, passing between Pearl Quay and Obsidian Marsh. Additionally, there are three wells providing potable water; located at Lapis Lookout, Crimson Song, and Basalt Moor, these gravity-feed down to a large cistern at the Trunk which supplies the remainder of the schools.

The water demands at the academy were enormous. In addition to the needs of the people for cooking, cleaning, and toileting, the horses and livestock required thousands of gallons each day. Finally, the swimming pool at Basalt Moor had its own well.

Students who were involved in the health, aquatic, or environmental programs were expected to tend to the water system—in some capacity—for at least one three-month term.

Eric was on the crew his first term at the school, anxious to get into the environment right away. While they were scrubbing out one of the large stock tanks, he asked Luke about the water shortage. "The Pacific Northwest is in the rain forest, but I heard on the news that Oregon is in a drought. Is this going to affect us?"

"Our county isn't, yet," said Luke. "But we have to be diligent, watch our usage carefully. We are vulnerable. It isn't like the old days, when we could just use water freely." He gestured to the others to get out of the tank before he turned on the hose. "Just like now. Used to be we would fill this and leave the hose running a bit, so as the animals drank it would continue filling. There was always water on the ground, puddles of it. We can't risk that waste any more." He turned on the power nozzle to rinse. "Here, you take this," he said as he handed the hose to Eric. "We may be on the ocean, but we can't use the salt water, and we can't afford to take *any* water for granted."

Chapter 16

Vulnerability

What is it we heartily wish of each other? Is it to be pleased and flattered? No, but to be convicted and exposed, to be shamed out of our nonsense of all kinds, and made men of, instead of ghosts and phantoms.
— *Ralph Waldo Emerson*

August

Seven in the morning and the air was already growing warm. Zeb took the stairway two flights down from the dorms, to the Trunk's library. On the same floor as the administration offices, it and the lobby are always open, though the offices are closed.

Because of the early hour and administration offices being closed until eight o'clock, there were few students in the library. Two were at the self-serve coffee bar, speaking quietly as they stirred their coffees with wooden sticks. Zeb hated this assignment, anxious to get it over with; he wanted as much privacy as talking with a stranger in a public place would allow. He meandered on the floor till he found what he was looking for.

She looks friendly, non-judgy, decided Zeb when he saw the young woman sitting at a table by the large east-facing window. She was wearing shorts and an aqua calico-print short-sleeve campshirt revealing strong, lightly tanned arms; her light chestnut hair clasped in a neat ponytail. She was drawing in a small sketchbook. He hoped she truly was an early-bird like himself, and not up at this dawning hour just because she'd had a bad dream or that she hadn't slept all night. He approached her. "Excuse me, may I bother you for a minute?" he asked gently.

"No problem, what's up?" She closed her sketchbook and smiled. The morning sun caught her eyes, and he saw that they were a beguiling deep green, like the mature leaves of the rhododendrons peppered throughout the campus.

"I'm taking an enhancement class, and we've been given homework which involves talking to someone we've never met before, reading off a few lists we wrote, and sharing something with them that's unknown to most people. I wonder if you and I could set up a time to do that?"

"Sure, I wouldn't mind. How about right now? I don't have a class till nine o'clock."

"Oh, yeah, that'd be great." He sat down across the table from her. He leaned over for a better look at her notebook. "I see you're an artist."

She cocked her head dismissively. "I try. It's just for fun, helps me wake up in the morning. That and the coffee."

"I'm an artist too," he said proudly. "I'm getting my associates in it. Associate of Arts. In Art."

She took a sip from the mug and smiled; she found his blend of nervousness and boldness charming. "I'm not that serious about it. It's just for me. By the way, I'm Natali." She extended her hand and they shook.

"Sorry, I should've introduced myself first. I'm Zebulon, but everyone calls me Zeb. What degree are you working on?"

"It'll be in Humanities, but I'm not sure which direction I'll go yet, probably social services. What term are you in?"

"This is my first."

"Me too. Wait, you're taking an enhancement class already? I thought we weren't supposed to take them till we finished our first term," said Natali.

"Most people don't, but we can take them if we want," said Zeb. "I like to space them out evenly."

"So you are spreading out twelve enhancement classes over

eight terms ... how is it possible to do that evenly?"

"It isn't, it drives me *nuts*," Zeb said, raising his hands, palms up, in frustration. "So I'm taking two now, one next term, then two, then one ...."

Natali put her hand up. "That's enough, I get it. Very clever." She emptied the mug. "So, how do we begin?"

For the assignment, Zeb read her his lists of ten life goals, ten personal insecurities, and ten former accomplishments.

"This is stupid," said Zeb, shaking his head halfway through the list of his insecurities. "This homework is stupid. I'm sorry I'm wasting your time."

Natali patted him lightly on the shoulder. "Hey, don't worry about it. I'm sure there's a good reason why they're having you do this; it'll probably serve you in the future. Besides," she leaned forward as if to tell him a secret, "you couldn't have found a better person to share with. I'm very discreet. You said that you had to find someone you didn't know, and you've found me. Let's finish the lists later. Now, you're 'sposed to share something about yourself that hardly anyone knows. Does that mean a secret?"

"I guess it can mean anything, whether it's meant to be a secret or not. Like, my middle name, which is William. It's not a secret or even embarrassing. I just don't use it much, because kids in school called me—okay, I guess this is kind of a secret—Zebilly."

Natali chuckled.

Zeb smiled. "I guess it doesn't bother me anymore; just don't let it get around."

"You 'guess' alot though, do you know that?"

"Oh, yeah; I gue ... I mean, I should try to watch that." He smiled again, more shyly than before. Natali decided that was probably his most endearing habit. "Anyway, sharing my name probably isn't adequate for the assignment." He paused, looking up at the ceiling as if to find the answer.

"Haven't you thought of this before, what you wanted to talk about?" asked Natali.

"Of course. I had a lot of thoughts, but they only gave us the assignment yesterday. I haven't decided which one to use. I was busy making up these damn lists." He quickly sat up in his chair. "I've got it. But if you don't mind, let's go up there." He pointed to the suspended loft, which encircled the room below. "It's a little more private."

They stood, gathered their things, and moved to a seating area with overstuffed microfiber chairs.

After Zeb brought them fresh coffee from the beverage station—hers black, his with two sugars—he began. "The thing is, the kids here talk about missing home, missing their parents, school or even work. I don't. Not at all."

"That's it?" said Natali. "Maybe you just haven't been away long enough."

"No, I mean I *really* don't miss them, particularly my folks." He took a slurp of the steaming brew. "I never will. I couldn't care less if I ever *ever* saw them again."

Natali raised her eyebrows, cocking her head to the side. "Ever? Ever ever?" Zeb nodded. "Wow, that doesn't sound good."

"I just really don't have any use for them. In fact, the more they need me, the less I need them. Just being treated like a farm hand doesn't make me feel like I owe them any allegiance."

"What about the rest of your family? Do you have brothers and sisters?"

"Yep, two sisters and a brother. They're okay, but we're not close. Dorothy's my mamma's handmaiden, always at her beck and call, never leaves the house now that's she's finished school. Georgina's married, with two brats already, and that's what they are. They live in town, but I don't see them 'cept on holidays. My brother's a wildcat, goin' off every night, coming home late and stinking of cigarettes and musk after screwing any girl or woman who'll let 'im." Natali cringed, but not for the reason he thought. "Sorry, that was crass." He sighed and shook his head as if to dismiss the thought, and the true nature of the relationships. "I do miss my room though. The rest of the place

I could do without, but my room is my own; it's full of books that I've collected, from floor to ceiling. And my bed is real soft, thick with real wool batting. It was my inheritance from my grandma."

"But that's not like missing actual people," said Natali.

"No, it's not. I guess ... I mean, I *suppose* I should feel bad about that." He paused, looking deeply into his dark coffee. "I do, on some level."

"What level is that?"

"Don't get me wrong, I'm loyal. Maybe to a fault. 'Honor thy parents,' you know all about that, I'm sure." Natali nodded. "I just don't feel a connection to them. They've never treated me well. Humiliations, being the brunt of their jokes; they let my siblings torment me, didn't do a thing to stop them or...." His voice trailed off. He continued in a lower tone, "They didn't even think it was worth me coming out here." Zeb's voice began catching on some of the words, stumbling on memories. "They think ... I'm not 'quick' enough, can't take the heat, can't handle conversations, or being away from 'ma and pa.' They think *so* little of me." Natali moved to the chair next to him, and instinctively put an arm around his shoulder, lightly rocking him. His emotions rising to the surface like goldfish at feeding time.

After some minutes had passed in silence, he gathered himself and said, "I haven't been entirely honest with you," Zeb said, releasing a big sigh. "I'm here because ... because I'm kinda running away." He seemed to swallow the last words.

Natali adjusted in her seat. *I knew he was holding something back. Please don't let it be illegal.* "Go on, I'm still with you."

"I don't know why, because it sure wasn't my idea, but I'm ashamed. I learned that my mom and pop aren't my real parents; they're my grandparents."

"That's not very unusual. Lots of kids get raised by their grandparents."

"But mine didn't tell me. And the reason why isn't pretty." He went on the explain the circumstances, and the need for him to get away from the whole toxic situation.

They continued talking through the morning, even missing their first class of the day.

Zeb had never felt so accepted and unjudged. A sense of peace and appreciation settled over him.

"Hey, we should record our numbers," Zeb said. "Want to? There's a kiosk downstairs."

"Sure. Here's my number: PA25NM3."

"Cool," he said as he wrote it down in his log. "Mine's PA14ZC1. Hey, I just realized, you got a three? That's unusual. Even a two doesn't happen that often."

Natali shrugged. "Yep, apparently there are at least two other Pangolins with my initials, born on the 25th. But I doubt that we have the same birth month."

"Why's that?"

"Because the chances of the others being born on Christmas Day are very slim."

He grinned. "I'll remember that."

While Zeb was lifted from the bog of his family secret, Adele was falling deeper into a not-so-innocent secret of her own. Their trysts usually occurred in Peising's office, but sometimes at a remote outdoor location. Whenever they got together, sparks would inevitably fly. Reciprocal arousal and mutual satisfaction made for a powerful narcotic, and Adele was hooked.

Chapter 17

Meditation

*Progress is impossible without change, and those who
cannot change their minds cannot change anything.*
— *George Bernard Shaw*

August

The ridge at the north end of Crimson Song allowed Zeb a
sweeping view down into the valley basin. Taking in a deep,
cleansing lungful of the camphor-scented air, he surveyed the
grounds from Cherni, a blood-bay with black tail and mane
matching Zeb's forward-combed mop. He marveled at his
journey so far: exactly two months ago, he'd never ridden a
horse in his life. Neighbors and others in Mullens had horses, to
be sure, but they were mostly used for plowing, or letting the
children ride the slow, gentle beasts. Other than that, no one
rode recreationally, or considered their horses as anything
more than livestock. And although Zeb was in awe of them, he
was uninterested in actually riding. Now one week into his turn
at Compound Alert, he was having the time of his life, and had
even decided to take on Cherni as his own horse, for now.

Classes were in session, students traveled to and fro on
horses, bicycles, or dual-sport motorbikes. Work study duties
were not limited to daylight or weekdays; especially animal care
and incident response teams who weren't always needed, but
who were always on-call. The end of summer was the busiest
time for campus security, as it was for the whole of the Oregon
coast. Vacationers from Portland to the east coast were rushing

to get in their last or only trip to the beach before going back to school or returning to work. But some members of the public become overly curious, going off into the private areas of the campus. If they don't leave when asked, they are trespassed off the property for at least twenty-four hours, and if the situation calls for it, barred for up to a year, or even banned for life. Zeb had already participated in one such exclusion. The sheriff was almost called, but the recalcitrant visitor finally left. Zeb had mostly watched the event, taking in all the procedures. He found it thrilling to be in on the action, but hoped he'd never have to actually confront a difficult person.

Escape Drive to the retail stores and harbor at Pearl Quay was open to the public during the day, with a passcode gate closing at ten o'clock. Every week on Mondays the passcode was changed. At the security headquarters at Basalt Moor, on Zeb's first day, portly Security Foreman Kevin Baer asked him for four digits. "Me? You want me to assign the gate code?" Zeb said. His heart was racing.

"Sure, why not?" countered Baer. "Any numbers will do, except you know, something like '5-5-5-5'."

After a momentary pause, Zeb said, "Okay, how about 1-9-2-0."

"Interesting, how did you come up with that?"

"It's the year that downtown Mullens burned[17]." He noticed Baer's raised eyebrow. "Mullens, West Virginia; it's where I'm from."

"I see. Well, it's kind of a dark reference, my man. But you got it."

Zeb trembled with the same excitement in making this small decision as he had watching the trespass. Everyone—for this week, at least—would have to use the gate code *he* selected. It may have been a small thing, but it gave him an odd sense of power anyway. It was unlike the feeling he'd had his entire life, not being in control of anything, including his life.

To expedite communication, and to be discreet, emergency codes covering almost all possible scenarios had been

---

17 www.wyomingcountyheritage.com/history/town_mullens.htm

developed. Zeb found them to be easy to remember, as the colors corresponded to the events.

Code Red = Fire

Code Blue = 911 which meant that the victim's life or limb was in jeopardy, ie trouble breathing.

Code Yellow = HazMat spill, HazMat being short for Hazardous Material, such as chlorine or solvents.

Code Green = General first aid, not critical enough to call 911.

Code Brown = Biohazard, which referred to human waste such as vomit, feces, or blood.

Alert codes were more specific. He enjoyed the challenge of learning that a "10-33" call meant that there was a possible theft in progress, for example. It was like a secret language, and he was a part of it. A part of something special and honorable. It was in that moment that he knew he'd made the right decision to leave his home far behind.

Opening up to Natali eased a burden he hadn't been aware he was carrying. Maybe it was guilt, or dishonor; whatever it was, it had never occurred to him that he felt badly about blowing off his family. He felt better, lighter, after talking to her than he had since leaving home. Unlike the gate code, it was a feeling of true power, that he could grow beyond his family's expectations and become the man he wanted to be. A new goal crystallized: He wanted to do something for Natali to show his appreciation. Maybe something for her birthday; whatever it was, he knew it wouldn't be enough. *Careful, Zeb,* he reminded himself. *You don't want to start hearing your family in your head!*

The crackle of the radio swept him back to the present. "All available hands, llama drama at Cedar Whiles, code 10-10," it said. Zeb waited for a break between other responders before pressing the button of the radio on his shoulder. "ZWC responding from CS," he reported. He reined Cherni down the trail to Escape Drive, moving him into a lope; when they were on its shoulder he kicked the horse into a full gallop. They flew in the dirt to the back of the ranch where the camelids were pastured, Zeb's heart pounding from exhilaration and absolute but denied terror of falling at such breakneck speed: he'd never gone so fast before. As Cherni bounced Zeb to a stop at the gate —Zeb astonished that he wasn't thrown out of the saddle—a student opened it to let them in, and they took off again to the action. Dust was churning in the middle of the pasture, while two advanced riders moved their horses around it, lassos in hand. In the midst of the dust could be seen cream and rust clashing and the tangling of long necks and legs as two alpacas silently fought each other, only grunts occasionally escaping their throats.

"We're trying to get them apart," called out one of the riders to Zeb. "If we can lasso them, we'll separate them before they damage each other or themselves."

"What can I do?" shouted back Zeb.

"Get in—" but before she could finish, the alpacas tore off running, one chasing the other so closely they almost looked harnessed together. The aggressor was trying to bite the other where the neck meets the shoulders. As they approached the herd of alpacas and llamas, it split, half going one direction, half the other. The fighting pair stopped at the fence, again tangling together, attempting to bite legs, ears, necks. Zeb and the other two caught up with them, and another responder on horseback joined them.

"Back off you guys, we've got to get them away from the fence." He rode up to Zeb and tossed him a blue tarp. "Go to the fence behind the brown one and wave that tarp. I'll do the same behind the white. With luck, they'll separate and those guys will catch at least one of them." Zeb moved Cherni into place; the tarps startled and distracted the alpacas enough to get their attention, while the horses danced but didn't panic. One of the alpacas bolted, the other momentarily behind but long enough for a rider to move in, prompting it to change direction. With the alpacas now more confused, within two throws of the lasso, one was caught. His body kept trying to go, but spun around as the lasso tightened around the upper portion of his neck. The first alpaca was down the pasture before it turned to see why it wasn't being pursued anymore.

Though to an observer coming on the scene each of them would've appeared calm and aloof, Zeb could see the lower lips of both alpacas drooping and loose, with thick, green saliva dripping heavily from them; their sides heaving with labored breath. The responders planned a strategy while they waited for the alpacas to truly became calm. Barry, the one holding the rope with an alpaca at the other end, said, "We'll have to confine this one to solitary, I think."

Branchmaster Senpaku arrived. He walked up to the roped alpaca and released it. Barry protested, tried to explain what happened but he was cut off. Senpaku said, "They've resolved their issue. They're done fighting till the next time." At that, the two contestants rejoined the herd, resuming the clipping of the grass as though nothing had happened. "Come on inside, you kids have reports to file."

The three responders rode their horses to the main building, giving the "all clear" radio call. Inside the office, Senpaku caught up to them with a pitcher of iced tea infused with sprigs of mint.

"Some fight, huh?" said Barry. "That was pretty exciting."

Senpaku sat down at the table with them. "It was, but not much compared to fighting horses. Consider today's incident your training. One of these days, you'll have another fight to break up, and it won't be as easy as splitting them up."

"What's the worst battle you've seen?" asked Tonya.

Senpaku thought for a moment. "I've been here at the academy for almost thirty years." He paused; he'd told the story before, but always considered his audience. "Years ago, we had a Lipizzaner stallion. He'd been injured during a practice for a show; even with his lameness, he was still too much to handle for most riders. We acquired him as a retirement animal. Because we will never breed horses, he was castrated. Although the hormones worked themselves out of his body after several weeks, he had the mind of a stallion because of, habit, I suppose you'd say. The stallion mentality never left him.

"Now, understand that he didn't have 'the drive' to reproduce anymore—we'd kept him isolated from the rest of the herd during his transition—he still needed to be the alpha horse. The mares understood this, and so did the other geldings. But I suppose we added one too many geldings.

"The second day it was in the pasture, that Lipizzaner attacked him. Chased him all over the field; the squealing could be heard all the way up top Lapis Lookout, I'm told." He paused and took a long draught of his tea. He set it down, seemingly lost in thought.

Tonya couldn't take it anymore. "Well?" she said. "What happened?"

He glanced at her and continued, "By the time Grounds Alert arrived, the stallion had brought down his victim. He didn't stop there. He was crazy with stallion madness. I won't go into details, but it is enough to tell you that they both had to be destroyed." He finished the tea and stood. "Don't let it scare you off patrol. That was a one-off, and unlikely to happen again. Just don't take any animal for granted, you never know what they might do."

Chapter 18

Envy

*Oh! my dear fellow beings, why should we longer
cherish any social acerbities, or know the slightest ill-
humor or envy! Come; let us squeeze hands all round.*
— *Moby Dick, chapter 94, by Herman Melville*

September

Most activity at Moon Caverns takes place on top. Many ancient layers of earth and rock protect the caves from weight added in the form of people, horses, and buildings. Numerous small cavities where purple martins nest are located in the cliff face between the base and the top. Of course, these holes can only be seen from the valley below, as the cliff is much too steep to observe from above.

Between a business management class and his final class on kindness, Eric stopped for lunch at the Moon Caverns cafeteria.

The girl at the next table in front of him was sharing her plans for the break. "My boyfriend and I are going to Disneyland in Paris for a week. I'm so excited, I'm almost packed already! To tell you the truth," she leaned forward to whisper, though everyone at the table could hear, "I'm not sure if I'm more excited to see him or go on the trip!"

Eric was annoyed at her insensitivity. Sure, it was fine for her to be excited, but her tone was braggartly. Didn't she realize that some people couldn't go home? Just three months into the school year, it was much too early for a cross-country trip back home, though he'd had several bouts of homesickness.

He gathered up his food and took it to an outside table. Something must have startled the purple martins, as hundreds of them shot out from the cliffs below. They congregated in the sky and swooped up, creating a murmuration over the valley. He knew even they would be leaving soon, migrating to South America for the winter. It made him miss his family even more. He did a quick calculation, determining that Kisha, Renae, and Obi would just be getting out of their school.

After his last class of the day, he called Amara again.

"Hey, what snooze?" she answered.

"I just miss you."

"You say that every time."

"Well, it's true. What's going on over there? It's noisy."

She laughed. "It should be! I'm over at your apartment. Renae is having a birthday party for one of her friends, that one in her class, remember?"

"Yeah, I think so. Lisa something. What are you doing there? A little old for eighth graders, aren't you?"

Amara scoffed. "I'm here for the party, but only as an escort. You never know what a bunch of these girls can do, and your momma only has one set of eyes." A crash of—he couldn't tell what—fell in the background. "Uh, I gotta go, daddy-bear."

"Okay, I love you, Sugarbu—" He didn't finish; she'd already hung up.

Eric found that as the term was wrapping up, he had a couple days off from classes and as luck would have it, he didn't have to be at work, either. He planned a day to get back to his secret pleasure of writing poetry. What would his basketball "bros" think of him? He could just imagine their taunts. He gathered up his notebook, a couple of pens, and his interactions log, and headed out to his favorite thinking spot at Obsidian Marsh, where the hydrangeas were in late bloom, in hues ranging from deep and light blues, periwinkle, white, to creamy green.

He took out his pen, and, thinking of an unrequited love from the past—his seventh grade teacher—wrote "A Short

Novel" on a fresh page. On this particular subject, he knew he could write a whole book. Instead, he wrote the essence of the story in the form of a poem.

The bus ride for Fred on No. 10 was a long, cold journey through
form, creation, and that woman.
　Seizing the moment, he passed
through the massive door.
　He rang the bell and waited—too long!
Katalin's voice feebly crackled,
　"Who is there?"
　"It's me," he replied.
The door did not open.
　He was not a man to ring twice.

Eric knew no one would ever see it; he didn't want them to. Let them think he had limericks inside of him. He received a great deal of satisfaction in composing poetry, and any recognition he got for it would demean his efforts. For Eric, praise was not only a source of embarrassment, but a hindrance to writing anything more.

"I've been here three terms now, and still haven't had a date!" The girl's broad shovel scrooped loudly across the concrete as she cleaned up soiled sawdust from the aisle.

"A boyfriend isn't everything. Be careful what you ask for." Adele was cleaning out Pickle's stall. The mare was tied in the aisle, snorting a confab with Amanda's white gelding. "They can be more trouble than they're worth."

"Do you have a boyfriend?"

"Not right now," she semi-lied. After all, Wesley was a fling, not a true relationship. They couldn't even be seen in public. *I can't even call it a friendship. For that matter, he's no boy.* She needed to change the subject, fast. She'd been wanting to tell someone she could trust about it. Why, she wasn't sure. But she was sure this girl wasn't the one; she was a known blabbermouth. What she did trust her with was her mare: the girl was an excellent horsewoman. "Before I forget, thanks again for taking care of Pickles while I'm on break."

"Sure, it's no problem. I've got about ten other horses I'm babysitting anyway. It'll keep me out of trouble."

Adele stopped raking. "*Twelve* horses? Alberta, don't you want to take some kind of break yourself?"

"Horses are my life. It'll be a lot of work, but it'll be a mental break. You know, there's a lot more to animal husbandry that even I didn't know about. That degree isn't going to be a piece of cake. Anyhow, it's not as bad as it sounds, 'cuz all the horses are here at the Trunk. If I had to run around to the other stables, that'd be another matter."

"Huh, okay. When I get back, I can help you move to your new dorm," she said as she pulled the obstinate mare back into the stall.

A Word About the Bird

Mascot of Moon Caverns, the Purple Martin[18] is the largest member of the swallow family in North America. Purple martins have, for the most part, taken to nesting in cavities that have had previous occupants, or that are man-made. The ancient practice of providing hollowed out gourds has been joined by the modern practice of building wooden or metal nesting boxes. But at the academy, the saxicoline birds have found natural nesting opportunities in the cliff face at Moon Caverns. Though they nest at the caverns, they can be seen swooping all over the academy's grounds.

Since they feed entirely on insects, they've found a feast at the academy. With horses and other livestock come flies, and the purple martin helps keep down insect populations to a tolerable degree so that chemical intervention is unnecessary.

18 www.purplemartin.org/

Chapter 19

Pride

Vanity and pride are different things, though the words are often used synonymously. A person may be proud without being vain. Pride relates more to our opinion of ourselves, vanity to what we would have others think of us.

— Jane Austen

October

Phoebe looked forward to the discussions in her enhancement class at Emerald Crag. Everyone had an opinion; some were easily swayed while others adamant about their positions. The verbal give and take, push and pull, highs and lows fascinated her, and her participation made her experience even more rewarding.

"There are two ways to think of pride," said Mr. Pequod, writing on the whiteboard with a purple dry-erase marker, making two columns. "There is pride in accomplishment, a feeling of pleasure and gratitude. Then there's vainglorious boastful, arrogant pride, a feeling of superiority and self-righteousness. Give me some examples of each."

The students considered for a few moments, then one offered, "Being a show-off."

Mr. Pequod wrote it on the board under the heading "Negative."

"Optimistic," said another student. Pequod wrote it in the "Positive" column.

"Generous," said another.

"Judgmental."

"Enthusiastic."

"The Academy." Pequod turned and looked at the student. She wore a short pink tutu over black leggings and had a full head of pink hair to match.

"Interesting. Why do you say that?"

"It's like, all about itself, isn't it?" Pequod raised an eyebrow quizzically, in a way that meant "go on." "I mean, here on campus, we meet almost all our own needs. We have our own water supply, grow a lot of our own food, have a medical team; it's almost like we're trying to exclude the rest of the world."

He drifted to her side of the room. "So I assume that I should list the PAA in the negative column? Does anyone else want to comment on that?" From this point, it was more about getting a discussion going than making lists.

"I kinda see that," said a boy in the front row. "But I think it's a good thing, being self-supporting. And it's necessary. Here on the coast, we're so far away from many services, and skills, we have to cultivate our own."

"Besides, we can take these skills out into the communities when we leave here," offered Phoebe. "Isn't that why we're here, to bring what we've learned to the world, the point of all education?"

"If you are in a guild."

"You don't have to be in a guild to have an impact," said Pequod. "Sure, the guilds are the academy's approach to setting it apart from other institutions, offering a specialized team to create a positive role model in the world. But you'll influence many people throughout your life too. Our hope is that you'll influence them positively."

A young man with freckles and a toothy gob interjected. "And we don't exclude—the public comes to Pearl Quay to shop every day, and to the community market there every Saturday and Sunday." The boy paused. "And the shops are rented by businesspeople, who hire us to work for them. I think it's pretty cool," he said, folding his arms over his chest as he leaned back in his chair.

"And you seem proud of that," said the pink girl. She waited for the double tease to sink in.

He opened his mouth to reply, but his eyes grew wide as he caught himself. "Oh, I smell what you're stepping in! Aaand," he drew out the word, "I guess I see your point. Aaand, I'm proud of you!" The room broke out in laughter.

After the students quieted down, Mr. Pequod said, "So you see how easily pride can shift, from a positive quality to a negative as easily as the permissive parent can slip into being neglectful. As it is said, 'Too much of a good thing is still too much.'"

Pequod reminded the students that there was no one who could be proud for being on campus based solely on their intelligence. They may be smart, but it wasn't a qualifier for attendance. Components of intellect are carefully weighed, however, and no one got in without exhibiting some type of mental agility, regardless of standardized test scores.

Since she had taken the cooking class as an elective, Adele thought that she should show off her new skills in the kitchen. She'd always taken some pride in her ability to follow a recipe to the letter; now she had more understanding about the nature of ingredients, and was becoming more adept at conjuring a meal without a template. Basalt Moor had a cafeteria, but kitchenettes were also available on the dorm floors. Adele wanted to cook a modest but fancy dinner for her roommates. Although she had arranged the time with each, she mailed them written invitations in her best and most elaborate hand.

She found china in the cupboards, leftover pieces from past students' meals. Though the plates, glassware, and flatware were mismatched and the dining cramped, she managed to make it formal and charming.

"Where's the grub?" teased Mari, the first of three to arrive. She carried with her a bottle of red wine.

With false haughtiness, Adele said, "It's not 'grub,' it's a delightful repast," as she took the bottle. "And it's still cooking."

Mari sniffed. "Whatever you call it, it smells good so far."

Another guest came in, this one with the fresh flowers Adele had requested. "Hope these asters work for you," said Dana, setting the bundle of purple and blue flowers on the counter. "I found them growing alongside the back road of Saffron Cascade, at the property line fence."

"They're perfect," said Adele.

"One of the perks of being on patrol," Dana said as Adele handed her a glass of the wine.

Adele turned to stir spaghetti sauce into the pan of ground seasoned sausage before adding the steamed cabbage shreds. "Anything interesting happen today?"

"Sure, there's always something to report!" She pulled out a butterscotch-colored bathing suit out of her satchel. All over the front of it were golden plastic sequins the size of silver dollars. "Look what I found by the waterfalls last week. There's no lost report on it, so today Baer said I could keep it. I think it'll even fit me."

"I don't know why you'd want it to, it's hideous! How did it get there?"

"Oh, I'm thinking someone probably went for a dip in Horsetail Basin and decided to go 'skinny' instead, and when they got dressed forgot about it. Since swimming in the falls is forbidden, that probably explains why they didn't file a report. Anyway, I think it's awesome!"

The last roommate came in just as Adele began to spoon the cabbage/sausage mixture over steaming rice. "Wonderful, you're right on time, Gretchen," said Adele, grateful for the distraction so she wouldn't be tempted to question Dana's taste in clothing.

Chapter 20

Conservation

Conservation must become before recreation. (sic)
— *Prince Charles*

October

Moon Caverns was most renowned for the caves below it, which were filled and criss-crossed with selenite crystals of all sizes, from pencil-thin to the width and length of cedar logs. There was more to the campus than the magical caverns though, and when Phoebe moved there for her second term, she explored the entire school, taking a tour of the caverns almost as an afterthought. For her, being outdoors amid beautiful flora was her ideal place in nature, not enclosed with minerals.

The southernmost school at the academy sits above the northeast-facing caverns, with the impressive main building—named Lincoln Terrace—facing the same direction. Across the road from this building, were paddocks built at the top of the cliffs, with a margin of safety between them and the ledge. Stables were built underneath the massive brick Lincoln Terrace, with runs coming out its other side, to the southwest. The dorms were smaller buildings on either end of Lincoln Terrace, but otherwise matched the main building in its Collegiate Gothic style.

During one of her solitary outings, Phoebe came upon a long-overlooked unpainted wooden structure in an overgrown garden on the far side of the orchard; it was designed to be open and airy, similar to a round gazebo. Taller than it was wide, it was the height of at least of two stacked fence posts, about sixteen feet high, she reckoned. Though sound and sturdy, it was obviously an amateur attempt, probably built by students many years ago as a class project. It was a far cry from the rigid architecture of the school. She could see something lavender inside, but she couldn't tell if it was a fountain, short statue, or birdbath. It was too obscured to make out.

The tower had a haunted quality; it was covered all over by a creeping vine, with thick trunks squeezing the lumber, sometimes distorting and even threatening the building's structure. It nearly enveloped the tower, creating more darkness within it than usual. Lesser vines meandered, turned, twisted, or shot straight out from the building, as if reaching for the skies. Upon most of these hung empty stamens, the flower petals having fallen to the earth, some with large pods dangling from their ends. Some green or dying leaves remained; the plant was going into its dormant period. Phoebe recognized the vine as a wisteria.

This was Phoebe's bailiwick; she had a knack for growing plants, specifically flowers of all kinds. Being among the greenery and caboodle of colors when gardening put Phoebe out of time and place; it was her form of meditation, her chance to disappear from the human world with its troubles and concerns, and get a fresh perspective. It was a mind-cleanse, and the crisp autumn air subsidized the effect.

The desire to work with this plant, to bring it to the glory for which she knew it could return, reached for her as it did for the sun. Though it was alive, it had been neglected. Its attempt to use this folly for its support reminded her on a subconscious level of her life before attendance at the academy: living adequately, but clinging to a fanciful place in hopes of climbing to a better quality of life; yet not working toward her potential. She decided to speak to the branchmaster for permission to prune the unwieldy plant.

Her introspective moment was interrupted by an odd crunching sound. She walked around the tower, trying to locate the source. She came upon a low bush, with a swishing black tail poking out from underneath it. Phoebe bent down to look: first she saw white paws, then the black body of a cat...munching down on what looked to be the remnant of a mouse. "Well, that's not a pretty sight," she said before standing upright. "In fact, *blech*," she said; her face wrinkled in distaste.

The tuxedo cat finished its meal, and came out to rub innocently against Phoebe's legs. Too fat and healthy, it was obviously not feral. She stroked its thick and shiny coat. "Where did you come from? Do you have a name, you little carnivore?" No answer but a loud purr. "Until I hear otherwise, I think I'll call you Carnie. Assuming I see you again." Phoebe sat on the ground and allowed the cat to curl up in her lap. She had seen dogs and cats at the schools, but they were generally kept inside or near the buildings to keep them safe from predators. But of course, cats were prone to wander, finding their way home when they needed it. Phoebe made a mental note to bring some catnip from Basalt Moor's herb garden the next time she came out, just in case.

Chapter 21

Research

Every path to a new understanding begins in confusion.

— *Mason Cooley*

October

Biodiverse marine habitats of the Oregon Coast make for an inclusive marine biology lab. Rocky and sandy beaches of varied substances, bays, harbors, and estuaries, isolated coves, both gentle and expansive sand dunes, sea caves, and the open ocean itself, create a virtual research paradise for inquisitive students and faculty. The academy's school of marine science provided several of these habitats on its campus.

Eric took an introductory course at Sandpink Beryl on marine biology to fully round out his ecology education. Since the Earth is covered by over 70% water, it's critical that its nature, inhabitants, and ecosystem be understood. He was somewhat familiar with the science already; one of his favorite places back home was the Georgia Aquarium. His favorite fish— the whale shark[19], largest extant fish known—made a home there. Whenever he felt the need for a mental break, he would simply close his eyes and imagine that he was back at the tank, watching the giant fish cruising through the water above him. Even living in the big city and his chaotic home life, the perspective quieted Eric's busy mind.

---

19 en.wikipedia.org/wiki/Whale_shark

Adele enjoyed running; not just because it was simple exercise, but it was an easy way for her to clear her thoughts. "Running away from my problems," was how she explained her need to hit the road whenever she was asked.

"Are you still seeing Mr. Peising?" asked Mari during their late afternoon mid-week run from Emerald Crag down to Sandpink Beryl.

And we were getting along so well, Adele said to herself. Against her better judgment, she'd finally told Mari her secret. She wished she'd never said anything about it. "Yeah, but I'm breaking it off with him, as soon as I get the chance."

"You know, I've noticed someone looking at you," Mari teased.

"You have? Who?"

"Just a boy. Now, don't give me that face! He's a student here. I don't think he's stalking you, I just notice him noticing you."

"Where at, in the dorm?"

"No...let's see, once when I went with you to the post station, and when we went to the main library, he was in the visitors' paddock; we were taking off as he was unsaddling his horse. I think he has a work study at Saffron Cascade." They slowed when they came up to the bridge over Pistoia River; Adele stopped on the other side, holding her ribs as they jogged in place. Exhaled white mists appeared and dissipated in the cool autumn air as they spoke.

"What does he look like?"

"Mmm, medium height, black hair. That's about all I remember."

"White guy?"

"Well, yeah. I mean, he's not blue."

"You say it like it's obvious. You know, at least a third of we "leaves" are different colors. Even in our little group; Gretchen is 'tinted.'"

Mari sucked in her lips and crease her brow. "Yeah, what is

she anyway? East Indian? Hawaiian? Hispanic?"

"I guess you'll just have to ask her." Adele took off toward the sun lowering into a cloud bank, with Mari close behind.

Chapter 22

Humor

There is, I confess, a hazard to the philosophical analysis of humor. If one rereads the passages that have been analyzed, one may no longer be able to laugh at them. This is an occupational hazard: Philosophy is taking the laughter out of humor.

— *A.P. Martinich*

October

American Sign Language at Saffron Cascade isn't a very popular class, compared to the speaking conversation classes of French, German, and Japanese that the academy offers, but more well-attended than Igbo or Cantonese. Those who took ASL were apt to have family members with hearing problems, were adding to their language abilities, or like Adele, wanted to learn a non-verbal language.

As the wind bore down on the building, the howling made such a racket that the mostly soothing tones of the oboe lesson nearby was all but drowned out. The ASL instructor had them share information about themselves, showing them how to sign key words as they went along. He signed, "*It's a good thing we don't have to hear each other.*" The students who read him put their hands in the air and shook them as a sign of appreciation of the little joke. During class, they learned where their fellow students were from, which languages they could speak, why they were at the academy, what term they were in, and their favorite pastime.

Adele was jealous that Phoebe could speak French fluently. After class let out, she invited Phoebe to join her for coffee at the cafeteria. Since cafeterias are naturally noisy, it was located as far as possible from the stables. It was built at the edge of the upper Pistoia River, just before the water disappeared into the woods. The girls took their hot beverages onto the deck where roaring elongated pyramidal gas heaters kept them warm on the outside, while strategically-placed clear acrylic panels protected them from the wind.

"*Oui*, but down home in Louisiana, it's not that *inhabituel* to speak French. I've actually had to work at it, because I grew up with Louisiana French. You may have an easier time learning it than I did, because I had to unlearn some," Phoebe said, as they settled onto the cushions.

"I don't think so; I've tried to learn another language so many times."

"What have you studied?"

"I started with German; oh, I do remember some Spanish before that. In California, they start you in grade school."

"That's the best time, when you're young and impressionable."

"I guess not young enough for me," said Adele. "Anyway, I did okay with German, but I haven't studied since I was a sophomore. I went to community college to learn Italian, but I didn't have anyone to study with. It's not encouraging when you don't have anyone to listen or even tell you when you've screwed up."

"Well, I will study with you. This'll be fun - we can send signals to each other, almost like a secret in plain site!"

"If you'll be my partner in ASL, help me study, I'll give you private riding lessons. How does that sound?"

"Fabulous idea, *mon ami*. I mean," she gestured with her hands, "*good idea. When do we start?*"

"*Tomorrow morning*," signed back Adele. Then verbally, "Right after breakfast, in the arena, where I can watch you and we can hear each other. At least until we learn hand signals, of course. *Good for you?*" she signed.

"*Yes, I love it.*"

Adele met Phoebe in the arena. Although close to thirty riders were also there giving their horses a morning workout, there was still plenty of room in the large arena. Adele was on Pickles, the horse she'd been assigned, and Phoebe had checked out a leggy, lean, strawberry roan for the session.

They rode counter-clockwise around the arena, walking their horses side by side as others passed them. The roan bumped into Adele's horse, causing the girls to hit their legs together and Pickles to jump ahead.

"Oh, *excusez-moi!*" Phoebe called out to her.

Adele laughed. "Don't worry about it, we'll do that lots of times. Pickles wasn't scared, she's just ornery." Changing the subject as Phoebe caught up, she said, "You know, I never asked you, why do you want to learn to sign?"

Phoebe shrugged. "It's probably a waste of time, but my uncle—my father's brother—is losing his hearing. At this rate, he'll be deaf in no time."

"Then why would it be a waste of time?"

"I don't know if he wants to learn sign language; it'll pretty much be a one-sided conversation!" After sharing a laugh, Adele said that it wouldn't be a waste, Phoebe could always use the skill down the road, with other people.

"Is your father going deaf too?"

Phoebe looked down and sighed. "We lost my father last year."

"Oh, I'm so sorry, I had no idea. Phe, please..."

Phoebe shook her head at Adele. "Don't worry about it, honestly," she said. "Truth is, I'm closer to my uncle. My papa was away most of the time, didn't really spend much of his days home with me. And, my parents are a lot older, I came along as surprise when they were starting to plan their retirement. So, as my uncle says, 'sixty-eight was old enough.' It wasn't the tragedy it sounds like. I guess that sounds cold, but we never had a 'warm' relationship anyway."

"It's always hard to lose a family member though."

"Yes, but I'm more concerned with my mother than my father. She's not exactly healthy, and without me at home, I don't know if she's taking care of herself."

"Are you going to go home at break?"

"We can't really afford that." That put a halt to the conversation.

When Phoebe sighed, Adele knew it was time to make their riding session more interesting, and to change the subject.

"Okay, let's pick up the pace. We're going to move them into an easy trot."

It took a bit to get Phoebe's gelding in the right pace. Once she did, Adele told her to relax. "Let go of the saddlehorn!" she called out. "You won't fall, I promise you." Phoebe complied, but kept a hand on the pommel. *Well, that's an improvement*, thought Adele.

After a few times around the arena, Adele gave Phoebe a choice. "We can either run the horses, or change direction and go clockwise. Which do you prefer?"

Phoebe shrugged. "I guess I should try running."

"Okay; it's called cantering or loping. Full out running is galloping."

Phoebe put her chin up. "I know about galloping, of course."

"Fine, but we're not doing that today. You'll have to get much more secure in the saddle first. When we've done a few sprints, we'll call it quits for today."

They rode to the far end of the arena. Adele and Pickles demonstrated first, running to the opposite end then back again. "Your turn," she urged as she moved Pickles around the back end of Phoebe's horse. Phoebe got her roan to a quick, hard trot right off, but couldn't move him into the faster, more comfortable lope. At the opposite side of the arena, she turned the horse around; this time he took off towards Adele quickly. Too quickly. At full-gallop, Phoebe grasped the horn with both hands, managing to keep in the saddle till mid-arena, but one bump too many and she was on the ground as the roan ran away from her, head and tail high in the air with empty stirrups flopping haphazardly from the vacant saddle. Adele and Pickles were at once at Phoebe's side. "Are you okay?" Adele said as she quickly dismounted and knelt by Phoebe. Several other riders stopped to observe. Phoebe sat up in the dirt, dazed.

"Wow, yeah I think so."

"You're sure?"

"Umm, give me a minute."

Adele took a seat in the dirt next to Phoebe. "Take your time." She waved to the others to let them know help wasn't needed.

After a few minutes, Phoebe confirmed she was a little dazed and shaken, but more pride-wounded than injured.

"Normally I'd say get back up on your horse, show him who's boss, and conquer your fear before it conquers you, but this time, I think you were assigned a horse that was beyond your skill level," Adele said.

"You think?" Phoebe replied more sarcastically than she'd intended as Adele helped her to her feet. Changing her tone, she said, "Adele, I think I'm okay, but I better get looked at just in case."

"Alright, I'll go with you to Moon Caverns clinic. Just let me put the horses up. Think you can go wait for the shuttle while I do that?"

Phoebe nodded, unexpectedly feeling contrite but not yet ready to voice it; she walked out of the arena as she rubbed her elbow, glancing meekly as Adele and two riders caught her horse.

As she'd predicted, Phoebe was fine though sore. Only her pride was truly hurt, and she'd never considered herself to be prideful before. After getting checked out at the clinic, Adele used her advice in earnest. "Let's do it again tomorrow, but you'll tell the barn manager that you need a *beginner's* horse, right?" During the shuttle ride to the clinic, Phoebe had confessed that she'd convinced the barn manager that she was no longer rated "beginner." She was sorry she'd been arrogant. This time, Phoebe rode in on a new horse she'd checked out for the day, a pretty little buckskin mare. She moved her into a trot towards Adele, Phoebe bouncing in the saddle. "I'm glad...I'm close...er...er...er...to the...grou...ou...ound...today."

"You've got to find your seat, or your horse is going to get upset with you very quickly!" warned Adele. She didn't want to witness another dumping; next time, Phoebe might not be so lucky.

"I know, I just can't seem to help it." Phoebe pulled up next to Adele, facing the opposite direction.

"Imagine your butt is glued in the saddle, first of all. Even if you're closer to the ground, if you bounce off your horse again, it's gonna hurt. I don't need that. And any notion you have of 'posting' is out the window."

"What's posting?" asked Phoebe.

Adele tightened her lips. "Phe, you really are starting from scratch, aren't you?"

Adele explained that English riders almost stood in their stirrups when trotting, pulsing up and down to the beat. Although it required muscles, it was less wear-and-tear on both the horse and the rider's rear end. "But we don't do that in Western. We 'merge' with the horse, move with them. When you've become one with the saddle, we say you've found your 'seat.' Until you do that, you're going to bounce all over the place, and like I said, bounce right out into the dirt!"

Although they were having fun now that Phoebe was matched with an appropriate mount, Phoebe noticed Adele's change in demeanor from the day before.

"Is something wrong?" she asked.

"Oh, no, everything's okay. I was just thinking about my horse back home. I miss him," said Adele. She told the truth; it was also true that she had Peising on her mind, but she had learned not to share *everything*. Besides, for today she wanted to forget about her growing discontent with the hollow affair.

"You have your very own horse?" Phoebe dropped her head forward and looked at Adele with wide eyes, open mouthed. "You never said! No wonder you know so much."

"Yep, my folks bought him a few years ago. I trained him myself when he was a yearling." Adele pulled out her iPhone. "Here he is, just took it on the last break. Feels like it's been a lot longer than two months."

"Wow, he's beautiful! Hey, you went home already?"

"Yeah, but I just live like, ten hours' drive down the coast, so it's not that much trouble."

"Okay. But now I'm jealous of you! You said in class that horses were your favorite subject, but you didn't say you had one of your own. You know you're lucky, right?"

"Of course," said Adele. She meant it with all her melancholy heart.

Students with permits could use the dual-sports to go to town, as long as they paid for gas and any repairs that might be needed. Though they couldn't bring their own vehicles, they could use the bikes freely.

But every Tuesday four shuttles are made available to take whoever wanted to go into Gilded Sand. Each shuttle would park for the day in different areas of the small town: one in the business district at the south end, one in the historic area on the west side of Clover Lane, one near city hall and the tiny library on the east, and one at the single-airstrip airport at the north end. At two miles long, one could easily get from one shuttle stop to another.

All along the west edge of town are beach access points; the entire shoreline in Oregon is public, so as long as a path is found to get to the beach without trespassing on oceanfront property, anyone can enjoy it.

Once a month, the shuttles took the students to Silica City, where they could run many more errands, and participate in more activities. With a population of 6,000, it still wasn't a large town, but had more to offer than Gilded Sand in terms of entertainment, shopping, medical and legal services.

One of the main attractions was a thriving cultural center,

publicly sanctioned but privately funded. Located in a large former schoolhouse donated to the center by the city, numerous activities and events were hosted by the SCCC. At the ground level were separate studios for fiber arts, ceramics, glass arts, and woodcarving. On the main floor, up several steps, one could find a gift shop, administration office, full-service kitchen, three dance studios, meeting rooms, auditorium, and a room for yoga or meditation. On the second floor, permanent art classrooms were established. The third floor was entirely open save for the restrooms and a small kitchen, a studio painter's dream. There was enough room with floor to ceiling windows for a flock of painters. The fourth and highest floor at the cultural center was dedicated to the administrative offices, storage, and archival records.

Another activity that draws many visitors is the local indian casino, offering gaming and a wide variety of events.

That evening, Adele sent Phoebe a text. *Hey, shuttle going to casino in SC tmrrw. Wanna go?*

Phoebe texted back, *Don't have much money.*

Have $20? Just want to try blackjack, I'll buy lunch in SC.

OK snds fun :o)

They met at the city shuttle stop in Pearl Quay, and chatted about their experiences with casinos as they took the 30-minute trip.

"I've never been in one, but my Dad goes to one in Geyserville occasionally," said Adele.

"There's a bunch of casinos in Louisiana, tribal and regular. I actually had an application in at the one in my area," said Phoebe. "I was trying to get into their dealer school."

"You didn't get in?"

"I did, but they called after I accepted my invitation to apply here."

"So you had a choice; nice. Do you regret it, not going to the dealer school, I mean?"

"It wasn't something I wanted to do, but it was good pay. I was going to do it for a year, save up money to go to Louisiana

State; they have a campus right in Eunice. But the noise, the cigarette smoke, and rude patrons I can do without. I have friends who work in casinos around there, and they hate it. So I'm not sorry I came here. Not a bit."

The shuttle slowed as it approached Silica City. The verdant journey through douglas fir and Sitka spruce gave way first to a flashing caution light, then to a view of the lake through shrubs, to a traffic light at a busy intersection with a half empty shopping center. The shuttle took a left, climbing up the casino's winding drive. Every foot of the ground was landscaped with box hedges, flowering azalea, asters, and blankets of petunias. Though not quite as crooked, the snaking curves of the road reminded Adele of Lombard Street in San Francisco. Phoebe noticed the effort, but was not impressed with the result. "Unimaginative," she told Adele.

They were dropped off by the door, with instructions to reassemble there in the afternoon; again with a warning that to miss the ride meant finding their own way home.

Adele and Phoebe linked arms, an unconscious show of unity. After they were greeted by a human—who politely checked their ID—they were greeted by a tasteful but in-your-face monolithic sign: *Must be 21 or over; No weapons of any kind; No smoking of any kind.*

Phoebe was aghast. *A casino without smoking? I wish I could've applied here!* she thought.

Bright, flashing lights seemed to be everywhere. Mirrors threw back exaggerated dazzle. There was a cacophony of colors and patterns from the carpet to the ceiling; slot machines blared whistles and sirens and bells; the overhead music was deafening, seeming to compete with shouts from the craps tables.

After being sufficiently overload with light and jangle, the girls made their way to the blackjack tables. They walked around them, looking for any dealer with a friendly face. Phoebe spotted an empty table with a dealer standing bored.

Adele pulled out two $20 bills and put them on the table.

The dealer cut out eight red chips. Phoebe didn't make a move. "Aren't you going to play?" Adele asked her.

Phoebe shook her head. "I was going to be a dealer, but I've never actually played. I'll just watch for a bit."

"I hope I last long enough for you to come in!" Adele won the first $5 bet, lost the next, doubled down and won the third hand. She pushed $20 to Phoebe. "Come on, I'll help you. I've played lots of blackjack with my dad."

"I can't take your money!"

"I'm ahead. Besides, technically it's not mine, it's house money. Please, it'll be more fun with you playing."

They won some, lost some. On the way to the casino they'd come up with a strategy to only play the minimum bet, no matter how they were doing. "My dad says that if you play long enough, you'll lose. So let's just make it last as long as we can!"

A serious man in a long overcoat and black leather slouch hat joined the game at the other end of the half table. He didn't acknowledge anyone, but put $500 on the table. He simply said, "Green and black." The dealer cut four each of green and black chips, and pushed them towards the man announcing loudly, "Black going out."

Phoebe and Adele watched moon-eyed as the man put one black chip on each of the three spots in front of him. The dealer dealt the next hand; He won the first two spots, lost the third. Phoebe and Adele lost their bets. The girls played for a while, but finally ran out of chips. It wasn't time to catch the shuttle for over an hour, so they stayed at the table, watching the man who was not only losing most hands, but playing poorly.

After a few minutes, a new dealer tapped in, a redheaded woman. The man spoke for the second time, seemingly to his dwindling stack. "Good riddance. Hope you can help me out better than that last guy."

"Good luck, sir," she said. But in short order, he lost all his chips.

They watched horrified as the man pulled out more money, his wallet bulging with cash. Phoebe whispered to Adele, "I don't think he knows what he's doing. Shouldn't someone speak to him?"

"Probably, but they won't."

He continued playing the three spots, continued losing more hands than he won.

More money came out of his thinning wallet.

The dealer showed signs of concern. She finally asked the man, "If you don't mind me asking, how is it that you have so much cash? Did you hit a jackpot?"

The man sat up and stretched as he tucked away the wallet. "My house was foreclosed, and this is what they gave me for it."

Soon, he was down to only green chips. He placed $50 bets on each spot. This time, the girls were no longer naive: they knew he would lose it all. Instead of watching him lose not only his shirt, but everything he possessed, they quietly walk away to wait for the shuttle home.

"I think I've had enough 'fun' at the casino to last me a lifetime," said Phoebe as they sat on the bench outside.

"Um, yeah," agreed Adele. "Hey, listen, I have an idea. The casino had its moments, but it kind of ended on a downer. Let's go to the cultural center, they're supposed to have some kind of bird show going on."

"Like owls and chicken, stuff like that?" asked Phoebe. Then, "Oh, I hope not stuffed owls and chickens?!" Both girls laughed.

"God, I hope not!" said Adele. "But whatever it is, it's got to beat this place."

Phoebe agreed, and they took the in-town shuttle to the cultural center.

The bird show wasn't at all what they'd envisioned: There were no caged birds, no raptor demonstrations, flapping wings over their heads. The show was in the gallery, all kinds of avian-related art. They breezed through the gallery, then checked out the visitors' information center.

Inside, they learned that Silica City was in the midst of celebrating its 50th year as an incorporated city, having brought together seven separate communities during the years.

They had just enough time to read brief descriptions of each of its districts before they had to return to the casino and catch the shuttle.

Poster for Silica City's 50th Anniversary

Silica City was so named for the sand at the beach, and its reputation as an art glass mecca, as silica[20] is a component in both.

Districts or "pearls" run from north to south starting with Lands Spit, the most recently included neighborhood. Laetus is the first district that westbound visitors come to, its name is Latin for "happy." Sealoch is a shopping area situated between the Pacific Ocean and a large natural lake. It was rumored that diabolical creatures inhabited the lake, so it had been named Lake of the Demons. The next community—Diabel—was similarly named for the legend; however, it does not live up to

---

20 en.wikipedia.org/wiki/Silicon_dioxide

its namesake as it enjoys a long history as a nice, quiet neighborhood.

Callfield is a quaint older neighborhood with a new name, as its residents decided to honor two of Oregon's more recent political icons: Tom McCall[21] and Mark Hatfield[22].

Wharrison was named for a former United States president as a counterbalance to "Tillacoln County" in which the communities are situated. Dewy Downs—at the south end of Silica City—is the most bicycling-friendly neighborhood, but at the greatest risk of being totally wiped out by a tsunami.

Phoebe looked at Adele. "That's a lot of town. Uh, for the time being."

"We'll have to come back someday when we have the time."

---

21 en.wikipedia.org/wiki/Tom_McCall
22 en.wikipedia.org/wiki/Mark_Hatfield

Chapter 23

Independence

*All deep, earnest thinking is but the intrepid effort of
the soul to keep the open independence of her sea;
while the wildest winds of heaven and earth conspire
to cast her on the treacherous, slavish shore.*

— *Herman Melville*

November

As a gambler is drawn to casinos, Eric feels drawn to Obsidian Marsh, compelled to experience the low-lying campus whenever he has free time. He visits at least once a week, even participating in fieldwork, whether or not he's enrolled in the class. Some consider it to be the gloomiest school of the academy. He doesn't feel that way at all: to him, it is teeming with life, from the primeval hornwort to the elegant black swans.

After his Conflict class, Eric rode a dual-sport to Obsidian Marsh. Already dusk, the headlights lit the gauzy layers of lowland mist. He parked in the usual place, at the end of the marsh so he could walk in to the campus, gathering his thoughts in the cool and quiet atmosphere. Rarely did he see anyone else about. Only this side of the water had a walkway. Without it, the land was too mucky to walk in. Skunk cabbage provided ample coverage for polliwogs and other freshwater creatures. Frogs hiding among the reeds leapt with a splash, so quickly that it was hard to catch sight of them. With Eric's weekly visits to the Marsh, some imagined him a crapehanger, but that was far from the truth. To others it was a bleak, oppressive place; but his vibrant, active mind longed for its calm. It was his retreat, his Camelot. Not surprisingly, the Conflict class always engendered heated discussion, in which Eric fully participated. When it was over, Obsidian Marsh helped him cool down, literally and figuratively.

But tonight he was on campus for another reason: His friends were throwing a party for his eighteenth birthday in the theater. He stopped at the swamp to clear his mind before going up to the school. The brume rose from the waters, swirling over the surface with the slightest draft.

A sudden rustling in the shrubs startled Eric; it couldn't be a frog this time, but something much larger. First a hand, then an arm emerged to push the thicket aside. He started breathing again when he saw it was the Branchmaster of Obsidian Marsh, Brandon Felix.

"Shit; man you startled me!"

"Sorry, guy, just doing some digging." Felix lifted a pail with a fetid, writhing mass. "Going fishing tomorrow, and the bog soil has the best night-crawlers. Wanna help?"

Eric's nose involuntarily wrinkled. "Thanks but no thanks. I'm actually on my way to a party."

Without responding, Felix set the pail down on the decking, and pulled out a pouch from his pocket. From that he withdrew what Eric recognized as a blunt. As he lit it, Eric remarked, "I didn't know you smoked weed."

After Felix took several quick puffs, he said tightly, "Yep, it relaxes me." Noticing Eric's troubled look, he added as he exhaled, "Don't worry, it's not illegal to smoke in Oregon."

"But smoking isn't allowed on campus, right?"

"Technically you are correct. I'm not worried about it. Besides, I only smoke outside, and never around others who aren't partaking." He held the blunt out to Eric. "So go ahead, if you want. You know, as a token of friendship, no pun intended!" he laughed at his pedestrian joke. "It'll get you in the mood to party."

Eric reached out and took the alternate-leafed cigar from his hand. He took a hit, pulling the smoke into his lungs.

"Looks like you've smoked before," said Felix.

"Weed? Yeah, but nothing like this. Just tried joints a few times." He handed the blunt back to Felix. "It's good stuff, but that's enough for me."

"Not into it, huh?"

"Oh I could be, but it relaxes me to the point of dullness. I want to be sharp. I've got lots to learn, and I'm trying to promote awareness, not oblivion. Pot takes the edge off, but that's not why I'm here."

"It's medicinal too."

"Yeah, I know. I know it helps a lot of people with lots of problems. But so does aspirin and stuff. Even alcohol can help, but it usually causes more issues than solutions. Anyway, I don't need it, I don't have glaucoma or pain or whatever."

"That's cool." Brandon Felix took another toke, watching the smoke rise to join the brume. He seemed to forget about Eric.

"Yep, well I gotta go, I'll see ya." Eric left Felix on the boardwalk, with his nasty bucket and self-induced tabula rasa.

It was time. Peising hadn't done anything to anger her really, but Adele had grown increasingly uncomfortable with the affair. She had tipped over on an emotional level from feeling good about feeling good, to feeling bad about feeling good: the cost to her psyche for physical pleasure was too much to bear. She texted him that she wanted to meet in his apartment.

"I just don't feel that we should go on, Wes," she told him in his dining room when he protested. "We've had our fun, but now I need to concentrate on my studies. First term was a breeze, but now I'm taking my degree classes so it's getting more intense." She was only partly lying.

He leaned across the table and grabbed her forearm near the

wrist. "*You've* had your fun, and now you think you can just kiss me off?"

"Let go," she said. He didn't, but glared at her. She repeated, slower and deeper: "Let go *now*." He complied; she looked at the red marks his fingers left on her skin. "Never do that again, don't ever lay a hand on me again." Fear rose in her chest. She finally understood the danger she'd put herself in.

He sat back in his chair. "You're a goddamn tease," he said. "You *asked* to come here tonight, to my apartment. To break it off with me, just like that? No. You owe me satisfaction." He pointed to the bedroom.

Adele considered walking out. But the excitement that he'd always roused in her still worked, even as she realized it was at least partly based on fear. As much as she hated it now, she still couldn't deny her physical yearning. She made a conscious decision to give in to her base instinct. *Besides*, she argued with herself, *if I give him what he wants now, he'll be less likely to come after me later.* She stood, and after a moment's hesitation, walked into the bedroom. He followed her, slamming the door behind him.

When he passed out she left under the blanket of night, but not to her room at Basalt Moor. Adele was too upset, too embarrassed, too humiliated. At being stupid? Or at being hurt? She wasn't sure, and it didn't matter. He had taken advantage of her compliance, and in his anger, been too rough. She didn't want to associate this night with her room, her sanctuary. So she went to the first place she could think of to spend the remainder of the night where there'd be little chance of being found, hiding in one of the art studios at Saffron Cascade.

Huddled in the darkness of the empty classroom, she considered reporting Peising to the academy; by the time the large east-facing window allowed early morning to bathe her in its blue light, she'd decided instead that she would rather forget the whole affair ever happened. She picked herself up to go home to a long, hot shower.

A Word About the Bird

Mascot of Obsidian Marsh, the Black Swan[23] is another aquatic bird. It can weigh up to twenty pounds with a wingspan exceeding six feet. In flight, broad white wingtips can be seen. Other than the young cygnets which eat larvae and crustaceans, the swans subsist on a vegetarian diet, consuming aquatic plants, algae, grasses, and grain.

Nadja Paunder suggested to her brother to use the black swan as a mascot because she learned that when it appeared in dreams, it could indicate that there are deep mysteries within us seeking to express themselves.

A native of Australia, Sebastian imported two breeding pairs. They took well to the setting, and have produced many generations.

---

23 beautyofbirds.com/blackswans.html

Chapter 24

Awareness

The awareness that health is dependent upon habits that we control makes us the first generation in history that to a large extent determines its own destiny.

— *Jimmy Carter*

November

After saddling Caberneigh, Phoebe bundled up in her jacket and alpaca scarf before donning her riding helmet. Adele had been right: there was nothing like having your own horse. Even though the Fell pony wasn't technically hers, the responsibility for him was. She stroked his neck; by January, the mahogany bay would be in full winter coat.

Phoebe put on her gloves and mounted up. Riding from Sandpink Beryl to her class at Obsidian Marsh would take about thirty-five minutes. The first frost of the season had dusted the trees and grounds so that it seemed as though someone had lightly sifted powdered sugar over everything. They arrived at the campus just as the cold was starting to penetrate through the gloves. She tied Caberneigh to the school's railing with the other horses, and headed toward the building. The black obsidian relief on the ramp's retaining wall was highlighted by the frost. Phoebe paused a moment to admire the carved black swans before she traipsed up to the second-floor classroom.

A posting on its door had advised the students to leave their coats on. "Yes, yes," confirmed Ms. Tangering when one of the students asked if they were going on a field trip. "We are all going to the gym. To expedite the trip, we will be taking a shuttle together."

"What about our horses?" asked another.

"They'll be fine, we will not be gone long. If you are concerned, you can tie them in the paddock."

Tangering brought her students to the main gym at the Trunk to experience physics in motion. When Phoebe first met her, she was as shocked as most people: Nearly every visible surface of Dorothy Tangering's translucent white skin was modified in some way. Tattoos covered her arms, hands, and fingers; even small ones dotted her face. Eggplant-colored hair was shaved close to her scalp on one side. Her earlobes were enlarged with holes large enough to pass a tube of Tangering's cherry-red lipstick through, and she wore a nasal ring in her septum. It was a terrible thought, but Phoebe couldn't help the visualization of leading her around like a bull on a lead. However, any preconceived notions of Dorothy's personality vaporized as her students got to know her: She was as helpful, kind, patient, and innovative as anyone Phoebe had ever known. Qualities that made her a perfect fit at the academy.

She demonstrated similarities between the weight machines and her body. "You see, we are a kind of machine too," she said. "We are made with levers, pulleys, gears. Our hearts are pumps, our brains the wiring in our system. Your homework for next week is to design a machine with these ideas in mind."

Predictably, students groused about the assignment. But Phoebe was delighted. This was what she'd had in mind: The dynamics of movement in the human body. She thought it might even make her a better rider.

"You are going to pick partners today. You must meet together to design your project. You may stay here now and find your way back to Obsidian Marsh, or come back with us and return here at your leisure."

This was not as welcome news to Phoebe. She preferred to work on her own, make her own mistakes and decisions.

Tangering instructed them to find a partner now, and together, begin to explore the gym's machinery while taking notes and making drawings.

Some students gravitated to each other right away, others meandered. Phoebe came around to a tall, intimidating machine, and watched the lean young man climb it and raise himself up. He reminded her of some of the black runners at her high school back home.

"I don't understand that machine," she said after watching him lift himself up and back down a few times.

"What don't you understand?"

"How you can get a workout with just twenty pounds of weight."

Eric stopped, suspended in the air, three feet off the ground. "You've never used a weight-assisted machine before?" His tone wasn't teasing or incredulous.

"Never even heard of it."

"It's pretty cool, let me show you. It helps you do pull-ups, dips, or chin-ups. The weight isn't how much you're lifting, it's how much you're being assisted. It's a counter-weight, see?" He demonstrated, then had her try.

She took the two big steps up into position on the platform. "This is kinda scary," she admitted as she looked down at him. "I'm about as high as I am on horseback."

He nodded. "Yeah, it can be dangerous. You really have to pay attention to what you're doing. When you get used to it, it'll be simple enough. But always be aware. Do it wrong, and you could literally break your arms." That really got her attention. She'd only been thinking about the height. "Now go ahead and grab the bars, and slowly pull yourself up."

After a moment's hesitation she did so, the surprise showing on her face. "Oh, that was easy!"

"Yeah, too easy. Step off for a minute. How much do you weigh?"

"A little personal!" she protested.

He chuckled. "Don't worry, I won't tell. But I want to make it about thirty pounds less than you weight, so I need to know."

"Well, okay. If it's 'scientific.' I'm about one-ten."

"You are a little thing!" He bent down again and set the machine at ninety. "Give that a try." She did, and found it was still easy, but a better workout.

They continued exploring the different ways to use it, forgetting about finding partners. Phoebe asked him, "Why are you taking this class? Didn't you say at the beginning of the term that you're in marine biology?"

"Yeah, I am. But I'm also interested in learning about oceanography. Besides, physics is a pretty basic science course. What about you?"

"I'm in the sciences too, but in medicine. So yeah, it's a basic requirement for me, too."

When they realized everyone was partnered up, they agreed to partner by default.

"Guess it's you and me," he said.

"I have no problem with that," she replied with a smile.

Chapter 25

Forgiveness

You must bear with me.
Pray you now, forget and forgive; I am old and foolish.
— Shakespeare, King Lear

November

Zeb and his grandparents had agreed before he left that he would not be coming home for any of the breaks. Zeb had felt they suggested it too easily, but he reminded himself that their relationship wasn't what he'd thought it was. He sat on the stage at Pearl Quay alone, the dorm room not providing much in the way of privacy. His fingers were beginning to tingle with the biting cold. No one in their right mind would be out here without good reason. *All the better to end the conversation as soon as possible.*

"You never wanted me around, not to be myself. I haven't even been here six months yet, so it doesn't make sense that you want me to come back now."

"We didn't think you'd finish the program. You'd quit by now and come home, help me at the shop. You know, I'm not getting around as fast as I used to. I could use another pair of hands. That kid from your school, he wants me to take that old Pacer he's got, and—"

Zeb interrupted him. "I told you Pop-pop, I don't want to be a mechanic," He felt his face get hot.

"I told you not to call me that, son."

"I told *you* not to call me 'son,' old man. And I'm not leaving the academy for you." With that, he terminated the call.

Two miles from Mullens, West Virginia, up a rock road, sits Zebulon's ancestral home. His aging mother, Henrietta, is a lifelong housewife; with three adults, four children, and several dogs going in and out, the house needs a full-time caretaker just to keep on top of the mess, if never ahead of it. His father, Noah, is a mechanic with remedial though adequate home repair skills, so although the farmhouse is old, it is relatively functional.

Zeb's bedroom is his sanctuary. His collection of hundreds of garage-sale and closeout books—most of which he's read at least once—line the wall above his bed. The books were a healthy combination of both fiction and non-fiction. While he often escaped reality by immersing himself in novels, he equally enjoyed reading about fascinating realities. One of Zeb's books has a section on the Cave of the Crystals in Mexico[24]. He sometimes fantasized about the caves being on another planet, where he made his solitary home.

Zeb sat on his bed in the alcove and thought about the argument with the man he had always considered his father. He thought too about the alpacas; how they'd fought, apparently ready to kill each other. No one could explain what had set them off, nor how they could seemingly "forgive and forget" so quickly, as though nothing had happened.

Could humans learn to move on from their conflicts too?

In the quiet of the night, he recounted how he'd come to be at the academy.

He'd completed his application form for the Graphic Design Technician program at Southern West Virginia Community and Technical College in Saulsville. It wasn't the fine arts degree that he'd wanted, but it was the best he could find in commuting distance. They asked for a copy of his birth

---

24 en.wikipedia.org/wiki/Cave_of_the_Crystals

certificate among other documents. When Zeb asked his father for a copy, he said he didn't have it. "I didn't save it, you don't need that for nothin'," was the answer he got. But of course he did need it, not only for the school but for travel later. Without cooperation from his parents, he did some digging on his own. He finally acquired the certificate, and received the facts as a kick to his chest: the names of his mother and father did not match the names of his parents.

Zeb confronted Noah and Henrietta at the kitchen table. "Who are Mary Caruthers and Doyle McAdams?" he demanded. "Why are they listed on my birth certificate?" He stood over them, feeling for the first time that he was bigger than them.

"You don't need to know particulars, son, but those were your real ma and pa," said Noah.

"That much is obvious, 'Pop'," Zeb said caustically. "I want to know who my parents were, and who *you* are. And I want to know *now*."

The couple looked at each other with resignation. Henrietta let her husband tell the story of how their daughter Mary went off with a suave stranger. All Mary knew about him was his name, and that he was an army deserter with green eyes and jet-black hair living on the road. The relationship hadn't lasted long; in fact, just long enough to leave a little something behind. Shortly before she had the baby, she contacted the father who had rejoined the army, involuntarily. He said he'd take her on, but not the infant; he didn't want anything to do with his own child. She agreed—her libido being stronger than her mothering instinct—and left Zeb with his grandparents. They never heard from her again.

"Why didn't you tell me before? Were you *ever* going to tell me?" Everything was falling into place; why they treated him like a second-class member of the family, why he was the only one with black hair. His grandparents didn't answer. "How about my name, why did she name me Zebulon?"

Henrietta was tired of being put on the spot. She swallowed hard and answered him honestly: "Because you were the last child she ever wanted to have."

Zeb glared at her, trying not to lash out at her. Instead, he faced his grandfather. "Don't ever call me 'son' again."

Zeb was hurt, and angry. He had been abandoned, never wanted. And perhaps worse, had been deceived all these years. He retreated to his room and promptly tore up his application to Southern. Although he still had his sights set on going to school, he now wanted to go far away, away from his family and the bleak future in Mullens.

The weekend of the horse seminar and adoption event was to follow Thanksgiving. Natali had been on the event planning team for the last two terms, and now the time was just around the corner. She called Ben. Her brother had a way of putting her at ease, even in her most stressful times.

"I'm just helping out this time, but I feel so involved. I really care about these horses. But I'm flipping out! I can't sleep, just turning over and over in my mind what has to be done, and what could happen."

"You need to focus on one thing," he said. "This is Thanksgiving, so why don't you focus on what you're grateful for?"

"I'm grateful for you," she teased.

"Gee, thanks sis," he snickered. "But c'mon, stretch a little."

She was silent on her end of the line. He knew to give her time to think. "Well, this is going to sound sarcastic, but I'm thankful that I'm not naïve about horse rescue anymore."

"How do you mean?"

"You can't help to change something if you don't really understand it. I used to think that just buying an old horse and giving it a home was rescue. But it's so much more involved. There's a lot to consider. But Senpaku—he's one of the branchmasters here—says that I have to understand sellers and kill buyers better."

"Why does he want you to understand them?"

"Oh, something about being judgmental clouds my judgment, that there's valid reasons for almost everything, stuff like that. But I just can't get beyond what they're doing. It breaks my heart that horses are put through auction, and it makes me so angry!" she said, nearly shouting.

It was his turn to pause. Then, "I still say, you've got to focus. Focus on what you can do, like this seminar you kids are putting on. Otherwise, you'll lose your mind worrying about what you have no control over."

Chapter 26

Creativity

If a man does not keep pace with his companions,
perhaps it is because he hears a different drummer.
Let him step to the music which he hears, however
measured or far away.

— *Henry David Thoreau*

November

It was no accident that the Enhancement Class of Creativity was taught at Saffron Cascade's School of Art. The wind blew hard against the classroom's windows; gusts sometimes sent raindrops pelting them like shrapnel. The class sat in a large circle to enhance discussion.

"I believe we're made in the image of God; as he is a Creator, so are we to be," said Zeb.

Tawny Port perched on her stool. "That's an interesting statement, Mr. Caruthers. Would you care to elaborate?"

"Sure. Uh, well, we think of 'image' as what something looks like, but since God doesn't have a human face—at least I don't think so—it's more about how we are like God in the way that no other creature is. I mean, what sets us apart from other animals. And I think that is in creativity."

Another boy in the circle said, "Lots of animals are creative. How about octopuses? I'm in the aquatics program. We have an octopus[25] that uses anything he can get a hold of to hide in, like the teapot he has now. He even carries it with him!"

---

25 news.nationalgeographic.com/2015/06/150605-octopus-tools-animals-ocean-science/

"Yeah, but they're creative for a *purpose*, they're trying to reach a goal," Zeb pointed out. "They're making a tool so they can get food, create a shelter, stuff like that. They don't create art for the sake of art. We want to express ourselves, or create a legacy, or—"

"Or make beautiful things to look at," said a pretty girl sitting near Port.

Without thinking, he said, "Yes, we appreciate attractive things." Hearing himself, he began to blush.

"Which is why God made you;" why didn't you say it to her?! You could've even said it after class, dummy. But now it's too late. Zeb chastised himself. Always too late with the flirtations. No wonder he couldn't get a date. Maybe it was self-sabotage; he still had the spoon-shaped girl with the crooked smile on his mind. Surely their paths would cross one of these days...the academy's population wasn't *that* big, even though its grounds were rather vast. Maybe he'd meet her in next term's enhancement class.

Then the thought occurred to him that if God could forgive, then, being in his image, humans should be able to forgive. Zeb could absolve his family. It wasn't that forgiveness was unique to the human race: even animals could forgive. But to stop playing the blame game was a divine act.

He decided that forgiveness was necessary to open up the channels of creativity. Replaying wrongs done to him kept him, his thoughts, his focus, in the past. Looking backwards all the time, at least in relation to his family, kept him from moving forward. Being creative was all about looking to the future. He resolved to quell this natural tendency, and focus on what he wanted: a content life with an honest, accepting woman. For that goal to be realized, he would have to forgive himself, too.

Chapter 27

Joy

It is not what we learn in conversation that enriches us. It is the elation that comes of swift contact with tingling currents of thought.

— *Agnes Repplier*

late December

Between each term, Zeb stayed on campus during the two-week break, except the autumn break when he enjoyed West Virginia the most with its emerald green, golden amber, and scarlet foliage, and before it became chillingly cold. Since Christmas was a major holiday in the Paunder family for generations, the tradition continued on campus. Students who remained were of course welcome to participate in Christmas festivities or not. Each major building—including the stables and barns—had a large Christmas tree, each independently decorated; culinary students cooked up a storm, both traditional dishes from their regions, and anything else they had a mind to create. Evergreen garlands adorned eaves, fence posts, and porch railings.

Feeling inspired by his Creativity enhancement class and the load of lightness, Zeb joined in a wreath-making party. When he'd shared his innermost self with Natali at the library, he was in a heightened state of attention, so that when she shared something about herself, it burned into his memory. He recalled that Natali said she got her name because she was born on Christmas day, so he wanted to craft a wreath with her in mind.

He didn't know where she was staying this term, so he'd have the academy deliver it to her.

Zeb was one of the first at the event. The first non-resident of Sandpink Beryl, in fact. He was given the choice of a styrofoam "donut" for a base, or a wire ring. He opted for free-form, giving the wreath a wire-wrapped base of noble fir, then added more greens: sprigs of variegated holly with pale green edged leaves, tough leather-like salal, and even a few rhododendron cuttings, to match Natali's eyes. Taking advantage of the assortment of decorations provided by the organizers, he attached small red glass balls with wire, along with washed and dried shells one of the residents collected from the beach. He hot-glued these evenly around the wreath.

He was too engrossed in the creative process to notice the comings and goings of people, sometimes singly, some in groups. They milled about, laughing, talking. Zeb didn't mind company, as long as they didn't try to engage him in "happy talk." He saw no need or entertainment value in conversation simply for the sake of talking. In fact, small talk was a waste of time.

A thick ceramic mug of steaming cider thudded on the table in front of him. "Complements of the committee," said a girl at his side with light golden-brown bouncy hair. "Unless you'd prefer hot cocoa or eggnog."

"This is fine, thanks," then glanced up. It was *her*; he was transfixed with recognition as the girl he'd been noticing since the tour on their first day at the academy. "I mean, thank you," he said stiffly.

"You're welcome," she said, and was off as quickly as she'd appeared, tending to the other tables.

He sipped at the cider as he watched her, trying not to stare. Something about her had caught his attention last summer. Maybe it was the way she interacted with people, her eye contact, her spoon-shaped figure. Zeb did appreciate girls with a womanly figure. He could never fathom how men and even his peers would be attracted to women with the figures of adolescent boys. Weren't women *supposed* to be curvy?

He finished the cider, and returned to his project. He glanced now and then to see where she was. He would catch her before she left, but not too soon so he wouldn't come off creepy. Deciding somewhat prematurely that the wreath was finished, Zeb made his way over to the girl—woman, really—and asked her what she should do with his leftover supplies.

"There's just scraps left; should I put them back where they came from, or someplace else, or just toss them out?"

"You can just leave them on the table. We'll sort through it."

"Okay, cool." Zeb held out his empty cider mug. "Any chance of getting a refill?"

"You had cider, right? Unfortunately we ran out. Would you like cocoa or eggnog instead?"

It was the right question. "Only if you will join me. Please?" He gave her a twist of his head and puppy dog eyes, and a slight pout.

She gave him a look that said *you've got to be kidding me with that face.* But she shrugged and said, "Sure. I'll come over in a minute."

Finally, you flirted! You old dog, you had it in your all the time. He was proud of himself. *I guess I was just saving it for the one I really wanted,* he mused.

Eric was flying home for Christmas. He hadn't intended to, but the jealousy and anger he felt in September had illustrated to him that he needed a dose of home. He could already imagine tasting his mother's scratch cooking. Her chicken and dumplings were beyond compare.

The family met him at Atlanta International Airport. His youngest sister Kisha was the first to spot him coming out the gate. "There he is!" She ran up and threw her arms around his slim waist. "My big brother's back!" Her hug felt like home.

At the request of her roommate at Lapis Lookout, Phoebe

helped throw together a party to celebrate Natali's birthday. "No green or red, because Christmas," she'd been telling the invited guests. "If you bring gifts, please bring food or something else ephemeral; hand-made small items would be nice." She explained what everyone understood, that during the break Natali didn't want to pack up any more than she needed to, and having lots of gifts would be a joy, but also a burden.

Natali returned from the errands she'd been sent on. It was a typical Oregon coast December day; the winds were down from their late-autumn gusts, and though nippy, it wasn't very cold. Just wet, very wet. When the rains let up, everything outside dripped with accumulated raindrops, till it rained and started all over again. Although it was nearly three o'clock, a blanket of clouds overhead made it seem much later. *No wonder people get SAD*[26] *this time of year*, pondered Natali.

The room exploded into "Hurrah!" when she came in. There were perhaps thirty in the dimly-lit foyer. Though the party wasn't a surprise, she was surprised at the number of guests who'd turned up, particularly since it was the middle of winter break *and* Christmas day, no less. She'd expected Phoebe, her roommates from this term and last, maybe a few people from her classes. She felt overwhelmed but delighted with the greeting. Someone relieved her of the parcels; she was so distracted she didn't even notice who it was.

"Wow, thanks everybody! and Merry ..." but Phoebe cut her off.

"No no, you may share the day, but this gathering is for *you*," said Phoebe, handing her a snifter of steaming peach pie moonshine. She motioned to the decorated room. "See, no green or red, just your favorites, orange, pink, and teal." Indeed, the room was aglow with warm colored streamers, balloons, and candle light from several clusters of candles in teal blue Mason jars. There was a table with gifts wrapped in one shade or another of her favorite colors, tied with ribbons or dyed raffia. She felt warmth and calm well up inside her, and

---

26 www.psychiatry.org/seasonal-affective-disorder

she hadn't even sipped her drink yet. Natali then noticed that most of the party goers were also dressed in the happy hues of her favored pallette.

"It's incredible, you guys are really coordinated!" she remarked. They laughed jovially, and baptized her with their presence.

Phoebe was pleased with the turnout for the party too, and more than numbers, how well it was going. Natali was happily visiting with her friends, there was plenty of food, thanks to the sharing, and everyone was having a good time. Despite the darkening day, the candles and soft electric lighting buoyed spirits.

One of the students from her public speaking class approached Natali as she helped herself to a slice of quiche from the buffet. "Hey, have you been doing any public speaking since our class?" he asked her.

"Not yet, but I've been asked to officiate a wedding in April. In the meantime, I'm helping the bride with coordinating the thing. How about you?"

He shuffled his feet. "Maybe someday, if I need to. But it's not something I'm planning to do. As a musician, I can just play and not have to answer to anyone."

"We'll be having live music, want to audition?" Natali asked. One of the benefits of helping with the wedding was an excuse to network. She wasn't the type to just go up and start talking to strangers for no reason.

He told her that of course, and she could post it on the bulletin board at Saffron Cascade if she wanted others to audition.

"Where will you be living next term?"

"I'm moving to Obsidian Marsh tomorrow," she said. "Not that I want to. I really, really don't."

"Oh, why's that?"

"It's not my favorite place, to be honest. And I've liked living here at Lapis so much, especially the sunrises...," she appeared lost in the thought. Snapping back to the present, she said, "I really don't foresee spending any more time than I have to there outside of my room. It's just so dark, and damp. You know, they always have to fight mold and dry rot. And even though the ocean and Pistoia River are close by, there's no view of them!" she exclaimed. Natali could tell that the alcohol was loosening her tongue.

"I guess it is kind of dreary," he agreed. "It reminds me of where I grew up, in Vancouver. It has its charm, there's some really nice places, but it can seem pretty down, most particularly on days like this." He noticed her face clouding over. "But hey, you can come visit me at Saffron Cascade any time! You can hear music playing from almost anywhere on campus. And although I don't usually get up in time for sunrise, the sunsets are spectacular."

"I'll keep that in mind; I think I'm going to be visiting a lot of people there next term!"

Chapter 28

Reality

In so far as the statements of geometry speak about reality, they are not certain, and in so far as they are certain, they do not speak about reality.

— *Albert Einstein*

early January

Zeb met Adele at the stables of Sandpink Beryl. The noon sky was sunny and blue, barely a haze streaking through the crisp atmosphere. Deceptively postcard-perfect.

"Do you think a winter ride is such a good idea for a first date?" said Adele as she rubbed her gloved hands together, watching Zeb saddle up her horse.

"Soytenly!" he laughed. "I figure it's a good way to see what you're made of. Besides, it's a beautiful day."

"It's a cold day, Zeb. But I'm not complaining, it'll be fun."

"The ground's dry, not many people are out in this cold so we'll enjoy some privacy, and when we get up to my chalet at Saffron Cascade, I'll make you a coffee nudge to warm you back up. But if you get cold before we get there, I've got you covered." He pulled out a flask from his Carhartt jacket. "See? 'Always be prepared,' that's my motto."

Zeb took Adele on a brisk tour of what he thought were the most romantic spots on campus. They started at Sandpink Beryl, watching the sandpipers dart and dip on the glittering pink shore. From there, they took a trail around the south of

Lapis Lookout. He led her to cross in front of the cave of Moon Caverns, taking a wildlife trail past it to Basalt Moor. They went up to the observatory, then down the other side to the academy's graveyard for horses.

Adele cocked her head at Zeb. "Uh, you think this is romantic?"

"Sure," he said levelly. "Just think of all the love that went into these horses, and the love they gave back."

It was an interesting concept, a viewpoint she'd never considered. She didn't say a word as she took in the scene. The mostly barren hillside gradually sloped down toward the neighboring property. Small basalt markers were laid flush with the surface. They rode through the site, noting that some of the markers were so worn they couldn't be read. They saw one with no writing, it instead exhibited the image of an American kestrel.

"I wonder if this was for one of the falcons, maybe someone's pet," said Adele.

"I don't know. Come on, I have something else to show you. A little secret." Zeb winked at her. They rode back up to the observatory, then down another trail to the valley below Basalt Moor. As they passed through the stubbled hay fields to Crimson Song, Adele stopped.

She propped her elbows on the pommel. "I gotta tell you, Zeb, I'm really enjoying this time with you. It's a unique date, just like you."

He walked Cherni closer to her. "I'm glad to hear you say that. But just wait till I show you what's next!" He suddenly kicked the horse into a lope, and Adele followed right behind till they got to West Peregrinate where they slowed to a trot up into the campus. Eventually they walked the horses down a sloping narrow side road, sometimes ducking under the bare limb of overgrown alder trees. "I'm on the maintenance crew this term. There's a little abandoned shop here. No one uses it."

Sure enough, just after they passed a tall, spindly rhododendron, Adele spotted the garage. They tied the horses to a post, and Zeb produced a key. The lock opened easily.

Inside was little more than a desk, an expired calendar, and dusty coffee mugs. Cobwebs lightly laced the window.

"This is kind of spooky," said Adele.

"It is right now, but there's plans to fix it up as a guesthouse for visiting teachers, other special visitors."

"That's cool, but why are you showing it to me?"

"Well," he cleared his throat, "I thought that once it's refurbished, we could use it as a little getaway. You know, assuming you agree to a second date."

Adele snickered. "You are presuming, sir!"

"Am I wrong?" he asked, doubt in his voice.

"Not at all. I'm already looking forward to our next outing."

A Word About the Bird

Mascot of Sandpink Beryl, the Western Sandpiper[27] is a tiny common shorebird, weighing in at about one ounce. Its long legs and relatively long beak make up for its short neck. Along with the larger killdeer and plovers, they can be seen scurrying on the sand while foraging for insects within. But in the summer, they migrate far north to breed at the coastal tundra in Alaska.

Being constantly busy and moving in groups, they brought to mind students rushing from class to class. Honoré therefore deemed them the perfect mascot for the sandy campus.

---

27 www.allaboutbirds.org/guide/Western_Sandpiper/lifehistory

Chapter 29

Curiosity

Curiosity killed the cat; but satisfaction brought it back.
— children's rhyme

mid January

At the beginning of each year, all students were given an updated exhaustive map of the entire campus, complete with occupancy limits, fire exits, water lines, and power sources.

Mid-winter was boring to Eric. It was either too cold or too wet to ride the bike very long, and though he enjoyed watching sports on television, he preferred to be active during his off time. In addition to his studies, he had two plans: to sleuth around the grounds—there must be some secrets—and to take the tour of Moon Caverns.

Examining the map they'd been issued, Eric noticed three stories for the Long House at Crimson Song were shown. But in person, it was clearly four stories high. He considered that it must be some kind of mistake, a misprint or less likely, a miscount. But after all these years, wouldn't the academy have found and corrected the error? The mystery intrigued him. He suggested an impromptu reconnaissance mission to his roommate.

"Let's go see what's really going on. From the outside, it looks like there's three stories, if you judge by the windows. But it's tall enough to have four," Eric pointed out.

"When ya wanna go?" said Joshua.

"No time like the present!"

"You mean now?" Eric found that Josh often needed to verify the obvious.

"Yeah, you don't have anything better to do tonight, do you?" Josh couldn't argue that; his classes this term weren't very demanding. They gathered together some supplies: a compass, the map, a length of rope. "What do we need rope for?" Eric asked.

"Never know what we might run into. Rope can come in handy for all sorts of things." Eric still didn't see the need, but it was his turn not to argue with logic.

They rode from Basalt Moor a short distance down to Crimson Song. The sky above was an inky purple; below it sank with deep red into the ocean as the sun was setting. They parked the dual sports near a dark corner of the main building, an enormous log cabin. Looking around the corner, there was just enough sunlight left for Eric to make out a narrow, unmarked door on the Long House's unused side. He pushed back some encroaching vines with his foot. "Come over here, I think I found something already!" he hoarsely called to Josh, as loudly as he could whisper. They looked; the door had no bolt or place for a key. There was no window either, so no way to know what was on the other side. Eric reached out, and began to slowly twist the doorknob. It was stiff and caught as it turned, but turn it did. It came free of the strike plate, the door's hinges squeaking as Eric pulled it open.

For a moment, all they could see was darkness. A cool draft escaped the opening, brushing their faces with its mustiness. Eric said, "Hand over the flashlight."

"I thought you had it," replied Josh.

Eric cleared his throat. This really could turn out to be an adventure. "You're honestly telling me you didn't bring a light. We brought a rope, but no light," Eric said flatly.

"Sorry," Josh volunteered.

"How about your cell phone?"

Again, "Sorry" was all Josh could offer.

Eric shook his head, then started up the dark and narrow captain's stairwell, with steep risers and shallow treads. His eyes were wide open, trying to take in as much light as possible.

Josh followed closely behind. "Do you see any doors?" he whispered, unable to see past Eric.

"No, but I can see that there aren't any, as far as I can see."

"What does that mean?"

Eric sighed. "I mean, there's enough light from little windows that I can see landings, probably where the next floor starts, but there's no door there. It's weird. I think it goes all the way to the top too."

"Are you going to the top?"

"Might as well. We've come this far."

Eric continued moving up the steps until he came to the last landing. Here the stairwell ended. This time, there was no window. There was just enough illumination from the landing below to see that there was a solid door instead.

"Are you going to open it or not?" urged Josh breathlessly. Eric couldn't tell if it was from his excitement or the climb.

"I don't know. It could be the girls' bathroom for all we know."

"Could be just a closet. Or locked."

"Yeah," said Eric. "I suppose we might as well try it." He reached out to turn the knob. This time, it was immobile. The coarse texture told him that it, like the other knob, was heavily rusted. "I can't open it," he said, stating the obvious.

"We could break it open," suggested Josh.

"No, I don't want to damage anything. We found what we were looking for: there really are four stories. I'll check around the library, see what I can find out later. Let's go back; I'm declaring this mission accomplished."

They turned around and descended the stairs, Josh now in the lead. As they neared the bottom of the stairwell, Eric saw with a start a roughly rectangular shape in the fading light to the right of the door. For a moment he stopped in his tracks, his eyes wide trying to make out the unexpected figure.

"Why'd you stop?" asked Josh.

"Look there, what's that?" As he said it, Eric realized just what it was.

"Oh, I didn't see it before," said Josh, now standing at the open door. "It's some kind of plaque."

Eric came down to the last step, behind Josh. "I know what it is," he said, recalling an article he'd read about the academy's mascots.

"Yeah, me too. It's a parrot."

Shaking his head slightly in the dark, Eric said, "Yep, you're right." He decided to leave it at that.

Chapter 30

Judgment

*Truly man is a marvelously vain, diverse, and
undulating object. It is hard to found any constant and
uniform judgment on him.*

— Michel de Montaigne

February

Adele was always hungry after her Introduction to Abnormal Psychology class. It started at ten o'clock, so she usually didn't have time for breakfast before leaving her yurt at Sandpink Beryl. She could take the shuttle instead of saddling up Pickles, but the shuttle's loop went the wrong direction for her. It may not have saved any time, but it was more direct—and enjoyable, even in this wet weather—to ride the horse to Emerald Crag. As was her habit this term, she headed for lunch in the cafeteria before going to her afternoon class.

Smack smack smack smack ... At the cafeteria, Adele tried to ignore the atrocious sounds nearby, of someone chewing with their mouth open: one of her biggest pet peeves. She was trying to enjoy her meal of pork chops and applesauce, but apparently this person chose a white-bread sandwich with jelly and a thick layer of peanut butter.

While he was still chewing, she heard him say, "My team played extra-ordinarily well yesterday. We only played against the Beryl team, but they were awesome." *Smack smack smack gulp ...* at that mispronunciation she had to look up from her plate to see who it was. *Smack smack smack ...* it was a boy that she'd seen several times at the Trunk in their first term. He had a fresh face, his flaxen hair was styled in a neat crewcut, and wore a clean "COEXIST" maroon t-shirt with letters formed of religious symbols which somehow irritated her even more. He reminded her of a California surfer dude. But his table manners, *oh!* She couldn't stand it anymore.

"Do you mind?" she asked with a voice of lemons, hoping her tone would speak for itself.

"What?" he said blandly, not bothering to swallow his mouthful. She saw globs of food swirling in his mouth with that one utterance.

"Your manners ... weren't you taught not to talk with food in your mouth?"

He took a big slurp from his glass of milk. "Nope." Then he took another bite of the sandwich and said, "Wasn't taught not to drink with food in my mouth neither." *Gulp, burp.*

"Gross!" she exclaimed. "You're disgusting." She started gathering her things, standing up from the table.

"Hey, don't go. I'll do better," he said, and she decided to give him another chance. But first she hesitated.

"Okay, for now. But please try," she said as she retook her seat.

"I will. Honest." *Smack smack smack* Strings of saliva were visible in his mouth. Adele's stomach tightened.

"REALLY?!" She stood up and slowly nodded her head at him. "Yes, you are an extraordinary asshole." She grabbed her tray. "But maybe you're right, you really are 'extra-ordinary,' as in 'particularly common.' I just can't decide." She wanted to move across the room, but didn't want to give the appearance that he got under her skin that much, so she sat at a table nearby. Adele hoped it was far enough not to hear him anymore.

"That was quite a little show," said a boy two seats from her at the new table. He was African-American, rather dark, like roasted coffee beans, she quickly assessed. His hair was closely trimmed on the sides, longer but still neat on top.

"And how is it your business?" She hadn't meant to be so

snide, but was still hot over the confrontation.

"It isn't. Just that..." he hesitated.

"Yes?" she demanded again. Adele started to feel her pulse in the arteries of her neck.

"Well, I agree with you, he's a jerk. But your making a big deal of it wasn't real cool either."

Adele shifted in her seat, feeling all-at-once exposed. She didn't not like the idea because it wasn't good, but simply because she didn't *like* it: something inside counseled her that it was *because* it rang true that she was uncomfortable.

But even this interior acknowledgment didn't stop her from lashing out in defense. "Why am I under attack? I didn't do anything wrong!"

"You don't think it's just as rude to point out someone's poor eating habits as it is to have them? You have a choice, maybe he doesn't. You can choose to ignore or move away. But instead you caused a scene."

She wanted to change seats again, but as upset as she was, the message she'd give would mark her poorly. This encounter was such a contrast to the delight she'd been enjoying with Zeb. They'd been on two dates, and it felt right, authentic. Being with him felt both new and comfortable. But this day was not comfortable. At all. She gave up on trying to eat any more.

She had no answer for him. In an act more of defiance than efficiency, she pulled out her journal.

"Are you a Pangolin?" she demanded. He nodded his head. "What's your code?"

"Yours first."

"Fine. PA19AS1."

"What's your name?" he asked.

Adele bristled. "I really don't think that matters."

"Maybe not. But just the same, I'm Eric, also known as PA09EW1."

She scribbled down this information furiously, then stormed out of the cafeteria without another word, leaving her meal behind.

Chapter 31

Regret

Have I not reason to lament
What Man has made of Man?

— William Wordsworth

February, same day

That night in her yurt, Adele's mind tossed and turned her body in bed. The scene with the boys in the cafeteria was an ugly one. Why did poor table behavior bother her *so* much? And Eric's attitude toward her bothered her just as much, maybe more. Yes, definitely more, because it was about *her*. If she were honest with herself, she'd have to admit that maybe she was the one who'd exhibited abnormal behavior. She'd always thought she was special, but not in *that* way. Was it she who'd made it ugly?

Her face flushed when she realized that if they ended up on the guild together, it could be very awkward. Reporting their interaction in the kiosk wasn't a bright move. Why didn't she say "no" just this once? At least she could have waited till she'd cooled off. Being on the defensive short-circuited her ability to think logically.

She had been carrying the burden of another regret: her nugatory affair. The unbidden thought that she'd been high-strung because she was afraid of running into Peising came abruptly to her. Teachers and students alike ate in the cafeteria. She'd remembered it on a subconscious level, and now with her mind trying to make sense of the day, she knew why she was on edge.

Regret teaches us to do better.

Adele decided she needed to reclaim her sexuality, make it something cherished again. A plan formed; she knew it wouldn't be met with resistance. This resolution allowed sleep to overtake her, at last.

Adele's slumber was so deep she overslept. At nine-thirty a.m., before getting out of bed, she sent Zeb a text, "*Where n when can we meet ASAP? Code rose.*" Because of his experience on patrol, Zeb had suggested that they come up with codes, a secret language between them. Code Blush was usually spoken aloud; it meant that one of them was embarrassing the other in public; the offender was usually Zeb. Code Lilac meant that one was feeling down and in need of comfort. Code Rose meant "I'm horny." This was the first time Adele used it. They'd been on several dates since December; she knew it was time to take their relationship to another level and she was ready.

Zeb was in a class on textures at Saffron Cascade. They were drawing a still life of marbles in a wood bowl on folds of satin, music from a piano lesson downstairs serenading them. He received *ting* alerting him of the text. When he glanced at the phone on the drawing table, his charcoal broke on the drawing.

His mind raced, then he picked up the phone with his sooty hands and texted back, "*45 min @ garage, n cs.*"

"*k,*" she replied, "*but make it 1 hr.*"

Zeb could barely contain his excitement. He waited till nine-fifty when class was over, then quickly gathered up his materials and dashed out the door to the paddocks and caught Cherni, bridling him in the field. Zeb didn't bother saddling up; he leapt on Cherni's bare back and trotted him down the road to the rendezvous point at Crimson Song. When Zeb arrived at the garage, it was vacant as he'd predicted. Now that he'd given up his resistance to learning mechanics—having gotten past his past with his family—he was discovering additional benefits: abandoned workshops. This one wasn't in use as a garage anymore, but its office was maintained as a kind of guest house. Several of them dotted the grounds, though they were rarely utilized.

Zeb tied Cherni in the garage; the pit was boarded over, the concrete floor and boards covered with dirt and leaves. He went into the office; the desk had been removed, and it had been outfitted with a kitchen table, a modest double bed, and a trunk with linens.

Adele came in; without a word, Zeb took her in his arms and kissed her deeply, passionately, lovingly. She responded back, delighted to be in his arms. The rest of the day was awash with passion, discovery, bonding, and some inevitable awkwardness.

But no more classes for either of them, not today.

Chapter 32

Toil

Toil is man's allotment; toil of brain, or toil of hands, or a grief that's more than either, the grief and sin of idleness.

— *Herman Melville*

March

When the coast experiences snow, it doesn't stick more than a few days. PAA was under an early-spring snow; the thick dusting revealed undone or underdone work. Two inches of snow was enough to hide small things, give larger things a uniform appearance; but it enhanced irregularities. Now it was easy to see that the previous season's crops weren't as thoroughly tilled under as they should have been, stubble and lumps poking and bulging like a man's skin after an inferior shave.

Forty-two Horticulture work study students met for a pre-season meeting to discuss which crops to plant after the last expected frost. They met in the dining room at Cedar Whiles, preparing to order seeds and other supplies so that the orders would arrive by the time they returned from break. They were going over the harvest maps provided by Luke; Phoebe knew well the fruit orchards atop Moon Caverns, while down below, she saw that nut trees provided a border between Escape Drive and Cedar Whiles.

"Cool, we have filbert trees!" said Phoebe. "I wasn't sure what those trees were."

Zeb corrected her. "No, they're hazelnuts."

Heated discussion ensued, until they agreed to disagree. "We've got more important things to talk about," interjected the lead student. "Let's move on."

She explained that not all the needs for vegetables for the entire PAA population would be met, but the more they grew, the less they'd have to order from big farms.

As they discussed such undebatable produce as spinach, kale, lettuces, carrots, cabbage, summer squash, and beans, the students grew more excited about their participation. One said that she'd help organize canning parties in the fall so they could literally enjoy the fruits—and vegetables—of their labor all year long.

"You know, our part is just getting the plants started," said the lead. "There will be other work crews following our term, to tend the plants while they're producing, and another after that to be involved with the harvesting itself."

During the discussion, Zeb's mind wandered to his rendezvous with Adele. Their relationship was really blossoming, which made him think of seeds—they were currently discussing carrot seeds, how tiny they were, and how fast they grew—which led to Zeb thinking of sex. The watering of crops and the equivalent sex act. A direct question snapped him out of his head.

"Zeb, you're from West Virginia, right? They grow a lot of hay there, can you give us any insight?"

He hoped they couldn't see him blush. Since he hadn't really been following, he had no idea how hay played into the discussion. "No, not really. See, in my area, Wyoming County, folks just grow what they need. Our main industry is, or was, coal mining. There are still some ginseng farmers though."

"Okay, thanks. Ginseng, huh? I never woulda thought it. I don't think we'll be planting that anytime soon. Senpaku says that we grow three kinds of hay: Timothy, Alfalfa, and Orchard Grass. His animal husbandry crew is in charge of that, but we have to coordinate with them, since we use some of the same equipment and irrigation supply. I'm sure you've noticed, they use the fields between Moon Caverns and Crimson Song. The orchard grass will be harvested first, right about the time our seedlings come up. Alfalfa will be cut shortly after that, then in the summer will be the Timothy. Other than harvest, we shouldn't be in each other's way at all."

After the meeting disbanded, students from first-year blocs brought out their interaction journals to record each others' codes. They found that eight were in the Auklet bloc, four in Zebra, ten in Saola, and six were in the Pangolin bloc: Cecilia, Jennifer, Mike, Phoebe, Fausto, and Zeb.

Chapter 33

Anger

Have no unreasonable anger, but be not without righteous anger.

— Chinese Proverb

March

The odors of gourmet cooking often wafted through the Crimson Song campus. This afternoon the enticing scent of barbecue from the Grilling and Smoking class reached Adele's small treehouse classroom, bypassing both the long, curved ramp up to it, and the more-often used spiral staircase.

Despite the exotic location between the arms of two giant Spruce, the Anger enhancement class wasn't a very popular course: most people aren't very keen on facing the ire of others, or their own. The ratio generally worked out to about seven students to the teacher. As a result, discussions could become heated very quickly. Many emotions surround the topic of anger, and Adele was not an exception.

"Who here believes anger is a secondary emotion?" asked Mrs. Tschannen. Several hands shot up. She called on one of them to expand on the thought. "Tell us your experience with anger being a result of another emotion."

"When my mom was embarrassed over something one of us kids did in public, like knocking something off the shelf in the grocery store, she'd flip out on us. It wasn't till much later that I understood she wasn't mad about what we did, but about how people judged her, like she couldn't control her own kids. I suppose to cover her embarrassment she'd deflect. What I still don't understand, is how she thought her anger would be better perceived than our childish clumsiness."

"I experienced that yesterday," said a guy Adele was familiar with from one of her psychology labs. "I'd taken my son to visit a friend in Silica City. When he played with their glass float collection for the third time, after I'd told him not to—I slapped his hand, kinda hard." He paused, his voice faltering. "He didn't cry. This...person...told me that I'm too rough on my kid, and that it's a bad sign that he didn't cry, that it shows he's afraid of me. I got really mad and told him to mind his own fucking business. When I looked back on it later, trying to think why I was pissed off, I realized that I was humiliated. I was just fighting back, because I didn't like feeling like a bad parent."

"Guess your fight defeated the purpose," said Adele.

"Yeah, that is stupid. But you don't think about such things at the time. You just, you know, react. All guns blazing."

Adele thought back to the scene in the cafeteria last month. That jerk wasn't behaving nearly as badly as her classmate had with his son. After all, though his manners were atrocious, they weren't *hurting* anyone. It had made her physically ill, but that wasn't physiologically based, just a physical reaction to emotional stimuli. She wasn't proud of how she came across, or of the anger she'd felt. What was *her* real emotion? What was *her* hangup? And most importantly, how could she respond better next time?

Zeb received a card on his twenty-first birthday, March fourteenth. The card was simply signed, "from The Family," but enclosed with the card was a letter from his sister Georgina, who he now knew to be in fact his aunt.

"You son of abitch, an I mean that litterally. Yah, I know what that means, you knowitall little fuck. You thik you got your future all rapped up, that your trust fund is goin to take care of you, you can just sit back on your hiney and collect. That maybe so, but you ain't

ever goin to be welcome back here, not while Im around. Get that!"

Clearly she was upset. Zeb didn't care. It barbed him a little, but she had always had it out for him so he was used to it. Now of course, he knew why. But despite her venom, what caught his eye were the words "trust fund." *What* trust fund?

Chapter 34

Honor

The purpose of life is not to be happy. It is to be useful,
to be honorable, to be compassionate, to have it make
some difference that you have lived and lived well.
— *Ralph Waldo Emerson*

April

When young adults are brought together, nature will run its course. As fruit flies drawn to vinegar, youth often don't know what's good for them. They may be drawn to the sweet call of the pomme, but also may drown in the masquerading acid.

Academy interactions were no different; students mingled and flirted, dated and dashed, mated and married. On this early spring day, the latter event was soon to take place at Lapis Lookout. An April wedding on the Oregon coast is unpredictable, but gorgeous when the weather cooperates. The noonday sun was shining, the sky was clear, and although windy—as it generally was—just warm enough to allow fashionable sleeves.

The betrothed had just completed their degree programs. They hired students from the culinary department to cater the event, arts to decorate, home science to design and make the wedding clothes—especially the wedding gown—the music department to provide the entertainment, and Natali from the Humanities department to officiate.

As avid alumni, they adopted the academy's colors for their wedding theme. The wedding began with a divertimento from

Haydn, played in the back as the guests took their seats, creamy satin-enrobed chairs tied with brown sashes lined up in rows facing west. Nearly all the seats were full when Zeb and Adele arrived. They sat in the back row. He couldn't be mad at her for making them "late": to him, she was only stunning, elegant in a natural silk blouse, deep blue pashmina over her shoulders, and tanned leather slacks.

Presently the groom joined Natali at the front. His tuxedo was ivory worn over a crisp white shirt, a brown satin vest with an embossed leaf pattern, lapis blue tie and a matching handkerchief in the jacket's pocket. The boutonniere was made with a single white rose and an accompanying peacock feather.

In traditional form, the bridesmaids came to the front with their escorts. The groomsmen were jacketless, otherwise dressed as the groom in brown satin vests. The bridesmaids were dressed in periwinkle tea-length dresses with three-quarter sleeves, tied in chocolate satin. They and the bride wore blue lycra bike shorts, just in case the wind grew too lively.

The bride arrived in a floor-length floaty organza gown with pearls thickly trimming the scoop neckline, chantilly lace caplets, and a chocolate brown satin sash around the waist; a headband of wrapped eucalyptus and peacock feathers with twisted pearl strands held back her rich brown hair.

Her bouquet was comprised of white roses, blue hydrangea blooms, and azure bluebells accented with a few peacock tail feathers and more fragrant sprigs of grayish-green eucalyptus leaves. The stems were bundled in the same brown satin as her sash.

The service was simple and lovely, excluding none. Natali was articulate, and had prepared an eloquent monologue on the ancient human tradition of honoring those who were loved, something she understood personally and deeply. No one of any creed or even lack thereof could have argued against her beautiful message.

After the ceremony and congratulating the new couple, Zeb suggested lunch to Adele at the Lazy Copper. "We're already dressed in our finest outdoor duds, and I want to show you off," he explained. They retrieved their horses from the attendant, and started down the elk trail toward Pearl Quay.

As she followed him, Adele considered that Zeb had never looked so good to her. It wasn't just that he was handsome in his white oxford shirt with blue-and-brown striped tie from the bookstore, or the authoritative way he rode and handled his horse, or his composure during the wedding. Maybe it was that he *felt* good to her; maybe it was deeper than making her feel good. Adele made a decision on the way, one that could make or break their relationship. They tied the horses to the rail behind the tea room and coming in the back entrance, were seated right away at a lace-covered table. He ordered a Naomi's Lunch for two to delight all their senses: black bread, Circassian cheese, borscht, boiled eggs, and fresh fruit with chocolate, all served with black tea, cream, and jam.

"Have you dated anyone here before?" Adele asked, as she sipped her sweetened tea.

"Here at the academy, or here at the tea shop? Well, it doesn't matter; either way, *god* no."

"Why not?"

"I'm selective, and besides," he said, leaning in, "I only wanted you, from the very first." He reached out and took her hand.

"Well, I think you should know, that I have," said Adele.

"Okay." Her tone was serious; he slowly pulled his hand back. "It sounds like you have something to say about it."

She nodded, looking down at her hands. "I do; that is, I think I should. It's not important, it's over now, but ... I don't want to keep any secrets from you. That said, it *is* a secret, an embarrassment really. so please don't share it with anyone. I mean it, *anyone*. Can you promise me that?"

"Of course. And I won't judge you either."

"You might. But it's to stay between us in any case."

Zeb smiled without enthusiasm, bracing for his heart to ache.

Adele said, "I met one of the teachers while I was working at night, our second month here. We started dating, and it was okay for a while, but I broke it off with him before Thanksgiving."

"Was it sexual?" Zeb asked. "Did you sleep with him?"

"That's a little personal, Zebulon."

"You don't have to answer, but I have to ask."

She sighed. "I suppose that's true. And I will answer, yes. In fact, it was the best part of our relationship."

Zeb cringed inside. That was the last thing he wanted to hear. "Then why did it end?"

"That really is too personal. All you need to know now, is I'm not seeing him or anyone else. In fact, I haven't been with anyone else but you since then."

Zeb felt an anger that he couldn't name well up from his core. "Who was it?"

She scowled at him. "Now, you *know* I can't tell you that!"

"It's sexual exploitation, you know," Zeb said. "He's an instructor, he took advantage of you, of his position."

"No, it's not. I mean, he did, kind of. But it's not 'abuse of power,' I let him do what he did." Zeb winced; this time it was noticeable. "Plus, he's—" she caught herself just in time. "He's in a different department. If he were in the psychology department or one of my enhancement classes profs, I'd have to agree with you. But he's not, he wasn't. So let's drop it, okay? Please?" She would never let him know that he raised a point of doubt for her. The humiliation of allowing—even encouraging—the misconduct would be greater than the exploitation itself.

They finished off most of the fare, but the glow they'd felt at the nuptials quivered and faded. Adele regretted casting a pall over their date, but she had to tell him sometime. She felt badly that she'd waited this long. Would it have been easier for her to forget about it, keep it a secret forever? Of course. But she had to honor Zeb's feelings, even if it meant hurting them.

A Word About the Bird

Mascot of Lapis Lookout, the Blue Peafowl[28]—commonly called peacock, although to be accurate, this term refers to the male bird, the female being the much-less showy peahen—is an import from India. Paunder bought two mating pairs locally, from farms in the nearby Yamhill valley.

They forage on the ground for berries and grains, but also hunt snakes, lizards, and small rodents.

Their call—which Bianca said sounds like a humiliated cat caught in a fence—can be heard from all the neighboring schools, and even high atop Basalt Moor. Honore jocosely noted that the peafowl was the perfect symbol for the school of communication.

---

28 en.wikipedia.org/wiki/Indian_peafowl

Chapter 35

Tolerance

If people can be educated to see the lowly side of their own natures, it may be hoped that they will also learn to understand and to love their fellow men better. A little less hypocrisy and a little more tolerance towards oneself can only have good results in respect for our neighbor; for we are all too prone to transfer to our fellows the injustice and violence we inflict upon our own natures.

— *Carl Jung*

April

Five o'clock in the morning was much too early for Eric. It was not a natural time for humans to get out of a warm bed. He dreaded this weekend job. He already missed the nightlife of Atlanta—there was always a party somewhere—and when back at Heritage Station, he was writing or reading. A true nightowl, he never got to bed before two a.m. But this wasn't home, and here, the thought that people counting on him waiting at the harbor jolted him fully out of his hypnopompic sleep as the song of his alarm couldn't. After shutting off Legend's "Glory" on his Tracfone for the third time, he rolled out of bed. His toes curled when his feet touched the bare wood floor. *Damn, that's cold!* he said to himself. *Just like an old man, I better get slippers.* He heard his roommate snoring softly across the room, so Eric knew the song hadn't bothered his sleep; it never did. Quietly he wrapped a towel around his waist, laid out a hoodie and

Carhartts on his bed, and walked to the bathroom down the hall to take a quick hot shower.

When he returned to the room at 5:40, the sky was beginning to lighten from indigo to deep sapphire blue, just enough to differentiate the sky from the blackness of objects below. The rosellas were also awake, chirruping and squawking loudly to the breaking dawn; they were Crimson Song's wake-up call. He hurried now to pull on his clothes and hurried to the kitchen to heat up a cup of yesterday's coffee and gulp down cold leftover corned beef and cabbage. "If you got up when your alarm went off the first time, I could've made you a German pancake," said a voice from a dark corner of the cold kitchen.

Eric managed to choke down a chunk of the beef. "Who's there?!" he managed.

"Sorry, I didn't mean to startle you," the young woman said as she stepped out of the shadows. "I'm fixing breakfast for the house today, just got here a little early." She reached out to shake Eric's hand. "My name's Marlene, and I know you've got to go. Here, I brought some muffins, you can take them with you."

"Oh, cool, thanks. Yeah, I gotta run. But thanks," he repeated, grasping the bag from her hand.

He dashed out to the bike shed, sneakered feet crunching on the crushed rock. The sky had lightened more; now objects could be seen, and the brilliant reds and blues of the rosellas now visible confirmed that he was behind schedule. *Yep, late again*, he thought while he loaded the saddlebags. Maneuvering the dual-sport out to Pearl Quay, he decided Marlene had the prettiest golden-brown hair he'd ever seen.

The April lawn at the Hip was wet with dew. A few vendors were already starting to unload. Eric parked the bike behind the storage shed, and met up with the market manager. "Running a little late again, my friend," he said to Eric.

"Sorry. But I am here." Pete gave him a raised eyebrow. "Uh, I didn't mean any attitude by that. Sorry."

"So you say—again. Let's just get to work, okay, Eric?" Eric nodded. "Good. Here's the layout for today. Go tell our early-bird over there by the fountain that he's got to move."

"Oh, he's not going to like that!"

"That's why you're the one who's telling him!" laughed Pete. "It's your punishment for giving me lip!"

Eric grudgingly took the map, grumbling loudly on the inside as he walked across the lawn. As he neared the fountain, he noticed for the first time how beautiful it was. The refracted rays of light in the long necks of the selenite egrets lit the fountain brilliantly, as though the sun were emanating from within.

Except for the stunning sight and sweet Marlene, the day hadn't started well. Pete's condescending tone didn't improve Eric's outlook, and in fact, discouraged him from making an effort. If he were going to be treated as though he were incompetent, maybe he should stop trying so hard.

Natali loved visiting the community market. It reminded her of the farmers market back home in Moscow. She especially enjoyed the craft vendors: organic soaps and lotions, blown glass, silk scarves, knit hats and fingerless gloves, watercolor paintings, tutus for girls and grownups, tie-dyed clothing and housewares of all types; clever items included hammered flatware, burlap bags made into skirts, wooden postcards and toys, and baskets woven from rug remnants. She stocked up on dorm-friendly packaged food like breads, peanut brittle, and soup mixes, plus food to eat on the run such as pocket sandwiches, donuts, kettle corn made in a huge vat, on site. Others favored pizza, hot buttered sweet corn, elephant ears, and bags of fresh roasted peanuts.

Farmers had a tendency to offer produce samples, delighting with whatever fruit happened to be in season, from autumn apples to summer watermelon. Fresh milk, cheeses, eggs, frozen chickens, other meats were on hand. Pickle and pepper relish, chutneys, and pear butter were among offered preserves. Even plant starts were available: strawberries, tomatoes, corn, watermelon, peppers, onions, leeks. Alpaca and chicken manure were sold by five-gallon buckets to enhance any vegetable garden.

A solo guitar player was singing "Purple People Eater" while children danced; a mostly-retired professional clown made balloon animals, told jokes to children of all ages, and performed magic tricks with cards.

Each market day had a theme. This week it was "Dress Alike Day," where vendors and market goers were encouraged to dress their spouses, kids, some even dressing their pets. All in all, it was a day both shoppers and vendors looked forward to, rain or shine. The vendors had a long day, but it was offset by being able to have a direct relationship with their customers. However, not all who worked the market were satisfied with their presence there.

It frustrated Eric even more to know that Obsidian Marsh was on the other side of the river, but he couldn't see it because of the cliffs between them. He felt very drawn to the calm solitude there, even more so on a day like today.

It was still early in the season, but more farms were bringing produce each week. The word had gotten out and more people than ever began attending. He was accustomed to crowds; he'd go to the Georgia Dome whenever he could to watch the Falcons play, as he was one of their treasured loyal fans. But it was a different kind of crowd as many people knew each other, visiting while they shopped or browsed. Here, he couldn't disappear into the throng of people. At least he had a purpose.

Eric walked from booth to booth, checking on their products, making sure everything was on the approved list. Sometimes vendors would try to sneak in items that weren't produced by them, hadn't yet been submitted for approval, or worst of all, had been rejected. It was part of Eric's job to find any of these offenses and deal with them accordingly, even so far as shutting them down and banning them from the market. It was unlikely he'd ever be required to take such action, though it wasn't unheard of.

When he got to the candlemaker, a young woman turned

suddenly, her head bumping into Eric's clipboard.

"Oh, excuse me!" she said. "I guess I shouldn't text and walk, huh?" she chuckled.

Eric took a step back to give her space. "Yeah, I guess not!" he said, mimicking a judgmental tone. "Hi, I'm Eric. I'm this term's assistant manager for the market." He put out his hand and she shook it.

"Natali. Nice to meet you. I was just telling my friend back home about these candles. Uh, sending pictures of the products is okay, isn't it?"

"As long as the vendor doesn't object, that's fine. But look, you can post them on our web page too, and that would help out our marketing." He showed her how she could upload the photo. "See, every time you want to share, share with everybody! So, I have to go to each of these vendors, wanna come along?"

"An insider's tour? How could I resist!" Natali said.

As they walked, they got to know a little bit about each other. How Eric missed his family and girlfriend, Natali's work with event planning, typical student issues. Most importantly, they discovered that they were in the same bloc: They were both Pangolins.

After exchanging codes, Natali said, "It was nice talking to you. Maybe I'll see you around sometime."

"You know where to find me, at least every weekend this term!"

Chapter 36

Resourcefulness

If necessity is the mother of invention, then resourcefulness is the father.

— *Beulah Louise Henry, inventor*

April

The campus at Pearl Quay was designed as both a business lab and a source of income for the academy. Besides running the farmers' market, students also design and test business ideas, and work at the existing businesses to earn some spending money. Work study didn't involve much in the way of actual remuneration, so students were grateful for the chance to make a little more spending money while staying on academy grounds.

In this working lab as well as in their business classes, students learned not only how commerce worked, but also about managing materials, networking, ingenuity, how to keep business documents secure, and more.

One of the oldest ongoing businesses in Pearl Quay was a creperie; the newest was an Russian-style tea shoppe. Regardless of their services or wares, they kept fairly consistent to the theme of an Italian fishing village by remaining homey in decor, small, and friendly. Not only did this result in a quaint ambiance, but most people felt quite comfortable and welcome, even if it was their first visit.

Phoebe saved some money from her agriculture job to send Cypress flowers for her birthday. She rode Caberneigh down from Lapis Lookout to the florist shop in Pearl Quay, tying him in back.

Walking in the shop was unlike being in nature; the atmosphere was humid and rich with new oxygen, yet cool and refreshing from commercial refrigeration. The combined scents from the flowers was pleasant, not overwhelming. Phoebe closed her eyes and absorbed it all slowly, filling her lungs and holding it in for a few moments before releasing it through her lips.

"Nothing else like it, is there?" Phoebe visibly popped out of her abstraction. Well of *course* someone was there; why did it make her jump? "My name's Kenny, I work here. I'm sorry; I didn't mean to startle you," gently said the young man in front of her. She only noticed his crystal blue eyes, like the pale blue delphinium she'd seen in the rocky fields of Saffron Cascade.

She blushed. "That's okay, I was just lost in the moment. This place is so *charmant*."

"*Oui, mademoiselle*," he responded. "*Ce est la plus belle entreprise à* Pearl Quay."

"You speak French?" she asked in the tongue.

"I am learning it, yes." They continued to converse in French, clarifying as they went: she with her French creole influence, he in his second year of conversational French. They talked about the courses they were taking, their backgrounds, how they came to be at the academy, and what jobs they'd been assigned to so far.

"I suppose I should get going," Phoebe finally said, then reverting to English, "I nearly forgot, I actually have an order to place!"

"Oh, then let's see what I can do. What did you have in mind, and how much do you want to spend?" Kenny walked behind the sales counter, pushing a pile of pink snapdragons out of the way.

"It's my mother's birthday in a couple days, and I have $35; is that enough time and money?"

"It won't be a huge bouquet, but a nice, modest one. What flowers do you want? This time of year, almost all flowers are available."

Phoebe chose a mix including white gerbera daisies, golden chrysanthemums, and purple stock.

"I can upgrade the stock to lilacs, if you like. My treat," winked Kenny.

"That's very nice of you, thanks," she said.

"*Mon plaisir.*" He smiled as he placed the order. He took her money, and as he handed her the receipt, held on to it. "Please join me for a drink tonight, *chéri.* I get off work at five." He released the paper.

Her subsided blush leapt back into her face. "I'm sorry, but I don't drink."

He took her hand. "Then let's have a picnic. It's a beautiful afternoon, *c'est pas*? What branch are you at?"

They made arrangements to meet at Lapis Lookout; he would provide the food, she would pick a spot and bring a blanket. As she left the shop and walked back to Caberneigh, she never once felt her feet touch the ground.

The majority of the businesses of Pearl Quay relate to fishing or boating in some manner, from chartered fishing vessels to the mouth-watering fish and chips joint. Shoppers buy off-the-boat dungeness crab and albacore tuna, or shop the fish market for these plus fresh-caught halibut, salmon, shrimp, steamer clams, and even live oysters. Those who have a desire to go onto the water but not into fishing have the option of whale watching excursions, venturing out a few miles from shore in search of the gentle, inquisitive gray whales. The academy's two passenger vessels are available for rent—crew included—when not being used to bring in new students.

A pastiche of businesses round out the Pearl's contribution to the academy:

A sweets shop offers seafoam, salt water taffy, and Swedish Fish by the pound; that's where anything remotely ocean-related ends. But children and adults—especially the students of the academy—indulge their sweet desires with an array of choices: spicy gumdrops, Turkish delight, candied ginger, jelly nougats, chocolate candy bars and bonbons, licorice, rock candy, Jordan almonds, caramel toffees, peanut and cashew brittle, violet mints, and spiralling lollipops of all colors. They were but some of vast assortment at Lavender Empress.

Patrons have a choice of eateries. At the deli, one can buy groceries to make their creations at home (or dorm room). They can also opt to purchase ready-made sandwiches, soups, and salads.

Motyl Hostel provides low-cost lodging for travelers. Once providing an income stream for the academy, in the present day it more often accommodates students' visitors than the public. It makes for a worthy hands-on "workshop" for those earning their degrees in either business, culinary arts, or hospitality.

Coastal Crystallography rock & crystal shop is filled to the brim with natural crystal and minerals of all types, but specializes in the stones of Oregon. Many of the items are said to have holistic, metaphysical, or healing properties, though most people simply appreciated them for their beauty. Raw minerals are sold, as well as polished and faceted stones. Jewelry and decorative items are also stocked and treasured by their purchasers.

Fiber arts studio participants take raw materials and turn them into finished products. The alpaca fiber is processed here, as well as wool from sheep. After picking out plant and other debris, and carding it so that the fibers were all going the same direction, it's woven, spun, or felted into usable materials such as yarn.

Along with baguettes, white cheddar cheese, green grapes and two small bottles of cranberry juice, Kenny brought an armful of blooms to the picnic.

"Oh, you shouldn't have!" Of course Phoebe didn't mean it. She felt any trepidation melt away as she inhaled their fragrance.

"Don't worry, these were going to get tossed. We can never sell all the flowers that are expiring, so we distribute them to whoever'll take them."

"In that case, hand 'em over!" Phoebe took the bundle and promptly buried her face into it, inhaling fully. She lifted her head and said, "Mmmm, I miss my flowers. You know, this is very resourceful of you. They would be proud of you in my Resource class."

"I know, I took it last term," said Kenny as he laid out their picnic on Phoebe's blanket.

"Did you?" said Phoebe. The surprise in her voice wasn't that she couldn't believe he took the class, but a registration of her realization that she didn't know something very important about him. "I never asked, what degree are you working toward?"

He smiled knowingly as he made their simple sandwiches. "I was wondering when you were going to ask," he teased. "I'm in Marine Biology, and taking business courses too."

Phoebe tilted her head and thought for a moment. "I give up. How can you use those together?" She pulled some grapes off the stems and popped them into her mouth.

"I'm going to be an aquarium curator. I'll oversee the work of aquarists, designers, and researchers, plus I'll act as a liaison for the aquarium."

"You sound pretty confident in the future."

Kenny said, "I am. If I had any doubt, I wouldn't work as hard as I do. What's the point of working toward something if you don't have confidence that it'll happen?"

They continued to chat and eat, but Kenny's advice sat at the back of her mind. She hadn't yet decided what her degree should be, let alone her career. Although she knew it would be in health care in some form, the question remained: In which direction did she feel more confident?

Chapter 37

Love

The shepherd-swains shall dance and sing
For thy delight each May morning;
If these delights thy mind may move,
Then live with me, and be my love.

— *Christopher Marlowe*

late May

A rapid klee-klee-klee-klee was heard overhead. Zeb silently pointed up to a hovering bird near where he and Adele were riding at Basalt Moor. Although the kestrel's wings beat briskly against the wind, his tail flexing as a rudder, he stayed in one spot in the blue sky. Suddenly he dove to the ground and was out of sight.

Spring was in the air; all of nature involved in the dance of life and love. Zeb and Adele were beyond the dating phase of their relationship; now they spent time together whenever and wherever they could, as time and scheduling would allow. They stole away on Cherni and Pickles to the observatory one warm evening after dinner. They tied the horses to the railing and once inside the building, sat on the thick sleeping bag Zeb brought. Adele set out the candles, red wine, dark chocolate, and a batch of cream puffs she'd made for the occasion. Their intent wasn't to look at the stars in the sky, but the stars in each other's eyes.

"Oh, that is *so* corny!" said Adele, though her amusement at his sweet nothings was transparent. "Tell me more!"

Zeb pulled her closer. "You are the flame to my candle, I can see my future in your soul." Then he pulled her even closer, and whispered in her ear, "I don't want to go, but I must. I've just gotten into this routine, and I don't want to break it now."

"Oh, how romantic," teased Adele. "And here I thought you were going to say how you dreaded being separated from me, how you couldn't live without me." She released an exaggerated sigh and pulling back from him, shook her head. "A whole week."

"You know I'm going to miss you." Zeb took her hand. "What you don't know is how much." He looked her directly. He seemed to miss her already.

Adele was startled; he was suddenly serious, and connected; not a combination that she'd seen in him before. Of course the impetus for his retreat called for him to be serious, but that usually resulted in him withdrawing, not reaching out.

"I think you should know," he continued, "That I have loved you since the first time I saw you at the Trunk."

Adele stopped breathing for a moment. "That's sweet," she said, aware that it wasn't enough.

"I'm not trying to seduce you. The first time I saw you, the way I saw you move and laugh drew me in, and how I saw you talking with others. Then I heard your voice, and I was enamored. But you can't say the same for me, even now." Zeb drew back slightly. "I know that's probably too fast, too heavy to lay on you. But it's the truth. I just don't want to go on my retreat, knowing that you don't know how I feel about you."

"It is fast for me. But that's one thing I admire about you, Zeb, your ability to lay it on the line, not think about the consequences of what you're saying." She leaned into him, resting her head on his shoulder. "It's also one of the more irritating things about you. But if you feel that way about me, I don't understand why you are going to be gone the whole break." She sighed, not expecting an answer. She knew he had his reasons.

He held her, and they shared a silence.

"You know I wouldn't leave at all, but there's some things I need to work out. This thing with having a trust fund, well, it's confused me. For once, I feel like my family might actually have some respect for me, like they consider me part of the family. I never thought my being in their lives mattered before."

"Whether it does or not, your presence matters to me," Adele said, her voice unexpectedly catching. Her words were prophetic; neither of them knew soon they'd be proven true.

Zeb told her the truth: he did love her. But it wasn't the entire truth. He withheld the fact that he was struggling with her confession. Ever since he'd discovered that his family was a lie, Zeb had little tolerance for secrets in any form or size. Knowing now that Adele held inside her a secret about a relationship with an unnamed teacher caused him angst. Honesty was paramount to him; could he have a relationship with someone who had secrets? Though the affair was over before they'd started dating, his perception of her had changed, and he didn't know if the innocence of his love for her could truly be restored.

If she wasn't the girl he'd thought she was, did it change his love for her? After all, maybe it wasn't like her to have a purely physical relationship; she *had* broken it off, that was to her credit. Was he afraid that she'd do it again, especially if they were together? What if this was a pattern for her; on the other hand, if she were a male, would he have the same character questions? He decided he needed to talk to someone more worldly. That night after he took her home, he called Eric.

"Hey man, what's up?"

Zeb cleared his throat. "Hey Eric, how you doing?"

"Not bad, I just got back from the gym. How 'bout you?"

"I'm okay, but I could be better. I'm planning a trip away by myself over break, to do some thinking. Can I talk with you before that? I'll buy lunch."

Eric didn't hesitate. "Yeah, of course. Anything, any time."

They agreed to have lunch at the end of the week at the creperie.

Meanwhile, Natali had just finished assisting at her second horse adoption/information seminar. Planning for the next event six months down the road always started right after the last, so that any issues or kudos were still fresh. Though most students are assigned to new work studies each term, she requested to stay in event planning for her first three assignments so she could learn it thoroughly. While Natali was on administration work study this term, she elected to stay involved with the event that had come to mean so much to her. In any case, the new position was exposing her to new skills which she could use for the program. Due to her diligent research, outreach skills, and immersion in all aspects of the planning, she was already moving into the role of consultant.

"I'm proud of you, sis," said Ben when she told him about her increasing involvement. "But keep your well-being in mind too. Know when to say no, and be sure to let it be known when you need help. You don't want anything—not even yourself—to prevent you from meeting your goals."

A Word About the Bird

Mascot of Basalt Moor, the American Kestrel[29] is a small, relatively colorful falcon. Of the thirteen species worldwide, it is the only kestrel in North America.

Its diet consists mostly of insects, but also small birds and mammals. If it weren't for the falcon and other predators, academy grounds would be overrun with bunnies. As they burrow, rabbits create holes and tunnels which are dangerous for horses as they can fall and break their fragile legs.

Kestrels can be seen all over the academy's grounds, particularly the open areas where they can perch and watch for prey. The academy encourages their residency by installing nesting boxes at Basalt Moor.

---

29 www.allaboutbirds.org/guide/American_Kestrel/id

Chapter 38

Fear

Let us not pray to be sheltered from dangers but to be fearless when facing them.

— Rabindranath Tagore

mid June

"It sounds to me like you're upset that she had sex with you before she told you about this other guy," Eric said.

Zeb groaned. Hearing him say it like that made Zeb seem petty and downright primeval. "I'll admit it, yeah. I know she hadn't been with him for months, but I think she shoulda told me."

"Why? Would it have changed how you felt about her? Would you have rejected her?"

"I don't think so. I don't think it would've made any difference, it's just—" Zeb wasn't clear, not to himself or Eric. He struggled to explain.

"What about this thing with your family? It's probably compounding your confusion. I mean, I assume it's bothering you too, right?"

"Yep. I thought I knew my place in their minds; that's why I'm out here. But I talked to my...I haven't decided what to call him, I guess just 'Pa' will do for now...anyway, I asked him what Georgina meant in the letter, and he verified: When I turn 25, I'll have a trust fund available to me. Eric, it means that if I invest prudently and live modestly, I won't have to work another day in my life."

Eric puckered and whistled. "That must be some trust. How'd he make so much money?"

"He told me that he bought plots of land all over Wyoming County as it came available, and years later would sell it at a profit, parlaying the money into more acquisitions. Didn't even work the land, plant on it or build or anything, so no one knew what he was doing. I don't know what to do now. Should I treat 'Pa' like I was, or be nicer to him? Out of what, appreciation? Guilt? I don't have to manipulate him; he can't revoke the trust. But I don't know what my honest response should be."

Eric patted Zeb on the back. "These aren't easy questions, and there's no easy answers. I know you're going off by yourself over break; if I were you, I'd take all the time I could. You have a lot to sort out, man."

After his talk with Eric, Zeb decided to go to Crater Lake for his entire break, not just the one week he'd planned. He took final exams, bid goodbye to a surprised and protesting Adele, "But we'd planned to spend a week together, just you and me, no studying or classes!" He told her that he needed this time alone. He put most of his belongings in storage—a simple matter for him, since he still didn't have much—and with his basic supplies and Latin books, took the shuttle into Silica City. From there, he rented a car. He sat behind the wheel to give himself a few moments. *Two weeks of solitude, no worries, no interruptions*, he sighed. Eric had given him a lot to think about, some perspective he hadn't considered before. Zeb started the car, and headed south.

"Don't touch me!" Adele shrieked, instantly regretting it. "I'm sorry, I'm sorry, but any movement affects my ankle." She made careful, minute adjustments in her position on the rocky surface. Her outburst didn't help, and now Alexis had her feelings hurt, just because she wanted to give her injured roommate a hug. Even in her current state, Adele knew that she wasn't the only one hurting. The pain Alexis was feeling wasn't physical, and there was no comparison when it came to the intensity. But of course, she was suffering in her own way. Adele momentarily wondered if the day could get worse. She sat without moving a muscle, aware of Alexis standing behind her, waiting for permission to help. Adele didn't speak, afraid she'd really lose it. Besides, even speaking resulted in too much motion.

"I'll get help. I'll get Ms. Horakova," Alexis said at last and ran off. Adele heard the sneakered feet crunching softly on the coarse dirt. As they quickly faded away, Adele felt a little colder, even though the day was brightening. Keeping as still as she could, her consciousness started slipping in and out of the present; her ability to focus diminished to mere moments at a time.

Just a few minutes ago—it seemed—she was sitting on the serpentinite bench with carvings of mallards, staring into Emerald Crag's Reflection Pond. In the early morning stillness, the pond was as solid and reflective as a mirror. The only clue that it was otherwise were the small, quickly fading rings when a koi made its way up from the darkness to kiss the surface from underneath. Legend held that if one got lost in the smooth reflection, managed to release the turnings of their mind, images of their guild would appear. Would Adele find her guild? Did she have a guild to find, or was she just one of an elite group of two hundred? And what about Zeb; did he really say that he loved her already? How could he know for sure? Could she love him? Did she feel the same, but didn't realize it yet? Finally, she had to ask herself how the affair would affect his perception of her. He said he understood, but some confidence seemed to wither in him. Or maybe she was projecting out of guilt or shame. If her intuition was correct, would he come back from Crater Lake with a different attitude or worse, a change of heart? She may not get the opportunity to know if she loved him or not.

Adele's mind was too active that morning to allow any revelations to be disclosed by the pond, her thoughts churning the metaphysical waters. Instead she walked over to the ledge overlooking the valley far below, the softly blue-green serpentinite escarpment so steep that the tops of sky-reaching pines were at or below her eye level. And now as she lay here in an awkward position, helpless, she saw a face beginning to form. Was this a new image, or a memory of a vision of a guild member just before the fall? She suddenly remembered taking an extra step, forgetting that she was already standing too close to the end of the rock ledge. She winced as it all came back in a flash: the rock giving way, her right foot abruptly sliding after it, the blinding pain of her left calf striking a large broken branch, her right hip landing hard on the dry, crumbling dirt and the jolting crack as her right ankle struck another rock. With conflicting purposes, Adele all at once tried to forget, yet wanted to commit to memory, the succession of events. While it upset her to relive the accident, it also distracted her from her current fear and increasing pain.

Once the descent had ended, she was still in a precarious position. Already in intense pain, she had enough presence of mind to know that she had to move to a safer position, off this steep slope, before she slid further down—and possibly off the cliff waiting below. A flash of memory, the story of a woman years ago in the early days, and the subsequent naming of this precipice. That woman had fallen too; she did not survive. She was found quite far down the rockface. Because of her sudden disappearance, the slope was named French Leave.

If Adele slid that far and went over, there would be no chance of saving herself. Her right leg was useless; though it was cut and throbbing, she didn't see any exposed bone; small comfort, as clearly bones were broken. With all the reasoning she could muster and despite her diminished proprioception, her hands and other foot had to do the work of scooting her backwards up to the ledge, which was just above her head. If she could get back up there, she would be safe from sliding further, and she could be found. The cliff was much too high for anyone who wasn't purposefully looking to spot her from below. So she continued scooting, screaming out each time her left foot pushed futilely against loose soil. Her palms were dry and caked with dirt, bleeding from cuts on jagged rocks. Perspiration poured from her scalp and forehead, despite the cool morning. As she reached the ledge, she turned onto her left side and pushed, pushed, pushed with that foot, forcing her shoulder and torso across the rocky soil, further ripping her clothes and skin. With a last effort, she heaved her hip onto the flat surface, and propped herself onto her elbow. Although the motion hurt her, she couldn't hold back great, heaving sobs. In fleeting moments of lucidity, she briefly recalled the arrival of Alexis; poor thing, Adele must remember her kindness later.

Still struggling for a rational foothold in time and place, Adele found that she was sobbing again. It was impossible for her to judge how much time had passed—she had been mentally traveling through many moments and back again—but now she heard a vehicle, followed rapidly by approaching footsteps. Alexis had been successful: help had finally—or quickly—arrived.

Chapter 39

Attention

Experience ... is a matter of sensibility and intuition, of seeing and hearing the significant things, of paying attention at the right moments, of understanding and co-ordinating. Experience is not what happens to a man; it is what a man does with what happens to him.

— *Aldous Huxley*

June, same day

As usual, Natali woke at the splinter of dawn, just as early light broke the darkness at Basalt Moor. Balboa House was oriented north-south, so she generally missed her beloved sunrises unless she made a point to go to the library on the main floor, or watch from outside.

Her classes for the term were out; she'd officially started her summer break. But not everyone was as lucky, so she couldn't relocate to Saffron Cascade for at least two days. With time to kill, she planned to spend the day riding the grounds. After dressing and performing her toilette, the first stop was the paddock. Recognizing her, Moonstone nudged his way through the other horses and was rewarded with an apple. Natali looped a piece of baling string around his neck and put him in an empty stall. She fed him a flake of alfalfa and a scoop of cob. The molasses and high-protein hay would fuel the horse for the day. While he ate, Natali went to the cafeteria for her own breakfast, and to pack a lunch and snacks. She and Moonstone would be gone till dusk, relishing the time to appreciate each campus, except Obsidian Marsh. Although she could stop at any of the several cafeterias along the way, she wanted to reserve the ability to eat anywhere, any time she got hungry. Of course the gelding could eat and be watered just about any place they went, but she brought some horse cookies. *Horses can have picnics too*, she mused.

By the time she returned to the horse barn, others were up working with their horses and related tasks. Natali exchanged pleasantries with them, but didn't want to waste time. She was giving Moonstone a vigorous brush-out in the wide breezeway before saddling up when a first-termer stopped by.

"He's looking really good, his dapples are becoming more prominent."

Natali continued brushing. "Thanks; with his winter coat gone, he'll be all sleek and shiny after I bathe him."

"Are you doing that today? I can help."

Here was Natali's chance to give the girl a clue. "No, I'll do it tomorrow. There's no time today, I've got to get us out of here soon. We've got lots of ground to cover." With that, she dropped the brush in the grooming pail and threw the saddle pad on Moonstone's back.

"Where're you going?" The girl wasn't taking the hint.

Natali adjusted the pad then hoisted the saddle onto it. *This girl is going to talk me right out of the barn,* she thought but said as she cinched the saddle, "I've got our whole day planned out, we're going to visit each of the campuses. I won't be back till at least dinnertime. Excuse me." She maneuvered behind the girl to grab the bridle.

"Okay, have fun. See you later," said the girl.

"Alright, see ya." *Finally*, Natali thought to herself as she bridled Moonstone.

She led him out of the barn into the morning light. Mounting up, she was thankful for the perfect day for a long ride. They went down the road from Basalt Moor, crossing Escape Drive to a wildlife trail up to Saffron Cascade. Under tall, lanky alder trees, Hypnos Trail wound through a carpet of blooming bluebells. The grey horse and rider created swirls and eddies of earthy, sweetly spicy fragrance as they passed through the rich azure blue, a canopy of bright green alder leaves above. It reminded Natali of springtime pea fields back home, only with the colors reversed.

At the top of the trail, the woods thinned and opened to a field. She moved Moonstone into an easy lope to the barns. As they approached, they slowed to a bumpy trot, then a walk as they neared the quiet barn. Here too students were about, but almost silently as they worked around the skittish horses. Natali tied her horse to a rail and went inside.

"Hey, how's it going?" said the barn attendant softly.

"Hi Fausto. I came by to see how our newest convalescents are doing," she replied in the same understated tones. "I heard there was some trouble before the auction last week."

"Yeah, this one over here caused quite a stir." He walked over to a box stall with a wide-eyed mare. The whites of her eyes flashed as she watched their every move. "One of the bidders opened the pen, and when they turned to talk to someone in the aisle, she bolted. She ran through the aisles until the staff closed gates and got her contained. Fortunately she didn't run into anybody, but did come close to some."

Natali looked over the quivering pinto. She had numerous scars—some freshly healed—on her legs, rump, and back; typical marks of whips and ropes.

"What's your prognosis for her?"

Fausto sighed, sticking his thumbs in his pockets. "Well, this is the place for her. She has an open run so she can go outside anytime she wants, but she usually stays in her stall. I'm guessing that trauma," he pointed to the mare's legs, "was done in a lunging ring, probably at the time she was learning what humans are all about."

"In other words, we're monsters."

"Yup."

It was too early to tell, but Natali agreed with the prognosis that the mare was ruined for a useful life: she would have to be content with being safe. When Natali left Saffron Cascade, she rode down East Peregrinate; she could hear the cascading stream waters to the right, enclosed by the forest. On the shoulder of Escape Drive they trotted jauntily as they passed Cedar Whiles. She waved to the work crew mending fences, and observed animal husbandry students shearing sheep. She turned Moonstone onto Charon's Alley before walking across the Pistoia bridge, his hooves clopping an echo on the boards. Upriver to their right, a group of students were braving a swim in the cold, churning water. Natali dismounted on the other side in the shade of a copse of trees to share a snack break with her horse.

Once refreshed, Natali remounted and took the shortcut toward the higher campus. The coolness didn't last long as she urged Moonstone up the declivitous switchback to Emerald Crag. She hadn't expected it would be too hot to take the wildlife trail, but the powdery dry dirt that the horse was kicking up, heat under her riding helmet, and sweat on her back proved her wrong. The mid-morning heat was unusual on the coast for the early summer month of June. At least she'd had the forethought to wear sunglasses.

Below them on Titanium Terrace, Natali saw the emergency Jeep speeding up the winding road to Emerald. Moonstone noticed the flashing lights too and nervously skittered a bit, but Natali held him steady. After the Jeep disappeared around a curve, Natali again urged Moonstone forward. In his heightened state, he obliged, trotting up the incline as Natali leaned forward to help him along. She hoped that no one was seriously hurt, or sick. Soon they were at the top, and caught site of the Jeep a few hundred yards away near the main lodge with a crowd of people. She moved the horse to a calculated lope, and as she got closer, saw Branchmaster Šárka Horakova holding back the crowd. One of the students grasped Moonstone's reins as Natali quickly dismounted. She pushed through the students to reach the victim; her stomach instantly knotted up when she saw that there was someone on the ground, evidently with a serious injury.

The girl was shaking, hard. Natali knelt beside her. "I'm here to help. What's your name, love?" Adele glanced up at her, and the tears she'd been holding back began to flow again.

"I'm Adele, please...I can't believe this happened!"

"Can you tell me what happened?" asked Natali, attempting to bring Adele into a more rational state of mind. But Adele couldn't form any more words.

"She's had a bad fall, miss," said one of the men, who was supporting Adele's back. Natali recognized him from her Wisdom class last term.

"You're Cody, right?"

"Yes ma'am, thank you. Adele here hurt her ankle pretty badly, it's probably broken. But we're trying to figure out if we can move her farther away from this cliff. The ambulance from Tillamook is on its way, but it'll be a while."

Natali took over supporting Adele, lowering her to the ground as Cody gingerly raised the ankle higher with cushions that Alexis had brought from the lodge. He lightly wrapped the ankle in cold packs. The Jeep's driver, Yousef, was helping her keep hydrated with crushed ice. Horakova said, "The ambulance is coming!" and the others then heard the siren's wail too. "Alright, everybody give us some room, it's all under control now," Šárka said as she shooed the bystanders away.

"A break to start break; hope you didn't have any plans to go home!" quipped Yousef.

Adele moaned at that, and a reluctant sob escaped her chest. "Why? Why me, why now?" she said.

"Don't worry, I'm going to stay with you as long as I can," said Natali. "And I'll help you any way I can as you recover. You *are* going to get better, you know." Adele glanced down at her leg and shook her head defiantly, rejecting the assurance. Natali took her hand. "Look at me, Adele. Look at me," she persisted. With hot tears pooling in her eyes, Adele complied. "I promise. It's going to be alright."

Part Three

CONFLUENTEM

Chapter 40

Compassion

Love and compassion are necessities, not luxuries.
Without them humanity cannot survive.

— Dalai Lama

July

"Knock, knock, are you decent?" Natali said as she cracked open the door to Adele's cottage. With a lilt she added, "I've brought a visitor." She walked in and nodded to another resident reading a book on one of the sofas, a blue heeler curled at her feet.

"You did? Who?" answered Adele as she clump, clump, clumped down the hallway with her crutches, the cast leg off the floor. "Oh my god, Phe! I didn't know you two knew each other."

Phoebe gave her an awkward hug around the shoulders. Adele could only accept it, her arms being occupied with keeping her on her feet. "Natali asked me if I wanted to come with her to bring lunch to an injured student at Crimson Song. When she told me that they had just come back from the hospital, I knew it must be you!" Phoebe helped set up Adele at the table, while Natali took the food she prepared to the kitchen. "So how's it going here? Are you enjoying your new quarters?" Phoebe asked.

"It's okay; as you said, I came back from the hospital yesterday and the two roommates who are here so far are very nice. They let me have the first bedroom so I wouldn't have to hobble any farther than I need to. They even set up a schedule for the next few days to pick up work from my teachers. But my moms still want me to come home."

"I thought you discussed that with them when they came to see you in the hospital. Didn't that get resolved?"

"I thought so, but they are adamant. Oh, and get this: they want to sue the academy! I told them no way, it was my fault. They're still pressuring me, but it's my decision. Anyway, the academy is paying all my medical expenses. I'm satisfied with that."

Natali came in and started laying out the food. "Why are they being so insistent?" she asked.

Adele sighed. "They think it's dangerous here. 'It wouldn't have happened if you'd stayed in Santa Rosa,' they said. But they don't remember I did fall at that campus, it just wasn't off a cliff. In fact, that fall is what prompted me to come here."

Phoebe swallowed a bite of her turkey and swiss sandwich. "Have you ever thought that you're a bit of a klutz?"

Adele twisted her head to give Phoebe a raised eyebrow. "I think that's been established, yes."

Early afternoon at Lincoln Terrace, first day back in classes since break, and Phoebe was having a hard time concentrating. From this vantage, the full-wall window allowed her to make out the tall eucalyptus trees of Crimson Song, where Adele was recuperating, trying to cope with the pain and frustration of the accident, and not having an easy time of it. Her parents weren't helping, ironically by insisting that she needed them, that she should come home and "forget about this silly 'philosophy' school." Never minding that this was probably the most fulfilled they'd ever seen their daughter, despite her accident.

"And that is the reason we're starting with self-compassion," said Ms. Talbot.

"What about unexpected pregnancy?" said a thick-lashed boy with sharp cheekbones and a sallow complexion at a desk directly behind Phoebe. The abrupt intrusion jolted Phoebe back to the present time and place. "I know a guy who got a girl pregnant, right here at the academy. I feel sorry for the guy, does that count as compassion?"

"It would depend," said Talbot.

"Hey, you feel sorry for the guy? What about the girl?" asked someone in the front row. Her tone was angry and indignant.

"Well, I don't know her, just the guy."

"Then I would say that does not qualify as compassion, Mr. Boste," said Talbot.

The discussion went on about human overpopulation, which led to the subject of raccoons. "I think it's mean, that we have so many scraps and don't feed them to the wild animals. Not even in winter. How can we say we're 'compassionate' when we aren't even allowed to share our food?"

One of the students Phoebe recognized as a biology student spoke up. "It's not compassionate to add to their troubles by creating a population boom. The more we'd feed them, the faster they'd multiply, and they'd be concentrated in the 'free feed' areas. They'd fight more between themselves—and if you've never heard a raccoon fight, you have no idea—and they'd get more aggressive toward humans; instead of respecting our hospitality, they lose respect for us. Our involvement would be a bad thing all around. For us, for them, and for other species that would be affected. Besides, when they become dependent on humans—being opportunistic, they eat what's easiest, most plentiful, and yummiest..."

"Sounds like most people!" said the interrupter, inducing a big laugh.

"Ahem," said the bio student. "If I can continue...they stop eating their natural diet, like slugs, mice, and dead animals. So if we feed them, we not only increase their number, but increase the number of slugs, mice, and carrion throughout the academy's grounds." That statement elicited not a few disgusted groans, "yucks" and extended "ewwwws."

After class, most of the students who weren't staying at Moon Caverns walked back to the left end of the paddocks. Phoebe walked with two other girls from the class. Sunlight was breaking through thick, billowy clouds, vivid blue sky beyond.

"I've got to go get my mail, want to come?" said Phoebe.

"Sure, I'll go with," said Poppy.

"My next class is at Lookout. I'll ride with you for a few minutes," said Jessica.

They found their horses where they left them, tied to rails of the paddock. Once they refitted the bridles and mounted up, the girls regrouped and headed north, descending down the shaded dirt service road on the western side of the campus. Several others were going the same way, some in groups up to six abreast, some solo. Through gaps between the towering Sitka spruce and beyond the high cliff edge, glimpses of the ocean far below could be seen.

"I wonder who the girl is," said Phoebe.

"She lives in my dorm. I don't know her very well, but her name is Toni, she's in her third term here." revealed Poppy.

"How far along is she?" asked Jessica.

"I think she just found out last week. She's been dating this guy since just before break, so she's in her first trimester."

"Apparently they found something to do besides beachcomb while school was out."

"Oh Jessie, you're terrible!"

Phoebe couldn't help nervously tittering with the girls, because it was something that could happen to any of them. "Seriously though, is she going to keep it?" Phoebe loved watching plants grow, and though heading off flowers was necessary at times, it made her uncomfortable; the thought of a human life being terminated was almost more than she could abide.

Poppy said, "She hasn't decided yet. She only turned eighteen last summer; a baby will make her life a lot more complicated and difficult."

"Thank you, Ms. Obvious," said Jessica.

Poppy continued, "The only thing she's decided for sure is

that she doesn't want to raise it with the guy. If she keeps the baby, she's going to have to deal with the father all her life. I know she can't afford to raise a family on her own, and her family doesn't have the means to help her."

A sympathetic pang centered itself deep in Phoebe's abdomen. If it were her, she'd definitely keep the pregnancy. Adopting it out would be a gut-wrenching decision, though like her flowers, perhaps necessary. Despite not being involved, she felt a wash of relief that it was a choice she didn't have to make. She said, "I think we should go visit her, let her know we don't judge, and assure her."

"Why us?" asked Poppy.

"Well, dummy, because we're supposed to be learning about compassion," quipped Jessica as they approached the back road to Lapis Lookout. "Fortunately, me and my girlfriend don't have to worry about unplanned pregnancy, obviously. But just because we don't, doesn't mean we don't care about what you people have to deal with."

"Why is that obvious?" asked Phoebe.

Poppy interjected, "Because lesbians can't get pregnant unless they want to."

Phoebe's eyebrows shot up; it hadn't dawned on her that Jessica's girlfriend was *that* kind of friend. Jessica nodded at her, affirming Poppy's statement.

"Here's my exit; text me when you decide what to do." Jessica maneuvered around the chained entrance and kicked her horse into an easy lope, disappearing around a bend in the woodland road.

"I guess that settles it, we're going for a visit," Phoebe said to Poppy.

They rode on, each mulling over the conversation. Breaking the silence, Phoebe said, "We gotta help that girl change her ways."

"What? Why?" Redheaded Poppy was instantly ready for an argument.

"Because her grammar is horrible! 'Me and my girlfriend,' I can't believe she said that. Plus she ended a sentence with a preposition. Don't they decline your application if your grammar is bad? I thought everyone here had a basic education."

"Oh...yeah, you're right." Poppy felt her face flush as her ire passed, and hoped Phoebe wouldn't notice. She did.

Phoebe smiled, then chuckled. "You thought I meant something else. If I were back in my grandparent's time, I would have. But come on, homosexuality nowadays isn't a big deal, is it?"

"For some people it is, I think they are scared of anyone who's not like them. But I say, if it's good enough for the black swans, it's good enough for me!"

"The black swans? What do you mean?"

It was Poppy's turn to chuckle at Phoebe. "I found out in my avian husbandry class that a fair number of black swans—about the same ratio of people, I believe—have same-sex pairings[30]. Male pairs will have a three-way relationship with a female till she lays her eggs, then they kick her out!" The irony struck both of them, and they laughed out loud.

Phoebe finally managed, "I'm serious though, we've got to tutor that girl on her grammar. She's gotta represent the academy better than that - we can't let her out in the world with that kind of mouth!"

"She makes mistakes sometimes, but she speaks three other languages. With her mad lingual skills, the academy will overlook imperfections."

"Pop, do you hear what you just said?" Phoebe was ready to burst from silliness.

"Huh? What do you .... oh! I hear it now!" They both lost it.

The trees thinned to an open area. Phoebe and Poppy decided to cut diagonally through the unfenced elk meadow to West Peregrinate between Lapis Lookout and Crimson Song. No elk were present; they were up the hill leading to Lapis Lookout, spending the warm day in the cool and concealing woods. The girls slipped the horses' bridles off while they walked, allowing

---

30 en.wikipedia.org/wiki/Black_swan#Nesting_and_reproduction

them to snatch mouthfuls of lush still-tender grass on the way—defeating any time-saving benefit that the shortcut would've given them. Phoebe and Poppy talked about sex. Phoebe and her boyfriend were choosing to abstain, each for their own reasons. For her part, Phoebe had decided long ago that she needed an unshakable emotional and confident connection with her partner before fully sharing herself physically.

"I have *zero* worries about getting pregnant. I'm on birth control, *and* I make my boyfriend wear two condoms," said Poppy.

"*Two*, at the same time? Sounds like you *are* worried about it."

"Taking precautions isn't worry, it's just smart. Since we're 'über' prepared, we don't have to think about it, we just take care of it automatically."

Phoebe sighed. "Kenny says wearing a rubber is like wearing a raincoat in the shower."

"Tell him to imagine he's showering in acid rain; that might give him a different perspective."

Phoebe laughed. "Yeah, that might do it!" She decided not to disclose that it didn't matter in her case.

"Somebody shoulda told Toni's guy," said Poppy.

"Maybe they did use protection. You know, nothing's 100% effective, short of not doing it at all."

"You sound like a disclaimer for a Trojan ad," teased Poppy.

"I just mean, we shouldn't judge. We don't know how things happened. He may be just as upset as I imagine she is. I think we should practice what we're learning, show *both* of them some compassion, you know, and decline judgment."

"When do you want to visit her? I can arrange it; I'll see her at the dorm tonight."

Phoebe reached down and patted Victory on the neck while she mentally reviewed her schedule. "I'm free Saturday afternoon."

"Okay, I'm pretty sure she's free then too, and it works for me," smiled Poppy. "I'll ask her where she wants to meet, and text you and Jessica to confirm."

They arrived at the Trunk, tying up their horses. They went to Mail Post on the main floor, a large room shaped like a W. All mail was delivered here.

Phoebe opened her box, and among other posts, pulled out an oversized ivory vellum envelope. Without even seeing the front with the logo, she immediately recognized it as being from the Academy. This was her second surprise post from them. Why would they send her a letter, when she'd already been there for a year?

"Open it!" demanded Poppy as she came up with her own handful of mail. "Here, use my nail file."

Phoebe sliced open the envelope, and pulled out a letter on the familiar matching paper. She began to read it silently.

"WELL?! Come on, share!"

"Okay, geez, you're as bad as my mother!" shot back Phoebe. "It's an invitation, they want me to show up in the executive offices upstairs next week."

"What for?"

"Doesn't say," said Phoebe. "It doesn't give any indication of what they want to see me about."

Poppy gasped, exaggeratingly sucking air into her lungs. "I'll bet you're in the new guild! We've been here for four terms, and there hasn't been one from any bloc since we started. Maybe it's time!" Phoebe shook her head in disagreement, and looked at the letter again. After a moment, Poppy added, "If you're going to be in the guild, I'm happy for you." She hung her red head and looked at the floor. "But it'll mean that I'm not in it."

"I'm sorry, Poppy. I mean, you're probably wrong. I hope you're right, I'd love to be in it, but yeah, that would—"

"Just kidding!" Poppy said, throwing up her head, laughing. "I don't want to be in it, I want to be free after graduation!" She pulled the journal out of her over-sized bag. "See, I use it for pressing wildflowers, not recording interactions!"

That evening, Phoebe and several others were on their various social networking sites in the great room at Cedar

Whiles. Some students eschewed electronic amusements and were gathered by the stone fireplace playing a game of Catan.

Phoebe was mindlessly scrolling through her newsfeed, tucked up in one of the deep leather chairs. Every once in awhile, some photo or update would catch her eye; Kenny was messaging her with the minutiae of his day. But her thoughts were mostly on the happenings of hers. She put aside Poppy's suggestion of the guild. She'd find out what the meeting was about in due time; in fact, very soon. In regards to compassion, she allowed herself some free association; maybe rationalizing, maybe just trying to cut people some slack.

It was easy to feel compassionate towards Adele: she knew her, she liked her, and she could relate to her. But what about those who were very different from Phoebe; not familiar with their lives or struggles? Could she separate the concepts of basic human rights from entitlement?

Even though the loudspoken boy sitting behind her in class didn't know what compassion was about, he deserved to have it. She imagined he came from a large, quick-talking family. He'd had to learn to speak up and speak loud to be heard. Did he mean to make her jump? Was his question sincere? Just because his approach wasn't suave didn't mean he was a jerk. Of course, she could ask him these questions, but decided against it. It didn't make any difference.

Her thoughts flowed to the blackjack player who was losing so much, and playing so badly. It saddened her more deeply than she would have thought, when she realized he might have *meant* to lose all his money. Perhaps he'd already lost everything else, anything, any *one*, who really mattered. Had he lost his family because he lost his house? Or had he given up on saving his home because he'd lost his family, possibly to some tragedy? She would never know; and that she decided, was what was important: what she did or didn't know didn't matter: everyone—whether they *earn* it or not—deserves compassion.

Chapter 41

Communication

Two prisoners whose cells adjoin communicate with each other by knocking on the wall. The wall is the thing which separates them but is also their means of communication. It is the same with us and God. Every separation is a link.

— *Simone Weil, French philosopher and mystic*

early July

Zeb was returning, just in time for the Pangolins' fifth term. He'd be back on campus in the next day or two; before he left he'd told Adele that when exactly depended on the traffic, that there would be many travelers on the road and he'd avoid congestion when he could. Adele's anticipation of his return was running high and she was nervous. In her convalescence, she'd reflected deeply on their relationship. Although he'd professed his love freely, she also felt that it was guarded. Was there a component of doubt in him? Her trysts with Peising had been physically pleasing. It was mostly fun and exciting; she'd loved the feeling of being sexy and desired. The chemistry between them was undeniable. But she'd made a terrible mistake. Who did she wish was there with her on the crag, while she was suffering and frightened? It wasn't Peising. Zeb truly loved her; devotion was longer lasting than combustion, and ultimately more satisfying and gratifying. She'd always heard about sparks flying, the earth moving, hearts pounding. But did she want fires, earthquakes, or palpitations every day?

Suddenly, someone authentic and steadfast seemed much more attractive. But she needed to know that he forgave her; if not for having the affair with a teacher, then forgiveness for not telling him early in their involvement. Could she forgive herself for not telling him before they were intimate? If not, she couldn't expect it from him. She put her distracting thoughts aside—after all, they'd gotten her in trouble before—and started getting ready for the mysterious appointment.

When Adele's shuttle arrived at the Trunk, she worked her way down the steps of the Peacock after everyone else disembarked. Hands appeared to support her as she took the last step to the ground. She looked up to say "thank you," but the words caught in her throat when she saw it was Zeb.

"You're here!" He caught her when she dropped the crutches, throwing her arms around his neck. They held each other tight. Adele whispered into his neck, "I'm so glad you're back."

They continued their embrace until someone behind them said, "Uh, you guys mind if I get on?" He held out Adele's crutches. Embarrassed, they released each other. Adele took the crutches and Zeb accompanied her as she went inside.

"I thought you weren't going to be here till at least tomorrow?" Adele asked breathlessly. The effort of ambulation, the excitement of seeing Zeb, and going to an appointment she knew nothing about sapped the brio from her, while Zeb's seemed to be bolstered.

He noticed her waning energy and motioned for her to sit at a bench near the elevator. "I just got back. I received a message on my way from Crater Lake that I had an appointment here, so I came straight from the road. In fact, later I have to go to Silica City to return the car. What about you, what are you doing here?"

"I've got an appointment too," she said.

"When you're ready, I'll walk with you. I'm a little early for mine."

She stood. "I'm okay, let's go."

They entered the elevator, Zeb pressed the 2 button. "How was your trip?" Adele asked. "Was it everything you hoped it would be?" She really was asking how he felt about her, if he wanted to be with her anymore.

He answered her with a deep kiss, ending it just before the doors opened.

As they entered the empty administration's reception room, Zeb asked her, "Do you have time to talk about what happened?"

"What?"

Mulier immemor, he thought. *I guess opposites do attract.* "The elephant in the room of course; your cast. Which way is your appointment?" She indicated the hallway to the left.

"Conference room three," she said.

"Huh, that's interesting."

"What? Why?"

Zeb looked at her, raising both of his arched eyebrows. "That's where I'm going too."

They were both early; he out of habit, she because she was learning to allow extra time for getting around. While they waited for the mystery meeting to start, Adele told Zeb about the accident: how frightened she'd been; who helped her, that she could remember anyway, but in particularly Alexis; the ambulance to the hospital; the visitors, including her parents; how she'd tried to reach him.

"I'm so sorry I didn't get your texts or calls while you were in the hospital," Zeb said. "If I had, I would've come right back. I wish you said what was going on though."

"I know; I figured you must not have coverage. I didn't want to tell you what happened without knowing I could reach you." She sighed. "We have some issues to resolve, but I was sure you weren't just blowing me off. I'm more confident in our relationship than that."

Their conversation was interrupted by an energetic black man striding into the room. He quickly glanced at them. She thought he looked familiar, but couldn't quite place him.

"Hey Zeb, I didn't know you were going to be here." The boys shared a friendly hug. "Good to see you, how was your trip to Crater Lake?" His voice was familiar to Adele as well.

"It was great, it's really a special place. Almost magical. Thanks for recommending it." Turning to Adele, he said, "I'm taking you there next year."

Just then, Phoebe and Natali arrived together. They had shared their letters, and discussed Poppy's prediction.

Now the pieces could start falling into place.

Zeb was surprised to see Natali; out of two hundred people, he was somewhat embarrassed that the only one who held his secret was here. He hadn't even told Adele yet. He realized it then: he was keeping secrets, just like his family. When he and Adele had a chance to discuss their issues, he'd fill her in on all his family's details.

Phoebe was surprised to see Eric, since he had been so adamant about being a "free agent." She was still working on the assumption that this was the coming together of the guild. If he wanted to be free, why did he report interactions at all?

Eric was surprised to see Adele, considering that their interaction was of animosity. He only recorded people he enjoyed being with; it had never dawned on him to do anything else.

Adele finally realized with a start why Eric looked familiar: he'd been the one who'd called her out in the cafeteria. She had listed him as a contact in her interactions journal because she recorded everyone with whom she interacted—she knew that the more recordings she had increased her chances of qualifying for the guild. But she never anticipated actually getting on a guild, let alone with him! She knew that her anger was her issue, but regardless, she didn't appreciate how he'd riled her up even more.

After visiting for a while and it seemed that no one else was coming, Adele spoke. "While we're waiting, why don't we introduce ourselves? Let's tell our names, where we're from, degree programs, languages we speak. I'll start: I'm Adele Stawski, from Santa Rosa. That's in northern California. I'm planning to get my associates in psychology, and go to Oregon State University when I finish this program. I've been learning sign language since October. What about you?" To exhibit confidence and challenge her discomfort, she looked at Eric, who was standing to her left. She enjoyed putting him on the spot, but then realized he probably enjoyed being the center of attention anyway.

"Okay, well, my name's Eric Wholm. I live in Atlanta, Georgia. Home of the Hawks." He pumped his fist in the air, "Whoop! Whoop!" The other two girls giggled. Adele was stoically unaffected. "I'm working on my degree in environmental science. I speak Spanish." There was an awkward silence.

Then Natali said, "I'll go next. I speak some German, and I'm from Boise, Idaho." She looked to the last man in the room, attempting to direct the attention away from herself.

"But what's your name, sweetheart? And what you studying?" teasingly prompted Eric.

"Oh, I'm sorry, I forgot, didn't I?" she said. "I'm Natali. Natali Marks. I'm still honing in on my degree." She again fell silent, and started fidgeting with her hands. "I may go into the ministry, or maybe public speaking. I have performed a wedding, so I used both disciplines." She smiled at Zeb for sharing that memory.

Phoebe then spoke. "You all know my name already. I'm from Eunice, Louisiana. Home of the *real* Mardi Gras! I speak French, and I've been studying ASL too, with Adele. I'll be working in the health field someday."

"That's a pretty big field," said Natali. "I know I'm not one to talk, but can you be more specific?"

"Probably emergency medicine...or maybe physical therapy. The classes I've taken so far can apply to both. I'll decide by the end of this term."

After a pause, all eyes turned toward the final one in the group. Without looking back at them, he reluctantly introduced himself. "Guess that leaves me. Name's Zebulon, but you can call me Zeb."

"You don't have to be shy, Zeb." Eric said.

"I'm not shy!" Zeb raised his voice. He looked up at Eric. "I just don't like talking about myself in front of strangers." At Eric's prompting gaze, Zeb's voice softened. "Sorry. I just don't respond well to being in a crowd."

Phoebe and Natali caught each others' grins at five people being a crowd. Adele was not amused; Zeb's outburst confirmed to her that there *was* something upsetting him, and it probably involved her. Or was she just being overly sensitive?

Natali said gently, "Remember though, Zeb, we're not strangers." Zeb nodded.

"So c'mon," prompted Adele. "Tell them a little about yourself."

Zeb said, "I'm sorry to snap at you all; I just came back from camping, and had to deal with heavy traffic. I don't like to travel in the first place, but I wanted to see some more of Oregon. For those of you who don't know, I'm from Mullens, in the hills of West Virginia. It's an old coal mining town; not a lot of people live there anymore."

"Home of 'Coal Miner's Daughter,' Christy Martin, female boxing champ," noted Eric.

"That's right!" Zeb finally showed some enthusiasm. "I have an aunt who went to high school with her, when she was still Salters. As far as language, I know Latin." Though his were rather abrupt transitions, the others were impressed with the information, glancing at each other in approval.

"Latin? That's awesome, not many people can say that," said Natali.

"I do a lot of reading. A *lot*," Zeb said with exaggerated emphasis.

Adele redirected the stalled conversation. "Okay, that's everybody...everybody who's here so far, anyway," she said, and set free a large sigh. "Well, let's relax while we're waiting to find out why we're here. These refreshments must be for us." She maneuvered to the buffet and picked out cheeses, strawberries, melon slices, and a bran muffin. It was a nice enough presentation, but simple, provided by second term culinary students. "C'mon, you guys, dig in - I don't want to be the only one eating!"

The others started to join her, and began loosening up. Zeb helped her with her plate. They chatted about the notifications they received to be at this meeting, how Adele broke her ankle, their new living quarters, and more details about where each of them called home.

"How are you doing with getting around?" asked Phoebe.

Adele looked to the ceiling and sighed. "It's been okay, I take the shuttle all the time. But I really miss my horse, it's been really hard on me." She rubbed her face with both hands. "To lose mobility, to be dependent on others has been bad enough. To add to it though, you know I already left a horse behind. Now to have Pickles taken away too, well, it's like a whole change in lifestyle, not just inconvenience. I'll be honest, the pain and being 'crippled' isn't the worst part." She turned to Zeb and rubbed his shoulder. "But I shouldn't complain, I've got this guy back."

Zeb explained that he'd been gone, that he only just was informed about the meeting. "There wasn't any cell coverage at all."

Eric changed the conversation. He said to the group, "Hey, this is cool. We just covered everybody, A to Z!" The four others looked at him blankly. "You know, Adele to Zeb, A to Z?"

"Oh yeah, that's right," Phoebe said. "That's kinda neat."

The conversation continued about life at the academy, courses they were taking and work study.

"Why are we here?" Eric finally asked the question that was at the back of everyone's mind. "My invitation said that Kimiko Paunder and Ms. Pepperburgh were going to be meeting us here, but not much else. Are we in some kinda trouble?"

Phoebe said, "Since there's five of us, I assume that we are the new guild." She heard and ignored Zeb gasp and sputter on his iced tea. She continued, "So, the first two years after we graduate are already decided. We're not going to have to wait until then to decide what we're going to be doing."

"If that's true" said Eric, "we're going to be spending the

next three years together, so we might as well get to know each other now." He playfully punched Zeb on the arm. Zeb flinched, managing a slight grin while he rubbed his arm.

"Actually, we won't see each other any more this year than any other student. Less, in fact." Phoebe noticed the others looking quizzically at her. "Because we won't be in any enhancement classes together, at all," she explained. "Assuming I'm right, we're the guild because between us, we will have taken all sixty classes, twelve apiece. Separately." Zeb and Adele shared a wink. They would find time to be together.

It occurred to them that if Phoebe was on the mark, they must have each had some kind of meaningful interaction with the others, that is was officially disclosed to the academy, and that none of them shared any of the enhancement classes.

Adele said, "If we're the guild, we've all interacted sometime in the past. I remember meeting each of you. Let's compare notes; if we haven't all met before, then we'll know we're here for some other reason."

"Why waste time?" asked Eric. "Kimiko will be here soon and will tell us what's going on."

"Do you have something else to do right now? Maybe a better idea?" Adele snapped. She had daydreamed about what an honor it would be to be in the guild, how exciting it would be to travel the country. But if he ended up one of her myrmidons, she wasn't sure she wanted the aggravation. His cool attitude rubbed her the wrong way, and she was sure he didn't like her. Besides, she was frustrated; she wanted to get out of here to spend time with Zeb. They had a *lot* of catching up to do. Then it dawned on her: If Eric and she were myrmidons, that meant Zeb was too.

"Look, it's simple," interjected Phoebe. "Do any of you *not* remember meeting any of us?" No one responded. "To make it real clear, raise your hand if you've met the other four people in this room before today."

All hands went up.

"There's our answer. Hello, myrmidons!" Natali said, raising her glass.

Presently, Paunder and Pepperburgh arrived. They did indeed verify Phoebe's assumption, and after confirming that everyone was on board, explained that the myrmidons have two months to work up initial ideas for their guild's project.

"This meeting is for you to get to know each other purposefully. Until now, it's been random and casual. Now, you will have to become familiar with each other in order to work effectively," said Kimiko.

"Let's go over the schedule," said Ms. Pepperburgh. "Within these guidelines, you as a group, will make decisions. Also, you will be getting together 'off schedule,' as a group and sometimes two or so of you. That is up to you. But for these meetings," she passed a printout with the schedule to everyone, "You'll run the show, and the academy will foot the bill. You'll tell us what you need for these meetings. As you see here, your first planning session is in two months. You'll discuss results of brainstorming and surveying, eliminate some of the ideas, and assign research for remaining ideas.

"In the second session, four months later, you'll discuss the researched ideas in depth, further eliminating some. At the third session, three months after that, debate and advocacy commences. You'll continue doing that in the interim, 'fighting' as it were, for your project.

"At the fourth planning meeting, three months later, you'll decide as a group on the project, and make a plan. You'll start implementing the plan after graduation."

Kimiko asked, "Does anyone have any questions?"

"I do," said Eric. "You said we're on our own, but what if we need help?"

"Ms. Pepperburgh will be your primary advisor. She won't 'babysit' you, but you can go to her as a group or independently if you seek guidance. You can also seek out assistance from any of the instructors from whom you took your enhancement classes. And remember, whenever you're on the grounds even after graduation, our resources are here for you to use, whether food and lodging, facilities, or materials." She leaned forward, pressing her palms together. "You are our greatest investment; the academy has a stake in the guild's success. Whatever help we can give you, please, don't hesitate to ask."

They spoke on all sorts of matters, including where they were expected to live after graduation. Kimiko said, "One of the perks of being in the guild is that you can continue to live on campus for the duration of your tenure, if you so choose. You're in the guild for three years, the first year is of course your second year in the academy. It's a planning year, which we've discussed. The next two years you'll be implementing your project. Where you live is up to you. In any event, you have a monthly stipend. This is to eliminate the need for a job, so you can be available to meet with your guild whenever necessary."

After more explanations of the program and getting everyone's agreement to participate, Pepperburgh and Kimiko Paunder officially welcomed them into the program. Kimiko said, "You are henceforth known as the Pangolin Guild."

They bid the new myrmidons goodbye, leaving them to explore their new status. Questions and comments flew between them.

"This is SO rad, I can't believe it!"

"I think someone should chair our meetings."

"We can take turns."

"We *should* take turns."

"How about as a reward, whoever volunteers to chair gets to choose the next location?" It was agreed, and Zeb volunteered to lead the next session. He knew right away where to go: Basalt Moor.

The girls went to the restroom together after the meeting concluded. Eric spoke to Zeb in the reception room as they waited. "So, *she's* the one you've been talking about? I had no idea, man. She's a spitfire!"

Zeb shrugged and grinned up at Eric. "That's what I like about her, she keeps me on my game."

Chapter 42

Opportunity

... the precipitate of sorrow is happiness, the precipitate of struggle is success. Life means opportunity, and the thing men call death is the last wonderful, beautiful adventure.
— *Alice Foote MacDougall, businesswoman*

mid July

The wheelchair wasn't Adele's least favorite piece of equipment, but it came close. What she really despised was using the crutches, especially in this heat. Of course they were a necessity; of course they allowed her to get around inside the cottage more freely; but they made her shoulders ache, it was difficult to carry anything, and when she wasn't using them, they were awkward and generally in the way; ironically, they were tripping hazards. She yearned for carefree mobility again; she even missed the recalcitrant mare she'd been assigned. As one of the more experienced riders, she was assigned a challenging horse; Pickles had a tendency to rub her riders against trees or fence posts. But since Adele wasn't allowed to ride, and certainly couldn't take care of her, Radegast had reassigned Pickles after Adele's accident.

All three of her roommates were out at classes or work study; for the first time since she returned from the hospital, she had the cottage to herself for a while. Adele took advantage of the privacy, and called Lorena. They had a long talk about the fall, the hospital's initial misdiagnoses ("It's not just a sprain," she'd shrieked; "You have to x-ray it!"), her parents, Lorena's finals, and when they thought Adele could run again. The conversation lifted her spirits, but at the same time, exhausted her. When they said their goodbyes, she realized how thirsty she was. Adele managed to crack open a can of coconut water, but didn't attempt to take it over to her chair. It was easier to just stand and sip it at the kitchen counter. For almost two weeks she'd been stuck here at Crimson Song, with a couple of trips to Pearl Quay to get supplies, and one back into Silica City for a cast change. Now past the shock, boredom was starting to set in. It was exciting to be on the guild, but it was too early to do anything. She wished she could spend the day with Phoebe in Gilded Sand again, though she knew she wasn't up for a trip to town yet. Adele had plenty of projects for classes to work on, plenty of visitors; she even had to turn some away. But it was all so very routine.

Today she had something to look forward to, but Sine wasn't specific. "Some surprise" was all that the branchmaster told her, that it would be delivered in the afternoon. Adele assumed it was flowers, probably from her father. From her infancy, he was adept at being involved from afar, doing what didn't matter. While in the hospital, he'd sent her the first bouquet she received. But he never called.

She hobbled outside and lowered herself into the wheelchair. She "paced" back and forth on the wide porch, wheels of the chair clattering on the cedar boards. She practiced making turns, spinning, and sudden stops; there wasn't much else to do while she waited for the arrival of ... whatever. She listened to the crimson rosellas vocalizing in the trees. Whoever named this place "Song" was apparently easy to please, or had a terrible sense of what music was supposed to sound like. Or maybe it was a playful joke. She couldn't imagine anyone would think of the rosellas chirping and screeching as anything but a cacophony. On the other hand, "Crimson Squawk" would be a terrible name.

Adele indulged her imagination of what else the surprise could be. A visit from her mother; a big box of Whitman's chocolate bon bons; a fancy Parisian gown; maybe a new leg. *Now where did that come from?!* Her fantasies were declining to the macabre, so she snapped back to the real world.

She became aware that the inside of her cast was hot, and her leg was starting to itch; she pushed a eucalyptus switch down into it to scratch her leg, being careful not to touch her wounds. Distracted by this small chore, Adele then heard the familiar sound of hoofbeats approaching, and the sound of creaking and wheels crunching on the gravel. She looked up to see a gorgeous, imposing chestnut pulling a market wagon to the front of the cottage. The horse was stunning: tall, with shimmering golden highlights playing across his copper coat. Then she caught sight of the wagon's passengers; her hands covered her mouth as her eyes began to crystallize with emotion.

"You guys! This is amazing!" she exclaimed, her voice trembling.

Among several other coeds, the myrmidons began to drop down off the wagon while Radegast tied the horse to the railing. Natali, Phoebe, Zeb, and even Eric surrounded her, and the Radegast said, "This is Augustus—" He realized he was ignored while everyone was chattering. "Excuse me, hey kids," he gently broke through the small crowd around Adele and caught her eye. "This here horse is Augustus, and he's yours."

That got her attention. "Mine? What do you mean?"

"For the duration of your time at Paunder, this is your horse. He's assigned to you as long as you need and want him. Unless you mind," he teased.

"*Mind?!*" she half shouted. "I love him already! But how can I … I can't take care of him, can't ride him."

"It's alright, we've added you on to the duties of the Incident Response team. They'll help you out with harnessing, hitching him to the wagon, all that. You'll be on their daily rotation until you can do it yourself," said Radegast. He walked back to Augustus and patted the horse's neck. "But, you're going to learn how to drive the wagon yourself tomorrow. You may not be able to ride for a while, but you'll get around anyhow."

The others whooped as Adele gasped. Eric patted her firmly on the shoulder, ignoring her flinch. "Bet you didn't see that coming!"

Adele dreamt all night of wagons, long, thick reins, and large red horses. Waking life was going to be a reprieve from whirling imaginary visions. She was ready to get the first day out of the way.

She fought to pull on her jeans. One of its legs had been sacrificed to accommodate the cast. She could've had someone pick up sweatpants for her, or a skirt. But that just wasn't her; she would be uncomfortable even though they'd be easier to manage. After dressing and cleaning up, she had a simple breakfast of her candy white coffee and an English muffin with avocado at the cottage's kitchen table. Popping over to the Song's main lodge for breakfast was one of the things she missed the most. Nowadays it was usually too much effort, especially for this early in the day.

In the middle of a bite of muffin, she heard the clatter of the wagon. *Shit, he's early.* Looking at the clock she realized that *she* was *late.*

"Okay, kiddo, lean on me now. Don't worry, I'm a tough old guy." Radegast helped her into the driver's seat. She was tenuous with her injured leg, easing up into the wagon. It was times like this that she'd wished her diet was more stringent. Her assistant, Max from the incident response team, was learning how to help her, and learning how to drive the rig too. He hopped in back as Adele settled in next to Radegast.

"I'll drive you around a bit, then I'll give you the reins," said Radegast as he signaled Augustus. "Let me tell you about this old boy as we go. He's a Frederiksborg[31], a rare breed nowadays. They're from Denmark, bred to be a harness horse; but when you're up to it, you can ride him too. Make sure you use a step when you do, I'd hate to have you injure that leg again trying to be tough. Anyway, Augustus is about fifteen years old; hard to

---

31 en.wikipedia.org/wiki/Frederiksborg_horse

know exactly, as we got him at auction a couple years ago, and the owners didn't volunteer any information about him." Adele knew from what Natali had told her that this could be the kiss of death for most sound auction horses. Health and usefulness alone weren't enough to keep them out of the slaughterhouse.

Crimson Song is laid out like a campground. Natural hedges and mature trees grow abundantly here, but kept trimmed back in the peopled areas. West Peregrinate winds through its campus, each curve wide enough for vehicles to turn around. Coming off of the winding road like legs on a centipede are fifty leveled clearings about sixty feet wide and two-hundred feet deep, large enough for a single oversized cottage with a small covered paddock and a workshop in back. Each cottage houses four to six residents. Tough-leaved salal, spiny Oregon Grape, rhododendrons, huckleberry bushes, and the adopted eucalyptus trees provide natural barriers around each cottage, so they seem isolated from the other cottages. It was the perfect place to learn how to drive a wagon, just challenging enough. As its name implied, Peregrinate had curves and slopes; but along with some rough spots, but nothing too narrow or steep.

She was pleased that Max was strong and had some lessons already under his belt, since all the information was a bit overwhelming: How to position the body, how to hold the reins, using the whip as a guidance system, and voice control. And this was just the first lesson! Surprise changes and adjustments were a lot to take in, especially since she was dealing with a cast and the discomfort.

"In no time a'tall, you're goin' ta be a pro driver," Radegast told Adele, imitating an old-timey cowboy. "Now, I'mma gonna set with yeh for a few more turns, then we'll go out in the open where yeh can go 'round yerself. With Max, a'course."

He had her drive off Crimson Song, West Peregrinate winding down the hillside through the eucalyptus with the rosellas chattering their mid-morning calls. The roadway straightened out between the maturing hay fields. They joined Breakthrough Way before turning to the base of Moon Caverns.

"That was right pretty, little lady. You two go on up now, ya hear, to the observatory up yonder on Basalt Moor. I'm gonna visit this here cave a spell. Be in radio contact if'n ya need me. By the time ya'll come back to pick me up," he cleared his throat, "I shoulda oughta have shaken off this here accent."

Adele laughed. The faux inflection was ridiculous, but he had a way of putting people at ease. She appreciated it now more than ever. She was enjoying learning to drive the wagon more than she would've expected, but it was still frightening: even though he was only one horse, Augustus was very powerful.

As soon as Radegast was off the wagon, Adele clicked to Augustus and he started moving out.

"Whoa whoa whoa!" shouted Radegast, and Adele instinctively pulled back on the reins.

"What's wrong?" Her heart's tempo shot up.

"First rule of dropping off passengers: make sure they're clear of the wheels before you move your wagon!"

"Did I hit you?" she asked, terrified she'd caused an injury, and not one minute into her solo drive!

"No, but damn nearly. Just be more aware, and know you've got plenty of time. You're clear now, go on ahead."

She looked all around the wagon this time, and around the horse before telling him, "Augustus, walk on." She wanted that to be the first *and* last near-miss.

She made a big circle in the drive right in front of the entrance to the caverns. She and Max couldn't help but glance in awe at the gaping chasm of the entrance to the caverns.

"Have you been in there yet?" asked Max.

"No, but I always wanted to. Now I don't know if I can." The instant she said it, she caught her negativity again. She would have to work on that tendency.

She doubled back, and continued up Breakthrough Way to the school at Moon Caverns. After they passed through the campus and through the woods, they saw the building on the hillside of the Moor; at three stories high, Balboa House was unmissable.

It was an enjoyable drive, and Augustus made it seem easy

as they climbed steadily to a higher elevation. His big muscles were fascinating to watch as they moved under his gleaming summer coat. Adele looked forward to the time when she could groom him herself, and with luck, be healed enough to ride him before she graduated. The wagon wasn't so scary anymore, and she recognized that she'd be able to do more with it than she could on horseback. Still, there was nothing like being in the saddle with a strong horse under you. The psychological transference of power was exhilarating.

The rock road was noisy under Augustus' hooves. The wagon clattered along behind him. Adele looked to her left, awestruck at the scene: the view from the Moor was incredible. She could make out the elk meadow, the mound that was Lapis Lookout, the hill of Crimson Song, and even a glimpse of the south end of Saffron Cascade beyond it.

Adele drove to the top of Basalt Moor, making the loop around the observatory as Radegast had instructed. Before they started back down, she handed the reins to Max. "Here, you take over for a bit." She pulled out her father's old camera, a 35mm from the 1980's. She took several photos of the landscape, a couple portraits of Augustus' rear, and some of Max's wide, closed-lip grin.

"This is an amazing thing, hooking me up with a horse and cart," she said while she continued snapping. "Is this something they do? I read a lot about the academy before I came here, but I never came across this kind of effort."

"Nope, this is the first time."

"I'm sure people have gotten hurt before."

"That's true; having a hard fall off a horse or dual-sport, usually; sometimes even a bad spill from a bicycle. But they get around with rides, or getting help using the shuttle."

Adele lowered the camera. "Then why are they treating me so special?"

"You don't know?"

"No, know what?"

Max said, "Augustus, whoa." Max turned and looked at her. "The academy finally agreed obviously, but it wasn't their idea, and there was a lot of debate. Outfitting you like this is above and beyond their responsibilities."

Adele flushed while her elation visibly deflated. She never wanted to be treated as though she were special. "I feel like a user. I had no idea—I mean, this is awesome, but—"

"I'm not trying to make you feel bad," Max interrupted. "You should be happy, someone thinks a great deal of you. And the academy must have agreed about that, otherwise we wouldn't be here right now."

"Who was it? A teacher?" The thought glanced through her mind like a hornet that Peising had arranged this. She mentally swatted it away. It was replaced by another racing thought. "Crap, was it my parents? Oh god, I'm so embarrassed. They'd do anything for me, but can't they realize..."

Max interrupted her, tapping Augustus to move out. "Nah, it was one of your myrmidons, Eric."

A Word About the Bird

Mascot of Crimson Song, the Crimson Rosella[32] is not a native to the Oregon coast, but is another of Sebastian's imports from his Australian homeland.

A small parrot—or parakeet—they prefer wetter forests and woodlands, from sea level up to the tree line. With the presence of both the kestrel and the pygmy owl, the non-migratory rosellas are rarely found venturing out of the shelter of the tall eucalyptus trees and at Crimson Song.

They eat a variety of food, including fruits, seeds, nectar, grasses, and insects.

Feathers of striking blue and brilliant red with black scallops are the dominant feature of this species.

---

32 en.wikipedia.org/wiki/Crimson_rosella

Chapter 43

Anticipation

There is no terror in a bang, only in the anticipation of it.

— *Alfred Hitchcock, filmmaker*

July

"On time is late," he'd say, so Zeb waited in the great lobby at Basalt Moor for the others to arrive. He had wanted to come with Adele, but she gave him two good reasons for meeting him there instead.

"Babe, this is our first planning session. All the more reason you have to be there early to make sure the room's ready, and have things to do beforehand, so I'll probably get there about on time. I know how you hate that," she pointed out. "Besides, I want to talk to Eric privately after the meeting about that thing I told you uh,...about. I don't think it'll take long, but I don't want you to have to wait for me." He agreed, but reminded her to do her best to be on time, at the very least.

The atrium was open to the three stories, with glass panels for the north- and south-facing exterior walls. Either direction, the view outside was breathtaking; to the north he could see the road to the rest of the grounds, and the line of trees marking the edge of Crimson Song. Farther up, he could just make out the cliffs of Emerald Crag. To the south, the view past the herb garden rose up to the top of the mound, then sky beyond. Most of this view seemed desolate, with scant vegetation, and mostly gray hues, especially on this overcast day. The starkness was beautiful in its own right.

Zeb turned his attention back to the interior. Its furnishings were sleek and sophisticated; similar in taste to the Trunk, but more austere. The floor was basalt, smooth and charcoal gray.

He could hear activity in the upper floors. At the west, early classes were just letting out. To the east were the living quarters, and students were moving about. On the main floor below that was the cafeteria, and below the classrooms were conference rooms, where the guild would meet to have its first planning session. He was both nervously anxious and excited.

Eric arrived next. "Hey Zeb, buddy, good to see you." They shook hands. "Seen the girls yet?"

"Nope. Maybe they got lost. I guess we shoulda drawn them a map."

Eric snickered. "No one knows how to get around the academy's grounds better than us, but it's not quite *that* bad! Anyway, let's go on in, maybe there's something to eat."

"Oh, there is, and plenty of it. I made sure of that."

"I forgot you're running this meeting. Are there any surprises in store?"

Zeb shrugged his shoulders. "Maybe. But we'll eat first."

The windowless conference room was tastefully appointed, as expected. The decor was "modern prehistoric," graced with fossils of fish and plants suspended on the walls, highlighted by spotlights. Light sconces made of agate slabs gave the room a warm glow.

"Whoa, look at this!" Eric examined the large table, bordered in spruce and inlaid with crosscut sections of petrified wood. Some of the slices were opalized, with creamy blues, purples, and carnelian hues filling in between tree rings. The table was highly polished, its surface cool and lustrous. Two filtered spotlights above it completed the room's lighting.

Phoebe and Natali came in together. "*Nice* room," said Natali. "This is a cave I could live in!"

"When you're done looking, come over here and start eating," said Zeb. "We've got enough for us to make a meal this time." The likewise fossil-enhanced sideboard was nearly hidden, loaded with trays of sliced meat, cheeses, assorted breads, fresh peaches, red and green seedless grapes, and pineapple, bowls of nuts, hummus, smoked salmon, and crackers.

As they loaded their plates, Adele arrived. Her crutches were gone, but she wore a hard plastic cast with velcro straps. "Hi, everyone," she said. Her tone was less than enthusiastic.

"Hi, Adele," said Phoebe. "Look at you, you're stick-less!"

"Yes, I got my walking cast a couple days ago. I'm still getting used to it."

"There's lots of food here, do you want me to make you a plate?" Phoebe offered.

Adele thought for a moment. She wanted to be more independent, not rely on people to help her. Learning to drive the wagon gave her some mobility and independence back, and she was grateful for it. On the other hand, her leg was hurting as it adjusted to bearing weight once more, and was still getting used to balancing without support. Adele chose put aside her pride once again. "That would be very nice, thank you."

Once they ate and caught up with what was happening with each others' lives, it was time to get down to business. They excitedly talked about their notions, as well as the processing they'd gone through individually to eliminate a laundry list of incompatible ideas.

Adele extolled dog parks so that owners and their pets could have an outlet for socialization. "When people take their dogs out, it's usually just around the block, so they may see each other in passing, but the dogs don't get to play with each other. If they have a place to socialize—and there should be at least one in every town—the people socialize too. I think that's really missing in communities."

Natali agreed. "Even on the beach, people and dogs just see each other in passing as they're going different directions."

"But they can take their dogs off the leash and let them play," said Eric.

Adele shook her head. "First of all, they're supposed to keep their dog on leash. That means attached at both ends. But more importantly, people usually don't do that. They're either in a hurry, or they don't want to socialize with some random stranger just because they have a dog too, or their dog is prone to either fighting or running off. A dog park would solve all that."

"Except for fighting dogs," Eric pointed out.

"True; but maybe a dog fights because it's not socialized or poorly trained," said Natali. "Dogs who can't behave just can't be brought to an off-leash dog park. Or they have to stay on a leash until they learn manners."

Zeb chimed in with, "Nothing is for everybody, and I guess that applies to dogs too. Anyway, this time is for sharing our ideas. In a while we'll talk about them. But let's save heavy discussion for our next session."

Adele also brought up the idea of promoting healthy cafeteria options at the college level, something near and dear to her heart based on her past experience at a community college. "Why should only 'free' schools be required to have healthy food for their students?" she implored. She also offered a self-proclaimed "fantasy" project: to expand the use of horses as transportation. "I know it would never work, we have too many people, too many miles to cover, and too much to transport on a grand scale. We can do it here at the academy, but it's not practical outside of a small area. But they did tell us to dream big!"

Eric said he'd like to share next. He stood and said, "I think we need to think about educating the public about endangered species. For instance, you know the academy gives a unique name to all blocs, so we can figure out which term someone came in, and in which year. It's always the name of an animal, and it's usually endangered, rare, or already extinct. Do you all know what a pangolin[33] is, the namesake for our bloc?"

Only Zeb answered in the affirmative. "They're related to anteaters, right?"

"Yes, and they're in danger of going extinct." He held up an

---

33 www.worldwildlife.org/species/pangolin

8"x10" photo.

Phoebe exclaimed, "It looks like a pine cone!"

Eric went on. "Those scales on their backs are harvested. Trouble is, it's not like shearing sheep; they are killed for these scales or plates. Humans are wiping them out by the millions each year. It's already illegal, but as long as there's a market, it will continue. People need to know not to buy products made from pangolins." He waited while the others scribbled notes. He then continued: "I have another idea; I've seen, and I know you guys have too, lots of broken down cars. Most of them are still serviceable, but people don't have the know-how or parts to get them running."

"Or time," said Zeb.

"Right. So I think we could work on developing a registration system for old vehicles which need repairs." They all looked to him to continue. "You know, so folks can help each other. One has know-how, one has spare parts...that's all I've got on that right now," he said, and sat down.

Phoebe stood next. "That reminds me of the machine we built for our physics class, remember, Eric?"

"Yeah, that was pretty sweet."

"What did you guys build?" asked Zeb. "My roommate last term built a working robot. Kind of a literal take on the assignment, and it didn't work very well, but it was clever."

"It was a light machine," said Phoebe. "But we'll have to tell you about it later. Right now let's get back to our ideas. I'd like to see us do a regional beautification project, remove debris such as abandoned cars, replacing them with fruit trees; something that would start a nationwide movement to bring not only the beauty of plants to populated areas, but also cleaner air and even free food to harvest. I'm also thinking of helping people be more self-sufficient through vegetable gardens."

"Do you have any other ideas?" asked Adele, knowing she did.

"Yes, I want to help people be more physically active, purposely. Some kind of program that would kill two birds with one stone, so to speak. Like, remember the idea of washing your clothes while riding a stationary bicycle? Purposeful and intentional exercise. That's what I've been thinking."

Natali said, "You sound like you're all over the board." Phoebe shot her a sideways glance. "I'm not criticizing, I'm all over it too. You know I'm upset about shipping horses to slaughter, and I want to make others aware of what's happening too; along that same line, I think there should be a humane horse euthanasia program, which would eliminate some horses' suffering, and make it easier for the owners to do the right thing. But I also want to start a suicide outreach program, or a self-esteem program for young people. It's really tough when there are so many needs, and not enough volunteers."

Zeb, usually the first to arrive but the last to volunteer information, stood up. He followed the lead of his heart to promote writing and reading programs. "Our society is so focused on electronic entertainment and stimulation. It's all about being 'fed,' with no effort or imagination on our part. Reading enhances mental imagery, and writing gets us not only to express our thoughts, but encourages us to *have* them." Then he brought out a posterboard with his splintered family tree. "My other idea is based on what I learned a couple years ago about my family: it isn't what I thought it was." He shared a knowing glance with Natali. "I would like to inspire others to take an interest in their family backgrounds, whether it's good, bad, or ugly," he said. "We as a people need to stop hiding the bad apples, not just be ashamed of them and pretend they don't exist. How else can we grow?"

They took a break before moving to discussions. Adele approached Eric. "Can we talk privately after the meeting?"

"Sure; is everything okay?"

"Yes, there's no problem. But I want to discuss something with you, and it doesn't involve our business here or the others."

Eric had predicted this time would come. His mother had told him never to get between two people, never get involved, even if asked. "It can't end well; one or probably both would blame you for their own conflict," she'd said. *Zeb must've finally told her he talked to me about their relationship. She'll probably tear me a new one, to mind my own goddamn business.* He tried to put the thought aside during the second part of their meeting. He'd take his lumps when she dished them up.

After further discussion and some elimination—Adele had to concede that horses for transportation on a large scale wasn't even worth the time to consider—Zeb terminated the meeting by reviewing plans for the next. "We have four months before we come together again. Let's make sure we're on the same page." They discussed different goals, what they wanted to accomplish as a group, an overall result. In addition to the academy's set of parameters, they came to a mutual agreement: whatever manifestation their project took, it wouldn't be an end unto itself, or something that didn't require participation during and after; a segment of their project would somehow encourage people to get involved, to keep the project alive and vital. Each myrmidon would use this as their guideline before bringing proposed projects to the next meeting.

Phoebe volunteered to chair: she chose the library at Saffron Cascade as the location for their next session.

As they said their goodbyes and disbanded, Eric approached Adele. *Might as well get this over with.* "So, what did you want to talk to me about?"

Adele pursed her lips and squinted. "I made a mistake. I owe you an apology."

"What for?" He was genuinely nonplussed.

"I misjudged you. Do you remember meeting me at Emerald Crag a few months ago? In the cafeteria?" He nodded. "Well, I thought you were arrogant, a busy-body. I hated that you defended that guy. But then I found out what you did for me." She saw a smile fleet across his face. Now she knew that he knew what she was talking about. "You set me up with the wagon, didn't you?"

Eric bowed his head and nodded. "Yes ma'am, I did. You had a need, and I saw to it that it was fulfilled. That's all."

"I want you to know that I am so grateful to you now. I'm grateful that you're a busy-body. Eric, I was really in the dumps before a horse and wagon pulled me out. And that's thanks to you."

Chapter 44

Faith

I always like to look on the optimistic side of life, but I am realistic enough to know that life is a complex matter.

— *Walt Disney*

August

Faith means different things, depending on who's being asked, or the situation one is in. Do we place our faith in a spiritual, unearthly being, to look out for us or at least do the favor of wishing us well? What about faith in ourselves to get through the day, to make sound decisions, to believe that we're good people? We wonder how much assurance we have in those close to us; our faith in them is often tested, and sometimes restored. Finally, what about drivers on the road, not to sideswipe our vehicles or ram us from behind?

Sometime faith is forced upon us, because without it, not much gets done, and we don't go very far. Other times, we discover that despite our intentions, our own judgments can be called into question. In the past month, Adele learned those lessons through Eric. She wouldn't be the only one.

Natali didn't enjoy Obsidian Marsh. The class itself she adored: To her, faith and love and hope and optimism were all closely related. But she found this setting gloomy; it felt oppressive and she had a heaviness each time she came here. Eric loved it, she knew, but couldn't fathom why he did. It was dark, damp, had no view of the ocean. She had to admit that the pond was beautiful, but unlike the man-chiseled Reflection pond up at Emerald Crag, completely natural. One could wade and perhaps even swim in the Marsh's putrid swamp, but it was deep with decayed plant life, animals, and God-knows-what-else, so rarely anyone took a dip, except to hunt for frogs and other creatures. If she were to tell the truth, the place disgusted her.

"Is faith like, something we decide, or something we feel?" asked one coed to the class at large.

"I suppose it depends on what it is," said another. "When you go to deposit money in a bank, you have faith that you'll see it again. You don't go up to the teller and think, 'Hm, I feel good about this person, they look honest.' No! You choose to decide to trust that person. But if you leave your child with a new babysitter, you have faith in that person because you feel good about them, maybe you get a vibe that they're honest and wholesome. You might leave your money in the hands of a grouchy, strange old man behind the bank counter, but you're not going to do that with your kid."

Natali followed the discussion with interest. Once her eyes had been fully opened to see how humans treated horses, her initial curiosity had turned into anger. She needed her faith in humans to be rekindled, and was hoping this class would eventually provide the spark. In order to champion the besieged species, faith that it could happen was critical. Otherwise, why try to change anything?

Chapter 45

Grief

*Death is not extinguishing the light; it is putting out
the lamp because dawn has come.*

— *Rabindranath Tagore*

September

Though Natali excelled at responding in a crisis—she kept her cool, did as instructed, and gave direction, if needed—she expected the aftershock. Not that it helped. Once the incident was over, or was in someone else's hands, she then fell apart. This time her response was no different, though the event was certainly nothing she'd encountered before.

The horse at her feet still looked beautiful to her. Webster's summer coat shone silver in the sun; the full tail flowed out behind him; his hooves neatly trimmed. But oblivion showed through his bones, and lifeless eyes and lips didn't fight off the relentless flies.

Natali brushed them away as she wept.

Though he was retired, she had admired the gelding from afar: still full of spirit despite his advanced age, he'd taken delight in nipping at the old mares' legs, teasing them like a frisky colt. She told the other responders that she was okay, and would walk home. They left her to mourn in solitude.

Natali stroked the horse's cheek. The rhythm paired with her sadness was mesmerizing. In an instant, her mind was transported to a distant but vivid memory, back to Dell's funeral. It was held in the style of the Renaissance, and all were welcome, whether they knew Dell personally or not. Natali wore flowers in her hair, while Dell's mother and the other older women wore garlands of rosemary. In memory of Dell's interest in authenticity, all of the family and most of the mourners wore black. After the funeral in the twilight of the evening, a candlelight vigil was held in his memory and for suicide awareness. Natali couldn't see all the flickering lights that surrounded the lake of the arboretum, not all at once. She had walked around the lake, and read each remembrance. Her favorite was an untitled poem that she took home and memorized.

> We are all lights
> A steady glow, then burning bright
> Flickering, then dancing again.
> Until finality; burning out.
>
> Many flicker down to the end,
> When the wick has terminated
> When the wax has sublimed
> And the flame vanishes.
>
> Other lights end quicker
> Never to reach the full potential
> Of their earthly form.
> But all matter, anyway.
>
> Tonight we marked one light passed.
> We marked our fear, our loneliness.
> We marked the times we felt cold
> Hurt, unheard, unsaved; lost.
>
> Dell bridged a fissure between us
> Even if some were separate, unspoken,
> Unknown to each other, gathering in body or spirit

Flames burning, never alone.

We shared a light's time together
Not many with recall, having unmet.
But Dell brought us together, in passing
For tonight, united lights.

Natali knew what came next. The horse would be buried at the far end of Basalt Moor, the only area of the academy that was at least three-hundred yards from a water source. There was no need for an autopsy; Webster was thirty-two years old, so had already outlived the average lifespan. Hearing the clanking, jangling tractor approach was Natali's cue to say her final goodbye and go home.

It was a pleasant walk from the west side of Crimson Song to Saffron Cascade, though she barely noticed it. But as she started walking up the road to campus, she stopped for the first time to take a good look at the obelisk at the entrance. She reached up and traced the shape of the hummingbird carved into it. The monument was made of limestone; it stirred something profound in her, she knew not what.

When she returned to her dorm, alone in her room, she reached under her bed. There tucked into the springs she'd hid a pack of cigarettes in a hard eyeglass case. She'd bought the pack the day after she attended the horse auction in her first term; by the time she got to Gilded Sand her desire to smoke was there, though diminished; she bought them anyway. Now she sat on her bed, and opened the case, then the pack. The aroma of cured tobacco, sweet and pungent, instantly brought back so many memories; she inhaled the scent deeply. Her mouth could already taste it. Taking one of the cigarettes out of the pack, she rolled it in her fingers. Dell had said to her on more than one occasion, "If you smoke even one you have to start stopping all over again." He was right; she'd stopped and restarted more often since his death than she'd care to admit. Still, she hadn't had a puff in the last eighteen months; did she really want to start again, with the horse and his memory to blame? She returned the cigarette to the pack, and replaced it in the case. But this time she stored it in her leather satchel; one way or another, she'd get rid of it, forever.

Chapter 46

Industry

*Industriousness and conscientiousness are often at
odds, because industriousness wants to pick the still
sour fruit from the tree, while conscientiousness lets it
hang there too long, until it falls and bruises.*
— *Friedrich Nietzsche, philosopher*

September

It can be a hardship, moving every three months. Most
students pack lightly when they come to the academy, making
the move much easier; at least they think they do. Oftentimes
there's a tendency for possessions to grow fewer with each
move; by their fourth or fifth move, residents typically leave
behind some of their belongings for the next tenants, or donate
to Silica City's charity of choice, a thrift store supporting a
family homelessness program. Whittling down to their essential
needs makes the move easier and less time-consuming. They
have two weeks to settle in; less than that if they leave PAA for
the break. The difficulty isn't so much not even that they're
moving, but that *everyone* is moving. By the time they've
finished their degrees, everyone is a master of packing up and
resettling, establishing new roommate relationships, and saying
goodbye to others.

Eric, however, loved the hustle-bustle. He'd even developed
a habit of helping as many Pangolins as he could to relocate
each term. Since she felt the need to "pay back," he and Adele
became a team, with he and their "customers" loading the

wagon, and she with Augustus delivering the cargo all around to the different schools. It was much easier and more efficient than using the shuttles, as they ran in a circle. Their team could go to any school from another, directly.

He'd packed up his effects even before the term ended, but Eric couldn't move into his own housing until the current tenant moved. Finally his new space was vacated, and he loaded up his belongings at Cedar Whiles for Adele to drive it to Pearl Quay. He was her last customer.

"Some 'break,' huh? These two weeks have been grueling." Eric said as he climbed up to sit by her. "I'll bet you haven't worked that hard for a while. Do you wish you'd gone home now?"

Adele told the horse to move on. "It's not been that much work for me; besides, you and Augustus here have been doing all the labor. Other than missing my horse Oliver, no, I'm glad I stayed. Besides, I got to know you better. And since Zeb got me this snazzy hat," she pushed up the brim of the sunhat, "I didn't get as dark as you!"

Eric laughed. "That's too bad, I think you would've liked it."

"You may be right. Speaking of something else you get that I don't, you'll have to tell me how you like living at Pearl Quay."

"You haven't been assigned there yet?"

"I don't get to be there at all!" she exclaimed. "I was hoping to, I'd like to live 'downtown' at least once, be near the shops and stuff. It kind of reminds me—on a microscopic scale, of course—of living in San Francisco. I did that for a month one summer, helping my cousin when she had her first baby."

"Have you thought about staying on as staff? There are some rooms for employees at each branch. You could request the Pearl."

"I did think about it. They'd let me bring my horse from home if I signed on. But now that I'm on the guild, I don't know. I think I'll think more about it after graduation. I've got too many other things to do now."

"Have you been cleared to ride yet?"

"Yes, but...with restrictions. I think I'll keep it simple and just keep driving for a while. I'm really starting to like it. But I must say, I think Augustus would be a hoot to ride; he's so tall, I'd tower over everybody! I'd love to be on my 'high horse.' It'll be a big improvement from being ignored in the wheelchair."

They arrived at the back of the storefronts. Eric finished unloading. "I guess I'll see you at the next guild meeting in November."

"We'll meet before that," Adele promised. "I've got to bend your ear some more about my proposals." She left him with smiles as she drove off.

Chapter 47

Perspective

Everything we hear is an opinion, not a fact.
Everything we see is a perspective, not the truth.

— *Marcus Aurelius*

October

Changing one's point of view isn't easy. Even less so when one *wants* to make the change. Both positive and negative associations are so entrenched in the subconscious mind, that when the conscious mind wants to release old ways of behaving, the unconscious rebels. Just as a child resists change regardless of whether it benefits them or not, as when a toddler fights moving into a "big boy" bed, even though he no longer fits comfortably in his familiar crib.

Natali had never experienced a class taught by fire before. In her high school, few lessons were "hands-on." They read books, watched films occasionally (at least a few students would fall asleep in the dark room), or listened—sometimes—to their teacher drone on and on about the subject in a lecture.

An attractive black woman originally from Nigeria, Marama Ndidi had an athletic build with wide squared shoulders and prominent collarbones. Her unique international experiences suited her to the Perspective class. "Fire can be a blessing, and it can be a curse," she said. "It's all a matter of how you perceive it. It can hurt, kill, even wipe out entire communities or forests. Yet it's a tool to keep us warm, cook our food, even purge things we don't want anymore. Its smoke is the same way; as you are experiencing right now, Jeanine," and she pointed to the hapless girl, "You are not having a good time in that smoke, are you? It's hurting your eyes, and filling your lungs with ashy air. In fact, I highly suggest you change your perspective and migrate to the other side of the fire. Yet, what is smoke good for?" Answers ranged from "smoking salmon" to "controlling bees."

The bonfire was being held in the "crotch" of the diverging roads north of the Pistoia bridge. Titanium Terrace split off from Charon's Alley to wind its way up to the top of Emerald Crag—where she'd rather be right now, in her dorm room— while Charon continued from its origin at Escape Drive to its terminus at Obsidian Marsh. The burn was being controlled by the work study crew. They'd cut back overgrown brush from both campuses and pruned hydrangea bushes after their flowers had faded.

Ndidi said, "Along the same lines, water can be a friend or foe. It is said that you can drown in as little as a capful of water, but we all need water to survive."

"I never drink water," quipped a new leaf. "I hate the stuff."

"That may be, but you get enough water from other sources, obviously. At least enough to keep you alive."

"You really ought to drink pure water," interjected a health student Natali recognized from the clinic when she'd gone with Adele for wound dressing after her fall. "It efficiently removes toxins, gives you energy, and helps you think more clearly."

While this discussion was going on, it occured to Natali that this would be the perfect time to purge herself of the burden in her satchel. She walked casually around the fire; at a time when the others were looking the other way, she opened the case and threw the entire cigarette pack into the flames. A feeling of resolution flooded her; it was finally done. She recognized the crazy urge to reach into the blaze and pull the burning pack back out, but she let it wash over her like a wave. A tidal wave. A low tide. A bog. No wonder she'd felt burden, bogged down with this habit. But with all that she'd been through since arriving at the academy, she'd passed through it without smoking, without panic. She felt stronger in her weakness; in the same way that there's no courage without fear, how could there be strength without challenge? It was a strange but not unwelcome sensation.

With that problem solved, she continued watching the flames as yet-unresolved issues taunted her. Paired with her work on the horse adoption program, the auction was a wake-up call. Getting on her own, out from under her parents' drama, and being of service to others were her primary passions. This revelation about the treatment of horses ignited a new passion. It would take her through hills and valleys she would've never dreamt of.

Chapter 48

Closure

In philosophical inquiry, the human spirit, imitating the movement of the stars, must follow a curve which brings it back to its point of departure. To conclude is to close a circle.

— *Charles Baudelaire*

October

Winters on the Oregon coast—though generally mild—come with high winds, starting during the last part of autumn. When people move away from the coast to go back inland because of the weather, the winds are more likely the reason than the rain. Cold, robust gales knock down the weaker branches of trees like a girl making wishes off a dandelion puff, and send dead leaves —among other debris—hurtling through the air. Although temperatures are usually above freezing, staying outside for long brings an uncomfortable chill and cold noses.

Even without wind, outdoor work that needed to be done was all the more difficult to do. Just as tasks were generally easier done in the summer, in the winter even many simple tasks were more challenging.

But much can be done to prepare for that coldest and wettest season, which when done in advance will make those tasks much fewer and unnecessary. The closing of the season around campus involved assignments from the simple to those requiring ornate orchestration.

Still other undertakings were not so straightforward.

Though she'd symbolically closed the door on smoking forever "not even one," Natali couldn't close all of the doors that needed metaphorical bolting. It had been several weeks since the horse was buried, but she kept seeing the lifeless body in her mind's eye. Also haunting her were memories of the horses she'd seen at the auction, and the worst of all, videos she'd viewed of horses being trucked out of the country and their eventual butchering. The grisly images of healthy, able-bodied horses crumpling while being destroyed played out over and over again in her mind.

She was losing sleep nightly, but dozing off in class; she ate only for fuel, taking no pleasure in the food. Care was slipping from her, and she knew it. The only thing that mattered to her was keeping horses out of auction yards, to rescue them before they were neglected, abused, frightened, and despondent; to keep them out of peril. What she didn't know was how close she was growing to needing rescue herself.

Chapter 49

Imagination

My imagination is a monastery and I am its monk.

— *John Keats*

November

Phoebe was in charge of the second session meeting. Consulting with Ms. Pepperburgh, she'd been warned that the meeting would likely get heated, as passions and excitement collided. The myrmidons would discuss their researched ideas in depth, further eliminating some, but never without resistance. After all, they'd now invested at least four months into their remaining proposals. "Handle everyone with tact and respect, no matter how outrageous and impractical the ideas may seem, including your own. Know that you all are coming at this with authenticity, so keep an open mind. It will all come out in the end, one way or another. The burden of making dreams reality is not your burden," Pepperburgh told her.

It was an eerie sensation to be standing alone in the reserved periodical room at the main library. Where students usually filled at least one-third of the seats, now the space was truly still. Phoebe smiled when the refreshments were delivered. She wasn't hungry, but it broke the isolated feeling. Libraries were never meant to be empty. Shortly after she set up the coffee and tea service, Zeb and Adele arrived together, followed by Natali, then Eric.

Everyone was excited to share their clarified ideas, so after helping themselves to a hot beverage or water, they were ready to jump right in. Phoebe stopped them. "Before we start, let's wish Eric a happy nineteenth birthday!" She took a box off of a table, revealing a glazed applesauce bundt cake. Eric was sufficiently bewildered as the myrmidons hugged him.

Phoebe shared that she was still torn. She had a fantasy of flowers blooming everywhere because of her, supporting the bee population. She'd become a legend, like Johnny Appleseed. "What happened to the beautification project?" she was asked.

"For it to be what I envisioned, it was too much; my research showed me that it was much more involved, with too many components, too much to bring together. So I've condensed it to planting sustainable flowers in unused areas for the bees. On the other hand, I want to help people to live out their lives being as physically active as possible. While I'm still torn, I wanted to share with you that at least I finally decided to get my associates in physical therapy instead of emergency response." The others congratulated her, and wished her the best in her career. But the question remained: how could she have two such divergent goals for their guild? Was there a way to put it all together, to meet both goals at once? Phoebe knew there must be an answer, somehow. But she found that she wasn't the only one struggling.

Eric had entertained many ideas, and felt strongly about each one. But his most burning desire at this time was to teach the public about endangered aquatic animals, such as narwhals, the unicorns of the sea; and the vaquita, a small Mexican porpoise with goth makeup.

Zeb's ideas about promoting writing and history and encouraging the examination of family backgrounds were closely related, but he didn't know how to pull them together as a singular project. He didn't want to compromise his proposals, and he told them about this inner conflict.

Adele was pretty clear about what she wanted, and though she brought a few ideas to the table, she didn't have passion for any but her one desired project: Installing dog parks all over the country. But she'd altered her idea of using horses for transportation to the flip side, promoting retired horses as pets. "Somehow I'm sure we can change the perception that once a horse is no longer working, they become livestock," she said.

Natali wanted to save horses, but wasn't sure how. Rescuing from slaughter wouldn't be necessary if people only knew what they were doing when they chose to continually upgrade their horses like they did cars, houses, or boats. How could she educate people that horses deserved better treatment than an object? To be treated as well as a dog or cat should be minimal. Of course no one could promise a forever home to anything, but they shouldn't take an animal of any kind that they knew they wouldn't keep or be willing to rehome. It made Natali so angry, and she was not easy to rile. Though the brutal end to the lives of many horses upset her greatly, she knew that the problem started much earlier, in overbreeding. But until that stopped, a national adoption program seemed necessary.

The location for their next meeting was chosen for them: It was a long-standing tradition that the third planning session took place in the archives at Crimson Song. Eric volunteered to lead that session; as organizer, he would have early access. At last Eric would be able to enter the esoteric chamber.

After the session, Natali reminded everyone to come to the three-day adoption event that she'd help plan, starting the next day. "I emailed you all invitations last week. It would mean a lot to me if you'd all come, and spend some time talking to people about what we do here for horses," she pleaded.

"But Natali, I'm really not a horse person," said Eric. "I kinda think of them like the railroad: they were once useful, or even necessary. But now they're a toy, a hobby." He missed seeing Zeb's icy glare. Zeb and his family hadn't been involved with the railroad directly, but it was historically and presently an important feature of Mullens. Eric clearly was ignorant of the subject.

Natali sighed as energy seemed to leave her body along with the breath. "You're not the only one who thinks that way, Eric. And that's fine, if you're a person who doesn't have horses. It's the people who have them and consider them as a toy or an amusement, that trouble begins. They don't think of them as living beings with emotions and memories. But they are." Natali lowered her head, and pushed back the edge of the table with open hands, as if to stop herself. "What I'm trying to say is, even if you can't volunteer, I'm giving a lecture, and I'd like you all there for moral support. I'm saying some things that will probably be heavily criticized later."

"When is your lecture?" Eric asked.

"Day after next."

"I'll be there," he said.

"I think I can safely say we'll all be there," said Zeb.

In the same large conference room at which the Pangolins had received their orientation, Natali and Adele stood behind the curtain of the stage. Natali reviewed her notes and drank sips of water to keep her throat hydrated. She'd performed several marriage ceremonies, but this time it wasn't words of love, life, or encouragement she'd be speaking; instead, it was a challenge, a call to action, a demand for change. She heard the murmur and bustling of the audience as they began to come into the hall.

"Are you sure you're up to this?" asked Adele.

"My heart feels like it's going to beat out of my chest, but I'm okay. I know it's just nerves."

Adele grasped Natali's hands, looking deeply into her eyes. "Okay, but look, if you feel like you need to stop—for any reason at all—just excuse yourself, and I'll come up to take your place. I pretty much know what you want to say. I may flub it up a bit, but I can deliver your message. Then I'll tell them mine about how we utilize horses here. They'll never know I came on early."

Natali nodded and gave Adele a hug. "Thank you, but I'm sure I'll be fine." As if on cue, the announcer introduced Natali, and she climbed the steps to the stage.

"Thank you all for coming to our program. My name is

Natali Marks, and I'm in my sixth term here at the academy. This is the third adoption event that I've been involved with. I'd like to share just a little history about the program." She went on to tell them how the program was started when the academy found that it had more horses than people who needed them, especially when the dual-sports were introduced and approved for student use. "Some of you are here learning about horses for the first time. Others are here to upgrade their horses, or to add horses to your stable.

"I am on a mission to put an end to horses being cycled through the auction, to be at risk of shipping to slaughter. Have you ever sent your child to a summer camp that provided horseback riding? Have you wondered what happens to the horses during the off-season? Conscientious owners find a way to winter over their herd. But others sell their horses at auction after summer, flooding the market so that meat buyers get their pick. In this way, they save money in not feeding horses that aren't making a profit. The next spring, the string owners buy all new horses at the auction, and the cycle starts again." Natali shook her head as a lump formed in her throat.

"But for now, I want to talk about what we can do individually. We at the academy understand that most families can't commit to a horse for life, giving it a 'forever home' as they can with household pets. For one thing, horses can live thirty or more years. Plus being a large outdoor animal, when lifestyles or living situations change, horses are left out in the cold, no pun intended." The audience lightly laughed. "And truly, unless people are able and willing to have a barnful of horses, children do outgrow their ponies in stature, then later in weight, so a horse-child will go through as many as four or five horses before they are out of the family home.

"I've thought of a new way of rehoming horses. The buy/sell model will always be with us. But for those who'd benefit from a less monetary-based program, and one that keeps the welfare of the horses in mind, I propose a solution. I've gone over it with advisors, tweaked some of the parameters, and researched what horsemen—and women—need and want for themselves, their businesses, and their families. This 'recycling' program would all but eliminate the need for auction houses, internet sales, and idle horses as they wait for a new home. And my sincere hope, that it would ultimately stop the unnecessary and irresponsible breeding of more horses."

Natali explained how the program would work, that owners would register their horses, that buyers would be specific about what they were looking for, if they wanted a new horse or an upgrade. She was feeling "in the zone," her passion for the subject outweighing her earlier anxiety. In the back of her mind, she grew more confident that this was something that really could work: she could make a real difference.

Chapter 50

Recycling

Fall, leaves, fall; die, flowers, away;
Lengthen night and shorten day;
Every leaf speaks bliss to me,
Fluttering from the autumn tree.
I shall smile when wreaths of snow
Blossom where the rose should grow;
I shall sing when night's decay
Ushers in a drearier day.

— *Emily Brontë*

November

As Zeb sat in the last row of his mixed media class—they were looking at slides of the Recology sculpture garden[34] in San Francisco—he wondered if he should have promoted the arts more in his proposals to the guild. He turned it over in his mind. He'd felt a bit like a recycled person himself: rejected by his parents as a discardable burden, picked up by his grandparents as a farm hand, and now allowing himself to be repurposed by and for the guild. In this iteration, however—thanks in part to the trust fund—he was going to be used for a higher purpose, this time with his knowledge and permission. With the concern of how he was going to take care of his needs lifted, his mind was free to think of others, and not just Adele.

He was worried about Natali. At the last session, a light

---

34 recologysf.com/index.php/sculpture-garden

seemed to be going out in her; a candle flickering in a draft had more spirit. When he first met her, she was glowing, animated and friendly. Now she was sullen, defeated, unkempt. He himself had been through some rough times, so he recognized it easily. How could he ignore her, when she had been willing to help him? As he grew in confidence and hope, she seemed to be balancing it with discouragement and despair.

He spoke with Adele after their classes to see if they could come up with a strategy to help Natali cope.

Adele said, "I don't know that she needs help, really. She likes to keep busy."

"She's taken on *so* much," Zeb said. "Even a busy person needs rest."

Adele agreed. "But she did a great job of giving her speech. She was in her element; I was so proud of her!"

"I know, I was there, remember? It was the first time in a while that I saw her come to life. But even good events can be stressful. Planning our next guild meeting, taking on the hostessing duties of the Bonobo guild, and working on the horse adoption program, not to mention her studies and work study too...what's she doing this term anyway?"

"She's on the bird management crew, feeding the peacocks, putting netting over the martins' nesting areas while they're gone, stuff like that. But I'm sure she enjoys it."

"Oh yeah. Well, all that work combined is too much for just about anyone."

"It is, but all we can do is be there for her. And to point out to her if we see signs that she's overloaded. Otherwise, we have to trust her to ask for help if and when she needs it."

"Is that something you learned in psych?"

"Sure, partly anyhow. People need a chance to work things through for themselves. It doesn't take a scientist to know that."

Zeb shrugged. "Okay, but let's make sure that we keep in touch with her. She's one of ours, you know."

Violence

*I am a violent man who has learned not to be violent
and regrets his violence.*

— John Lennon

December

The Universe began with an untold, unfathomably violent act. Many of the stars we see in the sky are not stars at all, but brilliant, massive explosions of suns light years away. A big bang was necessary for life to eventually appear, and from the ants we walk on to the spiders we unknowingly swallow at night, violence continues to be part of our everyday existence, whether we're aware of it or not.

Adele had known she wasn't going to like this class, but she knew she needed to take it. If she wanted to be a mental health professional, she needed to understand humans and human behavior as best she could. There was no species that exhibited violence in the same way as human beings. The swans at Obsidian Marsh were quite frightening as they attacked any perceived predators, including humans: some people were downright terrified of them. But they, and even cats which played and tortured their prey, didn't do it with the same planning and gleeful malice of some of our own species.

"During this term, we've talked about what violence is, who does it, your thoughts on the subject. But now, before we conclude and you go on your winter break, I'd like to know, how would you define 'violence' in two words?" asked the instructor.

Adele's mind ran through several types before anyone answered. All of them involved human interaction. Of course there was "big" violence, such as wars. Wars between nations, but wars between families and even within families. Her thought flowed to the way Peising performed when she broke up with him, their final goodbye. She reminded herself to put that in the past, to sink it in the mental file of "lessons learned," right along with her first—and failed—attempt at a Baked Alaska[35].

Zeb was so different; she knew, though he was physically capable, that he would never hurt her in any way, for any reason. Violence also included slow, covert violence, such as torture, starvation. Dachau passed through her mind; the horrors there and on the way there. It reminded her of what Natali told her about horses shipped to slaughter. There was incipient violence in the form of verbal assault, name calling, threats, neglect; indeed, the accursed "silent treatment" could be considered a form of emotional violence.

Adele heard several people offer answers to the question. Her attention was brought back to the discussion by one of them: "Unnecessary harm."

"Would you care to elaborate? When is harm necessary, for instance?" asked Thordicci.

"Like when we kill animals for food. It's harming them, even when done humanely."

Adele remembered a story she'd read about last year. "A casino worker in Silica City left her dog in the car last July when she went to work. She didn't leave the windows down or anything. The dog was found dead."

Thordicci combed fingers through his yellow hair to the back of his head. "I'm glad you brought that up. At the academy, we feel that violence is violence, no matter the method or the intention. Is violence necessary, or is it avoidable? Questions like these will be on your final assignment. Your answers, your thoughts, your definitions, are your right. But how you answer will tell me if you've been paying attention to our discussions

---

35 www.saveur.com/article/Recipes/Baked-Alaska

and readings." He motioned to a stack of composition books on a table. "Each of you take one book; the assignment is there. Feel free to illustrate, attach clippings, articles; whatever you desire to make your message. Drop it off at my office before Christmas day. Class dismissed, enjoy your break."

Chapter 52

Doubt

... How far the unknown transcends the what we know.
— *Henry Wadsworth Longfellow*

January

Natali was shouting at her roommate, "Don't you understand?! What these people do, it's barbaric! How can I express to you...." With her left hand, Natali deftly grabbed Jill's left shoulder. "They have these short, pointy boning knives they call *puntillas*, and stab it into the horse like this," she said as she pretended to stab over and over Jill's spine with the outside of her fist. "It doesn't *kill* them, but once they finally sever the spinal column, once they've gotten through *muscle* and *bone*, the horse collapses in paralysis but they can still *feel* everything that's being done to them. The lucky ones, the *lucky* ones, die quickly of asphyxiation, unable to breath while they drown in their own blood. But otherwise, helpless and in agony, they bleed out while they're *dismembered. ALIVE.* It's barbaric! It's...," she stopped as she choked on the words. Her breathing became rapid and shallow.

Natali released Jill, withdrawing to her bed. Natali's heart was beating so hard it felt like it would break through her chest. "And these were horses that were people's pets, or dude ranch horses, or racehorses, or working horses...I can't do this anymore, I just can't," she repeated again and again. "And I can't take this *place*," she screamed. "I hate it, I *hate* it! *What* am I doing here?!" She aggressively threw pillows and other articles at the wall in a combination of frustration and anguish.

Everyone has their tipping point, the thin divide between inaction and action. For Jill, flying objects were the last straw. "Get Felix, quick!" she shouted to a resident standing in the hall. "Tell him it's an emergency!"

It seemed to Natali that her world was upside-down, and each time she tried to right it, it would spin faster. She had a sharp ache in her left temple, her knees were weak, her eyes stinging from so many salty tears. Her entire body shook. Though he'd been gone for several years, each time she remembered that she forgot her cousin Dell wouldn't be sending her any more funny text messages, she would cry anew. There was so much she wanted to talk to him about. She had seen so much in the past year, horrible things she learned that humans in this day and age were still doing, and uncertainty about herself and her future mounted up. And this *place*, this place really was a swamp; it bogged her down emotionally, and here she was, back as a resident—despite protests—for a second term. This time, on Dell's birthday, Natali balled up in another round of crying. Despite her roommate's efforts, she couldn't console her. Natali's disturbed temperament was escalating.

After receiving Felix's text, two myrmidons hastily arrived at Natali's dorm room. Eric and Zeb had been nearby; Adele was on her way.

"It's all so pointless, I can't make a difference." Natali shook hard, uncontrollably. She'd stopped crying, but her shivering was as upsetting to the others as it was to her. "I can't even help myself, what made me think I can help anyone else?!"

"Hey, that's not true," Zeb said. "Remember when I told you about my family? Remember? C'mon Nat, think back. Not so long ago, right?"

"Yeah, that's how we first met."

"That's right, and you helped me a lot, did you know that?" She shook her head defiantly. Recalling her own kindness wouldn't serve her thundering self-doubt. "Well, it's true. I had no idea how it was affecting me, till after you let me share. You need to know what a difference you made for me."

Branchmaster Felix arrived with a med kit. With calm reassurance, he interrupted Zeb, and asked Natali if she had a history of anxiety. She said yes. As he put on the stethoscope, he said, "You're probably experiencing a panic attack. Just in case, I'd like to check your vitals. Is that okay?" She indicated her assent and he started by checking her pulse. Seeing him unpack various supplies shifted slightly her frame of mind. Her breathing began to become more steady. Eric spoke with Felix while Zeb continued, "I told you things I've never told anyone. I didn't know at the time how important that was to me, and you didn't know either. But I'm here to tell you now, because you're important to me too. Do you understand?" Natali nodded her head. "Good. Good. Hey, we need you. Just wait till you see what we can do together. 'More powerful than a locomotive,' you'll see!"

Mr. Felix sat at the foot of her bed. "Speaking of trains, you've been on a black engine, young lady. What do you say, let's slow it down a bit, hm? Eric just told me about a technique for grounding you; are you willing to try it?"

She was, and as he instructed, she first named five things she could see, four things she could touch, three things she could hear, two things she could smell, and one thing she could taste.

When she finished, he said, "Excellent; feeling better?" She nodded. "Well, your vitals were all good, so I believe you did have a panic attack. Now just think about slowing down your breathing, nice and deep; that's right." Jill handed him a glass of water, and he handed it to Natali. "Go ahead and drink that."

As she did, Adele breezed in the doorway of the now-crowded room. "Well, looks like a party!" she joked, attempting to lighten the mood while meeting Natali's eyes. Felix asked her if she needed him. She declined. "Why don't you guys give us girls a few minutes? I'd like some private time with Natali." She turned to the tear-streaked girl on the bed. "If it's alright with you?" Natali sniffled and agreed. Everyone else exited into the hallway, including Jill.

"Looks like you fell off a metaphorical cliff, sweetheart." Adele dabbed at Natali's hot glazed cheeks with a tissue. "Want to tell me what caused you to slip?"

"Adele, what they do to horses...do you know? Do you know what they do, when horses are butchered?"

Natali had told her before. Adele indulged her anyway. "You mean, like at slaughterhouses?"

"Yes. It's illegal to butcher horses in the US anymore, but horses can be shipped from here to be 'processed' in Mexico and Canada."

"Oh, that's so sad."

Natali shook her head. "No, no, it's not 'sad,' it's brutal." Natali told Adele the reality of the situation, how horses were inhumanely hauled in cattle trailers for thousands of miles with no food or water, and that was just the start. Pouring out what she'd learned since attending the first auction was exhausting her, but was also calming her.

"Look, I have something to show you." Natali went to her desk and pulled out a folder and her Chromebook. "I'm not the only person who has ever wanted to do something about it." She handed the folder to Adele. She looked at the clippings while Natali pulled up a web site. "Way back in the early 1900's this woman named Ada Cole campaigned for the welfare of horses[36]. She did a lot to educate the public and founded the International League Against the Export of Horses for Butchery, see?" Adele read through the web page; it made it more clear to her why this issue affected Natali so much.

Natali sat back on the bed, folded her legs up in front of herself cross-legged. When Adele was done reading, Natali leaned far forward with her forearms on the bed. "Oh god, I'm so embarrassed," she said into the comforter. That term for a blanket suddenly made sense to her. "I don't know...I just don't know what to do; I feel so...unpowerful."

Adele rubbed Natali's back. "Whatever project is chosen, we'll gain good experience and knowledge from it. You'll learn about things you can do, and can use the experience to make

---

36 www.worldhorsewelfare.org/Article/WW1--the-silver-lining

changes later. Didn't someone say, 'Knowledge is power'?"

Natali sat back up and breathed in deeply. "You're right. I can't remember who said that either, but it's true." She looked at her hands as if something had just slipped through her fingers. After a pause, she said, "Talking to you is like talking to my cousin. Today would have been Dell's birthday. He was my favorite relative; I could talk to him about anything. I can't tell you how much I miss him in my life."

"I'm sorry, Nat. Do you want to tell me about him?"

Natali shared how he'd always been part of her life, as a playmate and later as a confidant—he knew about her parents' conflicts; about taking her to Renaissance fairs, and showing her the adventure of learning history.

"How long has he been gone?"

"That's the thing, it's been years. So why is it hitting me so hard now, again? I don't get it."

Adele gently lifted Natali's chin. "Our subconscious doesn't know the concept of 'time;' when you say, 'it feels like it happened yesterday,' that is a true if inaccurate statement. With the stress you've been going through, you miss him more than ever. You can always talk to me, and really to any of us. We myrmidons have to stick together. But first, be kind to yourself, you need that. We all need that."

Chapter 53

Conflict

Change means movement. Movement means friction.
Only in the frictionless vacuum of a nonexistent
abstract world can movement or change occur without
that abrasive friction of conflict.

— Saul Alinsky

February

Eric was beside himself. After a year of suspended curiosity, he would finally get to see inside that hidden room on the other side of the locked door at Crimson Song. More than that, he'd be among only five students at the academy to have a right to be there. But he kept his enthusiasm under wraps, for Natali's sake. Her panic attack was only a couple of weeks earlier, and the last thing he wanted to do was upset her.

Eric arrived two hours early, ostensibly to set up for the third planning session and supervise the layout of the food. But the chance to get to know the room and its contents were the real motivation. The mysterious draw had been haunting him since he and Josh found the unmapped floor.

A cast iron wood stove stood in one of the corners. The chilly day warranted a fire, so Eric crumpled up newspapers, stacking kindling on top. On that, he placed several split pieces of seasoned alder and fir, then opened the damper and lit the paper. He left the door slightly ajar for a moment, until the kindling caught fire. Then he latched the stove's door securely.

He looked through the bookshelves next. A section of books

had been written by Sebastian Paunder. As Eric scanned the spines, a bare-spined, hand-bound book caught his eye. Pulling it out carefully from between the books titled "*My First Year in the Woods*," and "*Spanish to Modern: A Journey in Architectural Design*," Eric was impressed with the little book's quaint binding in brown, worn leather. The title, now visible, read "*Musings by Sebastian*." He opened the book and read a poem written in hand with blue ink from a fountain pen:

"The Inchworm"

"**Have you ever seen an inchworm crawl up a leaf or a twig,
and then clinging to the very end, revolve in the air,
feeling for something, to reach something?
That's like me.
I am trying to find something out there beyond the place
on which I have a footing.**" — **Albert Pinkham Ryder**

The inchworm of Albert Pinkham Ryder
Was not entirely made of whole cloth;
Like silkworms weaving a gentle wave,
To wild crashings upon cerebral
Journeyings of vision—light
dark
    wind
          rain—
A romantic hermit locked away
Forcing the muse to sing an unheard song
Of which he was only the vessel, not
The creator (to whom he prayed for
Balance against the storm within ART).

Slowly, slowly, the inchworm crawled on,
Across old boards and pieces of rag
Until mystery and sister beauty

Wed before him as priest (and lone witness);
Moody and somber—like a foreign film
Whose subtitles cannot be missed—
We search for the message indicating
Why the inchworm traveled here to us
And how it survived the heavy, thick,
And often bloody bootsteps of mankind;
How this sole flower rose above the din
And made love and light his masterpiece dream
From which he never awoke until death
Released the yoke of longings for
Immortality among the stars, he
(Within the pigments of humanity)
Sought stoically to reproduce on earth
These little works of one man's moon,
Clouds
    stars
        seas
           meadows
              trees
                color…

"NOW, IF WE LOOK A LITTLE BIT CLOSER…"

Eric put the book away before he became too engrossed, and made a mental note to read it later when he had more time. He pulled out another book written by Paunder. Judging by its blue canvas cover and professional binding, this one had been published. He turned to the chapter titled "Harnesses Aren't Just for Horses: Reining in the Power of the Subconscious Mind" and read:

"Contrary to *vox populi* concerning human psychology, we use 100% of our brain. But only 10-12% of our mind's activity is used consciously. The other 88-90% is subconscious, orchestrating functions such as maintaining and building our bodies, from instructing our hearts how fast to beat to performing housekeeping duties ie processing nutrients and expelling waste products; keeping us sane by filtering, storing, and venting information that deluges modern humans every day. It's said that we receive more message units in a single day than medieval man did in his entire lifetime.

"Our subconscious mind is also a storehouse for our experiences, emotions, beliefs, unconscious behaviors, and more. Both our positive and negative associations affect how we think, feel, and act.

"The subconscious mind doesn't know time. When we can 'remember it like it happened yesterday,' we're recalling how it felt because our minds can pull up those feelings because to it, it well may have happened yesterday.

"Likewise, the subconscious mind doesn't know the difference between fantasy and reality, which is why dreams can seem so real, even after we wake up, and before our conscious minds kick in with, 'That didn't make any sense at all!'

"On an emotional level, humans are about ten years old. As we get older, we gain experience and skills to deal with challenges, but our initial response to stress and conflict is of flight or fight. Panic attacks are a result of this inner conflict: on one hand, the victim wants to escape. Adrenaline is released into the system, so the heart beats faster, breathing accelerates while becoming more shallow; a prehistoric coping mechanism which we've never outgrown, and for the most part, rightly so. It helped us to escape prehistoric creatures such as the arctodus, an enormous, short-faced bear.

"But for modern conflicts, our prehistoric response doesn't often fit. We're expected to be civil, act rationally, even in the face of adversity. While that's a reasonable expectation, it's not usually possible. The 'flight' response is replaced by the 'fight' response. But what to fight? One can't punch out 'stress,' so a punching bag—or other appropriate object—can be a substitution. Panic attacks, though not dangerous in and of themselves, cause the victims to feel as though they're suffering heart attacks." This made sense to Eric; with adrenaline pumping through her system with no outlet, Natali's body essentially attacked itself. Could stress alone trigger an attack?

He heard the gears of the dumb waiter, and realized he had lost track of the time after all: Their lunch was on the way up. Reshelving the book, he decided to stay after the meeting to read the entire chapter.

"Hey, you guys know how Sebastian Paunder died?" asked Eric. "I've been doing some research here in the archive. I don't know if any of this stuff is secret or just not publicized. You wanna hear?"

"Sure," said Adele, munching on potato chips. "But if it's gory, don't give us a lot of details. We don't want to see our lunch twice, right?"

Eric nodded. "I don't think that'll be a problem."

"Go on then," urged Zeb.

"Well, you know how they have us wear masks when we go into the caves? You've all been, right?" All but Adele nodded. "You've really got to go sometime, it's not to be missed," he said to her. "Anyway, the masks are to keep your lungs from drying out, but also to filter out any particles. During Paunder's time, they didn't know that. Eventually he died of complications from pneumonoultramicroscopicsilicovolcanoconiosis[37] because of his work in the caves. He was sick for a long time because of it, that's why the Spreckles Foundation chose him to manage the land."

"Little comfort, I'm sure," said Zeb.

"But I don't get it," said Phoebe. "Why Sebastian?"

Eric explained, "He was one of their selenite miners. When he became ill and the cause was verified, they offered to pay him a cash settlement, or be designated as the superintendent of this property. He loved the land, so that was his choice. And you guys know about how the academy started, right?"

Natali said, "Sure, he had a dream, literally. Birds inspired him, and now each school has a mascot."

---

37 en.wikipedia.org/wiki/Pneumonoultramicroscopicsilicovolcanoconiosis

"Yeah, that's right. And stone tributes were made of each of the birds. There are ten throughout the grounds, one at each school, but not at the Trunk. Not many have found all of them."

A look of surprise leapt to Phoebe's face. Through a bite of sandwich, she said, "I think I know where one is!" She told them about the object she saw within the wisteria structure. "It's got to be one of them."

"I've seen one too, and it's in this building. I'll show you after the session."

Zeb said, "I think we've all seen one." The others looked at him doubtfully. "Think about our tour; I know for a fact that we all saw at least one."

Eric went on to share that he'd learned minerals or stones symbolize the ten campuses. A strand with beads of lapis lazuli, pearl, obsidian, lepidolite, serpentinite, sunstone, basalt, beryl, garnet, and selenite is given to each student when they graduate.

"Doesn't any stone symbolize the Trunk?" asked Zeb.

Adele quipped, "Yeah, concrete!" Laughter rang through the room.

Eric spoke again. "What's cool is, all of the minerals can be found somewhere here at the academy,"

"Not pearls!" Natali said.

"Actually, yes, from oysters at the north end of the beach. There's a little bay there," said Eric. "The pearls aren't exactly the greatest size or quality, but technically they are pearls."

After lunch, the sharing of distilled ideas began. Other than Zeb, Natali noticed the careful way the others were behaving toward her. She said, "Come on you guys, loosen up. I'm fine; I'm sorry I've upset you guys. Can we just get back to being normal, please?"

With this permission and subsequent apologies, the debating began in earnest.

Adele wants to start horse parks to start getting people to think of them as pets. How fun it would be, to bring horses to a big open field just to play with each other? There'd be a railing to put the saddles on, picnic benches for the riders to socialize themselves, while the horses galloped free around the pasture, enjoying their natural state of being a herd. She knew it wasn't practical on many levels, but she had fun with the idea nonetheless.

Eric was developing a speaking program about environmental awareness, how endangered animals were but of one indicator that the human race needed to make changes immediately. He was thinking about presenting to schools, but really to anyone who would listen. He admitted that he wasn't sure how to make this fit into the parameters for the project.

Natali was still torn in three directions; to go around the country planting seeds of small horse management and rescue operations, suicide awareness, or building self-esteem in young people. "Suicide prevention starts with becoming mentally strong, learning coping skills," she explained. "Young adults will always have something or other to deal with. Knowing that much in and of itself—that life isn't about being easy or uncomplicated—makes it easier somehow."

Phoebe wanted to do something horticultural, like community gardens, or something to promote physical fitness in the elderly population. Her idea of spreading flowers in unused areas wasn't enough to utilize the resources of the guild. Just finding a balance between projects that were "too small" and "too big" was proving to be a feat.

Zeb had clarified his idea further, to encouraging reading, and/or genealogical research. He hadn't though, worked out what exactly to do with his idea, or who his audience would be. He did have something to say about Adele's more concrete proposal.

"I'm sorry to say it, Adele, but it's going to take a lot to change people's idea that horses are pets," said Zeb. "Like where I come from, they're work animals for the most part. If we did this for our project, I think it would be a Pyrrhic victory. Or even worse, you don't want to be like Sisyphus[38], do you?" Adele understood his double meaning referencing the Greek

---

38 en.wikipedia.org/wiki/Sisyphus

myth of a king condemned to perform a grueling task over and over again, with no success. She rolled him the stink eye. He just blinked back feigning innocence. Unfortunately, he was probably right, just as he'd been right to be worried about Natali. Even though Adele was the psych student, Zeb was often the more perceptive when it came to understanding their friends. Adele admitted to herself that compared to the others' lofty and/or noble ideas, the horse park idea now seemed trivial, at least for this project.

Conflict didn't bother Eric much. He was used to it, and it could even energize him. So when his fellow myrmidons' arguments accelerated, sharing barbs and frustrations over the ideas they had for a project, Eric became animated and engaging while others were withdrawing.

"You guys, you gotta see this as a positive," he said. "No one is going to get exactly what they want. Let's see this as an opportunity to get creative, like compromising or even merging some ideas."

Zeb said, "My grandfather used to say, 'never compromise.'" As soon as he'd uttered the words, the irony of his upbringing hit him like a slap across the back of his head. Isn't that what his "father" had done with Zeb's entire life?

"I'm sure he meant—or at least the phrase means—never to compromise your principles, what you believe in. If we never compromised in the way of give-and-take, I don't think mankind would be as advanced as it is," said Adele.

Everyone had taken their turns discussing the ideas. They all became quiet, due more to fatigue from the deliberation than lack of enthusiasm. "I guess that concludes this session," Eric said. "Unless there's any last thoughts?" He paused a moment. Adele raised her hand.

"We're supposed to continue to contact each other before the final session, right? Continue to try to get support from each other for our project ideas?" The others nodded. Adele went on, "Well, I propose that we each can bring only one idea for the vote. By then we should know what we want to champion, and it'll make the selection process that much easier and quicker." They took a vote, and agreed unanimously.

Eric said, "Okay, we just need to have a volunteer lead the next meeting. We have one session left, and Natali, you haven't been chair yet. What do you think, are you up to it?"

Natali smirked. "Of course. Listen, guys, I really am okay. I just got a little overwhelmed. I'm still tired, but by May, I'll be right as rain. Besides, it's not that hard, is it?"

Adele said, "For me it came naturally. That's why I took charge of our very first meeting. At any rate, I think you're right; mostly it's coordinating with admin for the time and materials, with the Branchmaster of wherever we'll meet, and with the culinary department to provide dinner."

"Yeah, about that," said Eric. "Can we get a steak and shrimp meal next time? The academy wouldn't let me have it here."

Natali smiled and nodded in agreement. "I'll work on it."

Chapter 54

Dreaming

*"So I wasn't dreaming, after all," she said to herself,
"unless--unless we're all part of the same dream. Only
I do hope it's my dream, and not the Red King's! I don't
like belonging to another person's dream," she went on
in a rather complaining tone: "I've a great mind to go
and wake him, and see what happens!"*
— Alice, in Through the Looking-Glass by Lewis Carroll

February

Get off that horse, said a voice with no body. Zeb did as he was told, sliding off the bare back of the overly long-legged bay he found himself on. When he looked at the horse's face, it was Natali. She said, *what are you looking at? What do you mean 'why the long face?'* He hadn't remembered asking that. Then she was standing before him, her body returned to its normal slender shape, but her face was still long, from the area of the bridge of her nose to her chin which was stretched out down to her collarbone.

With that, Zeb jolted to alertness. The scuttlebutt was true: Emerald Crag caused dreams to be more vivid and memorable. He knew exactly what this dream meant; what surprised him was how literal it was. Why had Natali been so sad; why did it seem life brought her no joy? She was so supportive and accepting of himself and others. He knew her parents were divorced, but that didn't seem to upset her too much. What could have happened in the eighteen months he knew her for her *vim vitae* to sink so low?

The dream was a doozy, so vivid and lucid. But did he want to share it with the Dreaming class? Naturally they had asked for a report yesterday about their dreams. He'd signed up for the class to get inspiration for his art. But this one was pretty personal, and he didn't want Adele to hear about it. Visions of another woman—however innocent—could be misconstrued. He was pretty sure it would upset her, especially since it was the eve of her twenty-fourth birthday. He decided to just let it go. It was probably more a reflection of his concern than of Natali's current mental state. After all, she'd seemed fine at last week's session. That scene last month though told another story; he didn't show it at the time, but it shook him up. Which Natali should he believe?

A Word About the Bird

Mascot of Emerald Crag, the Mallard[39] is a beautiful if common duck species. A few nesting boxes with guards to keep out predators are available to the ducks at Emerald Crag, though most spend the majority of their non-breeding time at Obsidian Marsh. The koi in the reflecting pond are safe since Mallards are dabblers, eating aquatic insects and vegetation, as well as food they find on the ground such as seeds, earthworms, and snails.

Most people assume Emerald Crag was named for the minerals found there, but Honoré actually named it for the emerald green feathers of the male mallard duck's head.

---

39 www.allaboutbirds.org/guide/Mallard/lifehistory

Chapter 55

Health

*When I go into my garden with a spade, and dig a bed,
I feel such an exhilaration and health, that I discover
that I have been defrauding myself all this time in
letting others do for me what I should have done with
my own hands.*

— *Ralph Waldo Emerson*

March

"Health, that's the true wealth," Phoebe's grandfather would often say. "If you don't have your health, all the gold in Greece won't make you glad."

As a financial necessity, Phoebe spent most of her breaks on campus. Last summer, she managed to go home for the break in June, when her flower garden was in full growth and demanded the most attention. It was an excuse, of course. She couldn't ignore or put off the call of home soil any longer. The rest of the year her mother tended to the plants, but just enough to keep them alive, not to make them thrive. Phoebe's forte was growing things; her mother's forte was Phoebe. What would she do, if Cypress weren't in her life anymore? How could she cope? Phoebe was on her way home once more, this time with more to attend to than the flowers or even herself. It was on account of her worst nightmare: Cypress Hugo was gravely ill.

Since hearing the news, Phoebe often thought about how this could have happened. What if Phoebe had stayed home, made sure her mother ate healthy meals instead of going off to school across the country? What if Uncle Charlie hadn't visited that day; would her mother have died on that hardwood floor? Once settled on the plane bound for New Orleans, Phoebe took a break from the "what if?" game—a game she couldn't win—and instead replayed yesterday's events in her mind.

After her last class for the day, she had gone for a ride along the beach. She'd ridden to the southmost point of Sandpink Beryl, to the rubble of the road that had succumbed to gravity and unstable soil years earlier. At this end, the sand wasn't pink anymore, though the black mica still glittered. Caberneigh's hooves sunk slightly into the wet sand with every step, leaving small pools of saltwater in each hoofprint. Alone with her thoughts, Phoebe wrestled with the decision of which project of hers to champion; it was decided at the last meeting that each myrmidon could only bring one. But she felt equally passionate about community gardens and senior fitness. As an admirer of Johnny Appleseed, which would she want to be her legacy?

The tide was coming in, so they returned to the yurt barn. Phoebe unsaddled and brushed out the pony before putting him in the paddock, piles of dark red hair dropped to the ground from his shedding winter coat. She was on barn duty at Sandpink Beryl anyway, so cleaned up from him and the messes from other horses that their riders had missed. She had just about finished raking the dry sand in the breezeway smooth when she heard riders' voices approach. She smiled when she saw it was Natali and Adele. They rode as far as the barn's door; Phoebe walked out to greet them.

"Hi girls, what brings you by?"

"Well, his name is Razz," joked Natali, reaching down to pat her horse's neck.

"But really, we're here with a message," said Adele, riding high on Augustus. "They've been trying to call you at the yurt."

"Why didn't they try the barn phone?" asked Phoebe.

"I don't know," Adele said breathfully, like a balloon all at once losing its air. "Anyway, you're supposed to call home."

"Really? Why?"

"I don't know that either; maybe your mama misses you."

She began to dismount; Natali did the same.

"Come on, help us turn the horses out, and we'll go inside with you. You are offering us supper, aren't you?" Natali goaded.

"Of course, if you like Georgie's cooking."

The girls removed the horses' tack, swiped the sweat off their backs, and gave them a quick brushdown. They were put in the paddock with Caberneigh, fresh hay and water steaming in the cooling air. The late afternoon light was deepening yellow, the sun's rays bathing everything they touched in gold.

They went into the housing yurt that Phoebe shared with nine other girls. While Natali and Adele went to the refrigerator, Phoebe went straight to the phone. She hoped everything was okay, but it was unusual for Cypress to call. "I don't want to bother you, interrupt your fun or your studies," she'd explained. "But I'll always be here to answer when you call me, no doubt about that." And true to her word, she always was.

Phoebe punched in the number. "You have your Mom's number memorized?" asked Adele, as the phone rang.

"I didn't know anyone bothered anymore!" said Natali.

The phone continued to ring. Phoebe said, "Well, it is my number too, silly."

Reaching a worrisome number of rings, someone finally answered, a strange female voice on the other end. "*Bonjour*, Hugo residence," it said.

A moment's hesitation on Phoebe's end as she tried to process someone else answering her mother's phone. "Uh, *bonjour*, this is Phoebe Hugo. Who's this?"

"Phoebe darlin', it's Agnes from over by the creek." Oh yes, old lady Agnes, one of her mother's closest friends. She'd started watching over Phoebe when she was a toddler while her mother was at work. Phoebe could still smell the competing odors of mothballs and stale cornbread, if she wanted. She didn't. That woman always seemed to have cornbread in the house, but it never seemed fresh. *How was that possible?* wondered Phoebe.

"Oh, hi Agnes. Where's my mother?"

"Now don't you worry, but your mama's been taken to Acadian Medical."

"What? Why?" Phoebe's heart was racing.

Agnes hesitated for a moment, seemingly to gather her thoughts. "I was here playin' cards with your mama— Manipulation you know, her favorite—and she was holdin' the cards so tight they were bending. I said, 'Let up some, you're messin' up the cards!' She didn't say nothin', so I gave her a look. That's when I noticed her cheeks were bright red, and she was just blinking at the cards like she couldn't make 'em out. I called for Charlie and you know he couldn't hear me, so I had to go get him from in fronta the *tivi* and I told him to look at her. Well, he got on this phone lickety-split and called the doc."

Phoebe cut her off. "Agnes, please, what happened?"

"Well child I'm trying to tell you!"

"No, I don't mean the story, I mean what's *wrong* with Mama?" She was trying to be patient, but stifling the explosion of frustration in her chest was almost more than she could bear.

"Oh, I see. Charlie said it was a diabetic event, a uh, ketosis, something."

Phoebe clenched her teeth. "That can't be right. Agnes, do you mean ketoacidosis[40]?"

"Just so, yes." Finally she was getting somewhere. "Charlie got her in the car right away, so he asked me to stay here till I got aholda ya."

"Thank God for you, Agnes. Now you're sure they went to Acadian?" This was confirmed, along with some other details— especially the seriousness of Cypress's condition. Phoebe hung up the phone and told Adele and Natali what was going on. They had already surmised the situation; Natali had gotten on the laptop and pulled up the airline's booking page. Phoebe ordered a ticket for the trip to New Orleans.

---

40 www.diabetes.org/living-with-diabetes/complications/ketoacidosis-dka.html

Chapter 56

Advocacy

Life has taught me one supreme lesson. This is that we must—if we are really to live at all, if we are to enjoy the life more abundant promised by the Sages of Wisdom—we must put our convictions into action.
— *Margaret Sanger, activist*

March

Once the ticket was purchased, Phoebe applied for a leave of absence from the academy. With Kenny's help, she'd be able to keep up with her studies from home, but she was disappointed that she wouldn't be present for the first use of the lunging pen she'd helped build. Her work study this term was grounds maintenance. Being winter, most of the work in which she'd been involved was out of the weather to some degree: replacing soft boards of the stage at the Hip, installing lightbulbs over the Trunk's arena and stalls, cutting up firewood in the woodsheds.

Cedar Whiles, the Trunk, Obsidian Marsh, and Basalt Moor already had training arenas; her crew was just about to put in the fill material at the newly-built fifty-foot-wide pen at Lapis Lookout. The heavy work of flattening and leveling the ground was done by bulldozer, which she had a turn at running. She also learned how to build a retaining wall—necessary as the area was on an incline, and the pen needed to be flat—and how to operate the motorized posthole digger; the first time she was on it, she was nearly spun to the ground as the powerful augers gripped the soil. The work was hard and dirty, but the crew of mostly men was supportive and fun. Including Phoebe, they even called themselves "the brotherhood." Once the sand was in and the gate installed, they were going to have a party to celebrate the inaugural lunging. She was disappointed that she'd have to miss it.

Phoebe's absence broke the guild. Although the board of directors had approved her request for a leave from the school —with a warning that if she were gone too long, she'd have to transfer to the following bloc and would no longer be a pangolin —the academy's approach to this unique feature required that all five myrmidons were present and active; though they were scheduled for five official sessions, they were expected to engage regularly and independently. Absences exceeding one week were subject to disqualification from further guild activities, which, for all practical purposes, rendered the guild void.

Eric was in the Advocacy enhancement class. He had chosen it because it would be helpful in his work with the environment, advocating for endangered species and more comprehensive, enforceable laws in regards to pollution control, for instance. But he found now that he had to be an advocate for Phoebe. He knew she was worth fighting for, and so was the guild.

"When you advocate for something, or someone, you become involved, attached, permanently linked to them or even the outcome," said Ms. Pepperburgh. "Robin Williams, for instance, will always be remembered for his work with St. Jude Children's Hospital, to support their mission of research to cure pediatric catastrophic diseases. Most people know that he was much more than an actor or comedian."

Marlene raised her hand. She said, "But now he's the face of suicide prevention, postmortem." She lowered her hand and continued, "His death sparked many campaigns to treat depression, and I think it has helped to bring suicidal people out of the closet."

Pepperburgh conceded with a smile. "There were a slew of calls to suicide hotlines after his alleged suicide. There is always hope. One may not always feel hope, may not be aware of the people who care if they're surrounded by naysayers and critics. That's why we need to support each other, be compassionate, and fight our way through the negativity. We don't *bring* hope; we reveal it through the work we do."

Eric had fought for and won the use of a horse and cart for Adele. He was a natural negotiator; advocacy came under that umbrella. But this battle wasn't about enabling a student, it was about fighting tradition, something the academy held very highly. Though the academy itself was untraditional, the parameters and history it held were etched in stone. Eric hoped the stone was as soft as soap.

He would need the help of this class to accomplish his mission: To allow Phoebe to be involved long-distance.

It was time to make his move. Eric raised his hand. "Ms. Pepperburgh, we've talked about being advocates for groups and causes, but is it possible to advocate for just one person?"

"Of course, Mr. Wholm. Parents must do this for their children, an adult child for their elderly parent. Individuals can't and shouldn't rely on society to watch for their loved one's best interests. For instance, if we know of a person who is depressed, has isolated themselves, or any of the many signs that they're in peril, we must step in and fight for them, even if we have to fight with them. Did you have someone in mind?" She raised her hand to stop him before he could speak. "Remember, you don't need to share if you do, but if you do, don't give us any identifying details. Always respect the privacy of others." She had her suspicions of what he wanted to say.

Eric cleared his throat. "Yes, I understand. But on this it's okay, I think; she's not in any danger. It has to do with the academy's policy. As most of you know, I'm on a guild; but one of our myrmidons has had to vacate the grounds for an extended period to deal with a family matter."

"Who? When are they coming back?" asked a girl by the window.

"It's Phoebe, she ..." Ms. Pepperburgh gave him a tilt of the head with her expression reading *watch what you say, no personal details.* "That is, she needs three weeks to resolve this matter. At least three." His tone grew more worried. "I know the academy only allows myrmidons one week out, and that makes sense. But in this day of electronic communication, I don't think it's necessary that we have to stay on campus to have our meetings. And that's all we're doing right now, nothing 'hands-on' yet."

"So as far as this class is concerned, what are you proposing?"

"I want to do a mini-campaign," said Eric. "I think if we demonstrated the power of online communication, social networking, the academy will see that a lot can be accomplished electronically. In fact, it may be more productive and efficient to do what we have to do digitally. I want everyone here to tweet, post on your timeline, and pin on your virtual boards these words." He stood at the front of the class, and pulled out a white foamboard from behind a table. On it were words in six-inch letters:

Ponder Phoebe's Plight - Make the Guild Alright

"What do you think this will accomplish, Mr. Wholm?"

"If everyone does that, and sends emails to the board, I think it'll get the message across that we want Phoebe, and she can participate. The guild will be effective even if she's not physically present."

"Allow me to tell you now, that as your guild's advisor, I cannot help you in this matter. What you're proposing is outside of the scope of guild guidance. I can't help you, but I don't have to deter you. I'm afraid that you're on your own, but I can wish you the best of luck."

Chapter 57

Wisdom

The road to wisdom?—Well, it's plain
and simple to express:
Err
and err
and err again
but less
and less
and less.

— Piet Hein, Dutch inventor and poet

early April

Natali's face and the room behind her were awash in golden sunlight from the lowering sun. "Why are you checking out assisted living facilities? Your mom's out of the hospital, right?" She watched Phoebe on the screen, her face the only light in the room, as it was already dark in Eunice.

Phoebe's blue-light face nodded. "Yes, we brought her home yesterday. But she's still real weak, 'like a kitten,' she says. While I'm out here, I want to get information, just in case. The docs say let her rest, keep her diet strict, and she should be back on her feet soon."

"I hope so. You know, the way things go, by the time the board approves your e-participation, you'll be back!"

Taking advantage of the change in subject, Phoebe asked Natali how it was going with negotiations on her behalf. Natali reminded Phoebe that their efforts weren't just for her. "If the board doesn't approve of your involvement electronically, we all are dropped from the program." She told her that Eric's campaign was going well, most of the student body supported modernization of the policies.

The guild had decided to proceed with their communications as though Phoebe's absence were already approved. There wasn't time to wait for permission. If the request were denied, they would have wasted a lot of time and effort; but if the request were approved and they'd sat on their hands in the meantime, the result would be the same. So the decision had been made to forge ahead.

The girls' conversation continued about all manner of subjects. They found it easy to discuss any topic, never misunderstanding what they were saying. They had formed a strong, comfortable bond during the very first day at the academy, and it only grew stronger after Natali's panic attack. Now a new stressor was coming in the form of the visit of a past guild, just three days away.

"How are you coping with all that's going on; moving, hosting the Bonobo guild, your anxiety issue?" asked Phoebe.

Natali looked at her keyboard, considering her answer. Finally, she looked at Phoebe's image and said, "I can't deny that moving back here from Obsidian Marsh didn't vastly change my outlook. Lapis Lookout is where I belong, not down in that hole." She noticed Phoebe's tilted smirk. "Okay, I know it's not a hole, that's just my perspective. I'm not perfect, but I'm better. I'm learning to come to terms that I'm not perfect, the world's not perfect, nothing is perfect. I'm learning to let go, fight for what matters, and not internalize the bad things I see. I'm learning that my feelings are real, but they're not reality. I'm also finding more 'tools' to cope when I start to feel overwhelmed. Even when I do feel upset, I can usually remember that peace is my reality. That's sinking in more each time I meditate."

"Nat, I'm so glad to hear that! I think I can see it in your face that you're more relaxed. Either that, or it's the light from your monitor!" They both laughed, both truly connected in the same moment, two hours apart.

Nadja Paunder-Reese was an invaluable resource and mentor to Natali. They'd coordinated via email and video chats, planning both the session and the presentation to and of the twentieth guild. Nadja arrived at the academy two days before the Bonobo Guild members. Natali greeted her car at the Trunk.

"Good afternoon, Ms. Paunder-Reese," Natali said as she helped the woman from the black towncar. The driver took her luggage inside.

"Oh please, let's not be so formal. You can call me Nadja." She stood straight and smoothed out her clothes. She was more petite than Natali had expected, with a sleek gray pantsuit, perfectly manicured nails of coral red, and ropes of black silver-streaked hair piled elegantly on her head. "I'd forgotten what a long drive it is from Portland. But it's awfully nice to have made it!"

"It's so good to meet you in person, Nadja," said Natali as she took her first full breath since spotting the limo as it came out around the north point of Crimson Song. She paid the limo driver with instructions to return in five days.

"So kiddo, what's the plan?"

Natali motioned for her to go inside. "We've prepared refreshments for you. Come on in and meet everybody."

Just before they entered the foyer, Nadja stopped. "I understand that one is missing."

Natali nodded. "Phoebe is away in Louisiana. Her mother had medical issues, and Phoebe is working on getting that situation straightened out before she returns."

"Family is very important, she's doing the right thing. But we've had a long-standing policy that no member of the guild be absent for more than one week, and your Phoebe has been gone for almost three."

Fearing the worst, she began to object. "But Ms. Paunder-Reese..." Natali's body felt as though her blood was turning to bubbles, her face starting to flush.

"Please, it's 'Nadja,' you remember." She stroked Natali's

arm. "Let's go inside, I want to meet your fellow myrmidons. Then," she paused, "I have news to share with you all. Just take a deep breath girl, it's going to be alright."

A flash of memory for Natali as she remembered these were the exact words she'd spoken to Adele. Everything hadn't been "alright," but Adele had recovered. Natali took a deep breath, as suggested, and went inside with Nadja. Even if the guild had to be dissolved, Natali had learned a great deal that she'd be able to take with her in the world. And that really was alright.

Adele, Eric, and Zeb stood when Nadja entered the room. After the exchange of introductions, Zeb brought her a glass of iced tea. She turned to Eric. "Mr. Wholm, you have caused quite a stir on the behalf of Ms. Hugo. You are the kingpin of this movement to alter our tradition of the presence of all myrmidons to keep guilds intact."

Eric shifted nervously in the settee. "Yes, Ms. Paunder...I mean, Nadja," he stuttered. "We feel that with the benefit of instant communication, distance shouldn't matter."

"Well, I have news for you, Mr. Wholm. The board has decided to accept your proposal." The room exploded with "whoop whoop!" as the four myrmidons pumped fists in the air and shared hugs. She waited for them to regain their composure; when the exaltations subsided, she continued. "While tradition is important, we must also recognize human ingenuity, and human tenacity. You can all be proud that yours is the first guild to make this change in our policy, and it's mostly due to your efforts, Eric."

"Good job, man," said Zeb, smiling broadly.

"Who wants to tell Phoebe the good news?" asked Nadja.

"I will," said Natali. "But I'll have to wait a couple of days, because she's on the road checking out assisted living facilities. Otherwise she would've been here with us via video conference and you could've told her yourself. Anyway," she smiled wryly, "I want to see her face when I tell her."

Two days later, the Canary shuttle picked up the Bonobo Guild in Portland and brought them to the academy. Luke took

Nadja to meet them at the Hip. In the sunlight of the beauteous April day, the shuttle radiated like the sun. After greetings, Nadja directed them to the gazebo where the Pangolin Guild awaited. As they walked across the lawn toward the gazebo she said, "I'm afraid you won't be meeting one of the myrmidons. Phoebe Hugo is back home in Louisiana taking care of her mother."

One of the five said, "We heard. Is it true that the academy has changed one of its policies?" Jerri's tone was haughty.

Nadja hid her astonishment. She hadn't considered that it might be an issue for former guilds. "It is," confirmed Nadja. "I hope you don't see that as a problem?"

"Absolutely not! Isn't the whole purpose of the guilds to inspire change? If we didn't like change, we shouldn't have been on a guild. It seems obvious."

"We agree," said Nadja, secretly relieved.

They arrived at the gazebo whereupon Nadja introduced them to the new guild. "This is Adele Stawski from Santa Rosa, California. She is earning her associates in Psychology. Next to her we have Zebulon Caruthers from Mullens, West Virginia, who is earning his associates in Arts. Natali Marks is from Moscow, Idaho; her associates is in Humanities. Eric Wholm from Atlanta, Georgia, is working towards his degree in Environmental Sciences. And Phoebe, who I told you about, is getting her degree in Physical Therapy. Do I have that all right?"

"Yes, ma'am," affirmed Eric while the others nodded in agreement.

"Good. Now the hard part, let me see if I remember what you in the Bonobo guild are now doing," she motioned to the older guild members. "John Harel, the tall one here," nudging his arm, "is the Executive Director of the Grand Platte Visitors Center in Nebraska. Sheila Löfgren operates an RV park in Devils Lake, North Dakota. Ted Hashpaegho is a gunsmithing instructor at the community college in Altoona, Pennsylvania. Richard Effenberger owns a prestigious art gallery in Nashville, Tennessee, and Jerri Hajek from Centralia, Washington, volunteers at a horse rehab operation. Natali, you may want to speak to her later."

The two guilds and Nadja visited for a while, enjoying the spring day and refreshments. When the air started to cool, Nadja closed the meeting. "Luke will take you to your quarters for the week. We will meet up again the day after tomorrow. Natali has prepared a special presentation just for you at Obsidian Marsh. Have a good night, everyone!"

When Natali had her video call with Phoebe, she remarked to her how surprised she had been that one of the members was older, probably in his mid-fifties. The rest were in their early thirties.

Phoebe looked at her quizzically then smiled. "Naturally, most people who attend junior college are just out of high school, or take a year off traveling or whatever before they go back to school. But sometimes folks who've started careers or families decide to go on a different path. He must have done something like that. The academy guidelines are as long as a student is eighteen by the end of their first term, they're old enough to be there. But there's no upper age limit."

"I wonder how old the oldest ever student was," said Natali.

"I don't know, but it'd be interesting to know their stories." Phoebe's tone became sober. "Nat, I'm really sorry I'm missing the conference. I wish I could be there to support you, and see the results of all your hard work first-hand. I feel just terrible about it."

"Tomorrow night I'm giving them a talk. I'm not sure—" Natali was already shaking her head. "Well, it doesn't matter. Don't have any regrets. I wish you were here too, but I don't want you to feel bad at all. We're recording the conference anyway, so you'll get to see it even more up-close and personal than if you were here. Please don't apologize again. Besides, you won't be gone much longer, will you?"

Phoebe expressed that she didn't think so; the worst of the scare with Cypress was passed she said, as she knocked on wood. "And, she's complying with the prescribed diet and meds."

"I'm glad to hear it, on many levels. Not least of which because," she let the suspense build before blurting out, "your absence has been approved!"

"What? Natali! That's fantastic—I could kiss you right now!" Instead, she gave a dry smooch to the screen.

When you hate something that isn't intrinsically vile and has done you no harm, you should face it and embrace it, Natali decided. She abhorred Obsidian Marsh, though nothing specifically had provoked her disdain. She resolved to face the source of her hostility by studying its history. She would present what she learned as entertainment for the Bonobo Guild meet-and-greet.

There was little compiled information about the school at Obsidian Marsh. As a myrmidon, she had access to the archives at Crimson Song. She met Eric there, as he was now well-acquainted with its library and organizational system.

"I sure appreciate your help, Eric. This isn't like an ordinary library."

Eric agreed. "Over the years, there's been a lot of fingers in the pie, so it's kind of a mess. Just look at these stacks of maps. You wouldn't know it, but there's some damn important papers there."

"Where do you recommend I start?"

"How about the blueprints? It's easy to see which ones are oldest." He led her to a back corner of the room, where there were no windows. "Go ahead and use this table. Handle them carefully; if they're folded, put them back folded. If they're in a roll, roll 'em back up."

It was time for her presentation to the Bonobo Guild. Her fellow myrmidons, Nadja, and several of the faculty also attended. Natali stood in front of the screen. She was nervous, but had learned how to conceal it. "Never let 'em see you sweat," rang through her mind. She began, "Obsidian Marsh is the school of science and technology. But it wasn't always so; in the beginning, it was a hotel. As the second major building on the academy's grounds, it was built as an income-generating facility, but with an eye to its future as an educational and residential hall.

"The room we're in is used today as a classroom. It, along with the many similar rooms at this end of the structure, was originally used as a conference room.

"At the other end of the building, what is now a lecture hall was the theater, where the films of the day were shown, such as 'Casablanca,' and 'Journey to the Center of the Earth,' two of Sebastian Paunder's favorites. The screen is still there, so sometimes an A/V volunteer will run movies for anyone interested.

"The dance hall is now a sports court, where you can pick up a game of basketball or volleyball. Some students revert to their childhoods and play dodgeball or Red Rover; there's also a large closet accommodating mats used for gymnastics. And occasionally, we do still have dances there."

She went on to tell them about changes to the grounds over the years, and particularly improvements that had taken place in the last seven years. Natali concluded with a report of what the two guilds that had coalesced between them had accomplished: Making beekeeping a more mainstream activity for homeowners, and establishing a security system to protect ancient forests from unscrupulous wood poachers[41].

Later in the week, The Bonobo Guild was ready to present their program in the arena at the Trunk. A small stage and screen had been assembled in the middle, with chairs, microphones, and bottles of water. Natali introduced them to the students and other attendees with a short speech. It was estimated that over one thousand were in attendance. Natali told herself that she was only speaking to one person at a time; no one could listen for more than themselves. It was a convoluted thought, but it gave her confidence.

"Greetings, fellow students, distinguished alumni, esteemed faculty, and noble guests," she began. "We so appreciate your

---

41 www.sfgate.com/crime/article/Wood-poaching-Men-charged-with-slashing-5479004.php

interest in the report of the Bonobo Guild, the 20th guild. I am Natali Marks, a member of the 23rd guild. My fellow myrmidons and I have been able to spend time with these fine people, learning about what they've accomplished as a guild, and what they're doing now. We've thoroughly enjoyed them, and we hope you will too. Without further ado, please help me welcome Jerri, John, Richard, Sheila, and Ted."

The Bonobo guild explained why the students should care about the guilds, especially the active one, and how they can get involved. They talked about their own project to create remembrance centers for the benefit of those who had returned their loved ones' cremains to nature, the difficulties they encountered, how they overcame them, and what they learned in the process.

Richard said, "Our problem wasn't convincing people of the need; most of us can relate to not having a place to bring flowers to memorialize our deceased when their ashes have been scattered over the water, land, or even sent into space. Our challenge was not only with the communities we spoke to, but between ourselves. Where to put the centers, what they would look like, how large they'd be; there were times we almost felt like throwing in the towel, but we persisted."

Sheila stood next and said that conflict is like felting alpaca fiber: the more they rubbed each other the wrong way, the more tightly knit they became as a unit. "Like any challenge, conflict can help us to grow as individuals, as groups, as a society. Remember to be patient, consider intention, and be compassionate, even if the other guy is being a complete a-hole," chuckles rippled throughout the audience, "and everything will eventually turn out alright."

Chapter 58

Reproduction

Because the history of evolution is that life escapes all barriers. Life breaks free. Life expands to new territories. Painfully, perhaps even dangerously. But life finds a way.

> — *Dr. Malcolm, in "Jurassic Park" by Michael Crichton*

April

Cypress was on her feet, feeding and bathing herself without assistance. Daily deliveries from the Acadia Meals on Wheels program was arranged. A nursing aide came out every few days to monitor her meds. Cypress had protested, but finally relented: she could no longer deny that she needed help, at least for a while, at least until she fully understood and bought into the new regiment. Uncle Charlie was also trained in the new routine, with one of the directives, "No more crawfish biscuits." With him on board, Phoebe could return to campus at last.

Cypress came into Phoebe's room as she packed, carefully sitting on the boudoir chair. "This chair's a little low for me," she said, lowering herself.

"Well Momma, you didn't have to sit there. I coulda brought you another chair in. In fact, I'll go get one." Phoebe started out the door. Cypress gently grabbed her arm.

"No, child. I'm comfortable now. You'll just have to help me get up later. Right now, I just wanna talk with you a bit."

Phoebe sat on her bed. "What is it, Momma?" Cypress was

uncharacteristically somber; Phoebe worried that she had heard bad news about her health. "Did the doctor call? Are you okay?"

"Yeah, I'm as well as can be expected, for now." She leaned back in the armless chair. "But I won't be forever."

"Don't talk like that, please."

"I'm not trying to upset you, Honey. But there's things we gotta discuss."

Phoebe took a deep breath. "Of course, if you really need to." She really didn't want to have "the" conversation, but acquiesced.

Her mother told her things about her life she'd never known, mistakes and regrets she had as a young woman and later as a mother. "I was so proud when you came along," Cypress said. "I'd never expected to ever have a child. You know I was the happiest I'd ever been." Phoebe didn't know; she always felt her mother's love, but thought she was a mistake. She delicately said this to her. "Of course you was a mistake! But the best damn mistake ever made!" Cypress patted her daughter's knees. "Don't ever think you weren't wanted. If I had planned you I couldn'ta loved you more." Phoebe's eyes glistened.

"Momma, to hear you say that means a lot to me."

Cypress shook her head. "I've told you many times before. But you weren't always listening. When you're young, time seems to go by so slow, but life goes by so fast. You don't often catch the love that's said or shown to you. Girl, it's not your fault. It's just the way it is." She wiped a slow tear off Phoebe's cheek.

The thick silence they shared in the moments that followed was filled with a new love and understanding, each of them processing their strengthened relationship. At last, Phoebe said, "I've always thought of you as my momma, but right now, I see you as a woman."

Nodding her head, Cypress said, "I know what you mean. You aren't 'just' my little girl anymore," she said wistfully. "Now that we've got that settled," Cypress straightened out her back, "I want to settle up something else: I'm going to die."

Phoebe shook her head hard. "Yes, I am. I'm not dying *right now*, mind you!" she teased. "But someday, and it may not be long. And it'll probably be something to do with this diabetes that does it, of that we can be pretty sure." She grasped Phoebe's hands. "What I want you to know is, I've had a good life. One that I'll remember as long as the good Lord allows me to have a memory, whether in this world or the next." She told Phoebe her philosophy of life, of living, of the purpose of being alive. Phoebe never knew her mother had such deep thoughts.

By the end of the conversation, Cypress had instilled a peace in Phoebe regarding her death that was beyond comprehension. She knew that no matter how sad she'd be when her mother passed, Phoebe would eventually be able not only to go on, but to find joy again.

They heard the screen door creak open on its hinges, boots shuffling on the wood floor. "Time ta go," Uncle Charlie called down the rooms. "You don't wanna miss your flight, young lady."

The airport shuttle picked her up at Portland International. Springtime was naturally her favorite time of the year. New growth and vitality were in the air. In the Pacific Northwest there was still a chance that there'd be a frost, or even snow, but judging by the deep blue skies and upper sixty-degree conditions, a cold spell didn't seem likely.

The days were longer; some of the students would even start sunbathing on the warmest days. She hoped she'd be in time to see the alpacas give birth. Although the sight reminded her of a sci-fi movie involving slime and aliens, the cria—after being cleaned off—were adorable, all legs and enormous eyes.

Thinking of babies, Phoebe recalled that before delivery, Toni had been moved to the family apartments near the Trunk. She couldn't wait to hold Toni's baby, less than two months old. There was nothing in the world as delightful as newborn baby smell. With the difficulty she had just been through with her own mother, doctors, social services, and two days on the road to interview several ALFs, a vital, new life full of hope and promise was just the morale booster and change of focus she needed. She wanted to hear about the birth itself too; Toni had a hypnobirth, utilizing hypnosis to manage the pain and stress. From a healthcare standpoint, Phoebe was fascinated. But the visit with Toni would have to wait; Phoebe's first order of business was to *recommencer* the relationship with her beau.

The airport shuttle dropped her at its usual stop, by the postal station. After tipping the driver, she picked up her held mail then called Kenny. "I'm back. Where y'at, Sugar?"

Chapter 59

Healing

*It's when we start working together that the real
healing takes place... it's when we start spilling our
sweat, and not our blood.*

— *David Hume*

May

Natali took in a lungful of the cool morning from her third-floor balcony at Lapis Lookout, internalizing the sherbet colors of sunrise. The sweet scent of blooming honeysuckle drifted through the air. Her room didn't have a view of the ocean as those on the other side of the building did, but as someone who is up with the sun, this is where she felt most at home. She had volunteered to be in charge of preparing and running the guild's final planning session tonight. All was in place, and she planned to do nothing today but make sure of it. The meeting would be perfect; *or as perfect as rationally possible*, she reminded herself.

With the return of Phoebe to the academy, the guild was whole again. Many emails, texts, and video chats had passed between them from the beginning, but now such communication was blowing up their phones and other devices as they each campaigned for their final ideas.

Adele had a passion for developing a national network of dog parks—since there was still a dearth of this more widespread need, it was too early to promote horse parks—but she was starting to see that even this simpler goal wasn't the highest or best use of the guild. Before this meeting, she thought a great deal about how she could convert her passion into someone else's dream.

Zeb had narrowed his proposal to a campaign to write history accurately—not just from the viewpoint of the victor—one family's history at a time. He developed the beginnings of a program that encouraged reading by delving into one's past, discovering facts and secrets and scandals.

Phoebe had converged her ideas into gardening for senior citizens to help them get exercise, improving flexibility and mobility. Through the utilization of raised beds and specialized tools, senior citizens would not only be using their minds and bodies, but getting fresh air too. "Young people aren't the only ones engrossed in electronic amusements. Let's get old folks away from their T.V. sets, and back into nature! It's worked wonders for my mom."

Natali couldn't help it; though they had decided at the last session to bring only one idea to this session, she continued to advocate for two projects. She laid out the bones of the suicide prevention program with help from a staff member that Adele recommended: Simon Thordicci taught in the sociology department, specializing in the topic of self-violence. Additionally, on her own, Natali also began to develop a program for planting the seeds of horse rescue/adoption programs nationally.

Eric's focus became speaking to organizations about changing how they do things for environmental awareness, and inspiring them to contribute financially to clean up efforts. It became clear to Eric what he would do with his education and experience through the guild, but it also became clear to him that he'd have to do it on his own after meeting his obligation to PAA. Though he'd helped other myrmidons to continue in the program, he had to sacrifice his own dream. For now.

The selection phase was not as intense as Natali expected. They'd already agreed on how it would be done, so the process was objective. Each myrmidon was to give a final presentation of their proposal, then a straw vote would be taken. After each vote, degree of satisfaction for the outcome would be determined by taking a "fist to five" tally, where each person either raised their hand in a fist, which meant "zero support," or raised fingers: one finger meant "I'll support it, but I don't like it," all the way to five fingers up which meant "I love this project and back it 100%!" This would be repeated until everyone had at least four fingers in the air.

The process came off exactly as planned. At the end, two projects were left in contention until one was altered enough to reach consensus. The final decision was made.

Although Zeb's relationship with his grandparents was resolved, the animosity from his "siblings" wasn't; in fact, because he was now treated as an equal, the animosity was worse. It didn't matter that each of them had a trust fund as well. He wasn't privileged, just on the same footing despite being different. At any rate, he didn't want to return to West Virginia. But Adele invited him up to Emerald Crag to talk about her post-graduation plans, not his.

They sat on wintergreen-hued boulders by the footbridge over Upper Pistoia. The swollen river, roaring waterfall, softly rustling trees, and blooming rhododendrons created a romantic setting. But Zeb wasn't feeling very romantic: they were about to discuss major changes, one of his least favorite topics.

Adele held his hand as they faced the rushing water. She said, "I want to be with Oliver again, but I don't want to move back home either. I've grown so much in the last two years; I know my moms want me there, but I've got to move on. But what am I going to do about Oliver? If I don't go back, they're not going to want to take care of him anymore; that wasn't the deal."

"I know what you have in mind, just say it, Adele." His tone had an irritated edge. Zeb didn't have much patience for bushes being beaten. Clearly she'd been giving lots of thought to her horse; were any of her thoughts for him?

"Okay, I think I should move to campus, and bring Oliver

here. He'd love to be with other horses, I'd be totally independent of my moms, and I'd be available for any guild business." She got close and focused in on Zeb's scowling face. "And, I think you should stay here too." She waited for his response.

Zeb pulled his head back in surprise; although he and Adele had grown very close, neither had talked about their plans after graduation. They were living in the moment. But now the moment had arrived to make a commitment. Or in the words of his grandfather, "Pee or get off the pot."

He kept her hanging, mimicking aloofness. After hemming and hawing, he finally said, "I'd be delighted."

Chapter 60

Enlightenment

.... the more we know, the more ignorant we become in the absolute sense, for it is only through enlightenment that we become conscious of our limitations. Precisely one of the most gratifying results of intellectual evolution is the continuous opening up of new and greater prospects.

— Nikola Tesla

Later in the year

Phoebe was delighted that her proposed project was chosen, though it had been further morphed with the input from the other myrmidons. Having worked on and advocating for her project, sometimes strenuously, she'd felt a deep sense of guilt when she'd gone home for her mother. There'd been no choice in the matter, but knew the decision had put the guild at risk. She had to continue as if the guild were viable, but it almost felt like a lie. Now that all their efforts to change policy were vindicated, that liberation from guilt was its own reward.

With final exams and graduation behind them, they'd established some guidelines for working on the project:

Communication was a top priority. They verified addresses and other contact information, including social media and video chat. They had the advantage of already experiencing quite a bit of practice using the various tools, due to Phoebe's absence.

Timeline: They worked out a preliminary schedule of meetings, including who should lead the sessions. Sharing the duty had worked out well for them so far, and they did not anticipate that distance would be an issue.

Assigning tasks: They defined what they wanted to accomplish, and began a to-do list, knowing that it would be altered and amended as the project advanced.

Developing strategies: over the course of the next two months, they'd plan how to complete tasks together, and work out a timetable. After that, they'd set their plans in motion.

Based on their individual strengths and interests, roles were assigned: Adele would oversee the project; publicity would be handled by Eric; Phoebe volunteered to be liaison to the academy; historian was assigned to Natali; logistics fell to Zeb.

The myrmidons continued to utilize social media and video chats to keep abreast of progress, and how they were doing on a personal level.

Natali's brother was now working and living in Pullman, Washington (much to the consternation of their father, a die-hard Vandals fan). Ben invited Natali to move in with him until she decided what she wanted to do. It wasn't more than a day's drive from the academy, and maybe the guild would even come to her neighborhood on occasion. Besides, she wanted to be close to her family and the comparative stability while she learned methods of coping with her anxiety. It seemed that she may always be vulnerable to it, but she didn't have to let it inhibit her life.

Eric had been offered a position with the Sierra Club Inspiring Connections Outdoors[42] program. He'd leave for training after he flew home for a two-week vacation. The flexibility of his job plus the stipend and travel expenses related to guild work meant his energies could be used in multiple places. This was what he'd wanted: to be able to help wherever and however he could.

Phoebe went home to catch up on maintenance on the Hugo home. Cypress was doing well, but she and the aging Uncle Charlie weren't up to doing repair chores. Between weeding and

---

42 www.sierraclub.org/georgia/atlanta-ico

culling the overgrown flower beds, replacing damaged pickets in the fence, and shampooing the carpets, Phoebe had time to review the last two years. She had learned so much, made lasting friendships, and earned her associates of physical therapy. Being on the guild was the *cerise sur le gâteau*. Or for the sake of Cypress, make that the "peanut butter on apple slices."

She reviewed how they had all gotten together, she and the other myrmidons...the various ways they'd crossed paths. Though she had no regrets—or really any other choice—she still shivered at the thought of how her decision to put her family first imperiled the guild. It dawned on her that Eric had advocated on her behalf; if he hadn't done his campaign to demonstrate the power of remote involvement, there would have been no guild. But she wasn't the only one who benefited from his involvement: He'd made it possible for Adele to feel mobile and productive rather than an invalid. To a lesser though no less important extent, he had been instrumental in building Zeb's confidence, and setting Branchmaster Felix straight on Natali's condition, convincing him that she should remain at the academy, not sent home "for her own sake."

Phoebe pondered that despite what they'd already been through, anything could happen. What surprises did the future hold? What if someone were to drop out of the guild, or perhaps worse, prove to be unreliable? She couldn't think any of them would flake out, but one could never tell. *Ce qui sera sera*, Phoebe concluded. Although she knew that neither she nor anyone else could have control over their future, she wasn't so fatalistic to think that they shouldn't *try* to have a good life. She and the myrmidons would do their best to help people by planting seeds of hope, and encourage others along the way to do likewise with their own skills, talents, and interests. *Maybe I'm not so different from Johnny Appleseed after all*, she realized. Like the violets which symbolized affection, sweet fondness for the Pangolin Guild bloomed in her youthful heart.

Supplementary Material

Paunder's Table of Inspiration

Sebastian Paunder woke one night with images of a bird school. At first it was literal: Birds being taught school up in the trees. But then he realized this was a metaphor.

This page excerpt is from his bedside journal. He scribbled furiously before the inspiration faded.

In keeping with the bird theme, the primary campus is the "Trunk," and the other campuses are referred to as "branches."

Brown – Cedar Whiles
Red – Crimson Song
Blue – Lapis Lookout
Yellow – Saffron Cascade
Green – Emerald Crag

Black – Obsidian Marsh
Purple – Moon Caverns
White – Pearl Quay
Silver/Gray – Basalt Moor
Coral – Sandpink Beryl

Flora and Fauna of PAA

A partial list of the animals and plants inhabiting the grounds and waters of Paunder Avian Academy.

Alder, Dogwood, & Oak trees
Blackberry & Salmonberry
Bluebells
Buttercups, Violets, & other wildflowers
Clover
Crocus Pallasii
Cypress, Cedar & Pines
Darlingtonia
Dune & Marsh Grasses
Elderberry
Eucalyptus
Ferns
Foxglove
Fruit & Nut trees
Hay: Alfalfa, Timothy, Orchard
Heather & Holly
Honeysuckle
Hydrangea
Olive Trees
Oregon Grape & *Salal*
Redwood & Giant Sequoia
Rhododendron & Azalea
Sitka Spruce & Douglas Fir
Skunk Cabbage
Vegetable & Fruit Crops
Waterlilies
Weeping Willow
Western Hemlock
Wisteria

American Kestrel & other raptors
Bats
Black Bear
Black Swan
Bobcats & Cougars
Canaries & other songbirds
Cats & Dogs
Chipmunks & Squirrels
Coyote
Crimson Rosella
Crows
Deer
Frogs
Furry-tailed Woodrat
Geese & Ducks (esp. *Mallard*)
Great Blue Heron
Horse (numerous breeds)
Hummingbirds (esp. *Rufous*)
Indian Peafowl
Opossum, Raccoon, & Skunk
Oysters & Clams
Porcupine
Purple Martin
Pygmy-Owl
Rabbits
Roosevelt Elk
Salmon & Trout
Snakes
Snowy Egret
Western Sandpiper & Plover

Italic listings denote illustrations

Gemstones and Minerals of PAA

A partial list of the inert materials found at Paunder Avian Academy.

Basalt	Mica
Beryl	Obsidian
Emerald (industrial quality)	Oregon Sunstone
Feldspar	Pearl
Garnet (industrial quality)	Sandstone
Lapis Lazuli	Selenite
Lepidolite	Serpentinite

Referenced Materials

Sources and Resources

SAFE Act of 2015 – To put an end to the brutal export and butchery of live horses.

The Humane Society of the United States

World Book Encyclopedia

victorianbazaar.com/meanings.html Because flowers have a language, too.

www.allaboutbirds.org Lots of great details, and even songs!

www.auctionhorses.net Powerful stories and emotions here.

www.city-data.com Statistics for just about any US city!

www.dictionary.com Is it a real word, or did I make it up?!

www.thesaurus.com How many ways can you say "confused"?

www.wikipedia.org Lots of facts, but is it all the truth?

Current Enhancement Classes

Classes offerings may be adjusted from year to year.

1. Acceptance
2. Advocacy
3. Anger
4. Anticipation
5. Attention
6. Awareness
7. Closure
8. Communication
9. Compassion
10. Conflict
11. Conservation
12. Contentment
13. Creativity
14. Curiosity
15. Doubt
16. Dreaming
17. Education
18. Enlightenment
19. Envy
20. Faith
21. Fear
22. Forgiveness
23. Grief
24. Growth
25. Healing
26. Health
27. Honor
28. Hope
29. Humility
30. Humor
31. Imagination
32. Independence
33. Industry
34. Innocence
35. Intimacy
36. Joy
37. Judgment
38. Knowledge
39. Love
40. Meditation
41. Opportunity
42. Perspective
43. Pride
44. Purity
45. Reality
46. Recycling
47. Regret
48. Reproduction
49. Research
50. Resourcefulness
51. Sacrifice
52. Security
53. Toil
54. Tolerance
55. Trust
56. Truth
57. Violence
58. Vulnerability
59. Wisdom
60. Wonder

Afterword

This story was years in the making, though I didn't know it! In addition to the people who've influenced it, my experiences, the places I've lived, and jobs I've held have left their mark.

I've always wanted to learn a second language. I haven't been able to do that yet. It's not from lack of trying; I've "tried" German, Italian, Cantonese (my ex-husband and father of my children is from Hong Kong), French, and American Sign. But I believe it's from lack of practice—there's too many other wonderful things to do in the world, and I'm easily distracted! Perhaps as a result of my frustration, I've included a foreign language element in this book. Since my only language proficiency is English, I've relied on online translation to help me. For you native speakers, if there's an error, you know what to blame. For those of you who don't know, just go with it (use Google Translate[43], if necessary. At least then we should be on the same page!)

As a writer, I'm also influenced (knowingly) by my three favorite novels. Moby-Dick: The Whale, particularly in regards to the way Melville included sections of fact; The Source, where the location is the main character (as I'm hoping the setting of PAA will be) and Alice in Wonderland, with its remarkable ability to sweep us away and bring us back again, exalting the ability of the human mind to reach far beyond reality as we perceive it.

I would guess that at least 40% of my time in writing this novel was done in research. The more I learned, the more heartbroken I became in regards to the conditions horses are subjected to when they're no longer wanted. In fact, an ongoing situation came to my knowledge as I was preparing this manuscript for publication. That information was included at the last minute, I hope seamlessly. It is my further hope that this novel will open others' eyes to also see the injustices horses and other animals endure at our hands, and eventually put an end to it.

But mostly I wrote this novel to inspire the reader to consider many aspects of life. We're so busy and bombarded in this world we often don't take the time to decide what we think of it all. If you enjoyed and/or gained some personal insight, I'd love to hear about it. Thank you for taking your time to read!

43 translate.google.com/

Acknowledgments

I have many people to thank, starting with my second fiancé, James Hash, who in addition to giving me input when I was stuck or figuring out which word I needed (the thesaurus can only take you so far!) has allowed me to use some of his poetry. I would not have been able to write this book without his financial support, allowing me the time needed to work on it. Not least of which I am thankful for though, is his patience with me. Most of the time, anyway.

Special thanks to my mother, Jean Starr, who always believed in me and supported me throughout all my ideas and efforts, even after they didn't work out. Singular appreciation to my daughter, Jolene, who provided the counterbalance. Her challenges made me think deeper, and probably write better. I look forward to her insightful form of criticism for many years to come (I mean that with all my heart).

To my readers, your "fresh eyes" were invaluable, catching errors that I missed! I'm sure some still exist, but it's about as clean a text as my time permits. In no particular order, I'm grateful to Patricia/PJ/Tigerlily Crockett (who will always be Patty to me), Candace Paris, Joanie Helms, Ruthanne Taylor, Bobby Huffstetter aka Dad, and of course, Jim.

And to all those who've passed through my life at one time or another, parts of your influence may be within these pages. From those near and dear to me, to total strangers: Some aspect of you may be found within one or more of my characters. Thanks for your inadvertent help.

I must also mention gratitude to the Lincoln City Cultural Center for encouraging me and artists of all types; Lincoln City itself; the Thousand Trails system, especially in Pacific City; Turtle Ridge Wildlife Center in Salem, Oregon for taking in George and other creatures in need; Harmony New Beginnings Animal Rescue in Sheridan, Oregon, Duchess Sanctuary in Oakland, Oregon, and Eugene Livestock Auction for their work on behalf of horses in particular. There are probably others I'm not mentioning, so please visit my blog for updates and more information: www.quintetapproach.wordpress.com

About the Author

Julie Starr has been established on the central Oregon coast since 1993. She was originally from northern California, but was transplanted to Oregon in 1974. After ending up in Portland, she started her own family. Eventually she chose the Lincoln City area as her home.

Along with a love of horses, dogs, and other animals, Julie has multiple passions, the oldest of which is making art from drawing to glass; the most gratifying is helping people via hypnotherapy[44]. This approach has allowed her to work with her clients to discover their own self-worth and acceptance as they work towards self-improvement goals.

With the support of Jim, her life partner, she runs a small alpaca farm. It is their hope to someday be directly involved with improving the welfare of horses who've been discarded. She also writes fiction and non-fiction, enjoys managing their home and the woods in which it is situated, and loves the varied beauty that beach life offers.

The concepts of compassion, tolerance, and truly living every day are important goals for her as an individual and hopes for humanity as a whole.

The Quintet Approach, Pangolin Guild is her first novel.

Send feedback about the book to the author on Facebook:
www.facebook.com/juliekstarr

---

44 One last footnote! www.gemhypnosis.net

www.ingramcontent.com/pod-product-compliance
Lightning Source LLC
Chambersburg PA
CBHW071047250626
47159CB00002B/388